Satisfaction

Satisfaction

By K.M. GOLLAND
Book 2 in The Temptation Series

First Published 2013
First Australian Paperback Edition 2014

ISBN 978 1 74356 850 7

Published by Harlequin Mira
An imprint of Harlequin Enterprises (Australia) Pty Ltd.
Level 13
201 Elizabeth St
SYDNEY NSW 2000
AUSTRALIA

Printed and bound in Australia by McPhersons Printing Group

MIX
Paper from
responsible sources
FSC® C001695

ABOUT THE AUTHOR

"I am an author. I am married. I am a mother of two adorable little people. I'm a bookworm, craftworm, movieworm, and sportsworm. I'm also a self-confessed shop-aholic, tea-aholic, car-aholic, and choc-aholic."

Born and raised in Melbourne, Australia, K.M. Golland studied law and worked as a conveyancer before putting her career on hold to raise her children. She then traded her legal work for her love of writing and found her dream career.

For my parents.
Two of the most loving and giving souls on this earth.

PROLOGUE

Bryce

I've never really considered myself to be a lucky man. Yes, I have more than enough money to feed a small country — which I do, because I make damn sure a good percentage of my fortune aids people who genuinely need it the most. But having a rather large bank account has never truly satisfied me, nor has it ever fulfilled me. It was simply a result of working hard and keeping my mind from the emptiness I have felt ever since the day I lost Mum, Dad and my little brother, Lauchie. The day they passed away all the love, joy and playfulness I'd once known, vanished. And although I tried to recover those feelings, they always seemed to elude me.

For a long time, my sister Lucy was my focus and priority; she was all I had left. I promised myself that I would look after her, because I sure as hell was not about to lose her, too. But then she found her loving partner, Nic, and I had no choice but to reluctantly hand over the protective reins, once again feeling hollow inside.

* * *

It's the morning after the Tel V Awards, and I am sitting here on the edge of my bed staring down at the most beautiful creature to have ever walked this earth. I no longer feel hollow. Instead, I feel alive; I feel excited; I feel like I've just had the best night of my life. But more importantly, I finally feel complete.

Her silky smooth back is bare as she sleeps soundly on her stomach, and as I sit here and take in the sight before me, I cannot believe just how fucking lucky I truly am.

* * *

I think back to the time I first opened Alexis' application folder, to what felt like being slapped in the face when confronted with her photo. *Fuck me* were the words that came out of my mouth, followed by a dry swallow and the loosening of my tie. She was applying for the position of Concierge Attendant and if I had ever doubted the concept of love at first sight, I sure as hell didn't any more. I sat there and stared at her intriguingly innocent, beautiful face for almost an hour before reading her résumé probably twenty times. She was simply stunning. But it wasn't just her physical beauty that had me captivated. When I looked at her, I felt connected and somewhat drawn in, and that was a feeling I wasn't used to.

Her cover letter mentioned she was married with two young children, and I envied the man who was lucky enough to be responsible for that. Strangely enough, from that moment on, Alexis' husband existed only on that piece of paper and that piece of paper alone. It was as though my mind deliberately shut him out. Mr Summers was a nonentity where I was concerned. I knew it was wrong, but I couldn't help it.

I didn't hesitate to inform Abigail that Alexis was a successful applicant and that she was to concierge at City Towers in particular. I wanted her working in this building and as close to me as possible. I then asked Lucy to research her, or to put it technically, perform an employee background check. Lucy looked into things for me all the time, so my request was not terribly out of the ordinary for her. She had accessed Alexis' Facebook account which had given me an informal insight into her intriguing life.

From what I could see she was fun, had lots of friends, played Farmville, and she had recently been sick due to eating some fructose which had been hidden in a cake. I could also tell by her many status updates and photo tags that her alcoholic drink of choice was gin, that she loved her sports and admired cars. The fact that she liked cars had excited the shit out of me, because I couldn't wait to try and impress her with my own collection.

I had also noticed from a photo taken of her five years ago that she'd undergone a pretty impressive physical transformation. She had looked heavier back then in comparison to the photo I had been given with her résumé; but heavier or not, she radiated beauty from her angelic face and was still simply gorgeous.

* * *

The morning she was to start her traineeship at the hotel was downright crazy. It was also fucking weird due to the fact I had felt flustered, stressed, excited and all things strangely confusing and nice. Weird — but nice. *I never fucking feel 'nice'.* I had changed my suit three times, worrying about whether or not she would find me good-looking. I was turning into a bloody girl. I'm even surprised I didn't turn around that morning and look at my arse in the mirror, wondering if it looked big in the particular pants I was wearing. In addition, my palms had been sweaty, which I always thought was just a myth; a stupid saying, even. But it wasn't a myth, it was true ... palms actually do sweat when you are nervous as hell.

I had informed security to notify me when Alexis scanned her employee card at the staff gate, so I could position myself and catch a glimpse of the beauty in the photo who had captured my thoughts for the past three weeks.

I had spotted her hurrying across my casino floor, and the sheer sight of her had the head on my shoulders deciding to have a quick chat to the head in my pants. Then, as if I was an electrically charged moving particle, I was pulled by her magnetic force until we were both standing in line at Gloria Jean's.

I hadn't actually planned on talking to her until she was due to visit the penthouse floor. All I had wanted to do at that time was see her up close and personal, but once I did, I had found myself wanting more.

I'd stood directly behind her and the scent of her perfume and shampoo had nearly knocked me for six. Having been momentarily intoxicated by her presence like a lovesick pervert, I stupidly hadn't allowed enough room for her to turn around. Thank fuck I hadn't though, because the feeling of hot freaking white-chocolate covering my Versace shirt was one of the best feelings I had felt in a very long time.

The words that then floated out of her perfect mouth sealed my need to be around her as much as I could. She was not only breathtakingly beautiful, she was funny ... adorably fucking funny: 'Oh, shit! Shit! Jesus, that is hot! Oh, I am so sorry!'

I just wanted to grab her and swallow those cute little words directly from her mouth to mine, but it wasn't until she looked up into my eyes that I nearly fucking had a coronary. I swear my heart skipped a beat, if that is at all possible.

I wasn't sure what came over me next, because I lost control of my reason and grabbed her by the arm, leading her to God knows where. If my world was perfect, I would have led her to the nearest personal corridor and had her up against the wall. But that was not going to happen, so I had to think quickly before she screamed '*Psycho*' and kicked me in the balls.

She had seemed okay with me whisking her away at first, until she managed to pry herself out of my eager hold and ask me who the hell I was. In that moment, I came up with the idea of taking her to see Clarissa and lavishing on her a Versace dress that would be privileged to adorn her perfect body.

'Who are you and how do you know my name?' she'd asked. I had thought about opening my stupid mouth there and then, spilling out that the reason I knew her name was because I had thought about her every day since first laying my eyes on her. I'm glad I didn't though, because that would have probably sealed my fate and declared me borderline stalker.

My eyes had quite easily found her wet and slightly see-through blouse, which was lucky because this was how I noticed her name badge and was able to use that as the less creepy excuse for knowing her name. I also figured I would throw into the mix that I was her boss and see how she'd react.

The shade of pink her face had turned was adorable, and I knew from that moment I needed to make her blush a hell of a lot more — it was fucking awesome to watch.

I then placed my hand on the small of her back to keep her moving, and this had instantly snapped my dick to attention, like she deliberately sent an electric shock right through me in order to hit that very spot.

* * *

Bringing my thoughts back to the present, where I now sit gazing down at my sleeping beauty, it is quite apparent that Alexis still has that very ability to snap my dick to attention — even in her sleep. Just the sight of her naked back gives me a raging hard-on.

I smile to myself as thoughts of the first time I saw her naked back come rushing into my mind.

* * *

I remembered swallowing heavily right before I crazily opened her dressing room curtain with the dumbarse excuse of offering to zip her up. She had spun around quite eagerly for me; either that, or she had hoped I would leave, which I had no intention of doing until I had finished with her zip. When I'd placed my hand on her back, that electrifying dick-charge had coursed through me once again, and I knew I wanted to experience that feeling for as long as I possibly could. So, I deliberately zipped up the dress slowly, even having thoughts about pretending it got stuck so that I could hold her against me and tug at it.

She had flinched under my touch, and it worried me to think I might have icy-cold fingers that disgusted her, so I rubbed them desperately, nearly fucking producing a friction fire in the palm of my hands. I apologised for them being cold, but when she had said, 'No, not at all. They are fine', and then giggled, I relaxed and felt she was possibly flirting with me. That prospect alone was all I needed to take it up an extra notch, and I definitely had plans for doing that.

* * *

A small gurgling noise sounds from Alexis' stomach, snapping me out of my happy recollection. Even her stomach rumbling is sexy as hell. *She's hungry. I'll make her breakfast.* I quietly stand up from the bed and sneak out of the room. *I could make a quick batch of blueberry pancakes for her.*

I make my way to the kitchen and quickly produce a pile of pancakes, dressing them with yogurt and berries. I smile as I put them aside, then head back to my room to wake my perfect sleeping beauty.

When I return to the room, she is still sleeping soundly. *Fuck, I must've really worn her out last night.* I plan on wearing her out like this every night for the rest of our lives. The problem in my thinking, of course, is that when she finds out about my deal with Rick, we may not have the rest of our lives.

The fact he has cheated on her is in my favour, and knowing Alexis like I do now, she will not go back to him because of that. But will she leave me when she finds out about my part in all of it? I'm not quite sure. Just the thought of it terrifies me beyond belief. I can't lose her now. No, I won't lose her now. I have this week to show her just how much she really means to me, and to show her that what we have is magical, special and rare. I have this one week to prove to her that we belong together, and I'm not going to waste another second of it.

Now that I have her, I am never letting her go.

CHAPTER

1

There's a feeling you get when waking for the first time after an incredible night. It starts with your eyelids fluttering, slowly responding to a message sent from your brain, a message telling them to open completely so that you can return from your unconscious hibernation and feel the joy that begins to spread across your body as you remember what you had experienced before entering it. My brain was sending this message, instructing my mouth to curve into a smile as I slowly woke from my slumber, a slumber that was the result of a night full of passionate lovemaking. My eyes were heavy as were the muscles between my legs, but it was the tickling sensation I felt up and down my bare back that distracted me from my aching loins.

I opened my eyes, finding the morning sunlight to be unwelcome, but the realisation of what was tickling my back, or more so who was doing it, was probably the most welcoming thing imaginable.

'Alexis ... wake up, my love.' *Hmm, anything you say, you incredibly satisfying, sexy man.*

He kept trailing the object up and down my spine, sending tiny sensations radiating from the point of contact through to my breasts and right down into my pelvis.

Without hesitation, I rolled over.

There were many things I did not want to imagine in my life, one of them being what I looked like at that particular point in time. From last night's memories of Sex Up Against the Wall, to a Fuck On the Floor, to our wrestling in a bed full of roses, then Sex In the Shower, I could honestly take a guess and say that I looked well and truly fucked.

'Good morning,' I mumbled as a yawn escaped my mouth.

Bryce was sitting on the edge of the bed, wearing nothing but a pair of jeans. In his hand was a long-stemmed red rose, one of the hundreds scattered around the room. I couldn't help myself and smiled at him ... smiled because he was gloriously hot in the morning in his sexy jeans and because he had made me very happy.

Last night was, if I am going to be completely honest with myself, probably the best night of my life. He had tempted me for months, pursued me tirelessly and, when the opportunity arose, I succumbed to the temptation that was Bryce Edward Clark, a thirty-six-year-old billionaire, CEO of Clark Incorporated, my boss, and a man who was 'absolutely and undoubtedly' in love with me.

He placed the rose on my forehead then gently dragged it along the bridge of my nose, allowing me to breathe in its glorious scent. Continuing his sultry assault, he trailed it over my lips — the soft, silky glide of the petals a sensual tease.

I tantalised him by sticking out my tongue and licking the petal as it passed, initiating one of his telltale signs that I was setting a fire within him. He twitched his eye and held the rose still for a split second. If I was to hazard a guess, I'd say his pause was an indication of him deciding whether to pounce on me there and then, or continue his seductive tease. Presumption correct, then he opted to continue the rose's southern journey by dragging it over my neck and intensifying the sensations I was already feeling.

A burning need mixed with an excited thrill stirred within as the rose made its way down between my breasts, where he then circled each of them with controlled precision.

Watching the ownership displayed in his eyes, I relished his actions as he teased my nipples with the petals. The problem with his expression was that he didn't own me. By law I belonged with someone else — Rick Summers, my husband.

I quickly, but only to a very shallow degree, buried the memory from a couple of days ago, when Rick had confessed to having an affair. I was going to have to deal with him soon — that was inevitable — but for now, I wanted him out of my thoughts and out of my head completely.

Getting up on my elbows, I mouthed the words 'come here', but he didn't move. Instead, he just displayed that infuriating yet adorable and delectable smirk he possessed and so often fired my way.

'Bryce, are you deliberately torturing me?'

'No, I wouldn't dare.' *Oh, yes, you would, you sexy beast.*

Wanting to give him a taste of his own provocative medicine, I lifted my knee, allowing the sheet to drop to my foot therefore exposing the rest of my naked body. This inevitably elicited his carnal growl which, as per usual, sent waves of excitement right through me.

He placed the rose in between his teeth, turned, and began to crawl up the bed with a devilish glint in his eye. I loved his devilish glint, it meant one thing and one thing only: *Alexis, you are in for it now!*

Accepting the rose, I put my arms around his neck and kissed him passionately. This was, by far, my new favourite pastime, followed very closely — and I mean *very* closely — by what always comes next.

He tried to speak, but I was not about to let him leave my mouth, my refusal to set him free apparently not a deterrent as I could still understand his mumbling. 'I've made you breakfast, honey.'

'Thank you, but it can wait,' I replied without separating my mouth from his, and performing the same muffled speech. Breakfast was the last thing on my mind, so I wrapped my legs around his back and rolled him over until I was sitting on top of him.

Comfortably — and arrogantly, mind you — he placed both his hands behind his head. 'Hmm ... my new favourite view, Ms Summers.'

Hungry to have him in my hands, in between my legs — just to have him — I reached down and began to unbutton his jeans. 'Mine too, Mr Clark.'

I noticed a strange look on his face which made me stop after pulling down the zipper. 'What?' I asked with curiosity.

'Nothing,' he answered flippantly, his attempt to disguise his amusement not particularly good.

'Bryce Edward Clark, what are you trying to hide?'

'Nothing. Here, do you need a hand?' He tilted his pelvis up, thrusting me ever so slightly into the air which allowed him to pull his jeans down at the same time. *Cheeky bastard.*

Feeling his full erection pushing into my inner thigh, I reached down and positioned his crown so that it just touched my entrance. He smiled and tilted to progress admission, but I knelt higher, refusing him.

'What are you hiding from me, Bryce?' I asked again, raising my eyebrow and indicating that he had better confess.

'Nothing. You do realise you are not going to win this, either.' *I know.* This was another game I did not really want to win, but I was enjoying the pretence nonetheless.

He tilted again and again I refused. 'Are you telling me that you don't want my cock inside you?' he asked, calling my bluff. *No, fuck no.* He tilted yet again, and this time I lowered, allowing him to be entirely engulfed by my warm, lubricated pussy.

My acceptance prompted his teeth to grit and a loud groan to escape his mouth as I started pleasing his erection with my rhythm — which, in turn, pleased me. I craved the rawness he displayed when I gave him what he wanted. It made me want him even more. I was absolutely possessed and captivated by this man. Put quite simply, I was completely in love with him.

Bryce placed his hands on my hips, greedily holding me to him which only intensified the sense of empowerment I already felt. I liked riding him slowly, seeing the look on his face as I moved up and down his shaft. It was a position of control, of command, knowing that the rhythm I created was the root of his pleasure.

Leaning forward, I placed my hands on his chest then relaxed my arms so that I could flick my tongue across his lips; he opened his mouth and caressed it with his own, then moved his hands to grip my arse with sensational force. We were mesmerised, our eyes riveted on each other as he gripped my skin beneath his fingers with ferocious intensity, and as our pelvic movements escalated so did my orgasm.

I sat up, arched my head back and touched my breasts, sheer erotic waves coursing through my body and taking control of my limbs.

'Alexis, you are so fucking gorgeous, especially when you touch yourself.' *Holy fuck, the things you say to me, Mr Clark.* The lascivious words that rolled from his tongue helped peak my climax — Bryce's following closely behind.

As we began to regain our composure, he sat up and wrapped his arms around me, securing me to his chest. We didn't say anything, just hugged each other for what felt like hours. And honestly, I could have stayed like that indefinitely. It just felt right.

Unfortunately, the rumble that roared from within my stomach indicated I had to indulge in breakfast.

He laughed, pulled away, and looked down at my belly. 'Lucky for you, there's a big plate of blueberry pancakes downstairs with your name on it.' *Yum! I couldn't possibly love you any more, my smirky chef.*

I pressed a quick kiss to his lips. 'You're too good to me.'

I was quite eager to get the delicious circles of antioxidants into my mouth, when the thought of pancakes reminded me of my children. *I hope they are all right.* First thing after breakfast, I was definitely going to call Mum and see how they were, not to mention face the music.

I climbed off Bryce's now-fallen soldier and grabbed the navy satin nightie that had been discarded on the floor in the early hours of the morning. Bryce put his jeans back on and gave me the I'm-going-to-lift-you-up look.

'Don't even think about it. I'm walking!' I warned, displaying an expression that couldn't have been more definite than if I had waved my finger at him, placed one hand on my hip, and wobbled my head at the same time.

He put his hands up in defence and laughed at me, and again there was just something about his laugh that gave me the sense he was still hiding something. 'What?'

'Nothing.' *Bullshit, nothing. Grrr.*

Smirking, he grabbed my hand and led me downstairs.

* * *

The man was a god; a sexy, mouthwateringly sweet and talented god. And the dish he plated only added to his list of credentials. Placed on the table before me was a stack of heart-shaped blueberry pancakes with a dollop of yogurt and some berries on the side.

I stared at his culinary work of art, feeling loved, adored and a little overwhelmed. It was a simple gesture yet it meant so much.

I put my hands to my chest as the sentiment was truly adorable. 'That's so sweet, thank you.'

'It's what I do, Ms Summers.' *Oh, Mr Clark, I'll do you in a minute.*

Unfortunately though, I was now struggling to come to terms with the fact I was going to have to ruin his masterpiece by consuming it. I hesitated, but picked up my fork. *It looks so pretty, I can't do it. Alexis, stab the pancakes, you stupid bitch.*

Faltering for the slightest of seconds, I then speared the pile of berries instead and dipped them into the yogurt. I sheepishly looked up and noticed Bryce smirking at me, so I smiled sweetly back at him and then popped the blueberries into my mouth. *Is he just going to sit there and watch me eat? I hate it when he watches me eat.*

'For the love of God, Bryce, what?'

He chuckled loudly. 'Nothing.'

'Stop saying that. Clearly there is something you're not telling me.' I glared at him.

Lowering his head with a grin, he took in a mouthful of his own pancakes. I, however, continued to hover over mine. They really did look yummy. *How can I possibly devour this plate of love?*

With the tip of my fork, I lifted the top pancake and underneath it was another perfect heart. They were all equally impeccable, and I found them to be more and more untouchable the longer I looked at them. *Just do it, Alexis.*

I was still contemplating the angle of attack when Bryce got impatient and destroyed my blueberry tower of love with his fork.

'Hey!' I protested.

'Eat them,' he scowled.

'But they looked so cute and pretty, and I didn't want to wreck them.'

With my bottom lip pouting, I forked the sabotaged pile and placed some into my mouth. *Oh, these are just divine!* My pout quickly disappeared, and I followed with some more. 'You do realise you just broke my hearts?' I mumbled with a mouthful.

'Honey, if I ever broke your heart, I would mend it,' he said, with obvious sincerity.

I searched his stern face. 'But what if you couldn't mend it?'

'That's not an option.'

Our conversation had suddenly turned serious, the unexpected shift in mood unsettling. It was as though he was trying to tell me something or reassure me, but whatever it was, I didn't like it.

'It's simple then, isn't it? You won't have to worry about mending my heart if you promise to never break it,' I explained, aggressively stabbing the remainder of my leaning tower of pancake-love. His smile returned, which then magnetised my own.

I loved sitting out on his balcony eating a meal with him, a meal that he had cooked. It was so different to what I was used to back at home. I was used to slaving in the kitchen for hours, getting covered in pot splatter, sporting a blush of flour across my cheek and smelling of *eau de* garlic and onion. If that wasn't bad enough, I would then be told by Nate and Charlotte that they 'hate it, and it's the worst ever!' So, having someone else cook for me was a pleasant change and I was lapping it up. I did, however, regardless of their sometimes ambivalent attitude toward my cooking, miss my ratbags immensely and was dying to hear their voices.

Glancing up, I spotted Bryce's cheeky I'm-hiding-something look had returned yet again. 'Okay, tell me what the fuck is so amusing?' I demanded, viciously forking a strawberry and shoving it into my mouth. 'Or I will take back your permission to kiss me,' I mumbled.

He stopped chewing, put his fork down and stared at me wildly. 'Is that a threat, Ms Summers?' *Sure is, bucko!*

'It's a promise, Mr Clark,' I asserted, pointing my empty fork in his direction and murdering the strawberry between my teeth.

His fiery gaze was literally burning me and I could feel the radiant heat he projected. He stood up and tipped the entire

table over and out of his way. The sudden action forced me
to swallow the deceased berry and nearly choke. *Oh shit.* I
gripped my seat tightly, partly out of shock, and partly because
I had to hold onto something. The last time I challenged him,
I ended up in the pool.

He kicked his chair backwards and prowled toward me, his
eyes not leaving mine for a second. The way his stare penetrated me was indescribable, and already my breasts and pelvis
were vibrating with excitement.

Stopping directly in front of me, he leaned down so that
his face was level with my own. He went to kiss me but
stopped only centimetres from my wanting mouth, staring at my lips as if they were the most intriguing things
he'd ever seen. The pause and extreme close proximity were
excruciating. His soft breath was warm against my skin as
he moved his head down my neck. I automatically arched
back, giving him access. But his touch never came. *Holy
shit, this is hot.*

He moved back up to my mouth, again, coming as close
as possible without making any contact. Then, shifting to my
ear and hovering over it, he breathed and whispered, 'What
was that you were saying, about me not kissing you?' *Nothing,
absolutely nothing, do not listen to me.*

I moaned very lightly and that was enough for him to
caress my mouth, his lips warm and tasting ever so slightly
of blueberries. I gently licked them and savoured the taste.
Mm, he tastes so good. We deepened our kiss, but kept it very
controlled and sensual. It was simply wonderful.

Suddenly, he broke away and stood up. 'Don't make promises you can't keep, Ms Summers.' *Grrr, he is winning too many
of these challenges!*

'I hate you,' I said sulkily as I recovered from his spellbinding tease.

'No, you don't,' he sniggered back, then walked away. *No, I don't.*

* * *

Bryce began cleaning up the tipped-over table and leftovers from breakfast and watched me as I walked up the stairs. He still wore a secretive and mischievous smile, so I poked out my tongue and followed with a rather loud raspberry in response to his annoying expression. This only seemed to add to his already private joke, so I glared at him, then disappeared to his room to freshen up after our marathon of fuckery.

As I entered his bathroom, the reflection in his mirror stopped me in my tracks, finally revealing what his bloody secret was. *Are you kidding me? Oh, very funny.* Stuck in various spots amongst my hair were approximately five rose petals — I looked like a freakin' human bird's nest. I let out a little squawk in response. The joke was certainly on me. *Cheeky bastard. Alexis Summers does not forget things very easily.*

As I plucked the petals from my hair, ideas of revenge started floating around in my head and, as I stepped into the shower, I ran through them. *Right, the good old-fashioned hug him and stick a note to his back! Or kiss him on the cheek while wearing a bright red lipstick.* Unfortunately, none of these satisfied my building urge for retribution. *Patience, Alexis. Was it not Mr Hotpants Clark who said, 'Good things come to those who wait?' Well, wait I shall.*

* * *

Since it was Tuesday morning and technically a work day, I made my way to the walk-in 'stadium' with the intention of getting ready to do my job. *Yes,* stadium*! I still cannot get over how big his closet actually is.* Standing in the enormous space, I found it quite overwhelming to stare at the numerous high-end fashion choices. I think the fact that there were so many items to choose from actually made my decision all the more difficult. I did, however, finally select the Versace square-neck lace dress. I picked this one because I knew he would like it ... a lot. It was tight — very tight — clinging snugly to my breasts, and with the assistance of my Aubade push-up bra made them look about ten years younger. *Ha, check these puppies out! Not bad ... this will teach him.*

The dress was predominantly an ivory colour, covered in black lace. It had long sleeves, and the hemline rested just above my knee. I completed the revenge outfit with a pair of Jimmy Choo black patent Mary Janes, then blow-dried my hair and applied the very minimal make-up I was now used to wearing. I took one last look in the mirror and assessed my vengeful attire. *Alexis, you are getting quite good at this.*

Reaching for my phone, I noticed that the clock displayed 10 a.m. *Lucky you sleep with the boss, or you'd be fired!* There were also five missed calls and two text messages from Rick.

Message 1: *Babe, I'm sorry. It's not what you think, really it isn't. You never gave me the chance to explain myself.*

Please call me back — Rick

Message 2: *Alexis, obviously you need time and don't want to talk. I respect that, take the time. But if by the end of the week you have not returned my call or messaged me, I will track you down.*

By the way, you looked stunning on TV last night, and I miss you xo

It's not what I think? What am I supposed to think then? You accidently tripped over and your dick just happened to land inside of Claire? I closed the messages. I was beyond hurt, now I was mad. How dare he try and defend himself and brush it off as though it was nothing, our twelve years of marriage now flushed down the toilet. The worst thing about it, though, wasn't that he'd been tempted to cheat — I knew how that felt. It was the fact he had lied to me for so long about it; he had kept it a secret for five friggin' years.

Claire was twenty-seven years old and the daughter of my parents' friends. I had helped her get the receptionist position at Melbourne Mortgages as a favour.

Remembering back to when Rick came home after a late shift with Claire, I recall having picked up on the scent of Red Door, which I hated. I'd asked Rick outright: 'Is something going on between the two of you?' He'd said 'No' and told me she'd had a fight with her best friend and was upset, so he'd hugged her in the hope she would stop crying.

I knew that he hated crying, so I accepted his version of events. But I became more suspicious at his work Christmas party, when Claire seemed to hang off everything he said and did. She only worked there for another month or so after that, and apparently took off backpacking overseas — I hadn't heard or asked about her since. *I hope she is stuck in the fucking Sahara Desert somewhere and being spat on by a camel.*

I shivered all over and physically tried to shake the memories of her out of my head. *Right, don't think about it, Alexis. Deal with it at the end of the week.*

Who I did have to deal with at this point in time was my mother, Maryann Blaxlo. Mum was not a stupid woman. In fact, she was as sharp as they come, and I had no doubt she knew something was not right. Not only from my televised appearance the night before, but by Rick's and the kids' moods. The good thing about Mum was she didn't stubbornly force you to pour your heart out if you didn't want to and she never judged.

I sat on the edge of the bed and hesitantly dialled Mum and Dad's phone number.

'Hello, Alexis Elizabeth.' *Yep, she knows something; typical mother tactic of saying my full name.*

'Hi, Mum. I'm just checking in on the kids. Are they around?'

'Nate is on the tractor with your father, and Charlotte is helping me with the herb garden. So, Alexis, how were the Tel V Awards? That was quite some honour being named Best Dressed.' *What? Holy shit! Cool ... or is it? God, I hope I'm not being splashed all over* Sunrise *and* The Morning Show *right now. Crap!*

'Really? I didn't know that! Yes, that is an honour. It was a stunning dress, Mum.' *Change the subject, Alexis.* 'Look, I really can't be long. Can I speak to Charlotte, please?'

She murmured something and handed Charli the phone.

'Hi, Mummy. I saw you and Mr Clark on TV. You looked beautiful ... like a famous person.' *Charli-Bear, you silly little rabbit.*

'Thank you, darling. It was a very pretty dress, wasn't it? Hey, guess what? Guess who I met?'

'Who? 4Life? Who, Mum?'

If she was this excited at the sheer mention of me possibly meeting her favourite band, she was going to hyperventilate when she found out what Bryce had arranged for her the night before. The look on her face would be priceless.

'No, sweetie, not 4Life. Sierra Thomas ... she signed a napkin for you and I took a picture of her with me!'

'Really? Aw, sick, Mum!' *Sick? Oh no. Not you too.*

'I'll give it to you when I see you on the weekend, okay?'

'Cool! Do you want to speak to Nanny again?' *No, not really.*

'Yeah, put her on, sweetheart. Love you. Bye.'

Charlotte handed the phone back to Mum. There was silence on the other end at first, and I knew she was waiting for me to share some more information.

'Mum?'

'Yes, Alexis?' *Really? I'm no longer a minor, lose the patronising tone.*

'Rick and I are taking some time apart. I don't want to get into it with you over the phone. I will explain on the weekend when I come and get the kids. I just want you to know I'm fine, and I'm staying at work. I have my mobile if you need me for anything at all.' I waited for her response which did not come straightaway.

'Alexis, love, just take care of yourself and know the kids are fine and happy and that we love you.'

Tears began to well in my eyes. *No, Alexis, panda-eyes are not welcome here.*

'Thanks, Mum, I love you too. Can you tell Nate to ring me later before he goes to sleep, please?'

'Of course, darling.'

'Okay. Bye.'

I sat there staring at the phone for a few seconds. I loved my children and felt terribly guilty. Guilty because I was away from them at this particular moment. And guilty because I was here having the most wonderful time with a man who was not their father. *Alexis, you are entitled to a break from your children once in a while. They are in good hands, and they love spending time at the farm.* They did love it. Nate had even said to me once that he was moving out to live on the farm to help out my father, and that I could visit him whenever I wanted. I remember laughing at him, but the then four-year-old eyes looking back at me were very serious. I explained that he could move out when he was eighteen, but until then I owned him outright and he had to stay put.

I giggled to myself at the memory, when I felt the bed move and found Bryce was standing at the end of it. I hadn't heard or seen him come in. He walked over and helped me to my feet then wiped the few tears that had stopped on my cheeks.

He kissed me softly and then cupped my face. 'It's going to be all right. I promise. We were meant to be together, and that's what matters in the end.'

I wanted to believe him, more than anything, but it's never just 'what matters in the end'.

It's never that simple.

CHAPTER

2

Bryce gave me a soft smile, infecting me with his enthusiasm. Maybe always being optimistic was the key to his success? Unfortunately, optimism was easier said than done in my case.

'Now, no more crying. You are far too beautiful to be drowned in tears.'

'I'm fine, Bryce. Really, I'm fine. I'm just worried about the kids, that's all. Thankfully, though, they're at the farm, one of their favourite places in the world.'

'What's their other favourite place?' he asked curiously.

'McDonald's,' I replied.

Laughing, he kissed me on the forehead then stood back and inspected my payback outfit. I watched with delight as he ran his hand through his hair and, of course, now I knew my plot was beginning to have an effect.

'You, Mr Clark, are in big trouble!'

'Why?' he scoffed, as his private-joke face returned.

'So you like the whole bird's nest look, eh?'

He started laughing. 'You can pull off any look, honey.' *You'll be pulling off after my next move, Mr Smartarse.*

'It's fine, have your little joke. I'll remember this,' I retorted and raised my eyebrow at him. Then, turning around, I bent over and placed both my hands on the bed in an over-exaggerated stretch for my handbag, making sure I took my sweet time to retrieve it. 'I will see you shortly. I have *work* to do.' I took hold of my bag, stood upright and catwalked toward the door.

'Ms Summers,' he growled. 'You do realise you have the day off?' *No, do I?*

I slowly turned to face him. 'And why is that, Mr Clark?'

'Because your boss says so.'

'Well, if it's the boss' orders, I can't exactly argue with them, can I?'

'No, you can't.'

'So, what should I do on my day off then?' I asked seductively, as I leaned up against the doorframe. Sort of like the seductive pose Sandy does in *Grease* to 'You're The One That I Want'. *Alexis, no wonder he laughs at you. You're an idiot.*

His hands flexed, indicating my plot was continuing to work. *Good. Make him beg.*

'You should do what your boss tells you to do,' he said firmly.

'But it is my day off. Therefore, my boss is not the boss.' I turned around and exited the room.

* * *

I knew he would be in pursuit, so I picked up my pace once I was around the corner. The problem was, my Jimmy Choos were not made for running. Therefore, I only made it as far as the top of the stairs before his arms reached around my shoulders and held me to him.

I screamed.

'Alexis,' he whispered as he kissed the back of my neck. 'You cannot run from me.' *Oh, crap, don't give in. Remember, make him beg.*

'I could if I weren't in heels. You have an unfair advantage.'

'Really?' He let me go and moved around to my front. 'I can fix that.' And with his cheeky smirk, slid down a few steps and picked up my foot. Slowly, he traced his finger up and down my calf, untied the buckle and removed my shoe. He repeated the same process with the other foot. 'Right, we are on even ground now. You've got a twenty-second head start. Go!' *What?*

I looked at him confused. But he turned and started counting as he walked back to his bedroom. *Shit! Hide and seek.* I squealed, hitched up my dress slightly and took off — jumping over the last two steps.

Where was Charlotte when I needed her? To label her a professional at this game would be an understatement. She could hide in the smallest and most difficult spots imaginable. *Fuck, where do I go?*

His apartment was huge. However, after desperately scanning my surroundings, I quickly concluded that I really didn't have many options — especially on the first floor. I had no choice but to head outside.

Luckily, the bifold doors were open, allowing me to sneak out onto the balcony without him hearing. I ran past the swimming pool and around the corner, noticing the doors to his dining area were also open. *Thank goodness.* This gave me a second escape route if needed.

Still searching frantically, I spotted the large home-gym machine up against the wall and next to that wall was a window. *That will do.* I quickly slotted in behind it and crouched down, hopefully in adequate disguise.

I could see into the apartment without giving my hiding spot away thanks to a large potted yucca, so I peered through the leaves and watched him come down the stairs. *You can seek me any day, hot stuff.* The way he walked and wore the most adorable smile ever plucked at my heart strings. It was obvious he enjoyed his games, and I enjoyed playing them with him.

My heart started to pound as the adrenaline began to build in my body. I watched him look towards the bifolds then over to the kitchen. I thought he was going for the latter as he started in that direction, but he went straight to his front door and left the apartment. *Shit, where is he going? Or is this a trick?*

I didn't know whether to stay or run; the excitement over one simple decision was nearly overpowering. Surely, he had to be going to his office. There was no other alternative as far as I knew. It was either that or he planned on coming back through the door in the hope he'd spy me leaving my hiding place.

Looking across to his office window which was only approximately a metre to my left, I leaned over slightly and peered in. I was right, he was heading very quickly through his office toward the spot I was hiding in and he caught me peeping through the window. *Crap.*

I screamed and used my second escape route, running through the open bifolds and into the dining area. This gave me an advantage as my doors were open and his weren't. I thought back to when I got stuck in his office, trying to escape through that same door, and it gave me a sense of satisfaction. *What goes around comes around, Mr Clark.*

Running into the lounge area, I noticed the door to a room near the front door, a room I had not been in yet. As it was my closest option, I made the decision to go in there, hoping it would be unlocked. What added to this gamble was the fact I had no idea what was in the mystery room and that it could be a dead end.

As I turned the handle, the door opened. *Thank goodness.* I quickly went in and closed it quietly behind me, almost sure I had successfully snuck in without him knowing.

To be honest, when I turned around it didn't surprise me to find the room resembled a recording studio/man cave. Really, there was bound to be one here somewhere!

Quickly scanning my new surroundings, I noticed different types of guitars, a drum kit, microphones, many speakers and some computer equipment. There was also a pool table, bar and Nintendo Wii. The room had an obvious absence of windows. However, there were two skylights that went up some two to three storeys high. I looked up into one of them. *Shit, they would be a pain in the arse to clean. Poor housekeeping.*

The room was intriguing and, as I slowly walked around it, assessing its contents, I was able to gain further insight into my Mr Adorable Clark. It was a fun room, a typical alpha male's room and well used by the looks of the sofa and the scuff marks on the pool table. There were also various guitars leaning up against the wall, each of them very impressive. *Of course they are impressive, what do you expect?*

I had never played one myself, although I had always wanted to learn how. I loved listening to songs with a good

guitar solo. My body reacted with awe to the sounds that resonated from the stringed wonders — I just loved them.

As I stepped up to lightly touch them, I was able to identify
a Gibson acoustic, Les Paul, and the Fenders, but I had absolutely no idea what the rest were. I also spotted some sheet
music on a stand. *Hmm, I wonder what he's been playing?*

Walking over to it, I stopped and looked at the page. There
was no song title, or anything familiar. As I had no idea how
to read music, the notes floating around on the paper were as
clear to me as hieroglyphics. I could, however, clearly make
out the scribbled words. There weren't a lot of full sentences,
but some words were strung together.

> *You're all that I want and nothing else*
> *I've fallen hard and will never get up*
> *I cannot let go, I won't*
> *You're infectious, my love*

*Oh, shit. My love? He's writing a song about me! Oh, no, I
shouldn't be in here. Crap!* The only way out of the room was
through the door I came in by. *Shit, shit, shit.* I approached
the door and that's when I heard him call out.

'Alexis. Come out, come out, wherever you are.' His voice
sounded as though it originated from higher within the apartment, so, thinking he must be on the second level, I opened
the door slightly and peeped out. My assumption was horribly wrong. He was in the middle of the lounge, approximately
six metres away, and when he spotted my peeking face, he lit
up like a Christmas tree. I squealed again and shut the door,
finding a lock and, with lightning speed, snibbing it, making
sure he could not get in.

Almost instantly, the handle turned, but the door did not open. *Phew, take that sucker!*

I sighed with relief.

'Alexis, you do realise you are trapped.' He spoke confidently, his voice filtering through the door panel.

I *was* trapped. I couldn't stay in the room all day.

'Do you give up?' he teased.

Hell, no! Alexis Summers never gives up. 'No, you haven't won yet.'

Suddenly, I heard the clinking of keys. *Of course, he has a key.* My cockiness subsiding, I quickly ran round to the other side of the pool table, which seemed to be my only ally in the room. I wasn't about to throw guitars and instruments at him.

The pool table and I were now a pair to be reckoned with, so I braced myself on the edge of it as the door clicked. Slowly, he pushed it open, making my throat pause mid-swallow. To say the sight of him standing in the doorway was the most irresistible sight I had ever seen would not be an over-exaggeration on my part. His jeans hung low on his hips, his bare feet a sexy addition to the casual and calm aura that he conveyed. But it was the wicked grin on his face, with a triumphant expression to match, that had me catching my breath.

'Got you, my love,' he said slowly as he stepped into the room, making my body tense.

I could barely contain my trembling voice. 'Not yet, you haven't.'

'You've got nowhere to go.' *This is true, Mr Clark.*

I didn't say anything ... I couldn't. I just stood there with my eyes fixed on him. I was not going to surrender, not this time. Slowly, he stepped toward me until he reached the other end of the pool table, then — still smiling his victory grin — he placed his hands on the edge.

'Give up yet?'

'You are quite cocky, Mr Clark.' *In more ways than one, I might add.*

'I always win, Ms Summers.' *Arrogant, much?*

I had the break of balls up my end of the table, so I started rolling them in the hope I'd hit his fingers, the balls now bouncing from cushion to cushion. Bryce just kept his cool and triumphant expression. So far, with four balls, I had missed. But the fifth one, I rolled with force and accuracy, hitting him on his left knuckles.

'Fuck!' he hissed, quickly lifting his hand to shake it.

My face lit up. 'Bullseye,' I giggled. And that began the chase.

He ran to his left, which made me do the same. He was quick, but I managed to keep the half-table distance between us, stopping in virtually the same spot we had started after only three laps. My chest was heaving and I was out of breath, probably a result of unfitness or overexcitement.

'Out of breath, honey?'

'Yes, you seem to have that affect on me,' I puffed, trying to slow my breathing.

'Good.' He took off again but this time to the right, and this time much quicker ... or I was slower. Either way, I could not keep the same distance I had before, so I had to abandon the table and head for the drums. I managed to get in behind them, but had well and truly sealed my fate. I was now in a corner with only the percussion set between us, and my chances of victory looked horribly slim.

'Do you yield?' he asked, his voice now soft.

I backed myself up against the wall. 'No, I don't yield.'

'That's one of the things I love about you.'

'I don't yield, but I will give myself up in exchange for something.'

'Anything. You know I would give or do anything for you.' *Yes, Bryce, I know you would. It's one of the things I love about you.*

'Play a Fender for me.'

He slowly moved around the drum kit then stood right in front of me, putting his hands on my hips. 'What do you want me to play?'

'Anything ... surprise me.'

'As you wish, my love.' He took hold of my hand and led me over to the pool table, then, gently replacing his hands on my hips, he lifted me up to sit on it. I watched him walk over to the cream-coloured Fender up against the wall. He picked it up, plugged it in and began to play.

The chords were like music to my ears. '*Stairway to Heaven*' ... *I love this song.*

I shook my head at him with a smile. 'Show off.'

I called him this for two reasons: one, it had one of the best solo guitar pieces ever written. And two, this was more of his creepy research in action. He smirked back at me. *Yes, definitely creepy research. How the fuck does he know this shit?*

Sitting there mesmerised, I watched how his left hand moved along the fingerboard with such controlled precision. He didn't falter and looked so incredibly natural behind the guitar. It was a massive turn-on, not that he needed anything other than himself to turn me on.

Recognising the chords in the chorus, a smile crept across my face. He was good, VERY good.

I seriously loved this song, I loved how it escalated in steps; it climbed and you climbed with it. I put my head back and closed my eyes, singing the lyrics in my head. There is a part in the song that mentions there are two paths you can go by, and as I sang it in my head, I felt incredibly connected to it.

Reopening my eyes, I discovered him staring at me, displaying an expression of want. Or was it need? This only added to my already increasing urge for him.

As the invisible sparks exploded between us, he began to play the chorus, his hand going up and down the fingerboard in swift fast movements — making his body move to the rhythm. *Oh, fuck me, that is so sexy ... and he hasn't even begun the solo yet.*

The solo was coming, though, and part of me was coming as well. The slow lead-up had me wanting, yearning, and as he broke into that particular piece of guitar brilliance, I couldn't help but fidget on the table.

Bryce noticed my lack of control, so I bit down on my lip and tried to regulate my enormous urge for him. The sheer sight of him at one with the Fender resulted in me squeezing my legs for fear of involuntarily touching myself.

I watched intently as he played the song, while its tempo escalated my sexual resolve. The speed with which his fingers were moving as he played was driving me wild. I wanted those fingers moving that quickly in a different place entirely, therefore my attempts at regulating my desperation for him were failing.

Slowly, he walked over to me as he performed the final notes, and I found myself panting and positioned on the pool table ready for him to devour. I could see that he knew exactly how I felt; all it took was an exchange of eye contact between us. I adored this connection we shared. It was sexy, but also sweet that a simple look could speak a thousand words.

Placing the guitar down on the table next to me, Bryce moved to stand in front of my knees. Normally, I would react to this stance by opening them. However, the revenge outfit I had chosen was so tight it restricted my desire to do so. He realised this and proceeded to roll the dress up my legs.

'You picked that song on purpose,' I breathed out as his hands slowly crept up my thighs.

'Yes, I did.'

'You are incredible.'

'I told you, I make it a priority to know every single —'

'No. I mean you're an incredible guitarist. I loved it.'

He slipped his finger underneath my underwear. 'Yes, I can see that.' Then pulled it back out and slid it into his mouth. *Oh, god!* His actions forced me to let out a small moan, which was when he replaced his finger back inside me.

Surrendering finally, I laid back on the pool table. 'I yield, I yield,' I confessed.

He removed his finger and tore off my G-string. 'Very good.'

'You can't keep destroying my underwear, I'll have none left,' I panted.

He raised his eyebrow, indicating he liked the idea.

I just shook my head at him.

Bryce then rolled my dress up my body, exposing me from my navel down, gazing upon my bare form as if I were a blank piece of canvas. A canvas he planned to spend much time on.

Pressing his lips to my abdomen, he kissed the scar I bore from giving birth to Charlotte. I wasn't ashamed of my scar.

It was a part of me that signified what I'd endured to give life to my precious daughter.

'So beautiful,' he murmured as his hands gripped my sides.

I sighed and arched my back. The fact he was kissing me on my scar was sexy as hell and it told me that he, too, appreciated my wound. I adored this sweet-natured and practical side of him, finding that he was not only heated, raw and passionate, but also incredibly down-to-earth and charming as well. He was fucking perfect.

I brought my head up from the table and smiled at him.

'What?' he asked, bemused by my grin.

'Nothing.' *Ah, let's see how you like the whole 'I'm not going to tell you what I'm smirking at' thing.*

'Are you smirking at me?'

'What if I am? What are you going to do about it?' I threatened.

It was obvious that he thrived on my challenges, because as soon as I'd finished declaring one, his face would respond with enthusiastic acceptance.

Growling aggressively, he plunged his tongue between my legs. At first I squealed at his sudden tenacity, but then the sensation of his movements quickly spread over me and my squealing turned to moaning almost instantly. *Oh, fuck.* The devouring I had eagerly hoped for was now well and truly under way.

His tongue was beyond merciless, lashing me ferociously, and forcing my hands to stretch out, sending balls scattering in all directions. They bounced from cushion to cushion.

He continued his luscious assault on my pussy, twirling his tongue in every direction he saw fit. My body refused to remain stationary, a result of the incredible climax he had compelled me to reach.

I couldn't help but passionately call out his name. 'Bryce ...'

I flipped over eagerly and positioned myself on all fours as he climbed up on the table.

'No, I like to see you. I like to see your face — to watch you enjoy it.'

I rolled back over. 'Better?'

'Mm,' he groaned, then kissed me and entered my body enthusiastically. *Sex on a pool table? I wonder if there's a cocktail named after that.*

I did a happy-clap in my head, but my happiness soon faded as I felt my arse start to burn, my moans of delight momentarily turning into moans of discomfort. I must've displayed an expression to match.

Bryce slowed his movements to question me. 'What's wrong?'

'Nothing.' *Endure it, Alexis, you little wimp.*

'Alexis!' he growled, stilling his movements with a menacing look.

I started laughing, placed both hands across my face, and then hesitantly confessed. 'I think I'm getting carpet burn on my arse.' *Oh. My. God. How embarrassing!*

'Are you serious? Show me.'

He pulled out, so I rolled over to show him.

'Yes, so you are,' he chuckled, lightly slapping my tender spot.

'Ouch!'

He laughed again, bent down, and kissed my arse.

'You must be telepathic,' I stated, with misguided conviction.

'Why's that?' he mumbled as he gently nipped at my cheeks.

'Because I was about to tell you to kiss my arse.'

Before I knew it, he had me snagged across the waist and was hauling me over to the fluffy rug which lay in between the TV and couches.

I screamed and then giggled. 'You're barbaric.'

'If I was barbaric, honey, I would've continued to fuck on the pool table.'

He gently laid me down on the plush pile.

'Well, should I consider myself lucky then?'

He raised his eyebrow, suggestively. 'We'll soon see.'

I watched with dubious horror as he fell forward toward me. It made me squeal. I didn't think he was going to stop and my breasts — although they make good cushions — were not going to take the impact very well.

Closing my eyes, I waited ... but nothing happened. Curious, I reopened one of them to find he had stopped just above me with his elbows locked, the muscles in his upper region flexed and hard. Surprise and relief flooded over me, so I screwed up my face which made him laugh.

'Not funny,' I sulked. Although I did like the look of his impeccable arms, hard and taut as they were. I ran my hands along them, they truly were exquisite. 'Mr Clark, what big arms you have,' I murmured provocatively, giving him a cheeky grin. I then brought mine up and hit the insides of his elbows quite hard, forcing them to give way so that he would land on my chest. I grabbed hold of him and savoured his glorious mouth with my own.

'Remind me not to teach you any more self-defence moves,' he mumbled around my tongue.

Bryce smiled and took hold of both my hands, placing them above my head and holding them securely in place. Then, as if my knees were programmed to his instruction, they rose up, allowing him to insert his still firm cock inside me once again.

I indulged in his glorious rhythm and silently agreed that facing him during our lovemaking was undoubtedly the way to go. It allowed us to taste each other and this only added to our exhilaration. I also loved reading his eyes as we consumed each other entirely. It gave me an insight into the incredibly private and intriguing mind that Bryce had — a mind I wanted to know exclusively.

I gently closed my eyes as I moaned in delight, the feel of him just perfect. He kissed my eyelids, making me open my mouth wider for him to repeat the kiss there.

'I love you, Alexis. Please don't forget that. Whatever happens, know that I love you.'

His sincere plea had me reopening my eyes, and what I saw on his face triggered my stomach to churn. There it was again, a look of concern along with more of that unnerving talk I had heard earlier this morning. I really didn't like it.

'I know that you love me, but why do you feel you have to keep reassuring me? Is there something you are not telling me? If there is, please just tell me.' I kissed him again, hoping it would encourage him to open up to me, but instead, he kept pushing and pushing, harder and deeper, making me forget our discussion to focus on the pleasure he was bestowing upon me. Which I'm guessing was his plan.

I began to climb toward my climax — my body alive with sensations — and as he thrust into me with everything he had, it brought me undone and took him along with me. I dug my nails into his back as he emptied his erection, a harsh growl escaping him in the process.

He sealed his lips to mine almost desperately, caressing my tongue with his own to the point where I had to break away for the need of air.

'Bryce, what's wrong?'

'Nothing.' He touched my cheek lightly, but his eyes were betraying him. There was definitely something wrong, I could tell, and it left a sickly feeling at the very base of my stomach.

CHAPTER
3

Lying on the rug, I continued to search his eyes for a clue as to what secret he was keeping from me.

'Bryce, I don't like secrets, so if there is something you need to tell me, do it now.'

His expression was pained but then faded, a sly smile replacing it.

'Honey, there is nothing to worry about. Now, come and get dressed in something more suitable. You won't want to wear that where we will be spending the next couple of days.'

The fascinating thought of our mystery destination distracted me from the uncertainty I felt. But, more so, I had to respect the fact he was not ready to tell me. To be honest, I didn't like it, because I was well aware that burying it for now was only a temporary fix. The thing was, clearly he wasn't giving me a choice.

Bryce helped me to my feet, and we went back upstairs.

* * *

I looked over my shoulder as I turned on the tap to the shower. 'Are you joining me?' Bryce was standing in the doorway, watching me with a smile that melted my heart.

'In a minute, you go in,' he smirked.

'What are you up to now?' I asked, in an accusing tone. He winked and left the bathroom.

I stepped into the shower for the second time that day. Not that it really mattered, because I had to get changed again. Besides, I enjoyed having a shower, especially when he joined me. So, moments later when he appeared holding a towel out for me, I sulked.

'You're not coming in?'

'No, you know what will happen if I do. You need to get dressed, I need a shower and then we need to get out of here.'

'What do I put on? I don't know where we are going, remember.'

'I've laid it out on the bed for you.' He wrapped the towel around me, kissed my nose and got into the shower.

'I'm capable of dressing myself, you know.'

He chuckled and grabbed his body wash. 'Not when you don't know where you are going you're not.' *Grrr.*

I started to dry myself off but became distracted while admiring him bathe. What was it about a naked body, water, soapsuds and a large loofah sponge that was so fucking sensual? Whatever it was, had me standing there gawking at him like an idiot.

I swallowed heavily as the sexy mixture of ingredients fell down his neck, stopping momentarily on his lightly-haired chest and then continuing down his rippled abdomen, only to stop once again at his groin. At that point, I think I licked my lips, no doubt resembling one of those cartoon characters. The ones whose eyes bulge out of their heads a good metre or so then spring back in again. *Yoohoo, Alexis, there are other parts of your body that need drying.*

Snapping out of my mouthwatering perve, I realised I had already dried my chest and stomach several times. So I bent over to dry my calves and feet, once again becoming dazed by his soapy gloriousness. Unfortunately for me, I lost my balance and fell over.

He popped his smirking face around the glass. 'Are you all right?' he asked, stifling a laugh yet trying to sound concerned.

'I'm fine, thank you,' I answered between gritted teeth and a faux smile. *Alexis, you are a perving idiot.*

He stepped out from behind the screen, offered me a hand and secured me to his chest. 'I know how it feels, my love.' *What, falling on your arse and landing on cold bathroom tiles?* 'I've fallen for you, too.' He burst into laughter and managed to dodge my swinging hand.

'Very funny,' I grouched, pushing him back toward the shower and stomping out of the room shaking my head.

* * *

When I walked into Bryce's bedroom, I found an outfit lying on the bed. I picked up the Country Road denim shorts and tan-coloured suede ankle boots. *Interesting!* There was also a white tank top and a matching tan suede vest. It's not what I had expected, but I loved it.

As I was buttoning up the vest, Bryce entered the room with his towel around his waist, his eyebrow rising, indicating approval.

'Where are we going?' I asked, curiously.

'You'll see,' he teased as he entered the walk-in stadium. *Grrr, he is adorably annoying.* I put on the ankle boots and zipped them up.

Moments later he came out dragging two suitcases and was dressed in a pair of grey cargo shorts, a Quicksilver t-shirt and a pair of runners. This was the most casual I had seen him, apart from his birthday suit, of course. He looked gorgeous. *When did he not?*

'Ready?' he asked, looking quite pleased with himself.

I nodded, grabbed my handbag, and went to take a case from him.

He playfully lifted his leg to kick me on the bum. 'Alexis, get your arse over to the elevator.'

'So ... are you going to tell me now?' I asked as we stepped into the elevator.

'Tell you what?' he playfully asked as he pressed the basement button. *You fucking know what, you stubborn, sexy bag of goodness.* I shook my head at him and started tapping my fingers on the rail.

Diverting my attention from his obstinacy, I gave a thought to texting Mum in order to inform her I was going away for a couple of days. I assumed we weren't leaving the country because two days was not long enough, and I didn't have my passport with me. *Hmm, maybe I could get our destination out of him in a different way.*

'Is there phone reception where we are going?' I asked, curiously.

He laughed. 'We are not going to the moon, Alexis.' *Well, you never know, Mr Smarty-pants. You do like astronomy and you are incredibly resourceful.*

Feeling tenacious myself, I decided to play his game along with him. 'Well, now I'm really disappointed. I would have liked to have gone to the moon. I guess I've fallen in love with the wrong billionaire, then?' I crossed my arms and continued my act.

'No, you haven't.'

He let go of the cases and hit the red button. The elevator screeched to a stop and my legs nearly buckled beneath me. I braced myself on the rails and looked at him in shock. *Oh, shit, did I upset him? I was only playing.* He turned to me then pressed his body against mine, backing me up hard against the wall. 'Have you?' he mouthed my neck.

'Have I what?' I said, confused and mesmerised by the luscious feel of his lips on my skin.

'Fallen in love with the wrong billionaire?' he replied as he nipped at my neck and cupped my breast in his hand.

'No, I haven't,' I sighed, now intoxicated by his seduction. 'So, are you going to tell me where we are going or not?'

He breathed heavily onto my neck then ran his nose through my hair. 'Not.'

Grrr. 'I hate you.'

'No, you don't.' *No, I don't.*

He hit the button again, and we resumed our descent. *Well, that didn't work.*

* * *

Danny — Bryce's chauffeur — was waiting in the basement. He opened the door for us and placed our bags in the boot.

As I stepped into the limo, I smiled to myself, thinking of the antics my friends and I had gotten up to the last time we were in there. I was actually quite surprised I hadn't received any messages from the girls after the previous night's telecast. They would have all seen it. *It's still early days. This is the calm before the storm. You wait, Operation Let's-hassle-Alexis will begin soon enough.*

Bryce sat next to me and put his arm around my shoulder, prompting me to nestle into his side and breathe into his chest. *Geez, he smells good.*

The smell was familiar.

'What aftershave are you wearing?' I asked, sucking in another familiar whiff while he appeared to be racking his brain.

'Prada,' he said after taking a sniff himself. *I thought as much.* I had bought this one for Rick on his birthday because I loved it.

It's funny how a simple smell, if recognised, can instantly bring memories flooding back. Mind you, it's not particularly funny how this specific smell was doing that now. The last thing I wanted was to sit here in Bryce's arms and have memories of Rick — it saddened me, and I felt myself lulled a little. *Alexis, don't do this to yourself, what has happened is out of your hands.*

I tried to get thoughts of Rick out of my head, but he was buried in there somewhere and clearly able to be resurrected by smell. For the past couple of days I had been successfully keeping myself busy with sex acrobatics, which were a good form of distraction from the mess my life was currently in ... beneficial for diverting my thoughts, but not a permanent solution.

With all the smell-induced memories on my mind, I hadn't noticed us pull in to Essendon Airport and stop directly in front of a jet. I glanced out the window to the plane beside us, noticing that it didn't say 'Clark Incorporated'. Instead, on the tail was the designation, 'Challenger 604'.

Danny opened the door of the limo, and Bryce climbed out, offering me his hand and leading me to the jet.

'Don't tell me this is yours as well?' I asked with uncertainty.

'No, honey, I rent it. Why? Do you want it to be?' The teasing look in his eyes suggested he'd be more than happy to prove he could buy it if I wanted him to — which I didn't — so I glared at him and began to climb the steps.

Suddenly, I heard a low groaning noise from behind. I had a sneaking suspicion as to the source of the sound, and looked back at Bryce to see what he was growling at.

'Your arse in denim, my love, does things to my cock.'

My eyes widened in shock. 'Bryce Clark!' *He is very sexy and oh-so-naughty when he talks dirty to me.* He smacked my behind which quickened my steps.

As I was about to enter the aircraft, I heard a female's voice calling his name. At first, I thought I had imagined it, but after turning around and searching the tarmac to pinpoint where it was coming from, I discovered it was Chelsea and she was jogging toward the plane like a desperate lunatic. *Seriously, is this bitch always around?*

'Bryce,' she gasped, out of breath.

Bending over and putting her hands on her knees, she held up her hand to suggest she needed a second to regain her composure. Either that, or she was hoping he'd rush to her aid, thinking she was about to collapse. *I hope she collapses and a plane runs over her. Alexis, take that back. Okay, I hope she collapses and we leave her here.*

She looked up and noticed me on the top platform of the boarding stairs. 'Oh. Hello, Alexis.'

I smiled sweetly at her. 'Chelsea.'

'Bryce, do you have a moment?' she asked, giving him an important look.

He turned and glanced up at me, maybe to ask permission, I'm not quite sure? *Since when does he need my permission to do anything?* I was confused by the look, so smiled awkwardly and entered the plane.

A lovely young woman greeted me by name as I stepped inside.

'Ms Summers, my name is Amy, and I will be your hostess during the flight.'

'Hi, Amy. Pleased to meet you. So, where are we flying to today?' For a split second I thought she was going to let it slip. Unfortunately, that was not the case.

'I'm so sorry, Ms Summers, but I am sworn to secrecy.' She smiled apologetically and escorted me further into the plane.

Wow, this thing is stunning. It really was something else. From outside, the aircraft had appeared relatively small, but when you walked inside, it was actually quite spacious. Maybe that was because there was not row upon row of seating crammed together like commercial economy class. Instead, on the left-hand side of the plane were two cream-coloured, leather reclinable seats facing each other, and on the right-hand side were the same two seats but with a small table in between them.

'Can I get you something to drink while we wait for take-off, Ms Summers?'

'No thank you, Amy. I'm fine.'

'Very well. The bathroom is down the back through those doors if you need it. Please take a seat when you are ready as we will be leaving shortly.' She turned and headed back to the galley.

I walked further along the plane past two three-seaters which spanned both sides of the aircraft. They looked like futons and I imagined they probably folded out into beds. I went to take a seat on one of them when I noticed Bryce and Chelsea talking outside. They looked quite comfortable with each other and I'd probably take a guess and say they had known one another for some time. Maybe Bryce had learned to become a pilot at her father's training company? Or maybe they had known one another as kids?

I watched her bat her eyes at him while they talked. She would stand with her hands behind her back, then move one to her hip and put the other through her hair. It was obvious she was flirting with him — her body language suggested it — and it was this display, and his relaxed disposition, which made it quite clear they had shared a past. *I don't trust that bitch, I don't trust her at all.*

Bryce went to turn and leave when she placed her hand on his arm and leaned up to kiss his cheek. My face flushed red and I felt my nails dig into the leather seat with force. Chelsea's victorious smile crept across her face as she looked up at the plane and directly at me. *You know what? I really do hope a plane runs over you, you little tramp.* I glared at her and stood up. I was embarrassed, hurt and jealous — *very* jealous.

He broke away and followed her stare in the direction of the plane, but I had moved away from the window before he could meet my gaze. *I hate her. I hate that licking-lips, helicopter pilot, snotty little moll.* I turned myself in circles for a moment, not knowing what to do, then I headed for the bathroom.

Opening the door, I tucked myself inside, quickly locking it behind me. *What are you doing, Alexis? You can't hide in here the whole time. Get a grip. She kissed him, not the other way around, and it was a peck on the cheek, it was nothing.* The fact of the matter was it had hurt me. I didn't want anyone else touching or kissing him. I felt that Bryce's cheeks belonged to me. Or did they? He was keeping a secret, that was obvious. Maybe that was it: Chelsea was his ex and he still had feelings for her. Or she was a stalker? Or she was pregnant? *Alexis Elizabeth Summers, stop this now.* I started to hyperventilate, so I sat down on the toilet seat, bent over and stuck my head between my legs. *Alexis, for fuck's sake girl, breathe.* That's when I heard a knock on the door.

'Alexis, are you all right?' *Shit, I can't go out there yet.*

'Yes, I'll be out in a minute,' I replied, my voice shaky, the apprehension obvious in my words.

I grabbed a towel, dampened it and patted my rosy cheeks. *Alexis, you are thirty-five years of age, stop acting like a child. He loves you and has made that* more *than clear.* He had, of course he had, but when I thought about it, I didn't really know him. I had only been in his life for what ... a couple of months? He knew me inside and out, but I only knew him on the surface and I had only a very small insight into his past. It was nowhere near enough to comfortably say that I believed, beyond a shadow of a doubt, that he was 'absolutely and undoubtedly' in love with me. What I did know was that I was horribly jealous of Chelsea, which was strange because I had never been this jealous in my life, even when it came to Rick and Claire flirting at that Christmas party. *Argh!*

My rapid breathing increased, so I put my head back between my legs. *Alexis, what are you doing? Yes, you know nothing about him. But what you both feel is real, that is unde-niable.* I lifted my head and looked in the mirror. It was real, regardless of the time frame, but it was all happening so fast. *Right! Stop questioning everything, get the hell out of this hidey-hole and go enjoy your mystery flight.* Taking a couple of deep breaths, I opened the door to find him standing just outside.

He cupped my face in his hands, and I could see the concern in his eyes. 'Are you okay?'

'Yes,' I replied, looking down automatically. *Stupid, that's the first sign of lying.*

He tilted my head back up. 'I'm sorry. I didn't think she would still be here. I knew she wasn't going to be at the hotel today as she had a couple of late flights last night after the awards, but I assumed she'd be done with the Bell Ranger by now and then be gone.'

'What? Chelsea? No, it's not her, I'm fine.' I pecked his cheek in the same spot she did and almost wiped my mouth. *Eww, I hate her.*

He was about to protest my explanation when Amy walked in.

'Mr Clark, if you are ready, we can take off now,' she advised.

I took advantage of his momentary distraction and moved to the recliner, sitting down to buckle myself in.

'Yes, Amy, we're ready. Thank you.' He took the seat opposite me and looked intently at my face, trying to read my emotions.

I gave him a meek smile, then looked out the window. Amy briefly checked that the cabin was secure and that we were buckled in, then took her seat back in the galley.

Still looking out the window when the plane began its taxi to the top of the airstrip, I could feel Bryce's gaze upon me and found it incredibly difficult not to return his stare. Thankfully, the plane stopped, the engines roared to life and we took off down the runway.

Sitting upright, I peered out the window, resembling the child I still was at heart when it came to flying. The fact that people, houses, cars and trees became tiny during the climb still amused me.

Looking out of the window the entire flight was obviously not an option; therefore, with reluctance, I turned in his direction and met his concerned stare. We weren't speaking, yet our eyes were in deep discussion. I could see he was pained at my cool disposition, and I could also see he was distressed by the fact that he was deliberately keeping something from me. It was clear he was desperate to confide, but for some reason he couldn't.

The captain's voice came over the speaker, momentarily breaking our eye contact.

'Good afternoon, Mr Clark and Ms Summers. We have now reached an altitude of 30,000 feet and will arrive at our destination in approximately four hours' time. You may now remove your seat belts, and please enjoy your flight.'

I have never seen someone move so fast in my life. Bryce's belt was off, and he was on his knees at my feet within a second.

'Alexis, please tell me what's wrong? Have I done something to upset you?' he pleaded.

My initial stubborn, jealous reaction was to brush him off, but as I looked into his desperate eyes, I couldn't do it. 'You and Chelsea were once a couple, weren't you?'

He put his head down on my lap. *Oh, shit, here we go.* 'No, not really. Well, yes ... sort of.'

'Oh. please, Bryce. Did you fuck her or not? It's not that hard a question,' I snapped, as I rolled my eyes.

He raised his head and looked at me, still displaying evidence of worry. But now, he also seemed somewhat amused.

'Yes, we did fuck, but it never went anywhere. We didn't have a connection, not like the one I have with you.'

'When were you last with her?' I needed to know it wasn't recently. I didn't think I could take it if it were.

He paused for a minute. *You'd better be calculating, Mr Clark, rather than concocting a story.*

'It would have been about two years ago.'

'So were you a couple or not?' I asked again.

His posture slumped, and I think at this point he realised I was more than jealous. I was upset, upset that I knew nothing about him.

'Honey, please don't be mad. There is nothing between me and Chelsea, I promise.'

'Bryce, you didn't answer my question. Were you a couple or not?'

'In my eyes, no. In her eyes, yes,' he answered quickly.

'So what are we, then? You know ... just to clarify we are both on the same page.' My voice had an edge of sarcasm and hurt to it.

He rested his cheek on my knee and resembled a pleading puppy. 'I love you, Alexis. I've never loved anyone like I love you, and one day I hope you'll become my wife.' *Oh, okay, you can't get any more clarity than that.*

A lump formed in my throat and my eyes began to flood with tears. I think the built-up hurt I felt was not only due to the realisation I knew nothing about him and that Chelsea was his ex, but it was also due to ending my twelve-year marriage that I had thought was rock-solid. I couldn't contain myself any longer and tears now streamed down my face.

He knelt higher and gently touched my cheek. 'Don't cry. I'm sorry.'

'No, I'm sorry. It's just ... I don't know anything about myself any more. Up until a few weeks ago, I was in what I thought was a happy marriage. Now I'm here in a private jet, on the way to God knows where, with a man I'm in love with and know nothing about.'

I put my head in my hands.

Bryce stood up, took my hands away from my face, and pulled me to stand flush with his chest.

'Come over here.' He led me to the three-seater lounge and sat down, then patted his thigh as an invitation to sit. I obliged and curled into his lap. 'Okay, we have four hours. What do you want to know? And by the way, we are going to Uluru.'

CHAPTER
4

Uluru, Ayers Rock! Oh, wow, I've always wanted to go there. He could not have discovered this by creepy research, as I didn't think I had ever actually made it known that I wanted to go there. Then again, the question of how he was always able to gather such personal information about me remained a mystery, so I could not entirely rule out that our trip to the Red Centre was a result of me secretly wanting to go there.

'Why Uluru?'

'I've never been and neither have you. I thought you could add this to your list of firsts with me.'

He really was quite thoughtful and sweet, even if it had a small element of his mysterious creepy research.

I wiped my eyes and nose and sniffed away the remnants of my outpouring of emotion. 'Sounds wonderful, thank you, but tell me ... How do you know so much about me? How do you know I haven't been there before? How do you do your creepy research?'

A small smile crept in at the corner of his mouth. 'A magician never reveals his secrets.'

'You're not a freakin' magician, so spill it.'

'I've told you before. Lucy,' he answered. *Grrr.*

I sighed in exhaustion, not wanting to argue, or fight, or worry any more. I felt somewhat deflated.

'Honey, you need to understand this is new for me as well. I want to tell you everything you want to know, and I want you to feel that you know me inside and out. Screwing this up is not an option for me. I will not lose you.' He pressed my head to his chest and ran his hand down the side of my face. *I don't want to lose you, either.*

'Bryce, all I can fathom right now is that I have a week to share with you unconditionally,' I said quietly as I hugged his chest. 'My children are happy at Mum and Dad's house, not to mention safely away from all the shit. I'm not ready to confront Rick yet, and I won't be for some time, so this week is what we have right now.'

I pulled away from his chest to look into his eyes. 'I honestly do not know what is going to happen in the long run, but I do know that I will have to go back home and dissect what Rick's infidelity means for me and my children. I couldn't possibly be with him again knowing that he cheated on me so long ago and never said a word about it until now. Five years is a long time to hide such a betrayal. And anyway ...' I trailed off. 'He won't want to be with me either, knowing that I have fallen for you. He's a proud man. This is as much as I can comprehend right now, but I have to consider what it will do to my children. They are my first priority.'

'I understand you need to sort out what is best for you and the kids. The thing is, *I* am what is best for you, and I will do whatever I can to make you realise that. This is not just some one-week whirlwind romance to me, Alexis.'

I snuggled back into him. 'I know, really I do. It's just ... I don't know a hell of a lot about you. I know a little about your family, and I know your talents ...' *Boy, do I know your talents.* 'and your interests, but that's about it.'

'What would you like to know?'

The questions started to swirl around in my head, lining up patiently and taking a number. *Have you been engaged before? Better still, have you ever been married? Do you have any children floating around? Have you told Chelsea she has no chance with you? What are you hiding from me?*

'Have you ever been married or engaged before?' I asked with baited breath.

'No, before you I had never met anyone I wanted to share the rest of my life with.' *Oh, shit.*

'Why?'

'Don't get me wrong, I have been in relationships before, if you can call them that —'

'Hang on, hang on. "If you can call them that"? Really, Bryce? Do you not know the definition of a relationship?'

He moved me away from his chest. 'Ms Summers, what one person perceives as a relationship may not be what another does. This was the case with me and Chelsea. A relationship to me is one where two people connect on a level that could lead to forever. Yes, Chelsea and I connected, but it was never going to be "forever". I couldn't see a future with her. I tried, but it just wasn't there.'

Thank fuck for that.

'Was there anyone else who could've been a "forever"?'

Answering my questions hadn't seemed to faze him thus far, and the fact he could be so open with me about his past was endearing.

'When I was twenty-three, I met Sarah. We both went to a "group", a group that Jessica had arranged. Sarah, too, had lost her parents suddenly, and we could relate to one another. At first I thought maybe she could be a "forever" because we shared something so personal. But, after a couple of months together, I realised that was all it was; a mutual connection of loss. We are still friends and catch up every so often for a coffee.'

His answers so far were open and honest, but they left me feeling as confused as ever.

'What is it? You look worried,' he asked, removing my chewed thumb from between my teeth.

'I'm not worried. I'm just a little confused.'

'What about?' he smirked. *Oh, stop that.*

'You shared connections with Chelsea and Sarah. You had something in common with them both. With Chelsea, you are both pilots. And with Sarah, you shared a deep understanding of loss and grief.'

'Yes, and how is that confusing?'

'Well, we don't share anything like that. We have nothing in common. What's so special about me, then? I'm just Alexis, a thirty-something mother of two. I don't get it.'

I honestly didn't. I couldn't fly a paper plane let alone a helicopter, and the greatest loss I had suffered was my pet dog of thirteen years — which was horrible, mind you — but it was nothing compared to the loss of both your parents and brother.

He shook his head at me. 'Just Alexis, eh. What is so special about you? Oh, honey, you have no fucking idea what you do to me. I can't get you out of my head. I think about you 24/7. The way you look, the way you smell ... your confidence in everything that you do. I love how you read between the lines and the way you challenge me. I love your innocence, your kindness, your nurturing ways and your jealousy. When I'm with you I feel alive, like you are the missing part of me. And when I'm not with you, I can't stand it, I literally feel lost. It is fucking unbearable.' *Oh, shit, is that all?*

I sat there speechless, taking in what he had just declared, the heartfelt words bringing tears to my eyes. The honesty behind the admission of his true feelings for me penetrated my chest and completely ensnared my heart. I had never been spoken to like that before and it blew me away.

Repositioning myself astride him, I pressed my forehead to his. I couldn't possibly top his extremely heartfelt confession, but I opened my mouth to offer my feelings for him anyway. I owed him that at least.

'I have never felt like this either, Bryce. Don't get me wrong, I loved Rick — and I still do to an extent — but what I feel deep in here ...' I pressed his hand to my chest. 'What I feel deep in here when I am with you is like nothing I have ever experienced before. You control the tempo of my heart. You make it beat like crazy when you read me with your eyes. You make it beat like crazy with your selfless gestures. You make it beat like crazy when you make love to me.'

His hand twitched ever so lightly on my chest.

'You make it beat like crazy every time you smirk at me. You make it beat like crazy every time your lips touch mine. You just make it beat like fucking crazy full stop,' I whispered as I pressed my lips to his. Some of my salty menaces escaped my eyes, running down my cheeks and into our mouths.

He held me tightly and deepened our kiss, our tongues tangoing like never before. I knew now this was another form of communication we shared with each other, a communication without words, just like our silent exchanges of eye contact. This kiss said everything. It said, *I love you* 'absolutely and undoubtedly', it said 'it's not going to be easy but we will sort it out,' and it said we were 'one'.

Continuing our oral message, it started to convey we were heading towards the mile-high club. So I pulled his t-shirt up and ran my hands down his back making him groan. He placed his hands on my arse, pulling me into him, making me moan. I thought we were about to change gears from kissing to let's get naked when, simultaneously, we slowed ourselves down and took a deep breath, jumping back into neutral and resuming our silent discussion. It was the most overwhelming and romantic kiss ever.

'Are you hungry?' he asked, his eyes still closed.

'Yes, for you.' *I want a bowl of Bryce soup with a side of Mr Clark, please.*

Standing up with me still attached to his waist, he walked us over to the recliners and table.

'We can eat each other later, Ms Summers.'

'Good.' I unwrapped my legs and slid off him then we both sat down.

Bryce looked over his shoulder toward the galley. 'Amy, we are ready for lunch now.'

Moving the curtain aside swiftly, Amy stepped out. *Oh, shit! I forgot she was there. She would've heard everything we just said, including the notion of ourselves being on the menu later.*

My cheeks flushed red as she approached our seats. No ... delete that, they flushed fire-engine red.

'Certainly, Mr Clark, Ms Summers. What can I get you both to drink?' *Fuck! Do you serve anything that makes you disappear into thin air? If so, I'll have that thanks.*

I was so morbidly embarrassed that I couldn't even bring myself to look at her. Bryce, on the other hand, just raised his eyebrows at me. *I don't know. You choose. You seem to do a good job of that.*

I shrugged my shoulders.

'Alexis will have a gin and squash, and I'll have a Scotch.'

Amy nodded then turned back around. *Oh, my god, thank goodness.*

Just as she exited the cabin, my phone started to ring, surprising me a little. I fumbled as I tried to get it out of my bag. *Alexis, calm down, you moron. The plane is not about to take a nosedive.*

'Oh, crap. I forgot to turn it off,' I whispered apologetically.

I picked it up, seeing it was Tash.

'You can answer it. Paul is confident it won't affect the avionics.'

'Who is Paul?'

'The pilot,' he laughed. *Okay, good, a reputable source for information!*

I hit accept, and before I could even say 'Hi', Tash began singing 'The Lady In Red' by Chris de Burgh. I quickly hit the speaker button and let her continue.

Bryce tilted his head to the side, so I mouthed the word 'Tash'. He smiled and nodded then cringed when she hit a high note.

'You finished?' I asked her.

'Yep,' she answered confidently, sounding pleased with herself.

'Say hi to Bryce, Tash.'

'What?' Her confidence had seemingly disappeared.

Bryce put on his stern voice. 'Hi, Natasha.'

She went quiet for a second, and I struggled to hold my laughter.

'Oh. Hi, Mr Clark ... Bryce.'

I couldn't help myself and lost it, laughing and clutching my side. 'Hi, Mr Clark, Bryce. Tash, you idiot.'

Bryce chuckled also.

'Alexis Summers, take me off speaker right now,' she demanded, clearly unimpressed. So I hit the 'speaker off' button and put the phone to my ear, giving Bryce a cheeky self-satisfied wink.

'How can I help you, my lovely?' I asked, sounding obnoxiously cocky.

'You bitch! I'm going to kill you.'

'Serves you right!'

'Well, you were wearing red last night, I thought it was appropriate. So, how was the Tel V Awards? Can you talk right now?'

'No, hon, I can't. I'll try calling you later though.'

'Fuck trying. You *will* call me later.'

'Okay, will do. Mwah,' I said, making a kissing noise at the phone. 'Talk to you soon.'

She reciprocated and hung up, then, almost instantly, I received a text message. It was one word.

Bitch — Tash

Did I not predict Operation Let's-hassle-Alexis would begin eventually?

Putting the phone back into my bag, I smiled politely as Amy walked in with a trolley containing our lunch and drinks.

'Ms Summers, seafood dumplings in a lemongrass and coconut soup.' *Aw, yum!*

'Mr Clark, red wine braised beef short ribs, with polenta.'

She placed both dishes in front of us, together with our drinks. The food looked fabulous, better than any in-flight meal I'd ever seen.

'Enjoy. Please let me know if you would like anything further.'

We thanked her, and she returned to the galley.

'Did you pick this?' I asked as I picked up my spoon.

'Of course!'

I noticed him watching and waiting for a reaction as I dipped my spoon into my bowl.

'Eat your lunch and stop watching me.' I glared at him.

'Yes, ma'am,' he saluted.

I tilted my head to the side. He was so cute and cheeky. Squinting my eyes at him, I sipped the soup from my spoon. *Oh, holy fuck! My tongue just fainted in sheer indulgent pleasure. If it could scream and climax, it would have.*

Glancing back at Bryce, my eyes nearly bulged out of my head. 'Whoever made this has just given me my fourth orgasm for the day! Wow!'

A large smile spread across his face.

'You didn't,' I gasped. 'You did!'

He put a forkful of beef into his mouth. 'I'll take responsibility for all four then, shall I?' *I'm sure you'll rack up about ten by the end of the day.*

'You are a genius. This is the best thing I have ever eaten.'

He raised one eyebrow seductively, stirring my insides. *Oh, it's going to be like that, is it?*

Picking up my spoon, I kept my eyes on his and sipped the soup again. This time, though, I put the whole spoon in my mouth then slowly pulled it out again. I licked the tip of it and dragged it along my tongue, making him shift in his seat.

'Mr Clark, can I taste your meat?' I asked, smiling seductively at him.

He forked a bit of beef and leaned over. 'Ms Summers, you can taste my meat anytime.'

'Is it thick, rich and full of flavour?' I asked, innocently.

'You won't find one, thicker, richer or tastier!' he smirked, his expression nearly making me giggle.

I opened my mouth and he gently placed the fork inside. Immediately, I pressed my lips together, surrounding the fork entirely as he slowly pulled it out.

'Well? Was that the best meat you have ever had in your mouth?'

I swallowed and licked my lips. 'I've had better.'

Bryce glared at me, causing my heart to pound in my chest.

I licked my lips again as he picked up his Scotch. 'So, Mr Clark, would you like to taste my fish?'

He choked, nearly spitting his Scotch out, then, struggling to swallow his mouthful he grabbed a napkin and wiped his mouth.

'Is it good fish?' he choked out, still trying to clear his throat.

I bit down on my lip in order to supress my laugh. He was very good at this game, and I didn't know how much longer I could keep this performance up. *Alexis, stay strong. You have this one in the bag.*

Regaining my composure, I answered. 'You won't taste better. My fish is like no other.' I spooned a dumpling, stood up, and then leaned over, putting my hand under his chin to feed him the contents before waiting for his response. 'That's good fish, isn't it?' I asked while pulling the spoon out of his mouth. I then sucked it and trailed it down into my breasts.

'Yes, you have delicious fish, Ms Summers.'

'Why, thank you.'

He cracked up laughing, me along with him.

'I do believe that win belongs to me, Mr Clark.'

He continued chuckling as he ate the rest of his lunch. 'Yes, honey, you can definitely have that one.'

* * *

I savoured my dumpling soup right down to the very last drop. The two of us continued talking during the remainder of the flight which was just what I needed. He shared some more about himself, and I asked him if he was going to set Chelsea straight once and for all. He assured me he would do it the next time he saw her and that I had absolutely nothing to worry about where she was concerned. I also discovered that he had no love children floating around, no hidden gay or threesome tendencies — which he found highly amusing — and that he had a phobia about clowns.

'So, no romantic dates at Cirque du Soleil, then?' I enquired, teasingly.

His eyes widened. 'No, definitely not!'

'No movie nights watching *IT*?'

'Are you quite right there, Alexis?'

I was fairly sure he wasn't enjoying my joking at his expense, but I continued anyway, his nervous squirming fun to watch.

Cueing my baby voice, I stood up and made my way over to him, settling myself on his lap. 'Aw, baby, I'll protect you.

I'll yank on their big red noses, pull their curly orange hair and stand on their big floppy feet,' I pouted.

He glared in return and poked his fingers into my ribs, tickling me.

'Stop it, Bryce.'

'Oh, you don't like being tickled?'

'No, I hate it. Please stop,' I begged. 'I'm sorry.'

He ignored my plea and kept tickling, making me wriggle and squirm. I struggled to get free of his grip, but we fell on the floor.

'I'm sorry. No more clowns, I promise.'

He stopped momentarily, lying on top of me. 'Alexis, tell me you love me.'

'I love you, Bryce.'

'Tell me you'll never leave me.'

His eyes were pleading for the answer he so desperately wanted. But could I promise it to him? I wanted to, really I did, but I was not a single entity. I came in a package of three.

'I will try with everything I have in me to never leave you,' I offered, knowing it was not what he wanted me to say.

'Tell me you will marry me one day.' *Oh, shit!* Again I wanted to, really wanted to, but talk of remarriage was not even in the picture right now.

'Bryce, if we make it through the toughest of times and you ask me, then yes, I will one day marry you.'

He smiled in satisfaction and leaned in for a kiss, a kiss I was happy to oblige. I was not fobbing him off ... I'd meant it. If, down the track, we were in a position to do so, then yes, I would marry this man. Of course I would.

'That's all I need to hear, my love.'

CHAPTER

5

Captain Paul's voice came over the speaker, breaking the intense conversation we were having about future nuptials which, if it wasn't so hot and romantic, would be utterly crazy at this point in time.

'Excuse me, Mr Clark and Ms Summers. Would you please fasten your seat belts. We are about to begin our descent into Connellan Airport. The estimated time of arrival is 5 p.m., and the current ground temperature is 32° Celsius. Thank you.'

Bryce stood and helped me up, and we buckled ourselves into our seats. Momentarily locking eyes with one another, I took note of the smile radiating from Bryce's face, his obvious glee quite clearly a result of the promises I had made to him. Not to mention the fact we were about to land in a place neither of us had been before.

I smiled back at him and looked out the window, spotting a hefty lump of red-brown on the ground. 'I see it, I think I see it!' I exclaimed, elated at identifying a ginormous mound of sandstone rock.

Just as I was about to shout further elation, Captain Paul's voice sounded from the speaker. 'Excuse me, Mr Clark and Ms Summers. You may notice out the right-hand side of the aircraft what you think to be Uluru. This is, in fact, Mt Connor and is mistaken for Uluru quite frequently.'

Deflating like a pierced balloon, I pulled a sad face. Bryce tilted his head to the side in sympathy.

Paul the pilot continued. 'If you keep looking out the right-hand side of the aircraft, you will be able to see Uluru in approximately five minutes.'

I kept looking out of the window like an excited child. I had wanted to visit Ayers Rock, as it was then, ever since learning about it at school. And despite the fact I was now an adult, the bizarreness of a monstrous rock in the middle of nowhere was not lost on me.

My anticipation grew as I scanned the reddish-brown dirt searching for it. Bryce also leaned forward and then pointed to just behind where I was looking.

Turning back round completely, I covered the window with my head, spotting the impressive monolith. *Wow, it's freaking HUGE!* It literally looked like it fell from the sky and hit the ground with a thud!

'That's incredible,' I mumbled, my eyes opened wide.

'That's nothing,' he smiled, with an excited glint in his eyes. *What now? Does this man plan everything?*

* * *

We landed at Connellan Airport and thanked Amy and Paul for their brilliant skills and hospitality. A young man greeted us as we exited the aircraft and offered to help with our luggage. As we followed him across the tarmac, Bryce comfortably held my hand. I tried to recall the last time Rick had held my hand and, for the life of me, could not think of a time post-having children. *Surely not!*

I stopped straining my brain for a memory that appeared not to exist when I noticed that we were heading in the opposite direction to the terminal.

'Where are we going?' I asked.

Bryce looked at me quizzically and with his free hand motioned up ahead. I followed his finger which I soon discovered was pointing at a helicopter. My eyes widened and I swear my stomach did a backflip. *Can stomachs backflip?*

'Are we flying around the rock?'

Bryce lifted my hand to his mouth and gently grazed the top of it with his lips. 'Of course we are, honey.'

The young man who was assisting us opened the door to the cockpit and loaded our luggage into the back. Bryce then led me to the passenger side and lifted me up and into the cabin. And, by the look on his face, I would say he was more excited than I was.

Fastening my belt for me, he then handed me some headphones and closed the door. I watched as he spoke to the young man, who handed him a clipboard. He seemed utterly relaxed and I realised he possessed an uncanny ability to be able to communicate with absolutely anyone.

They shook hands and Bryce headed toward the cockpit, beaming like a beacon and radiating joy; it was infectious and spread over me like wildfire.

'Okay, we are about to see this beautiful rock at sunset from the best seat in the house.'

I looked out the window to find that he was right and that the sun was near the horizon. *Oh, my goodness.* I'd heard so many wonderful things about Uluru at sunset, but to see it from a helicopter with the man of my dreams was truly amazing. If it wasn't highly childish, or wouldn't have looked utterly ridiculous, I would have bounced up and down in my seat and shook my head like a maniac.

Bryce started flicking switches and — compared to the last flight I flew with him — I paid a little bit more attention. It probably had something to do with the fact that this time I didn't have a woman in labour next to me making whale noises, nor was I suffering concussion after a car accident.

I noticed just how delicious he looked as he took hold of the control sticks, one of which looked like a handbrake. *I know that's not what they are called, but that's what they look like to me.* He pulled the handbrake-thingy up, enabling us to rise high in the air.

We headed in the direction of what could only be described as a giant wall of red-orange and, as we flew closer, the wall got bigger. The sheer size of Uluru was beyond belief; it looked as if you were only a few hundred metres away, when in fact, you were kilometres. It was simply phenomenal.

The top of the rock was actually quite wide in area, but when you looked at it from the front, the impression was that it was long and skinny. But it wasn't. It was nearly as wide as it was long.

We were flying quite high, especially when you took into consideration the height of Uluru from the ground. Curious, I posed that very question to the extremely talented and sexy pilot sitting next to me.

'How high are we?'

He gave me a strange look. 'About 6,500 feet. Why?'

'How high can one of these things go?' I looked directly down — which in my case was never a good thing to do — then I looked back at him, waiting anxiously for his answer.

He smiled. 'Approximately 14,000 feet, but you wouldn't want to go any higher than 9,000 feet, especially if you need time to safely get to the ground in the event of a fire,' he casually advised.

I turned my head to him. *What freaking fire? Why would there be a fire?*

'Don't worry, you are perfectly safe,' he smiled, reassuringly.

I believed him, always feeling very safe around him. I just didn't like hearing the words fire, helicopter and ground all at the same time.

He lowered the chopper down to a height that made us level with the top of the rock. I think he did this to ease the concerns he thought I had. Either that, or he did it to get the full effect as the sun began to descend.

Uluru changed colour like magic right before our eyes: one minute it was bright red, and the next it was orange. It was truly beautiful. I reached over slightly to put my hand on his leg. He glanced down at my hand, then back out towards the rock.

'This is simply beautiful. Thank you.'

'It's nothing in comparison to you, Alexis.'

I rolled my eyes and blushed. He winked at me, then turned the chopper quite sharply. I screamed. Not out of fear, but more in excitement at the sudden change of direction and angle.

'Shit, Bryce! A little warning would've been nice.'

He laughed at me. 'Do you like being upside-down?' *Upside-down? In a helicopter? Hell no!*

'No, don't you dare! I mean it! Anyway, this thing can't go upside-down.'

I hoped I was right, although I had no fucking idea. He gave me a do-you-dare-me face and, instantly — metaphorically speaking — I began to shit myself.

'No, no, no. Please, no. I'll do anything you want,' I pleaded, regretting my promise as soon as it left my mouth.

His face returned to a shade of calm, but now he seemed quite satisfied with the advantage he had just managed to secure. 'Anything?' he questioned, raising his eyebrow.

Ah, fuck. 'Yes, although that's not fair.' I crossed my arms over my chest.

'Did you want to go round one more time, or head to the lodge?' he asked with a cocky smile.

I shot him a what-the-hell-do-you-think look. His smile broadened before he manoeuvred the chopper to take us around one final time.

* * *

As we headed back in the direction from which we originally came, I assumed the airport was to be our destination. But it wasn't long before I became aware of a diversion, when I noticed what looked like a group of white spots on the ground not too far ahead. They stood out because the only other colour around them was red. As we got closer, it became apparent the white spots were, in fact, white tepee-style buildings. There was a helipad next to them; therefore I knew that was to be our target.

Bryce landed the chopper with ease, climbed out and came around to my door. He attempted to help me down from my seat, when I just stopped and sat there, staring at him.

'Are you coming?' he asked with confusion.

I tilted my head to the side. *Yes, in more ways than one, Mr Clark.*

'Thank you,' I said, sincerely.

'For what?'

'For everything.'

I aggressively pulled him to me and attacked his mouth. He let me, but only for a short while before breaking away.

'It's what I do, Ms Summers.'

Hearing my surname in that moment — the surname of a man that had betrayed me — tore at my heart and had me feeling terribly sad and hurt. I didn't want to feel sad. I didn't want to feel anything toward Rick. In fact, for now, I wanted to pretend that he didn't exist. Deep down I knew this notion was ridiculous and that it would — in the near future — inevitably need to be confronted. But for now, I just wanted to be happy. I wanted to live in the moment and enjoy my time with Bryce.

'I'm not sure I want to be called that any more. Please stop calling me Ms Summers.'

He touched my cheek. 'What do you want me to call you, then?'

I shrugged my shoulders. 'Who knows ... one day you might call me Mrs Clark.'

I watched the joy of what I had just stupidly said wash over him like a tidal wave before he scooped me up into his arms and carried me toward one of the white cone-shaped huts. I was so overwhelmed and overjoyed, it was like a dream. But I should not have said it ... Summers was my name, and it was my children's name, too. And despite the fact that the man who gave me that name betrayed me, it was still my name nonetheless. *Alexis, you idiot.*

* * *

We were greeted at the edge of the helipad by a woman dressed in a short-sleeved shirt and khaki shorts.

'You can put me down now,' I whispered as she approached.

'No,' he answered quite sternly.

'Welcome, Mr and Mrs Clark.'

I coughed and subdued a coincidental laugh.

Bryce squeezed my leg and whispered into my ear. 'I like the sound of that.' He beamed and waggled his eyebrows up and down. I had to agree with him, it did sound nice, but it was still way too soon. *Alexis, you are caught up in the moment. What were you thinking? You should have kept your mouth shut.*

'My name is Dorothy, and I will be your host here at Outback Hideaway. Please follow me and I'll show you to your hut.'

She called out to a middle-aged man to fetch our bags from the chopper, then led the way.

'Bryce, you can put me down now,' I whispered again.

'No,' he replied.

We followed her along the boardwalk covering the thick, auburn dirt of the Red Centre. At least, it looked like dirt. Although, I guess it could be some kind of sand, too. Out of the corner of my eye, I noticed something scurry through the dirt and go under the boardwalk. I swear I even caught the glimpse of a scaly tail. *What the fuck was that?*

I was suddenly quite glad to be in Bryce's arms, or I probably would've screamed. I hate reptiles. Frogs, I love, but creatures with scales, I do not.

'This will be your private lodge. It's unlocked and everything you need should be inside. Dinner will be delivered shortly. If there is anything further you require, please do not hesitate to contact me on the in-house telephone. Enjoy your stay.'

'Thank you, Dorothy. Could you please deliver our meals at 7.30 p.m.? We would like to get settled in first.'

'Certainly, sir.'

Dorothy practically curtsied, then walked away. *Settled in? Is that what we are calling it now?*

Continuing to display a contented smile, Bryce carried me up the steps and opened the sliding glass door with his foot and elbow. I couldn't help remembering the last time I was carried over the threshold and into a hotel room, just like I was now. I also couldn't help cursing myself the very second that memory entered my mind.

Forcing it back down, I buried it with the other memories that seemed to want to rear their ugly heads.

'Here we are,' Bryce said proudly. 'Home for the next three days.'

As I took in my new surroundings, I was struck by how beautiful the room was. Unique and beautiful. As you walked in, the first thing you noticed was a king-sized bed in front of a dark red feature wall. *That was the first thing I noticed, anyway.*

The flooring was a dark hardwood, in striking contrast to the crisp, white linens. The roof went up into a point, like a tepee, and was made of a white canvas material. To me it resembled flowing curtains and gave the room a touch of both elegance and romance.

'You can put me down now, Mr Clark.'

Finally granting my request, he set me down and I took off to explore my new environment. The feature wall worked like the entrance to a labyrinth: when you walked behind it and turned to the left, you found yourself in another room, a room with a small kitchenette and dining area, which then led out to a private balcony and swimming pool.

I stepped onto the balcony and was struck with awe at the fact Uluru was pretty much smack-bang in front of me. I couldn't believe my eyes, it was just stunning. Everything was perfect. Our getaway was perfect. Bryce was perfect. And this little tepee lodge was perfect. Different — but perfect.

I wandered back to the bedroom in search of Bryce, finding him accepting our luggage and talking to the helpful man who had delivered it. I took this opportunity to further investigate our perfect love nest.

I had not yet found the toilet and was extremely close to peeing my pants, so I was beyond thankful when I found it behind the feature wall and to the right. *Brilliant!*

I relieved myself instantly, but realised I had not locked the door. *Oh, shit, what if he comes in and sees me sitting on the toilet?* I wasn't ready for that. *Oh, but you were ready to tell him you would one day marry him, Alexis. Figure that one out.*

I was so overwhelmed it wasn't funny. And I wanted nothing more than to bitch-slap my conscience which was currently being a sarcastic moll. Taking a deep breath, I told myself that all I needed to do was gather my bearings and take one step at a time. Yes, I was currently in what resembled a fairytale with a new man, but I was still married and my husband had no idea where I was, let alone what I was doing.

Suddenly, I felt terribly guilty. *No, Alexis, he admitted to sleeping with Claire and, at that stage, you had not gone that far with Bryce.* True, I had not gone that far when he confessed, but I had now, numerous times, daily. *Alexis, stop thinking of Rick. You are with Bryce, he loves you and would never cheat on you.* But how could I be so sure? I was sure Rick would never have cheated on me, either. *Argh, stop it, stop it, fucking stop it.*

This time, I did mentally bitch-slap myself in the face. I was not about to go back and forth examining this whole situation any longer for, if I did, I'd probably explode and self-combust on the spot.

Washing my hands, I splashed a little water on my face. It was hot in Uluru, and I definitely needed some cooling down.

Bryce came up behind me and placed a single white rose in front of my nose. My gaze climbed to look up at our reflection in the vanity mirror. *Do you really need to deliberate on your situation, Alexis? Take a good, long hard look in that mirror. What do you see?*

I did just that and calmness washed over me, removing any doubts and confusion I'd had moments ago. Taking hold of the rose, I placed it to my nose with a gentle sniff, taking in the alluring scent I adored. I couldn't help but to smile brightly at Bryce. He wrapped his arms around me and kissed my neck, then joined me in my assessment of our reflection.

'You think of everything, don't you?' I said softly, drinking in his adoring stare.

'It's what I do, Ms Summ—' He broke off. 'It's what I do, my love.'

I turned to him. 'Yes, it is, and you do it so well.'

Bryce leaned in, caressed my lips with his own, then let out a breath and whispered, 'You are exquisite.'

I moaned, wanting him to enter my mouth. His deliberate pause and the fact he was hovering so close without touching me with his tongue was excruciating yet perfectly unbearable. And the anticipation of when that touch would come was about the hottest thing imaginable.

I whispered back to him, making sure my breath entered his mouth. 'So, how do you plan on "settling in" exactly?'

He pulled away, and his look of pure, unadulterated lust hit me like a ton of bricks.

CHAPTER

6

I turned to face him, gripping the basin behind me in anxious but excited anticipation. Bryce stepped forward and grunted as he gripped my arse, all the while lifting me to his waist.

'I thought so,' I replied with an arrogant tone.

He mashed his lips on mine, intensely licking my tongue with his own.

Gripping the back of his head, I pulled him to me, forcing him further into my mouth and deepening our hungry kiss. He then gently bit down on my bottom lip, exciting me all over and making me moan with pleasure.

'I love your little moans, Alexis. They are so fucking sexy.' *Oh, in that case, I'll give you another.* I let out another 'sexy moan' for him, prompting him to groan fiercely and squeeze my arse with passionate force, taking my breath away.

'I love your ferocious groans, Bryce. They are so fucking hot.'

The sound he then gave vibrated through his chest into mine, stimulating me into a state of extreme need. With me wrapped around his waist, he made his way out of the bathroom. We bumped into the wall near the doorway, making me gasp. Not because it hurt, but because it was raw and utterly hot.

Bryce held me there for a short time, looking deep into my eyes. I assumed it was because he thought the bump had hurt me, as his eyes were intense, remorseful and full of worry.

I put my finger to his lips to reassure him. 'I love you, Bryce Clark.'

His mouth returned to mine, this time harder and heavier than before, his probing hardness now felt between my legs. *Mm, I love feeling him grow with pleasure.*

He stumbled out of the bathroom and over to the bed, leaning forward to place me down. 'So, I vaguely recall you telling me not too long ago that you would do "anything". Do you remember?' *Damn it! I did vaguely recall saying that as a result of his helicopter manoeuvre and subsequent threat.*

'Yes, I did, but that's only because you don't play fair.'

'I play very fair.'

I raised an eyebrow at him and spoke in a teasingly low voice. 'So, what is it that you want?'

'I want a striptease.' *Really? Shit! I'm no Jamie Lee Curtis.*

The thought of performing a striptease scared me to death, but at the same time a rush of anticipation filtered through me at the prospect. So, mustering my *True Lies* Jamie Lee Curtis courage, I scooted back across the mattress while deviously eyeing Bryce. 'If that is what you want, Mr Clark,' I said as I stood by the side of the bed and slowly began to unbutton my vest, swaying my hips to non-existent music, 'then that is what you'll get.'

This type of move would normally have me laughing hysterically, but when I saw the thrilled expression on his face, I subdued my typical response and continued to please him with my teasing moves.

Bryce stepped back to the wall and aggressively fisted a button that made the electric blinds cover the doors and windows, giving us complete privacy.

His assertiveness sparked my resolve to continue my tease, so I slowly removed my tan suede vest and twirled it around my finger. Initially, my plans had been to sling it onto his head, but, unfortunately, my twirling accuracy was a little off and it bounced off the feature wall and landed on the bed. *Massive fail, you idiot.*

Bryce raised an amused eyebrow and nodded for me to carry on and, being the team player that I am, I decided to shrug off my vest-twirling malfunction and move to my tank top, inching it up ever so slightly a little at a time. As a result, both of Bryce's hands fisted then relaxed, and seeing this assured me that I was truly tantalising him.

I pulled my tank top over my head and scrunched it into a ball and, without thinking, I threw it at him. Only this time my accuracy was just fine, the tank top hitting him in the face. *Bingo!* He groaned and practically tore off his t-shirt, flicking it with precision directly at me. I caught it, startling us both. Gloating and giggling, I shot him a happily self-satisfied look, then tossed his t-shirt over my shoulder and continued my amatory tease, unbuttoning my shorts and wiggling my arse as I pulled them down. The more I let myself indulge in the role play, the more empowered I felt as each item of clothing fell from my body.

Seductively, I stepped out of my shorts and kicked them toward the door, then, still swaying my hips from side to side, I stood before him in my white lace matching set. I could feel the burning heat as his eyes set me on fire, his carnal growl again sounding from deep down within his throat.

'Alexis ... keep going.'

I watched salaciously as he adjusted his shorts, indicating the swelling of his erection which was fast filling the space within them.

Licking my lips at the sight of him grabbing his cock, my body yearned for his touch. He really was mouthwatering. And seeing him cup the very appendage I wanted deep in between my legs, depleted me of all cognition. *Focus, Alexis.*

I snapped out of my Bryce-fog and continued my provocative display, lifting a foot to rest it on the bed in order to unzip my ankle boot, and exposing just a fraction of the precise spot he desired the most. Slowly, I ran my finger along the edge of my G-string seam, lifting it away and giving him a small glimpse of what was to come. This move elicited a crack of his neck to the left and again to the right, which made me tingle. *Fuck, he is sexy.* I repeated my moves with the other leg and dropped the boots to the floor.

'Bryce, I can't possibly continue when you have so much clothing on you. All that material is just not doing it for me,' I explained with an eyebrow raised. I then returned my gaze to my fingers as if to indicate I was bored.

He obliged and kicked off his runners.

'Not good enough. You'll have to lose more than that.'

I kept swaying to the music that was not there then provocatively ran my fingers over the top of my bra, sensitising my nipples.

The look of lust he so often directed my way was the biggest turn-on, but this look trumped them all. It not only had my heart pumping, but it also had my pussy screaming for some relief.

I turned my back to him, removed my bra, and held it out, twisting my head around to catch his expression — an expression that could only be described as seriously hankering.

Smiling to myself, I dropped it on the floor then hooked my thumbs into my G-string. I bent over, baring my arse to him and pulled it down, which was when he let out the loudest, hungriest growl to date.

'Fuck, you have the sexiest arse,' he said through gritted teeth.

I loved the way he spoke to me. I loved it when he was romantic and pouring his heart out, but I also loved it when he was dirty, raw and scandalous. *Alexis, snap out of it before the blood runs to your head. What?* Not realising it initially, I finally noticed I was still upside-down. *Again, I have nothing on Jamie Lee Curtis or Demi Moore. Maybe I should watch* Striptease *and get some tips! Alexis, stand up. Shit!*

I slowly stood up and stepped out of my underwear, allowing him to stare at my 'sexy arse' just a little longer. But the ache between my legs was now intense and only he could cure it. Therefore, I spun back around, ready to give us what we wanted and what we needed.

Upon turning to face him, I found him standing there naked and ready, the remainder of his attire nowhere to be seen. The sight of his full and overly-stretched cock was gloriously mouthwatering and had me aching everywhere at once.

'Mm,' was all I could manage to let out of my mouth as I crawled across the bed to where he was standing.

He looked down at me, knowing what I had in mind, and the knowledge of his yearning and excited expectation, filled me with even more desire. Greedily, I opened my mouth and tongued the tip of his erection in the hope he would growl again. He didn't disappoint, making me shudder with pleasure and forcing my mouth to clamp down on him, hard.

'Fuck, Alexis. Your mouth, it's ... grrr ...'

My smile circled his shaft at that very sound. I just couldn't get enough of it.

He placed his hands on my head, but he did not take over in guiding me up and down his luscious length, knowing that I needed absolutely no assistance whatsoever when it came to sucking his cock.

I continued to run my tongue up and down his smooth hardness, and taking him into my mouth entirely, as far as he would go. When he tensed and twitched within me, I knew I was not far away from my goal. He pulled out and directed me to stand up on the bed. I followed his cue, and he lifted me onto him. *Yep, there it is!*

'Oh, fuck,' I moaned, feeling my pussy expand in ecstasy, and the sensation of him holding my arse, securing me to him, only added to it.

He walked me over to the bench by the wall near the front door and, in one quick swipe, thoroughly cleared its contents onto the floor. *Shit, that was hot.* It was the perfect height for him to pound me, continuously, and he did ... in and out, over and over. I swear the tepee was shaking, but I didn't care.

It would have been fitting if the whole thing collapsed on top of us.

'Bryce,' I murmured incoherently.

'You like, my love?'

'Uh huh.'

He was sensational, and the momentum he created was perfect.

I couldn't help myself and let go, throwing my head back and crying out. 'Oh, fuck!'

It occurred to me in that moment that I had never before had this much sex in the space of twenty-four hours, and I was almost certain I wasn't done yet. It was blatantly obvious that we both couldn't get enough of each other. We were insatiable.

He jerked into me and released himself, expelling his fierce groan and leaving me breathing hard and covered in sweat. As our foreheads touched, I could finally see what he had seen from the beginning. We belonged to each other, and I had to start allowing myself to believe it. It was just that everything had happened in such a short space of time and it felt somewhat surreal, like a dream or a fairytale. And the fact it was happening to me, of all people, only made it that much more unbelievable.

'What are you thinking about?' he asked. as he looked into my eyes.

'Oh, it's nothing. I guess I'm just waiting to be woken up from this dream-nightmare.'

'Nightmare?' His expression seemed shocked and a little hurt.

'No, I don't mean it like that, not at all,' I said reassuringly, before kissing him quickly. 'I mean the nightmare of having a husband who destroyed the sanctity of our marriage. I guess

I'm just feeling that what is happening to me right now is so unbelievable. I thought I was happily married, leading a somewhat normal life, and now I'm here in your arms and incredibly satisfied. The enormity of it all is only just starting to sink in. It's just happening so fast. Do you know what I mean?'

'Yes, honey, I know what you mean. But it also feels like ... we have been together for a very long time,' we both said, simultaneously.

He took a deep breath, then moved my hair away from my face. 'Alexis, sometimes it's wise not to dwell on the incomprehensible, for if you do, you waste those precious moments of actually accepting it for what it is.'

He was right. *Geez, he's good at clarifying things! All right, no more wasting time thinking this is a dream. It's not. It has happened — is happening — and I'm going to accept it.*

I shook my head as if to shake the nonsense away. 'I'm sorry, I'm being an idiot.'

'You are my idiot.'

'Thanks, you can put me down now.'

'No,' he playfully teased as I felt him come to life again inside me.

'Mr Clark, you couldn't possibly go again.'

He moved his head back. 'Is that a dare?' *No, because I know you'll win.*

Before I could answer his challenge, there was a knock at the door.

'Ha ha,' I said and poked my tongue out. He responded by continuing to hold me on the bench and tease me with his twitching dick. 'Put me down,' I whispered.

'Why? Don't you want to answer the door like this?'

I giggled, 'No. Bryce Edward Clark, put me down now!' I pursed my lips at him briefly and called out to the visitor in an innocent voice. 'Just a minute.'

Bryce surrendered and let me go. So I dashed to the bathroom, leaving him in his naked glory and evidence of our fornicating scattered throughout the room.

* * *

We ate our dinner on the balcony next to the pool, the temperature still quite humid. And, apart from the horrid winged devils that were mosquitos, it was lovely. I decided I enjoyed watching him eat, too. Maybe it had something to do with his tongue movements, or the way he licked his lips when some sauce or juices escaped. Whatever it was, I now relished it.

'Do I have something on my face?' he asked with an amused tone.

'Do you want something on your face?' I offered, while raising my eyebrow, still in a teasing mood. Sadly, my phone started ringing, disturbing my new challenge. I dashed to the bedroom to retrieve it and, when I realised who it was, the irritation I'd felt moments before disappeared.

'Hello, little man.'

'Hi, Mum.'

'I missed you this morning while you were out on the tractor.'

'Yeah. Poppa and I had to move some hay bales for the cattle.'

Nate loved helping his poppa do things on the farm.

'Good work, my little farmer. So, how was the drive to Nanny and Poppa's yesterday?' I asked curiously, figuring I'd find out if he had picked up on anything where Rick was concerned.

'Yeah, all right, except Dad was in a bad mood.'

'Oh, was he? Did he say why?' *He'd better not have.*

'No, he just didn't want to talk to us much, so I played my DS and Charlotte listened to the iPod.'

'Oh, okay.'

'Hey, Mum, I saw you on TV with Mr Clark. You looked very pretty, and you looked like you were married. Is that why Dad is mad?' *Oh, shit! Um ... what do I say?*

'No, I don't think so, mate.' *Crap, change the subject.* 'Hey, Mr Clark said he will take you for a ride in the Crow soon, if you'd like?' *Oh, Alexis, of all the things you could have said, you chose that.*

'Yeah? Sick! How soon?' *Ah, fuck.*

'Maybe next week,' I said briefly. Changing my tone of voice, I also opted to change the subject. 'Okay, sweetheart, it's getting late. Is Charlotte still awake?'

'No, she's already in bed.'

'Oh, well ... I love you, ratbag. Have a nice sleep. I'll speak to you in a couple of days.'

'Okay, Mum, love you too. Bye.'

I had chest pangs as I disconnected the call. Nate was such a switched-on child and had already pieced a few things together regarding me and his father. How was I going to explain to my children that Mummy and Daddy were breaking up? How was I going to explain to Nate in a way that he wouldn't hate his father, or me for that matter?

I sat there momentarily with my head in my hands. *What am I going to do?* The thought of having to explain any of this, without actually explaining it, was just too much. Unable to even attempt to figure out my plight at that point in time, I walked back out to the balcony.

'Nate?' Bryce asked.

'Yeah,' I responded. 'He knows something is wrong.'

'He's a smart kid, Alexis. I'm guessing he takes after you.'

'Sometimes too smart.' I sat down and put my head in my hands. 'What have I done?'

'There's nothing you can do right now, so stop torturing yourself,' he instructed, sounding a little angry.

I looked up, shocked and offended by his tone.

'I don't like seeing you do this to yourself. You have done nothing wrong. None of this is your fault. So give yourself a fucking break,' he spat out, before standing and clearing the plates from dinner.

At first I didn't know what to think, everything was going so well, and now I had pissed him off.

'Here, I'll do that.'

I started picking up the rest of the dishes. I seriously felt quite lazy. I hadn't done a single thing since the Sunday night I drove into his garage resembling a panda.

'No, I've got it,' he retorted, then stacked them all and went inside. *Shit, well done, Alexis. You've pissed him off with your constant worrying, fickleness and toing and froing. He has organised this dream getaway for you both, has thought of absolutely everything right down to a single rose, and all you have done is feel sorry for yourself. You're a selfish bitch, no wonder he is shitty.*

I watched him angrily move about in the kitchen and I felt awful. *I need to make it up to him. What can I do?* An idea instantly popped into my head. It wasn't a grand gesture like he was capable of, but it was an idea and a good one.

Standing up, I made my way to the bedroom, opened the freestanding wardrobe and grabbed a blanket. I placed it on the bed then headed to the bathroom, snatching up the candles that were positioned around the bath. *I need these and some matches. Shit, I need matches.* I walked back into the kitchen where Bryce was finishing up. He looked at me strangely, but didn't say anything.

'Excuse me,' I said quietly as I slipped past him. *The cupboard under the sink: good place to start.* I crouched down and opened it, but there were no matches. *Shit. Crap. Balls! I need matches or this won't work. Dorothy, yes, surely she'll have some.* I stood back up, walked past him again, and went back to the bedroom to scoop up the blanket and candles.

'I'll be back in a minute,' I called out as I shut the door and took off.

I made a quick getaway to the reception office and opened the door. Dorothy was sitting behind the counter. 'Hello, Mrs Clark.'

I smiled at the sound of her slipped tongue again. 'Actually, Dorothy, we aren't married.'

'Oh, I'm terribly sorry. I thought you were on your honeymoon. You both look like honeymooners.' *We are acting like it too!*

'That's quite all right. Look, I was wondering if you could help me. I want to set up a romantic picnic out near the helipad. Mr Clark is a keen astronomer and seeing as it is an incredibly clear night tonight, I was hoping to surprise him with a bit of stargazing.'

She smiled, which then turned into a sneaky grin. 'Ah, yes. I most certainly can help you,' she informed, while looking at my items. 'No, they won't do. Come with me.'

Dorothy led me out the back of reception and into a store-room. She grabbed a large flat trolley then dragged out two sunlounge mattresses and placed them on top.

'Put your blanket on here too,' she instructed.

I did as I was told.

'And in here we have some heavy-duty, big, pillar candles, in case of a blackout.'

She opened the box and pulled out six enormous cylindrical candles. 'And over here are the binoculars.' *Oh, even better.*

'Excellent, thank you. Oh, I need matches, too.'

'Yes, not a problem.'

She pushed the trolley out of the room, so I followed.

'Wait here just a minute Mrs Cla—' She stopped and looked at me for an alternative.

'Alexis, you can call me Alexis.'

'I'll be back in a second, Alexis.'

Dorothy sounded very excited. I think she liked the whole organising a 'mission' thing. I liked the thought of it too. It felt nice being able to do something for Bryce for a change.

Minutes later, Dorothy returned with a box of matches, a bottle of champagne and a bowl of strawberries. 'Here you go.'

'Oh, Dorothy, this is just wonderful, thank you.'

'Take this flashlight, Alexis. I know just the place to set up your picnic.'

I followed her out past the helipad and down a small mound, stopping at the perfect spot. She helped me set up the candles in a large circle then we dragged the mattresses into position.

'Thank you so much, Dorothy, I can't tell you how much this means to me. He is going to love it.'

I surveyed our handiwork again, satisfied with our efforts.

'You're welcome, my dear. Anything for young love. Now, when you are done, give me a buzz and I'll come and pack it up for you,' she advised as she touched my shoulder and headed back up the mound.

Examining the area once again, I was quite happy with its perfection. The sunlounge mattresses now looked like a bed surrounded by a circle of candles. The champagne and strawberries were in an ice bucket. The binoculars were neatly placed in the middle of the bed. And, most importantly, the stars were out and shining brightly. I clapped my hands and headed toward the tepee.

When I opened the door, Bryce was sitting on the edge of the bed looking as pale as a ghost. He shot up and at first I thought something terrible had happened.

'What's wrong, Bryce?' I asked, walking up to him. 'Are you okay?'

I waited for an answer I may not have wanted to hear.

'Where have you been?' he questioned, sounding somewhat traumatised.

'I ... I ... I told you I'd be back in a minute.'

'I didn't hear you and you left your phone. I didn't know where you had gone or if you were coming back.' *If I was coming back? We are in the middle of the freaking desert. Where would I go?*

'Why wouldn't I come back?'

It was still painfully clear that there was something tormenting him and, for some reason, he had it in his head I was going to leave him. 'Bryce, how many times have I told you? I'm not going anywhere.'

He pulled me to him and held me tighter than ever before. Looking up, I noticed the colour start to return to his cheeks.

'Honey, I'm so sorry, I'm sorry I snapped at you before. I thought you were upset and left.'

'Oh, no, you had every right to snap. You have been so amazing, organising this incredible escape for the two of us, pampering me, and giving me everything I need. Then, I go and ruin it by sulking, whingeing and feeling sorry for myself. I'm sorry. I wanted to make it up to you, so I organised a surprise.'

He pulled away and looked at me, stunned. 'A surprise?'

'Yes, come on.' I grabbed his hand, and we headed out the door.

* * *

There was not a cloud in the sky, nor was there a breeze. The conditions for my stargazing picnic were perfect.

'Okay, close your eyes.'

'Alexis, wait —'

'Bryce, just shut up and close your eyes.'

He did as he was told, so I grabbed his arm and slowly led him down the mound.

'No peeking. Now stand here. Don't move and don't open your eyes until I say so.'

Letting go of his arm, I then positioned myself in the middle of the makeshift bed. 'Okay, you can open them.'

It took a second for his eyes to adjust to what was in front of him. He blinked a few times, then realised what this little candlelit circle in the middle of the desert was.

'I know it's not your amazing observatory, but the sky doesn't get any better than this. So, I was hoping you could teach me a little of what's up there,' I explained with a hopeful smile.

He shook his head at me, stepped into the circle and dropped to his knees. 'Alexis, I love you. Marry me.'

CHAPTER

7

Um, yeah, can't quite do that right now! I touched his face and smiled at his request.

'You seem to have forgotten that I am already married.'

'Minor details, my love. Don't worry about them,' he said playfully.

Bryce then took both my hands in his, an expression of renewed determination appearing in his eyes. 'I *will* propose to you properly one day, trust me. But until I do, I want you to promise that no matter what we come up against, you will one day walk down the aisle with me.'

He was obviously pleased with my surprise, but he also seemed anxious ... and terribly eager. Sitting with him in that moment, it appeared the confident man I had fallen for had suddenly become unsure of himself ... and of us. It also appeared that he was still harbouring a secret of some kind.

'Bryce, you need to tell me what it is that you are afraid of.'

He fell back on the mattress and put his arm out for me to rest upon. 'I'm afraid of losing you.'

Shuffling over, I placed my head where he had indicated. 'You won't if you are honest and upfront with me. I've already been with a man who took that for granted, and I will not make the same mistake again.'

He squeezed my arm momentarily, then a sly grin spread across his face. 'So, Ms Summ— sorry, Ms Sexyarse.'

'You can't call me that,' I admonished while rolling my eyes at him.

'Yes, I can, Ms Sexyarse.'

'No. You. Can't,' I reaffirmed, then softening my tone, I continued. 'It's all right, Summers is just a name. I was being silly before and sulking. I'm stronger than that. Anyway, at this point in time it is my name and will remain my name until I change it.'

'Very well, Ms Summers it is ... although, I do like Ms Sexyarse.' An almost devilish smile appeared on his face. But he must've noticed my look of disagreement because he quickly changed the subject and gazed toward the sky. 'So, do you know any constellations?' *Um, apart from the Southern Cross, no. Stars twinkle, Madonna has a 'Lucky' one and you can wish upon a shooting one, but that's as far as my knowledge goes.*

I pointed to the left and quite low near the horizon. 'I know those ones over there are called the Southern Cross.'

'They are also known as Crux, Ms Summers, and it's the smallest of eighty-eight constellations.' *Ooh, he sounds very sexy when he is Mr Teacher Clark.*

I put on my best schoolgirl voice. 'Very interesting, Mr Clark. And those two really bright ones near Crux, what are they called, sir?'

Bryce leaned up on his elbow and smirked down at me. 'You really are quite cute,' he said softly, before he touched my face and kissed my lips.

'Oh, I've never been kissed by my teacher before. How naughty of you. Is that the end of my lesson, sir?'

'I'm glad you've never been kissed by your teacher before, and no, Ms Summers, it's not the end of your lesson. Those two bright stars you referred to are commonly known as the Southern Pointers, or Alpha and Beta Centauri.' *Alpha, Beta, what?* I kept surveying the sky.

'I know what that one over there is. It's the Saucepan. It's sort of on its side,' I said with a tilt of my head.

He laughed. 'Yes, you are correct. However, you only score a B minus.'

'A B-minus? Pfft! Why?' *Surely my knowledge of the saucepan was A-plus worthy.*

'Because the Saucepan is not a constellation. It actually forms part of Orion, or the Hunter. The bottom of the saucepan is his belt, the sides of the saucepan are the tops of his legs and the handle is his sword.' He picked up my arms and pointed to the stars that formed Orion's body. 'Those two bright stars there are his shoulder blades, called Bellatrix and Betelgeuse.'

'Bellatrix? That's a character in the Harry Potter books!'

Bryce scoffed at me and buried his nose into the crook of my neck. It felt lovely. *What? Bellatrix is in Harry Potter. She's an evil wench!*

Apart from the Saucepan and Southern Cross — or 'Crux' as he put it — I couldn't really see what he was pointing at. To be honest, I was more fascinated in listening to him passionately talk about something he obviously enjoyed and knew a lot about.

Continuing with my schoolgirl voice — because he seemed to like it — I asked another question. 'What's that really bright one over there, Mr Clark?'

'That is Aldebaran, or the Bull's fiery eye. It is one of the brightest stars in the night sky and forms part of the zodiac constellation of Taurus.'

'What's that little group of stars there, near the bright one?'

'That's a star cluster called Pleiades, or the Seven Sisters. You can only see the seven brightest stars with your naked eye, but the cluster actually has hundreds of stars. I'll show you properly when we get home.' *Home? I liked the sound of that, but his apartment was not my home.*

We laid together in silence, gazing up at the crystal clear sky for several minutes.

'I really can see why you enjoy this. It is very peaceful and relaxing.'

'Yes, that is one of the reasons. But I really enjoy how the night sky is endless. It just continues on and on. There are no boundaries. I like the fact there are things in life that do not know boundaries.'

'Boundaries can also be a good thing, you know.'

'Hmm, sometimes.'

I sat up and gave him a sceptical look; he was so stubborn. 'So, would you care for some champagne, Mr Astronomy Teacher Clark?'

'I wouldn't say no to my favourite student.'

I poured us both a glass of champagne and opened the bowl of strawberries, plonking one each into the bottom of our glasses.

Bryce looked into his. 'I've never understood why people do that?'

'What?'

'Put a strawberry in the glass.'

Our roles of teacher versus student had now reversed. 'Well, Mr Clark, you will now learn something from Ms Summers, and might I add when you sit in *my* classroom you need to sit up straight and pay attention.' I hit his leg with the top of my hand, indicating he should do as he was told. He did, but with a sarcastic smile on his face. Mustering the most posh, toffee-nosed voice I could manage, I continued my lesson: 'The strawberry is placed in the glass to simply enhance the flavour of the champagne.'

'I know something that enhances the flavour even better,' he advised with a devilish smile as he placed both our glasses down.

I had only a second to foresee an attack — which wasn't long enough — because he grabbed me around the waist and wrestled me down until he was on top of me, pinning me to the mattress.

He slowly began to unbutton my vest, revealing my white singlet top. 'Have you ever been to second base with your teacher, Ms Summers?'

'Um ...' I thought for a second, purposely drawing out the hum in my voice. 'There was that one time ...'

His eyes began to widen.

'No!' I laughed. 'Of course not, but you can be my first.'

'Good.' He smiled greedily then grabbed my tank top at the neck and tore it apart, exposing my white lace bra and making me gasp.

'You can't keep tearing my clothes off, Bryce.'

'It's what I do, Ms Summers.'

'Yes, it is, but you can stop it.'

'No, it's the quickest way to get them off you.' *Well, if it's good for you, then it's good for me.* I reached up and grabbed his t-shirt at the neck and pulled as hard as I could. It tore, but only slightly. *Damn it.*

'Stupid thing,' I said, annoyed at the pathetic rip. He mockingly laughed at me, which only provoked my second attempt. So, gritting my teeth — because for some reason that helps — I wrenched it apart. Only this time I was successful.

'Ha, take that.'

He smiled then held up his glass of champagne and tipped it toward me very slightly.

'What are you doing?' I shrieked.

'I told you, I know something else that enhances the flavour.' He tilted it further, sending the champagne splashing over my chest. I squealed and closed my eyes; it was bloody cold.

Before I had a chance to reopen my eyes, he was licking, sucking and kissing my chest and neck, and the contrast between the cold champagne and the warmth of his tongue was divine. It also tickled like hell.

Sliding his hands behind my back, he tried to unhook my bra. 'I hate these silly things.'

My laughter increased. 'They really aren't that difficult. How is it that you can fly a helicopter, run a multibillion dollar company, cook like a god, yet you cannot unhook a bra?'

That devilish glint I loved, and sometimes hated, crept across his face again, and I knew what he had planned.

'Don't you dare. I love this bra,' I said in warning while putting my hands behind my back and unclipping it with ease. Bryce then basically wrenched it from me, exposing my breasts. I did the same with his shredded t-shirt. *Fuck me, his chest is glorious.*

I would never get sick of seeing this man naked; he was simply sex-on-a-stick, and I wanted to lick him all over like a lollipop. The ripples of his abdomen were perfectly etched, and just the sheer sight of them had my tongue tingling with expectation.

Propping myself up on my elbows, I invited him to tip a little more onto my chest. This time when he did it, he quickly caught the drips with his tongue as they went down my stomach. He then trailed that delicious tongue of his all the way back up to my nipple and engulfed my breast with his hungry mouth. The feeling, sensational ... champagne cold against my skin, his tongue warm and neutralising the temperature exquisitely. Bryce picked a strawberry and placed half of it in my mouth. He then wiped the remainder of the berry down my stomach and around my bellybutton, leaving a pink juicy trail. It was sticky, but when he ran his tongue up and down me, cleaning the traces, it was very sensual.

I rolled him over and sat on his hips while grabbing the bottle of champagne. I tipped it to pour the liquid on him — not gently, mind you, because I felt he needed a little punishment for tearing my tank top. Bryce screwed up his face just a little, but smirked at me and kept his eyes fixed on mine. *Geez, he is so stubborn.*

Sliding down his legs, I began my consumption at his happy trail. 'You're right, it definitely enhances the flavour,' I mumbled as I continued licking and sucking around his navel and up over his six-pack.

He groaned with vigour, his muscles vibrating underneath my tongue.

Sitting back upright, I put the bottle to my lips, taking in a mouthful. Then I leaned over and kissed him, transferring some of the contents. We continued our kiss, both swallowing champagne, and even when he sat back upright, we still maintained our lip and tongue lock.

I pulled away, grabbed another strawberry, and stuck it half out of my mouth. He leaned forward and bit down on the exposed half, until our mouths met once again.

'Have you ever seen the movie *Lady and the Tramp*?' he mumbled as he ate his half of the strawberry.

'No, believe it or not, it is one Disney classic I have not seen. Why?' I answered, sucking the strawberry juice from my fingers.

'You remind me of Lady.'

He grabbed my hand and placed my fingers in his mouth so that he could suck them clean for me.

Correct me if I am mistaken, but Lady was a dog, yeah? 'Are you saying I remind you of a dog?'

He laughed. 'No. Well ... hang on, bark for me.'

My eyes widened, and I pulled my hand away from his mouth. 'Really?'

He just laughed.

Right, let's see how funny this is for you.

Lifting the champagne bottle, I poured the remainder of it on top of his head, watching with delighted satisfaction as he just sat there with me atop him, displaying a shocked smirk on his face.

'Woof,' I playfully barked.

'Are we playing dogs now?'

'You started it.'

'In that case ...' He shook his hair and sprayed me with droplets.

I screamed and screwed up my face as they landed on me.

'I know another way dogs play, Mr Clark,' I voiced with a seductive tone while wiping my eyes.

'I'm sure you do.'

'Yes, and so will you.'

Leaning over, I grabbed my vest, and put it on. I didn't bother with the bra, because it wouldn't be on long enough when we got back to the tepee.

We both stood up and I looked down, feeling terrible that Dorothy would have to clean up this mess. Maybe I could come out bright and early and beat her to it.

I went to grab the flashlight, but Bryce was faster. 'You, Ms Summers, are not walking.'

'Says who?'

'Says me.'

The look on his face suggested he was ready to take me across his knee and give me a spanking, and that thought actually excited me. Unable to help myself, I shot him a seductive smile as I blew out the candles. He flicked on the flashlight and walked over to me, luring me in for a kiss. Unfortunately, that was all it was, a lure, because he bent down, grabbed me from underneath my arse, and lifted me over his shoulder.

'Bryce! You'd better not put me in the pool.'

'Is that a dare, my love?'

'No.'

* * *

He walked me back to the tepee and threw me onto the bed.

'Right, you had better be naked by the time I get back,' he demanded and disappeared into the bathroom, only to return moments later.

I had obediently done what I was told.

'Very good girl. Come on, come on, Alexis,' he said playfully while patting his thighs, calling me like I was his pet.

My mouth dropped. I didn't want to smile at him, because he was being beyond cheeky, so I pursed my bottom lip, which then turned into a pout. His face changed from playful to concerned in an instant.

Slowly, he walked over to me and grabbed my face, kissing me with force. He then lifted me into his arms, not breaking the kiss, not even a little. I knew his doggy antics were only a playful joke, but my little pout was enough to tell him to stop, and this kiss showed me that he was sorry.

Bryce stepped into the spa still holding me — he was so strong. He never flinched when I was in his arms, always so controlled in his movements.

I kicked my legs down so that I was standing in front of him. 'Sit,' I demanded, now demonstrating that I was in charge and that he was the one obediently doing what he was told. I stood above him and his eyes were full of sorrow. 'What?'

'I'm sorry for making you feel belittled.'

'What? The dog thing? No, don't be silly, I was playing too.' Sitting down astride his lap, I placed my hands on either side of his face. 'You make me feel more loved than I could possibly ever imagine.'

He gripped me tightly and kissed me until I felt him stiffen beneath me.

'Again?' I questioned, playfully. 'My goodness!'

'Have you had enough?' he teased, knowing that I hadn't.

I shook my head and his face lit up. So I lifted and allowed his cock to enter me. The water was warm, and we slid up and down each other with ease, keeping our rhythm slow and subdued. I'm not going to lie ... I was slightly sore and the muscles in my thighs were exhausted. But I had no plans to tell him that.

'Thank you for tonight. No one has ever done anything like that for me before,' Bryce said, sincere emotion in his voice.

His admission prompted me to think that he may never have had anyone fuss over him in the past. Of course, women threw themselves at him all the time, but to have someone put him before themselves may not have been something he experienced after his parents' death. It was obvious that Lucy — in a heart-beat — would drop everything for him, but as she had said, she was 'selfish and made his life a living hell' for a long time.

'You are quite welcome,' I answered, honestly. 'I enjoy doing things for you, too.'

He embraced me tighter, almost desperately, and I could feel him tensing within me.

'This is not how dogs do it, you know,' I mumbled into his mouth, as I moved up and down his hard length.

His smile broke our kiss. 'How do they do it?' he asked, with a slight tilt to his head, and an expression on his face which clearly showed he was fully aware of how.

I eased myself off him, stood up, and turned round. Then, bending over, I leaned on the tiled shelf.

'And look,' I said as I turned my head around to see him, 'a mirror. So you can watch me enjoy it.'

Turning back to face the mirror, I opened my legs, entic-ing him to enter. He growled and moved forward, but didn't stand right away. Instead, he lowered his head and licked my sensitive clit. *Oh, holy fuck!* He then thrust his finger deep inside me as his tongue tantalised my core.

'You taste so good,' he said between tongue strokes.

I whimpered at the mixture of sensation and words I was experiencing — what this man could do with his mouth was a true talent.

Bryce continued to lick, suck and please me with his tongue and fingers until I could take no more, climaxing and releasing onto him. My legs weakened and were about to give way when he was up with his cock inside me almost instantly, holding me in place. He put his hands on my hips and pushed into me as far as he could possibly go.

Yes, I was spent and my pussy slightly raw. But the thrill and excitement of his eagerness to fuck like a dog overpowered the soreness and I soon forgot all about it.

Holy shit, the length on this man. I cried out as he touched deep inside me, and it was obvious from his reflection in the mirror that he enjoyed watching me at his mercy, revelling in his control.

Biting down on my lip to stop any further screams of pleasure, I stubbornly held my cries at bay. He smirked at me, knowing what I was doing, and pushed harder and deeper, forcing me to completely let go.

I did, as did he along with me, his head falling back and exposing the flexed veins in his neck. Then, leaning over me, he fingered my clit, helping my climax settle itself down.

I dropped my head and placed my elbows on the shelf, completely and utterly exhausted. My arms were jelly, and my insides were well and truly satisfied. When I lifted my head up to look in the mirror, he was looking back at me and his look of absolute satisfaction mirrored my own.

He pulled out and helped me stand back up, piercing me with his intent gaze. 'You are truly beautiful, honey, from here,' he said as he traced his finger from my earlobe, down the side of my face and neck to my chest, just above my heart, 'to here. Especially here.'

Placing my hand over his, I tilted my head back to kiss him. His sincerity and words penetrated the heart he had just claimed as beautiful.

'Come with me, I wish to continue our dog theme.' *What? Oh, no you fucking don't. My cave is well and truly in a state of hibernation for at least tonight and possibly tomorrow ... um, tomorrow morning anyway.*

'Bryce, you are going to render me useless if we keep this up.'

'Fuck, we can't have that. Come on, it's not what you think.' He helped me step out of the bath and passed me a towel.

My body had literally been on a sexual rollercoaster, climbing slowly, ticking and ticking, momentarily teetering on the edge, then speeding up and exploding — up, down; up, down — until it slowed to a stop. And just like a rollercoaster the feeling stayed, throbbing inside even after getting off. I loved rollercoasters.

After drying ourselves, we both climbed into bed. He put his arm out and pulled me to his chest so I could lay and watch the television. Still interested as to how our dog theme was to continue, I eagerly watched as he switched the TV on and tuned into an Internet movie channel.

'What are you up to?' I asked, curiously. But he didn't answer. Instead, he just pressed the buttons until he finally downloaded *Lady and the Tramp*. A huge smile crept across my face; this man was so romantic. 'You never cease to amaze me, Bryce.'

He smiled and kissed my forehead.

The sound of 'Bella Notte' began to fill the room, automatically drawing me into the wonderful world that is Disney Classics. The kids and I often sat down and watched one on a lazy Sunday afternoon, Charlotte and I adoring *The Little Mermaid*, and Nate's favourite being *Peter Pan*.

At first, watching the movie had made me feel a little homesick or, more to the point, a little Charli- and Nate-sick. But I was curious as to why he wanted me to see the film, so I snuggled into him and watched the animated story unfold.

He had been running his finger along my arm as we lay there together, but it wasn't until about a third of the way into the movie — maybe when Lady found out her owners were to have a baby — that I noticed his finger had stopped.

Gently, I shifted my head to look up, finding him fast asleep. This was only the third night we had shared together, yet it felt like one night out of many.

Enjoying the opportunity to watch him sleep, I observed his chest rise and fall as he breathed, deep, relaxed and completely comfortable. I could have observed him sleeping all night, but Lady had just met Butch and he was taking her to Tony's. I watched as 'Bella Notte' began to play again and I found the scene extremely cute. These two dogs were not meant to be together and yet, there they were, at a little dinner table about to eat a big bowl of spaghetti meatballs, courtesy of the restaurant's chef. My heart fluttered as I watched Lady stand her ground, yet shy away from Butch when he looked at her. It reminded me of Bryce and I when we first met. *Maybe this was what he meant when he said I reminded him of Lady?*

It soon became apparent that it wasn't what he meant, the moment he referenced being when their lips met as they ate the same piece of spaghetti. *Oh, how adorable.*

Looking at the face of the man with me, my heart pumped wildly from within my chest. He was such a romantic at heart and I loved that about him. It was the small gestures that made me melt, not the grand and over-exuberant ones — although, most of them were really nice, too.

I could have easily fallen asleep with him; after all, I was so exhausted, but I hated missing the end of a movie. I had a hard time starting something and not seeing it out to its end, so I kept my eyes open and watched Lady and Butch live happily ever after with their puppies. *What a beautiful movie.*

Propping myself up on my elbows again, I gently moved a bit of Bryce's hair from his eye. He was my Butch. He pursued me with the intention of showing me there was more to the life I knew, but was I Lady? Lady tamed Butch, captivated him and changed his outlook on life. Would we live happily ever after? Could we?

I switched off the TV and snuggled into him. Maybe we could.

CHAPTER
8

The brain's ability to recall sensations is an incredible compe-
tence, this time my brain recognising the tingling sensation
before I had even opened my eyes. I could quite easily get
used to waking up by rose-tickle, the action purely divine.

Bryce was once again sitting on the edge of the bed trailing
a rose up and down my back. 'Good morning, Lady. So how
was the movie?'

'I loved it, Butch.'

He raised his eyebrow and got up. 'Come on, no rest for
the wicked. We have climbing to do.' *Climbing? Oh, the rock,
how exciting!*

'Are we allowed to climb it?'

'Yes, but warnings have been put in place by the landown-
ers as to why they feel people shouldn't climb it and why they
ask us not to.'

'Oh ... should we climb it then? Why don't they want us to climb it?'

'Because the site has sacred significance to the Aboriginal owners, not to mention it is quite dangerous to climb. The traditional owners feel responsible for people who get hurt on their land. Therefore, they ask you not to climb. However, it is perfectly legal to climb it. Listen, if you don't want to climb it, we don't have to.'

'No, I want to.'

'It's your call, honey. I know it's controversial, but let's have some breakfast and decide later when we get there. If you don't want to climb it we can take a tour around the base.'

Crap, if I don't climb it, I will regret it, I know I will.

We ate our breakfast on the balcony, and I couldn't help staring wide-eyed at the huge monolith situated directly ahead. Now that our climb was upon us, the sheer size of the rock had become quite intimidating. I hadn't been to the gym in months, so I knew this trek was going to be really punishing.

The size of the rock was really quite deceptive; it must have something to do with the surrounding area being so flat. There was nothing else close enough to compete with its enormity. The Olgas, also known as Kata Tjuta, were the only other mountains in the area and they were around thirty kilometres away. So, Uluru had no rival in its immediate vicinity.

* * *

Bryce arranged for a transfer by 4WD into Uluru–Kata Tjuta National Park. When we pulled into the car park at Uluru there were buses and people everywhere.

'So, what are your thoughts?' he asked, looking up at the trail.

I didn't want to disappoint him or myself, for that matter, and there were many people already climbing it, so I decided to make the trek.

'Yep, come on, let's do it.'

As we walked past the warning sign, guilt washed over me. Warnings were usually put in place for a reason, but I kept going and began the journey on what is referred to as Chicken Rock. My runners were firmly secured to my feet, and I had also opted for some cotton shorts, a hat and a tank top. Bryce was in shorts, a t-shirt and runners, and he was also carrying our backpack with some drinks and bananas in it.

By the time I got to the link-chain rail, my calves were burning like never before. What was also burning was the heat that radiated from the surface of the rock. It was only 7.30 in the morning and maybe 24° Celsius, but it felt much warmer.

'Are you all right, honey?'

'Yeah, I'm fine. My calves have just reminded me they exist, that's all.'

'Would you like me to carry you?'

'Oh, you are so funny.'

We continued our trek, and the view was breathtaking. Before I knew it, the incline of the rock became steep, and we were a good sixty storeys above ground. I also realised it really was treacherous and I now completely understood the warnings.

Many people had stopped on their way up, some of them quite elderly. I was concerned for most of them and asked if they were okay. There was one particular lady who appeared extremely exhausted. Bryce offered to lead her back down the rock, but she politely declined and said she would rest and take in the view for a while, so we continued till the chain stopped. Apparently at that point you were only a third of the way.

'Shit, I need a drink,' I admitted, in need of a break. I knew I wasn't the fittest person alive, but I was really feeling the hurt.

We sat down as there were a few flat areas where we could rest.

Bryce gave me my water and began to rub my calves. 'I think you will need a training session when we get home.'

'Oh, you do, do you? Are you going to train me?'

'Of course.' He looked radiant, and although he had broken a sweat, he was very fit and healthy. Me? Well, I was drenched. *Thank god I didn't wear my white tank top today; oh, that's right, I couldn't — it was torn apart.* A smile crept across my face as I remembered our little romp in the desert the night before. But the smile disappeared as quickly as it came when I also remembered the mess we had left behind. *Oh, crap! I hope it is still there when we get back.*

We ate our bananas and continued the walk across the top of the rock, which was still quite long, but not as difficult as the original incline. At the end of the trek there was a sundial and, as we stopped next to it, Bryce beamed with satisfaction. The achievement obviously made him very happy. I was just relieved that I hadn't collapsed.

To say I was pleased with my decision to climb the rock was an understatement, because the view and standing there atop Uluru was very special and something I would treasure for the rest of my life.

Gaining my breath and rehydrating for the journey back down, I propped myself against the sundial and guzzled some water. Bryce stopped a young couple and asked if they could take our picture to which they agreed, so he handed the young woman his camera. I smiled at his thoughtfulness and hugged him as the young lady took our picture. He asked her to take another one and, as she did, he dipped me for a kiss, surprising me. She then took this opportunity to snap a few more shots.

The idea of the trek back down was not as worrying as I had originally thought it might be, until we reached the chain again and my calf muscles reawakened, deciding to punish me for ignoring them for the last few months. What didn't help was the fact I had to use said calf muscles constantly due to the surface of the rock being quite smooth, no doubt a result of hundreds of climbers over the years. You had to descend very slowly, as slipping at such a height was not recommended.

We finally made it back to ground level and, after some reflection, I completely understood the Aboriginal owners not wanting people to climb. It really was very dangerous. Unfortunately, you didn't realise that until you were at the point of no return.

* * *

We arrived back at Outback Hideaway and headed to the tepee.

Remembering the mess we had left behind, I took off toward our little stargazing spot. 'Hang on a minute,' I called back, heading to the top of the mound. When I got there I discovered everything had been packed up. Apart from the flattened area of grass and dirt, there was no evidence of my romantic surprise and our sexy little dessert-tasting session. *Shit, I feel terrible.*

Bryce displayed a concerned look as I walked back to where I had left him. 'What's wrong?'

'I didn't clean up our mess, Dorothy did and I feel awful.'

He smiled at me and shook his head.

'What? She was very kind to have helped me last night, and although she said she would clean it up, I didn't really want her to.'

'Don't worry, Alexis. I'm sure she wouldn't have minded.'

'I'll have to buy her some flowers or something. Which reminds me, can we head into Yulara today? I want to buy the kids a souvenir.'

'Of course. I thought we could cool off in the pool first, then head there this afternoon for a look around and then some dinner.'

'Great, sounds perfect. I could do with a swim right now.'

And, as quickly as I'd said it, his devilish glint appeared.

'No,' I squealed and pushed him away.

As I took off, my calves decided to penalise me once and for all, seizing up and disabling my getaway. He captured me in no time and hauled me into his arms as naturally as you would pick up your bag.

'Alexis, you cannot run from me, and don't tell me I have an unfair advantage this time, because clearly your footwear is not a handicap.'

'No, but my aching legs are.'

He displayed no sympathy. 'Bad luck for you, then.'

'Meanie.'

'Meanie!' he scoffed. 'I haven't been called that since ...' Bryce's voice trailed off and his head dropped. He didn't finish his sentence.

I instantly had a dreadful sense I had stirred up something that had been buried deep within him. My heart ached. 'Since when?' I asked softly, although I had a good idea that I already knew.

'Since Lauchie,' he replied, taking a deep breath. He kissed my forehead and carried me inside, kicking his runners off. I didn't probe any further; he would open up more about his beloved brother when he was ready. 'I suggest you remove your runners, because I am not putting you down.'

I leaned forward and untied my laces. I wasn't about to call his bluff. 'You are going to have to put me down or you'll destroy our backpack and the camera inside it.'

He raised his eyebrow at me, that small facial gesture alone indicating that he wasn't going to waver. I was starting to get used to the looks he owned; this one was the epitome of cocky determination and control.

Bryce walked me outside to the edge of the pool where I assumed I was defeated, so for once, I didn't put up a fight. Not that I minded this time, the cool water of the pool seemed inviting after the strenuous climb we had endured this morning.

To my surprise, he placed me down near the edge and walked back inside, taking his shirt off as he went. *What was that?*

I wanted to go in after him, but I just stood there a little dumbfounded, not knowing what I was supposed to do.

Mustering my own new-found courage, I stripped off completely and jumped into the blissfully cool water. Bryce came out seconds later in his board shorts, sunscreen and Ray-Bans.

'Aren't you forgetting something?' he inquired, displaying a somewhat surprised smile.

I was in the far corner of the pool with my back to the rock and my arms out on the ledge, looking as smug and proud of my daring self as I could.

'No! What could I possibly be forgetting?' I asked innocently.

He pursed his lips together and nodded his head, then glanced past me.

'Good morning, Mr Wayne,' he announced, waving and acknowledging the gentleman who had helped bring our bags to the tepee, the gentleman who also just happened to be crouched down beside our balcony doing some gardening. *Oh, shit! Crap! Balls!*

Instinctively, I crossed my arms over my body and submerged myself under the water, surfacing seconds later wearing my infamous beetroot shade. Bryce appeared highly amused then disappeared back into our room. *Oh, that's right, arsehole. Leave me here.*

'Hello, Mr Wayne,' I said hesitantly as I pressed myself up against the wall so that he could only see my head.

He didn't look up, which was proof he had seen my brazen skinny-dip. 'Hello, Ms Summers, I'll be finished here in just a second.'

'Oh, that's okay, take your time.' *Take your time? Alexis, why not invite him the fuck in with you?*

Bryce returned with a bathing suit for me ... a bikini. I never friggin' wear a bikini. Mind you, I never normally wear absolutely nothing in an outdoor area, let alone in front of strange maintenance men.

Dangling the bikini from his finger, Bryce teasingly asked, 'Do you want it?'

'Yes.'

'You'll have to come and get it then.' *Grrr, is he bluffing? He is so arrogant at times.*

I swam over to the edge where he was standing and tried to grab the bathing suit without exiting the water, but it was useless. He was too tall. *I'll show you, Mr Smartarse. But am I brave enough to do it? Yes ... yes, I freakin' am.*

Mr Wayne had already seen my naked body, so what was the harm? I glared at Bryce with renewed courage and made my way to the steps, confidently taking one at a time. Bryce's smile faded and a look of shock replaced it. He glanced in Mr Wayne's direction then back at me as I strutted to the sunlounge.

Taking a seat, I casually, but with intended seduction, laid back, placing one hand above my head.

Bryce grabbed a towel and tossed it to me.

'I won't be needing that, thank you.' I smiled sarcastically at him.

'Thank you, Mr Wayne. You can finish that later,' he called out quite firmly.

Mr Wayne quickly packed up his tools and basically ran off.

'Alexis, are you trying to torture me?'

'Yes, you deserve it.'

Sitting on the edge of my sunlounge, he threaded my feet through the holes of my bikini bottom then lifted it up. I tilted toward him, allowing the completion of his covering. He then handed me the top, which I dropped by the side of the sunlounge with a smile.

Bryce shook his head and took a deep breath, then sighed. 'What am I going to do with you?'

'You can start by rubbing some sunscreen on my back. And let this be a lesson to you, Mr Clark. I am not as timid as you may think I am.'

'Oh, I know you are not timid, honey. You have proven that time and time again.'

I smirked triumphantly at him and rolled onto my stomach, waiting in anticipation for my UV protection to be applied. I didn't have to wait long at all. Bryce's hands were gloriously strong and firm, and as he massaged the sunscreen lotion into my skin, I fell into a deep indulgent trance. *Mm, that feels so nice.*

* * *

It must have been a couple of hours later when I started to rouse. The first thing I noticed was that Bryce had moved the patio sun umbrella over me so that I would not burn to a crisp.

Lifting my head, I spotted him sitting next to me working on his iPad.

'Hello, sleepyhead,' he said while putting the tablet down and moving to the edge of my lounge chair. 'Exhausted, are we?'

'Just a little. I have had a few busy and strenuous days recently. Plus I watched the whole movie last night. You didn't.'

'Touché, my love. What would you like for lunch?'

My stomach rumbled in response. 'What's the time?'

'Nearly 2.30 p.m.'

'Oh, I did sleep for a while, didn't I? Have you eaten?'

'Yes, I just had a sandwich.'

'Sounds good, I can make it. You go back to your iPad. Are you doing work?'

'Just a little, but it's fine and it can wait. I like making you things.' He kissed my shoulder and then walked inside.

He was heart-stoppingly handsome and sexy. He was sweet, romantic and smart. He could cook, play an instrument, and was obscenely wealthy. The man was simply too good to be true.

I watched in delight as his firm arse strode away from me, and relished the fact that I really had hit the jackpot.

How the hell had that happened?

CHAPTER
9

Bryce soon returned and placed a heart-shaped sandwich on my lap.

I giggled. 'Are all my meals going to be heart-shaped?'

'Most of them, yes.' He sucked his finger and walked off. *Jackpot, all right! Alexis Summers, you have landed yourself the most incredible man alive.*

I bit into the sandwich and once again my taste buds went into meltdown: turkey, cranberry sauce, Camembert cheese, alfalfa sprouts and avocado on white bread.

'How did you get hold of all these ingredients? We are in the bloody outback for frig's sake,' I called out, hoping he was in earshot.

'It's what I —'

I cut him off. 'Don't even bother.'

His chuckle resonated from the kitchen, filling me with love.

'Dinner is booked for 6 p.m., so we will head into Yulara about 5 p.m. Are you happy with that?' he asked.

'Sure, I need a shower first though.'

I finished my romantic sanger, got up from my sun-lounge, and stretched before walking into the bedroom. As I approached the bed, I noticed he had laid a black cock-tail dress out for me. I had to admit that I liked it when he chose my clothing — it showed he cared. This dress, however, seemed a bit formal for the outback, but knowing Bryce, he had something planned.

* * *

I think it's safe to say that most of us think we do not have many — or even any — bad habits when, in fact, we all har-bour a few. I was one of those people, although you only had to ask my family and they'd tell you otherwise. I had been made aware of one bad habit and that was my singing in the shower. I did it unconsciously, whether I meant to or not. It never bothered me, of course, but Nate seemed to hate it, especially when he had one of his friends sleeping over, as he had often told me.

The acoustics in the bathroom were complimentary — or so I thought. However, I think the reason I did it was because I was in a small space, by myself, with no interruptions, and songs would come filtering into my head.

I had been singing and humming away as usual, and was just about to turn the taps off when Bryce stopped me.

'Oh, for shit's sake! You scared the crap out of me,' I breathed, my heart pounding in my chest.

'Where do you think you are going?' he asked, stepping into the shower.

'To get dressed,' I replied, now knowing that was no longer the case.

He pressed himself against me, and I stumbled further back until I was pressed against the wall. 'Not yet you're not,' he said firmly, his strong and protective arms wrapping around me and lifting me ever so slightly.

Our mouths met and I threw my arms around his neck. Water cascaded down our faces as we stood there taking each other in. When we kissed it felt as if the world stopped, like everything around us stood still in time.

Lifting me higher, he indicated I should do what I always do — wrap my legs around his waist. I'm guessing he liked the feeling of my thighs gripping his hips; I knew I did.

'I could kiss you all day long,' I said, in between kisses.

'No, you couldn't,' he mumbled as he continued assaulting my mouth.

'Why not?'

'Because you talk a lot.'

I grabbed his hair and yanked it hard, pulling him away from my mouth. His eyes grew wide and he looked fiercely at me.

'Is that a problem, my talking?' I asked, still holding his hair.

'No, but it is if you want to kiss all day.'

He growled and shook his head free of my grip then penetrated me with force.

I gasped. *Fuck, I love his cock.*

We seemed to mirror each other's actions when we made love; if he was rough, I'd be rough back. And if I was soft and slow, he'd reciprocate.

We consumed each other in the shower and I decided not to talk much, especially after his cheeky feedback, but it was still incredibly hot and sensual, and although he had been a bit naughty, he was still oozing love for me through every pore of his body.

* * *

After we'd showered and dressed, I did my hair, finding the humidity and constant washing was starting to turn my normally obedient locks into a crazy, rebellious shag pile. I gave up trying to tame it and fixed it into a loose bun with some pins.

Upon entering the bedroom, I found that Bryce was already dressed, his appearance taking my breath away. Without even realising it, my mouth fell open.

He had on a black shirt with the sleeves rolled up and the top two buttons undone. Grey suit pants fell beautifully over his hard, muscled legs, and were finished off with a pair of black dress shoes. He looked utterly handsome.

Slowly, he walked over to me and lifted my jaw back up. 'Thank you,' he said with a knowing smirk as he kissed me, then walked into the bathroom.

Still remaining in my Bryce-daze, I put on the Wayne Cooper dress. It was black, tight, mid-length and had one shoulder strap. Bryce had also left out a pair of champagne-coloured Jimmy Choo strappy heels for me — they were exquisite.

Assessing myself in the mirror, I once again concluded that he really did have great taste. I loved everything he'd ever chosen for me; the man knew me better than I knew myself at times.

I caught his reflection in the mirror as my gaze rose from my feet to his face. He was now leaning on the doorway to the bathroom and, funnily enough, his mouth was agape, too.

I slowly walked over to him and lifted his jaw up with my finger.

'Thank you,' I said, mimicking the kiss he had given me.

'No, thank you, Alexis. You have no idea how satisfying you actually are. From the moment you strolled through my casino, you have captured and engulfed me entirely.' He leaned forward and pressed a gentle kiss to my lips.

I pulled back momentarily, still hovering my lips over his. 'Thank you for rescuing me, Bryce. I really didn't know what love was until I met you.'

He rested his forehead against mine and closed his eyes as if he were in pain. His expression briefly had me perplexed.

'Honey, it's the other way around. You rescued me.'

Before I could question his confusing demeanour he took my hands in his, kissed the tops of them and we left our room.

* * *

The helicopter flight was very quick as Yulara was only some five kilometres from Outback Hideaway. After setting the chopper down, Bryce took my hand and we walked a small distance to the shopping centre. I felt very overdressed when we entered a souvenir shop and other patrons gave us second glances.

Mere seconds after we arrived, Bryce placed his hand on my hip and whispered into my ear. 'I'll be back in a minute, honey.'

He hurried off and I assumed that maybe nature was calling, so strolled along the aisles, waiting for his return. I was looking at the numerous stuffed kangaroos and spoons with pictures of Uluru and Kata Tjuta on them. *I should get Tash a spoon!* The thought thrilled me, as it was a private joke between

me and my crazy friend. I had come across a spoon once that
looked like a penis. Tash had thought it was hilarious, so from
then on in, whenever I saw a strange-looking piece of cutlery, I got it for her. My problem was that these particular
spoons looked quite placid, except for one. I picked it up and
smiled, happy that this souvenir of the Olgas resembled a pair
of boobs.

I continued to browse, coming across a gold miniature tele-
scope on a stand. It was very cute and reminded me of Bryce.
There was no way I could leave it behind, so I hid it behind
the stuffed dingo I'd already found for Charlotte, together
with a necklace that had an Aboriginal design pendant. Nate,
I thought, would no doubt have fun with a boomerang, and I
couldn't possibly leave without a didgeridoo.

So, with great difficulty, I scooped up one of those as well,
along with a tea towel for Mum to satisfy her particular linen
fetish. I swear to God she had a cupboard at home filled with
the things.

Hauling my souvenir loot to the counter to pay, I noticed
they had a bucketful of lovely posies by the door. I grabbed
one of those as well.

As I awkwardly stumbled out of the shop, purchases in
hand, and feeling quite pleased with my shopping efforts,
I cursed to myself when I heard my phone start to ring.
The ringtone informed me straightaway that it was the one
assigned to Rick. I froze. *Shit, what should I do? Answer or
decline?* I didn't want to talk to him, but was I delaying the
inevitable?

I hit decline. *Not tonight. If I speak to him now, my night
will be ruined, I know it will.* Panicking, I quickly dialled Tash.

I didn't want him to ring again, but maybe if he did, he would know I was already on the phone and would give up.

Tash answered.

'Lexi, you were supposed to call me back yesterday. What's happening? I rang your home, and Rick said you were away.'

'I am, Tash, I'm fine. Listen, Rick and I have separated.'

She gasped. 'You told him about your feelings for Bryce. Oh, no.'

'No, not really. I don't want to get into it with you over the phone, but Rick had an affair a few years back and he only just told me about it. So I've left him and am currently in the Northern Territory with Bryce.'

'Fuck, Lexi. Shit!' She was silent. 'I'm so sorry. I ... I ... I'm at a loss for words. He cheated on you, really? Oh, god!'

'Yes, so as you can imagine, I'm heartbroken and furious as hell. I don't want to deal with him at the moment. I need time, which is why Bryce has flown us far away for a break. We'll be back tomorrow, and I will face Rick when I'm ready.'

'So what does that mean for you and Bryce? Have you ...?'

'Tash, I love you, but it's none of your bloody business.'

'Okay, fair enough, hon. You just take care, and I'll see you when you get back.'

'Thanks, Tashy. Bye.'

I ended the call just as Bryce came up behind me and placed his hand on the small of my back. 'Someone has been shopping.'

I had a bag hanging from my arm and a rather large didgeridoo in my other hand. 'Yes, I didn't think about having to carry it around with us, though.'

'Never mind, give it to me.' He carried my loot in one hand and held my hand in his other.

* * *

We arrived at the restaurant and were greeted by a young waiter.

'May I help you, sir?'

'Yes, I have a reservation on the private dune tonight.'

'Oh, yes, Mr Clark. Firstly, let me take your things.' The young man happily accepted my bag of souvenirs and didgeridoo, right after I snuck Bryce's gift into my clutch. 'We will see that these are taken to your helicopter, Mr Clark.'

'Thank you,' Bryce replied courteously.

'Now, if you'd like to follow me.' The young man escorted us past the diners seated inside and led us outside, down a candlelit path where I could see a private dining setting on top of a sand dune. The path stopped and it was thick, red sand from there on in. *Oh, shit, there's no way I'm going to climb that dune in these heels.* I stopped and went to lean on a post and remove them when Bryce cut in.

'No you don't.'

'You are not carrying me, Bryce. I might not be timid, but I am not flashing my arse to the patrons inside who are watching quite intently through the window.' He looked in their direction and grinned, then positioned himself as a shield and scooped me up.

'Bryce Edward Clark! I said no.'

'Shh. Since when do I ever listen when it comes to carrying you?'

'You don't.'

'Exactly.'

Arriving at the top, he placed me down next to the table. In the centre of it was an orange rose in a vase, surrounded by candles.

The sun slowly setting below the horizon, and the rock in all its sunbathed glory was majestic.

'Quick, come here,' I said in a hurry, grabbing him and pulling him close to me. I knew how quickly the appearance of Ayers Rock could change in an instant. So, reaching into my clutch, I retrieved my iPhone and took a selfie of us both, Bryce kissing my cheek as I pressed the button. A smile crept across my face, together with a tear in my eye. It was beautiful. The photo really captured the moment perfectly. I blinked back the tear, not wanting to be an emotional wreck.

We watched as the sun completely melted into the horizon, its amber glow seeming to ooze like syrup onto the distant ground. Bryce had his arms wrapped around me, and I couldn't have been happier. At that moment, I knew that no matter what happened with Rick — no matter how hurt I would feel when I faced him — I would always have these arms to come back to. And it made me feel safe, warm and loved.

We were entranced by the rock's beauty, but eventually sat down and listened as a local Aboriginal man played the didgeridoo, both of us enjoying the cultural ambience as we ate our four-course dinner. It was a magical evening and a fitting way to spend our final night in the Red Centre.

'I have a present for you,' I said with a grin as I placed my hands on top of my clutch.

'I have one for you, too,' he smiled, reaching into his pocket and pulling out a jewellery box. It was too big to be a ring box — thank god — but whatever it was, I could imagine it would be immaculate.

Suddenly I didn't want to give him my stupid present any more.

'Well, where is it? My present?' he asked, excited expectation plastered across his face.

I hesitated as I placed my hand inside my bag and removed it from its confines. 'It's stupid. You are going to laugh at me.'

'I always laugh at you.'

'Very funny. No, you are going to think its daggy.'

'I will not. Anyway, I never get presents, so give it to me.'

I handed it to him and covered my eyes, peeping through semi-open fingers. He unwrapped the tissue paper and held it in his hand, rotating it as he made his inspection. *How embarrassing. He gets me jewellery and I get him a stupid trinket.*

Placing it down on the table, he stood up and walked over to me, stopping by the side of the table. Then, delicately grasping my hand, he brushed his lips against my knuckle and pulled me up into a passionate embrace. 'I love it, Alexis, and I love you. Thank you. Thank you for sharing yourself with me.'

I kissed him back. 'And I thank you for sharing yourself with me.'

A very faint applause sounded from afar, so I peeked over his shoulder. There were people inside watching us and cheering our romantic interlude.

'We have an audience, I think.'

He turned and grinned at the onlookers then reached for the jewellery box and held it in front of me. I opened it, and inside was a stunning white gold snake necklace with a huge teardrop opal, surrounded by at least thirty diamonds.

The sight of its beauty nearly resulted in an awkward stumble on my part, Bryce steadying my stance with his arm.

'Oh, my goodness, that is the most gorgeous thing I have ever seen.' I went to touch it and he snapped the lid down on my finger, the very same way he had done it with the earrings. 'Bryce Edward Clark!' I admonished playfully, laughing and hitting him on the arm. 'Stop doing that.'

He laughed too, but this time a lot harder. 'I'm sorry, I can't help it.'

I squinted my eyes at him in mock ferocity, but even I couldn't hide the absolute joy I was feeling.

He pulled the necklace out of the box, put it around my neck and clipped it shut. I tried to look down but could only just see the tip of it. It felt stunning, and I could only imagine that it looked it as well.

'It's beautiful, thank you.' Faint applause sounded from the dining room and, hearing the appreciative clapping, Bryce waggled his eyebrows, dipped me and kissed me in an over-dramatised show for our audience. They showed their appreciation by clapping even louder.

'You're such a show-off,' I murmured as I broke away from his mouth.

'It's what I do, Ms Summers.'

'Yes, I know.'

* * *

After dinner, we thanked our host, before Bryce piggybacked me down the sand dune. We walked hand-in-hand back to the chopper, talking about places we had been and places we wanted to go. At the top of my list was Paris and Rome. I'd always wanted to climb the Eiffel Tower, see the Colosseum, walk under the Arc de Triomphe, and stroll the halls of the Louvre. Bryce, however, had already been to both cities to oversee the construction of Clark Incorporated hotels. He was very worldly and had visited many countries, mainly for business. However, as strange as it may have seemed, I had been somewhere he hadn't: New Zealand. As we flew back to our lodge, I asked him why he wanted to go there.

'I like *Lord of the Rings*,' he said proudly.

'So do I!' I exclaimed with a smile.

I remembered back to the time I visited New Zealand for a family holiday. Rick had arranged a surprise, booking our accommodation at a Hobbit Hotel. I was so excited stepping into our room through a round door: I was happy back then. *Geez, how things change.*

Quickly burying thoughts of my husband for the umpteenth time, I prepared myself to exit the helicopter. My feet were killing me and, as gorgeous as these shoes were, I was in a world of hurt.

'Bryce, can I ask you something?'

'Yes, anything.'

'I can't believe I'm about to say this.' I crinkled my nose and he looked at me curiously. 'Can you carry me? My feet are so sore.'

His face lit up, and he gathered me into his arms. 'I could carry you forever. You do realise that, don't you?'

I wrapped my arms around his neck and rested my head on his. 'I do.'

'Say that again.'

'What? I do?'

'Yes.'

'I do.'

'Hmm, I like the sound of those two words.' *I did once, too.*

Wanting to change the subject before he spoke of marriage again, I remembered the flowers I had bought. 'Oh, I need to give Dorothy something.' I motioned my head toward the reception building. He smiled a cheeky smile and carried me in the direction I'd indicated.

'You can put me down now.'

'No.'

I tutted, followed by a roll of my eyes.

As Bryce opened the door of the reception building with his foot, we were greeted by Dorothy who was sitting at her desk. She smiled brightly as he carried me toward her.

'Mr Clark, Alexis, to what do I owe the pleasure of this visit?'

I timidly glared at Bryce. 'You are going to have to put me down so I can get them,' I said, smiling apologetically at Dorothy. Bryce surrendered and lowered me to my feet. I reached into the bag hanging off his arm and pulled out the posy.

'Dorothy, these are for you. I just wanted to say thank you for helping me organise the picnic and for cleaning it up.' I handed her the bunch of flowers.

'Oh, thank you. It was a pleasure. But I didn't clean it up, dear.' *Oh, you didn't? Then who did?* The ever-so-tardy light bulb switched on in my head, prompting me to spin around and catch Bryce smirking a mammoth smirky fucking smirk.

Turning back toward Dorothy, I closed my eyes briefly and shook my head. 'Well, thank you for all your help, I appreciate it.'

She nodded, which was when Bryce scooped me up back up again, startling me in the process.

I squealed.

'Good evening, Dorothy. Alexis and I have some business to attend to.' *Bryce Edward Clark, she doesn't need to know that.*

She smiled and blushed as he carried me back out the door.

'You cleaned it up, didn't you, that morning when I was asleep?'

'Yes, honey, I did. It was the least I could do,' he answered with a smile.

'Thank you for what you do,' I whispered before kissing his cheek. As he walked along with me happily content in his arms, a sudden feeling of anxiety for what the future held washed over me. 'What am I going to do when we get back to Melbourne?'

He glanced down only fleetingly before opening our door once again with his elbow and foot. 'You are going to face the truth.'

Gently, he placed me down on the bed and undid my shoes then rubbed the soles of my feet. At first, I wanted to flinch, but my feet were sore and his rubbing actions were quite soothing.

'The truth hurts like hell,' I admitted.

'It always does, my love.' He removed his shoes and socks and crawled up next to me.

Both of us lay propped up on our elbows, looking at each other.

'How you overcome the truth is what really matters. Yes, it hurts like hell, but it's how you look at the situation and how you deal with it that will heal the hurt in the end.' He touched my face. 'You are going to hear things that will wound you deeply, but remember, not everything is black and white.'

I looked at him confused, his words sounding like a defence for Rick.

'Are you defending him?'

'Who, Rick? No, not at all. I'm just trying to prepare you in the hope it softens the blow.'

I took in a deep breath. 'Oh, I don't think you can soften the blow of my husband cheating on me.'

His eyes dropped and he got up and left the room.

'I'll be fine. I have you,' I called out to him.

Moments later he was back with a Scotch for him and a gin and squash for me.

'Yes, you do have me, and don't ever forget it,' he declared, with a tone of indisputable promise. Then, holding up his glass, he continued. 'Cheers to the best three days of my life.'

'Cheers to the rest of our lives,' I offered.

We lightly tapped our glasses together and both took a drink. Bryce didn't stop, so I continued as well, turning it into a race to see who could finish first. Of course, he won.

I swallowed my last drop and handed him the glass, then moved closer and softly pulled him into a kiss. I didn't want clothes tearing, wall bumping or legs wrapped around his waist. I just wanted to hold him, kiss him and make love to him tenderly and slowly. I think he understood my needs, because he caressed my face gently as we kissed.

I got up on my knees and unbuttoned his shirt, deliberately taking my time. The shirt slid off his shoulders as I ran my hands along his skin, completely removing it as I pushed it down his back. His biceps were invitingly luscious, so I pressed my lips to them and tasted his warm skin.

Trailing my lips to his shoulder then to his neck, I found my way back to his mouth again where our tongues gently stroked one another's, over and over — it was so nice.

He reached to my side and unzipped my dress, helping me out of it. I then unbuckled his pants as he kissed my shoulder and neck.

He stood up momentarily, allowing them to fall down his legs, taking his underwear along with them and exposing his glorious erection, an erection I would never get sick of.

I smiled at him, wanting him to know I appreciated his body and what he did with it.

Mimicking my appreciative regard, he moved toward me and kissed me again. I unclipped my bra for him as he slowly pulled down my G-string, kissing the insides of my legs as he went. No words were spoken between us. There didn't need to be, we were saying all we needed with each touch and kiss we gave one another.

We made love that night: real love, soft love, sensual love. Pure and lasting love. It was our last night at Outback Hideaway and we wanted to make the most of it.

CHAPTER

10

I felt slightly dejected during our flight home. We'd had such a wonderful time at Uluru that it saddened me to leave. I wished I could have just collected the kids and gone right back to our perfect little tepee forever. But I was a realist if anything, so I knew I had to return to my life in Melbourne and face it head on whether I liked it or not. It didn't change the fact I was dreading it though.

While in the air, I'd received a call from my insurance company informing me that my car was now fixed. The repair shop was not far from the airport, so Danny detoured and dropped me off so I could pick up my car. Bryce had offered to stay with me, but I assured him I'd be fine and that he should return to the penthouse. I told him I wouldn't be long and blew him a kiss as the limo pulled away.

Seeing my car looking healthy again filled me with happiness. Don't get me wrong, I had more than enjoyed driving the Porsche, it was just that my Ford Territory was familiar, and I'd missed it.

* * *

I decided I would quickly stop in at home on my way back to the hotel, under the assumption that Rick would still be at work. My goal was to get in and out quickly: collect my mail and grab the few things that I needed.

Opting to park a couple of houses away, I felt this made surveillance easier, just in case — for some unknown reason — Rick was there. I'd seen this type of precautionary covert act on TV and it seemed like a good idea. Or I was just completely paranoid. *Alexis, you will have to face him soon.* I knew facing him was inevitable, but still, I wasn't ready. Would I ever be?

Thankfully, there was no sight of him when I walked inside. However, the feeling I got when I entered my house was not what it normally was. For starters, the kids weren't there, which automatically took away that sense of homeliness. And, secondly, the house was in a terrible mess.

There were dishes in the sink, clothes on the bedroom floor, and remnants of a broken picture of Rick and I on our honeymoon on the kitchen table. I shook my head. This surrounding disarray wasn't like Rick. He had always been relatively neat and tidy, and although he had a temper at times, I was the one out of the two of us who would throw something in anger, not him.

I picked up the broken picture, which resembled my broken heart. *What went wrong? What did I do, or not do, that would make him actually have sex with another woman while we were happily married? Maybe it was because I was heavier back then?*

I don't fucking know. If he had been tempted by Claire, fine ... I got that. But why not just break it off or tell me sooner or ... fuck! I threw the frame across the room. It hit the wall and smashed into even more pieces.

Now angry and in an even more emotionally wrecked state, I went through the letters which had been thrown on the kitchen bench: bills, bank statements and more bills. I figured he would see to them, he always had. Being a mortgage broker sort of earned him the role of handling our finances, and as far as I was aware he did a good job of it — I never had reason to worry about any of it.

Quickly, and now in a rush to get the hell out of there, I grabbed some extra clothes. Not that I didn't have more than enough back at Bryce's apartment, because I did. I guess I just wanted some items of my own that were familiar to me, like my slippers, for instance, having secretly pined for them the last few days.

I also grabbed my hairbrush, some medication and a photo of the kids. I didn't want to dawdle or hang around any longer — just in case he came home early — so I gathered my things, got back into the car and drove to the hotel.

* * *

As I pulled into the basement car park, Bryce was beside my car before I had even opened the door. 'What took you so long? I've been worried.'

'I went home to get a few things.'

His expression turned ashen.

'Hey, don't worry, Rick wasn't there. I knew he wouldn't be. He doesn't normally finish work until 4 p.m.'

My revelation appeared to provide him with a little relief. 'You should have told me you were going home, I would've come with you,' he said, sounding slightly annoyed.

'I didn't think of it until after I'd collected my car. Anyway, I have to face Rick on my own.'

'No, you don't.'

'Yes, I do. Thank you for the concern and for wanting to be my knight in shining armour, but this is between me and Rick.'

'I know, Alexis. It's just I don't want you to see him, not until —' He stopped, cutting himself off.

'Not until what, Bryce?'

Slowly, he slid his hands into his pockets. 'Not until you are prepared.' *Prepared? I'll never be prepared, really.*

Reaching for the sides of his arms, I gently squeezed them and peered into his rich blue eyes. 'That's sweet, but I'll never be prepared to hear the details of when my husband decided a young slut was more satisfying than his loving wife. You cannot possibly prepare yourself for that.'

Bryce removed his hands from his pockets, placed them on my hips and then dropped to his knees. 'Nobody is more satisfying than you. Nobody!'

He pressed his face into my abdomen, just below my belly-button. My short, white, cotton slip dress clung to his face as he sucked a large deep breath in through his nose. His sharp intake of air, together with the feel of his clenched fingers as he inhaled, triggered my recognition of his hunger for me. I had felt this need many times before, one of those times being in this very garage.

I put my hands in his hair as he began kissing my stomach through the cotton dress, generating that wonderful tingling feeling in the very spot he was kissing me on. He started to scrunch up my dress with his hands, making me grip his hair in anticipation of what I knew was coming. I helped him lift it over my head until I was standing before him in my underwear and brown leather sandals.

He looked at me and gritted his teeth, repeating what he had just said. 'Nobody is more satisfying than you. Nobody.'

Scooping me up in his arms, he walked me over to the Charger. 'I believe we have some unfinished business here.'

'That we do, Mr Clark,' I smiled at him, allowing him to see the excitement that now covered my face.

He placed me down on the bonnet, the very spot where I had nearly succumbed to him weeks ago. I leaned back and propped myself up on my elbows.

'You have no idea how often I have thought about the last time you were lying here. How much I wanted to taste you there and then.' *I wanted you to taste me, too. I want you to taste me now.*

'Well, I suggest you stop thinking and start tasting.'

The look in his eyes told me he was going to rip my lace knickers — it's what he does — so I didn't argue when he tore through them like a hot knife through butter.

He placed both his hands on the bonnet of the car and hovered over me with his greedy eyes set on one target. I put my foot up on his chest stopping him, staring hot and wanting into his hungry eyes. I did it because I needed to remember the very look on his face, the look that told me I was everything he ever wanted. However, I could tell the suspense as to when I was going to lift my foot was already adding to his increasing urge. So, lifting my foot and placing it back down again, I watched with delight as his head disappeared between my legs.

His first touch always sent my body into a frenzy, forcing my head to fall back in sheer pleasure. I gripped the bonnet with both hands, but my fingers were moist with perspiration and slipped just slightly on the glossy purple finish of the Charger. My mouth was open, releasing moans of enjoyment as his tongue moved up and down, increasing my wetness.

I watched him lift his head and his eyes met mine. They were so sexy and alluring, and I could read them like a book. Right now they were saying, 'You belong at the tip of my tongue,' and mine were replying with, 'I know.'

He trailed his tongue over my clit, then continued to trail it up across my Caesarean scar and over my abdomen until his very delicious tongue was in my mouth.

Pushing myself up from my elbows, I reached forward and unbuckled his jeans, ripping hungrily at his underwear. To my absolute delight, they tore with ease. *Ha, good work, Alexis.*

His mouth fell open in surprise. 'We may have to go underwear shopping soon.'

'Yes, we may,' I agreed, as I guided him in and, as always, he fit me like a glove.

The sensation I felt at his mercy was wonderful, but it was the look in his eyes, as always, that tipped me over the edge.

'I can't get enough of you,' he breathed out.

'Good,' I panted, 'I don't want you to.'

He lifted me up and walked over to the Bel Air, placing me down on its bonnet.

'Ooh, on the Chev as well, Mr Clark?' I asked, greedily.

Bryce mouthed my neck. 'I'll do you on every one of them, if you like.'

The excitement his words provoked spread across my face as I looked around the garage — there were *a lot* of cars. *Fuck, that's a lot of sex.*

'Even the Aston and Reventon?' *Surely not. One slight dent and it's fifty thousand dollars in repairs just there.*

I slid off the bonnet to stand on my feet, and Bryce took a step back. 'Especially those.'

'No, you can't, I would cringe thinking we'd do damage.'

'Yes, we can,' he asserted, his devilish glint appearing. But I was one step ahead of him and I took off, managing to get behind the Lexus and giggling as I paused.

'No, Bryce. You'll seriously do damage.'

That devious grin grew wider.

I took off again and ran behind the Ferrari, looking at him through the windows on the opposite side. For a brief moment, I noticed the beige interior and imagined his bare arse on it. *Alexis, snap out of it! You are in the middle of being hunted down.*

'Alexis, I will always beat you on foot.'

'Ah, but could you beat me on four wheels?' I challenged.

'We'll have to find out.'

'Yes, we will.' I took off yet again toward the McLaren which was where he caught me, pinning my back against the golden-orange door panel.

He spread my arms out across the windows as he kissed my neck and chest, then hooking my leg over his hip, he penetrated me once again. The moment his cock slid into my pussy was simply divine — my nipples hardened, my back bowed, my hands were clenching the hair on the back of his head.

'I love you, Bryce,' I promised as our eyes locked onto each other's.

'I know, honey. I love you, too.'

He lifted me completely and walked us over to the lowline Reventon, gently placing me down so that I was sitting on the roof. *The roof, fuck!*

'What are you doing?' I shrieked.

'Shh.'

Hesitantly, I moved backward, having the feeling that I was sitting on thin ice — one move and the roof would crack or cave in.

He walked around to the front of the car with a lascivious smirk and stepped up onto the bonnet. *Oh, fuck, no!* I threw my hands over my mouth as he lifted off the ground, the sound the bonnet made as it bowed vibrating right through me. I was horrified and extremely fucking turned on at the same time.

'Bryce Edward Clark, stop!' I begged. 'You are ruining your car, and stop smirking, it's not funny.' He took another step and placed his hands on the roof, eye-fucking me disobediently. Then, with a greedy growl, he scaled the windscreen with his feet and made his way toward me.

Instantly, I felt myself moving backward along the roof as he hunted me down like prey. I had nowhere left to go, so laid back completely and put my hands over my face.

'I can't believe you are doing this,' I mumbled through my closed fingers.

'Believe it, honey.' He lifted my pelvis while on his knees and entered me once more. *Oh, shit. Hot sex on the roof of a 1.6 million dollar Lamborghini Reventon. It doesn't get much better than this.*

My hands were still covering my face when he leaned forward and removed them, pinning them down on the roof above my head. 'Don't hide from me, Ms Summers. I want to see your face as we dent this fucker.'

My mouth fell open and I raised my head ever so slightly. He pushed harder and harder, and the noise of the roof panel as it buckled in and out got louder and louder. He was loving it, as was I, but for entirely different reasons I'd suspect.

We climaxed together, and he groaned like never before, my cries matching his as I relaxed every part of my body while resting on the newly-fucked Reventon.

Bryce lowered himself on top of me and kissed my cheek, a satisfied aura radiating from him.

'You just fucked your car. You do realise that, don't you?'

'No. I just fucked *on* my car, and it was well worth it.'

I laughed and shook my head at him.

'Are you telling me you didn't enjoy that, honey?'

'Of course I did, very much, but I'd hate to hear how much that session just cost you. You're crazy.'

He smiled mischievously. 'So, you think you can beat me on four wheels, eh?'

'I don't think, Bryce. I know.'

'You are on, sweetheart.' He jumped off the roof and put his arms out for me to follow. I took the plunge and he caught me, then we retrieved our clothing and headed up to his apartment.

* * *

'I've got a few things to do in the office first,' Bryce explained after we unpacked. 'Ring the hotel's kitchen and choose something for dinner, okay? I should only be half an hour to an hour at most.'

'Okay,' I replied.

He kissed my forehead and headed into his office.

Hmm ... dinner. Maybe I could cook him something? I went to the fridge and opened the door. *Let's see ...* A few things jumped out at me: parmesan, eggs, cream, garlic and pancetta. *I hope he has fettuccini.* I made my way into the pantry. *Holy shit! He has everything.*

Overwhelmed and, quite frankly, jealous of his butler's pantry together with its contents, I grabbed a packet of dry fettuccini pasta and made my way out of there, grouping the rest of the ingredients I had found in the fridge.

I found Bryce's iPod sitting on the kitchen bench and plugged it into a speaker jack, so I thought I'd switch it on. Before I could do so, I heard Bryce yelling, the harsh and menacing sound curdling my insides. I froze and my heart started to pound. I'd never heard him speak that way.

Slowly, I crept up over to the office door and put my ear to it.

'It's not fucking good enough, do you hear me?'

'Yes,' a man answered, a man I soon recognised as Gareth. He was in the office with Bryce.

'I'm serious, Gareth, I'm sick of this shit. I don't want to hurt you, but when you do this you give me no choice.' *Fuck. Hurt him? No choice? What's he talking about.* 'You need to fucking keep on top of this, or so help me God, I will have you locked up.' *Locked up? Locked up where?* My heart was now well and truly beating in my chest, and I knew whatever they were discussing was very serious and very private.

'Bryce, I'm sorry. I'll try better, I promise.'

'You'll do more than try, Gareth. I will not risk anyone I love being hurt. It's not only me and Lucy any more.

There's Alexander, and Alexis now. Don't look at me like that, Gareth. Take your fucking meds and tell Scott he doesn't control you.' *Scott? Who the hell is Scott, and what meds?*

I walked back to the kitchen, now knowing I had been right; there was more to Gareth than meets the eye. If Bryce was worried about my safety, I had to know what was going on.

With my mind frantically trying to piece together what I'd just overheard, I started to dice up the pancetta, desperately trying to remove the vision of Gareth being yelled at by Bryce from my head. *Music, Alexis. Put on some music.*

I turned on the iPod and flicked through the songs. 'Edge of Seventeen' by Stevie Nicks. I love that song.

Pressing play, my tension eased as the sounds of a guitar kicked in. Instantly, I started singing along and dancing around the kitchen in my own little world. I often did this when I was cooking at home as it was a welcome distraction from the daunting task. Unlike Bryce, I didn't actually enjoy cooking the majority of the time. Let's just say I had to be in a certain mood to enjoy it, like I was now — after removing Gareth from my mind. I was, in fact, looking forward to cooking Bryce something for a change.

With the pot on the stove and the pasta boiling away, I whisked the eggs together with a small amount of cream then seasoned it and set it aside, singing along loudly. I then crushed the garlic and added it to a pan with the pancetta to fry it off.

The song finished as I was chopping up the parsley and 'Go Your Own Way' started up.

Draining the pasta and putting it aside, I then cut the crusty bread into star shapes. *He gives me hearts, I give him stars!* I placed them on a plate and smiled to myself, then added the cooked pasta to the pan together with the egg mixture and parmesan cheese, tossing it for a couple of minutes on low heat. I dished it up on a plate and sprinkled it with the parsley, while dancing around singing to myself.

Looking up briefly to see where we should eat, I noticed Bryce standing at the door watching me. *Oh, my god! How embarrassing. Not only have I desecrated his immaculate kitchen, I have sung and danced through the entire spectacle and he has now borne witness to it.* I stood, frozen solid, wanting to disappear in a cloud of smoke. Unfortunately, that was not an option though, so all I could manage was, 'Hey, I cooked.'

He slowly walked over to where I was standing, cupped my face and kissed me. *I really do love it when he does that.*

Flapping my egg and cheese mixture-covered hands in the air, I mumbled a warning for fear of him getting dirty.

'I have stuff on my hands.'

'I don't care about your "stuff". You, my love, are an angel. Have I ever told you that?'

'Yes, right after I sucked your cock for the first time.'

There was a pause, then both of us started laughing.

'Where would you like to eat?' I asked, still giggling.

He raised his sexy eyebrow.

'I'm serious, you insatiable man.'

Bryce kissed me again and then pointed to the dining table. He went to the fridge to grab a bottle of wine while I placed the plates down on the table. When he returned, he noticed my plate of stars and smiled, picking one up and admiring it.

This action cued my 'student' voice. 'So, Mr Astronomy Teacher Clark, what is that star called?'

'This, my dear, is the most precious star of them all and is known as "the Alexis".'

I beamed at him.

He put it down next to his plate and grabbed another one.

'Are you not going to eat "the Alexis"?'

'No, she is too precious to eat.'

'She will go mouldy then.'

'I won't let her.'

I shook my head as I began to eat. My cooking was nothing in comparison to what he usually conjured up, but I was confident he wouldn't spit it out, or at least I hoped he wouldn't.

I screwed up my face as he popped in his first mouthful and then raised my eyebrows in anticipation of his evaluation.

'What? It's lovely, thank you,' he replied.

I let out a huge sigh of relief. 'So, did you get your work done?' I asked, my intention now to probe him in order to find out why he had yelled at Gareth.

'No, not really. I was interrupted.'

'By Gareth?'

He looked up, confused by my knowledge of his interruption.

'I'm sorry, but I heard you yelling at him. You really are quite lethal and loud when you are angry.'

He nodded but with a sad look on his face.

'Bryce ... who is Scott?'

Sucking in a deep breath, he put his fork down on his plate and wiped his mouth with a napkin. 'I was hoping I wouldn't have to tell you, but I now realise I will. Not only because I don't want to keep it from you, but because it's for your own good.'

All of a sudden my stomach dropped, and I felt as nervous as hell.

CHAPTER
11

The atmosphere surrounding us had changed dramatically.

'Gareth has DID with positive symptoms of schizophrenia.' *Oh, shit! That, I had not expected.* 'Scott is one of his "alters".'

'Alters?'

'DID, or Dissociative Identity Disorder, was once known as Multiple Personality Disorder, so his "alters" are also known as his "identities".'

'Oh my god! How long has he had DID?'

Bryce put his head in his hands and looked down at the table. 'Gareth was in the car with Mum, Dad and Lauchie when it crashed. He suffered head injuries and post-traumatic stress disorder which they think led to his DID.'

I was completely stunned. Shocked. Devastated for Bryce. But more so, devastated for Gareth.

Reaching over the table, I grabbed Bryce's hand. He looked up at me, misery plastered across his face. It broke my heart.

'I'm so sorry, I had no idea.' *This entire situation makes more sense now.*

'You didn't know, honey. Like I said, I'm telling you because Gareth's "alter", Scott, can be dangerous. You see ... how can I put this? Scott is very protective of me, he loves me and in a sense he feels I belong to him.'

'Oh ... he loves you?'

'Yes, his "alters" are very different to Gareth himself. On a mental level they are completely separate from him. Scott is obviously gay and has deep feelings for me, so he can be very possessive.'

'Has he ever hurt you, or anyone else for that matter?'

'Not really ...' He hesitated. 'But Scott can get quite desperate. Look, when Gareth is taking his antidepressants, his antipsychotic medications, and he goes to see Jessica weekly, he does quite well. I'll need to speak to her, but I think maybe you might be triggering Scott's latest reappearance.'

'Me? Oh no.' *I feel sick.*

'Alexis, this is not your fault. Gareth has been skipping his meds lately and that has a lot to do with it.'

I sat in shock. The revelation was a lot to take in. 'If Scott is obsessed and protective of you, then why is he in such close proximity to you? I don't know anything about DID, but wouldn't it be best if you spent less time together?'

Bryce started to eat again, so I followed suit. 'It's not that simple. Gareth and I have always been close. On the day the accident occurred, I was meant to pick him up from a friend's house. He'd had a couple of drinks and was not fit to drive.

I completely forgot about him. Mum and Dad were in his vicinity, so they picked him up for me. He should never have been in that car.'

Bryce put his head in his hands again.

I got up, walked over to him, and knelt by his chair. 'This isn't your fault. You can't blame yourself.'

'I don't, I blame the arsehole that ran the red light.'

'What happened to him?'

'He was found guilty of culpable driving causing death and was sentenced to fifteen years imprisonment.'

It was obvious from his angry tone and tense features that this conviction infuriated him; it would infuriate anybody who'd lost three people they loved dearly. I shook my head. 'What do you need me to do? Obviously you are worried about Scott, or Gareth, or both of them?'

He glanced in my direction. 'I just need you to be aware that Gareth is not always Gareth. And when Scott is around, he can be quite aggressive where I am concerned. Scott is not stupid. He is actually quite smart and cunning. He can see my feelings for you are very different, and he is jealous.'

'That explains the Tel V Awards,' I mumbled, feeling terrible. I'd stood on Gareth's foot when it had been Scott who'd hassled me. But they were one and the same person, or were they? *Oh, this is so complicated, I really need to do some research.*

'What happened at the Tel V Awards?' Bryce asked, his tone now menacing.

'Nothing, it was nothing.' *Crap.*

'Alexis, what happened?' *Oh, shit, I'm just making it worse.*

I walked back to my seat and sat down. 'Gareth, or Scott — I don't know which one, but I'm now assuming

Scott — approached me outside the toilet. He grabbed hold of me, so I stood on his foot with my heel in self-defence and got free.'

Bryce aggressively stabbed an innocent piece of pancetta.

Pushing my plate to the side, I decided I had finished eating. My appetite was now gone anyway. 'Bryce, I can handle Scott. But, Gareth, it's not really his fault is it?'

'In a sense, no, but he needs to take his meds. That is his fault, he knows better. Gareth cannot control Scott, and most of the time he has no recollection after Scott has appeared. Gareth is what they call "the primary identity" and is passive by nature. Scott is an aggressive "identity" and is somewhat dominant over Gareth and the others.'

'The others?'

'His other "alters", although I have not seen one in a very long time. The meds together with the psychotherapy have been really good for Gareth. In recent years we have only seen Gareth, apart from anniversaries and birthdays and the like, when his memories of the trauma come back. Deirdre seems to make an appearance on these dates. She is a caring "alter", sort of like a mother hen. Deirdre helps keep the peace most of the time.'

I sat there amazed, listening to the complexity of Gareth's condition. 'So, there is no cure?'

'No. From what Jessica has explained the best thing is to keep him on the meds and make sure he visits with her frequently for psychotherapy. The therapy concentrates on helping the "alters" live in harmony together. This enables the primary to have a sense of control which can help Gareth lead a normal life, not a punished life. This assists him in the long run.'

Bryce stood up and cleared the table.

'Wow, that's a lot to try and keep in control of.'

I thought about the situation a bit further while helping him stack the dishes next to the sink. 'You said helping him lead a normal life? Is that why he is still vice-president of Clark Incorporated?'

He clasped my hand. 'Come with me. I need a stiff a drink and a more comfortable seat, then, I'll tell you everything you want to know.'

* * *

We left the kitchen and went to the lounge. Bryce fixed us both a drink from the bar then sat down. He took hold of my legs and placed them in his lap.

'You asked if helping him lead a normal life is why he is still VP? Well, yes, in a sense. He is closely monitored by the board, and little does he know, all of his executive decisions are almost always run past me or Arthur.'

'Arthur?'

'You've met him, Arthur Gordon.' *Oh yes, Santa from the Tel V Awards.*

'Like I said,' Bryce continued, 'when Gareth takes his medications and attends his sessions with Jessica, he does quite well and, believe it or not, he does a decent job as vice-president.'

I caught a slight sense of uncertainty in his tone. 'Isn't that a huge gamble, though?'

'Yes and no. It would be if he was not monitored properly.'

'It seems like a lot of work on your part. Bryce, tell me to shut up if I'm overstepping, but are you taking on this burden of having him as VP because you feel slightly guilty about the accident?' *Oh, I hope I didn't offend him. Alexis, keep your mouth shut.*

'Maybe a little, but it has more to do with the fact he saved Lauchie's life. Even if it was only for a few days, those few days meant everything to me and Lucy.'

'How did he save Lauchie's life?'

Bryce let out a weary sigh. 'Mum and Dad died instantly, but Lauchie was still breathing and somewhat conscious. Gareth pulled him free of the wreckage only seconds before it blew up.' *Oh, fuck.*

I put my hands to my mouth in surprise, then moved them onto his arm for comfort. 'Oh, my goodness, I'm so sorry.'

Sadness engulfed me. Just the thought of losing your parents like that was horrific. What a terrible thing to have to endure at such a young age.

'Don't be sorry, it is what it is and it can't be undone. I've learned to accept that over the years, with Jessica's help,' he admitted while reassuringly touching my hands. 'As I was saying ... Lauchie fell into a coma and was pronounced brain dead shortly after. Gareth was absolutely devastated. He adored Lauchie. We all did. Gareth is an only child, so Lauchie was just as much a little brother to him as he was to me and Lucy.'

My heart was literally breaking while listening to his words — it was such a horrible story.

'Should I speak to Gareth or Scott and tell him I'm not a threat?'

'No, definitely not! You are a threat to Scott. Scott wants me for himself and he thinks that with you around it cannot happen.'

'So, what do we do?'

'I'm not sure. As I said, I need to speak to Jessica about it. Gareth knows he needs to take his meds, and I've asked him to take them in front of me on a daily basis which he has agreed to do.'

'That's a good thing, you know. The fact he is cooperating. Maybe you need to ease up on him?'

'I know, it's just ... I don't want to have to commit him, it's the last thing I want, but I will not put you or Lucy or Alexander at risk because of Scott. He should not be underestimated.'

Bryce's talk of Scott had me worried; there was something in his manner and tone that made me think that Scott was a major problem and that Bryce knew a little more about his capabilities than he let on. *Oh, fuck, Samantha!*

'Does Samantha know about Gareth?'

He took a long drink from his glass and deliberately avoided making eye contact. 'Not unless Gareth has told her.'

'But she could get hurt. She has a right to know,' I complained, genuinely concerned for her safety.

'Maybe she does, but that's none of my business. I can't involve myself in all of his personal affairs. How is that helping him lead a "normal life"?'

'Well, it's not, but she has a right to know. Anyway, you would have a responsibility as her employer to warn her, wouldn't you?' I was starting to get anxious. *How could he not tell her, warn her?*

Bryce placed his middle finger and thumb on either side of the bridge of his nose as if he was feeling the onset of a headache. 'Alexis, what do you want me to do?'

Suddenly, I realised that Gareth's illness and the problem it imposed was a massive stress and strain on him, and my anxiety about Samantha was only adding to it.

I climbed on his lap and placed my hands on each side of his face.

'I'm sorry, I don't mean to add to the stress you already have. I want you to tell me what I can do to help you. You shouldn't have the burden of Gareth solely on your shoulders. What can I do?'

He placed his hands on my backside.

'Just stay away from him as much as possible. I don't need to worry about you as well. Listen, I'll keep my eye on Samantha, and if I feel something is wrong, I will get involved.'

I ran my fingers through his hair. 'Thank you, and thank you for telling me this. It could not have been easy for you.'

'Sharing things with you is the easiest thing I have ever done in my life.' *Funny thing that. Me too.*

Bryce stood up with me still attached to his front. 'Now, enough of this Gareth stuff. I vaguely recall you throwing me a challenge earlier today.'

I shot him a sceptical look. *Oh, yes, my beating him on four wheels.*

'Yes, I did.'

'Well, how about we have a practise run? A little warm-up?' he suggested, clenching his fingers around my arse.

I was becoming accustomed to not using my legs as much any more, so I did not always put up a fight when he carried me. This was one of those times.

* * *

We entered the man cave, which had me a little perplexed.

'What are you doing? There are no wheels in here.'

'Practise, my love, I said practise.' He put me down on the sofa in front of the TV and booted up the Wii, handing me a controller clipped into a white plastic steering wheel. 'Mario Kart,' he explained with a smile, 'you won't find a better form of practice.'

He jumped onto the sofa I was sitting on, displaying a similar boyish grin to Nate's when Nate was sitting in front of a gaming console. I couldn't help but smile.

'Fine, but I'm Mario,' I declared, shooting him a don't-argue-with-me look, which he didn't.

He chose to be Luigi and, before I knew it, we were lined up on track with lots of other characters in go-kart style racers. There was a blonde princess in a pink dress, and a turtle. *I think it was a turtle, or a dinosaur maybe?* There was also another really nasty-looking turtle. Again, it could've been a nasty dinosaur.

Little did Bryce know that Nate actually had this particular game at home, and I had played it before — although I'm guessing, not as often as Bryce played it.

I remembered Nate showing me a trick once, after I had gotten shitty at him. Nate always managed to speed off at the start of every race, leaving me lagging behind. I didn't know how he did it, and I refused to give him canteen money until he showed me how.

As the countdown came up on the screen, I got ready, holding down the accelerator button as the number two faded. This was the trick Nate had taught me, giving me an acceleration boost when the game began. Bryce was aware of this trick as well, because Luigi flew alongside Mario, leaving the rest of the pack behind them. He glanced over at me with a so-that's-how-it-is smirk, having realised I was not a Mario Kart virgin.

We raced through the track, each of us collecting bonuses along the way. Luigi shot out ahead, having secured a power boost thingy. *Damn it.* Lucky for me, one of the other karts launched a green turtle shell at him, spinning him off the track.

'Ha ha,' I laughed.

I could see the finish line ahead and still had my banana skin, so I dropped it and claimed my victory. 'Winner! I told you,' I boasted while jiggling in my seat, laughing, but also secretly relieved and proud of myself. *Empty threats are just that, Alexis. Empty. And they make you look like a fool.*

Bryce was smiling, but he also seemed to be slightly annoyed. 'Beginner's luck. Best out of three?'

'You're on.' I wriggled and sat cross-legged on the couch. He cricked his neck on both sides and, as per usual, eye-fucked me at the same time. *Fuck, he's sexy when he does that. Alexis, stop it. It's a ploy. He's trying to distract you with his sexiness.*

The countdown started once more, and again we both hurtled past the other karts using our boost trick. This time though, he crossed the finish line first. *Ah, crap.*

'Ah, Ms Summers, it seems we are now even.'

'You cheated!'

'How? I did not,' he refuted, looking offended. I, however, could see past his charade.

'That's okay. If dirty is how you want to play, then dirty it is.' I turned my head toward him and slowly ran my tongue across the top of my teeth. Then, leaning over, I hit start on his remote.

The countdown started for the final time, and our karts took off again. For the first couple of laps we exchanged the lead, but by the last lap we were dead even. *Now, Alexis, use your secret weapon.* I slowly moved forward, continuing to drive while getting on all fours on the rug in front of us.

Hitching my dress up over my bare arse, I gave him a perfectly good view. *Ripping my underwear is going to come back and bite you, Mr Clark, because now I have the ultimate weapon at my disposal and it is being waved in front of your face.*

I heard him groan and noticed his kart veer off the track a little, so I continued to move forward until I was lying on my stomach, with my dress still hitched high above my waist and my legs bent with my feet up in the air.

Having only half a lap left to race, it was now or never to execute stage two of my plan. I drove my kart next to his and bumped it slightly while opening my legs and revealing my ultimate weapon at the same time.

His kart hit a cow.

I won the race.

He didn't say anything.

Neither did I.

Smiling from ear to ear, I waited, still lying flat on my stomach. When I realised it was me who had to make the first move, I slowly turned my head back to where he was sitting.

He had one hand still grasping the remote and the other in his hair. I gave him the biggest smirk I had in me, got up on all fours again and circled round to face him. Slowly I crawled in his direction, giving him the burning gaze he so often fires at me. I crawled up to his legs and lifted the remote away from his hand, then climbed up on his lap and straddled him.

'I win,' I whispered against his lips.

He didn't respond, just lifted me up and carried me to his private elevator, en route to the bedroom. The doors slid shut, and I found myself being pressed up against the wall. I noticed that he never hit any buttons, so I knew our destination was now exactly where we were.

There was still dead silence between us, but our eyes were, as usual, in deep discussion. *He knows I've beaten him, and he can't handle it. Can't handle that he finds it hot.*

I lifted my dress off as he held me against the wall, still not saying a word. What was he waiting for? For me to kiss him? *No, Alexis, you won. Make him be the first to kiss you.*

I leaned forward, allowing my breasts to caress his chest. Then, hovering my mouth as close to his lips as possible without touching them, I held my position for seconds.

Neither of us closed the gap that would seal the touch of our mouths, so I trailed my lips to his neck, across to the other side of his face, until I was breathing warm and heavy into his ear, whispering again, 'I win.'

He was quicker than lightning and had his mouth on my neck and his hands on my breasts. *Oh, fuck.* I gripped the railing and shrieked at his ferocity and need for me. It was so sexy.

His hands were forcefully gripping and holding my tits as his mouth found my own. He let them go momentarily and wrenched his pants off, still managing to keep me up against the wall. He was hard and full and he didn't hesitate in entering me forcefully, sending excitement and wild pleasure right through me. He fucked me hard up against that elevator wall, pulling out his cock to the very tip and driving it back into me, over and over again. I can honestly say it was the wildest sex I had ever had. We didn't talk during it, not once, until the very end when he came with a luscious vibrating groan.

'You win,' he said softly as he placed light kisses on the corners of my mouth.

Breathing heavily, I replied, 'I know.'

He then leaned over and pressed button number two, stepped out of his pants, and when the elevator reached its destination, carried me to bed.

CHAPTER
12

The next morning, we woke up at the same time which was rare. He always seemed to get up at the crack of dawn, unlike myself who utilised the privilege that was a sleep-in. When you have children, sleep-ins are the ultimate treat. You only need to ask my sister Jen, who has three children under two. I don't know how she does it, but Jen survives on little to no sleep at all.

I was looking forward to seeing them at my parents' house on Sunday. Jen and her husband Steven lived just out of Shepparton, so I didn't get to see them as much as I would have liked. Therefore, whenever I visited Mum and Dad, I made sure I visited them as well.

I rolled over and placed my head on Bryce's chest. He wrapped his arm around me and secured me tightly to him.

'Good morning, beautiful. Did you have a nice sleep?'

'Yes, thanks to you.' I could feel the satisfied smile on his face without even looking to see if it was there. 'So, what are the plans today? Am I still on paid holiday leave? Or am I required back at work?' I traced my finger along his superb abdomen.

'You are working. Today your job is to participate in the "real race".'

'The real race? What do you mean?'

'I told you, honey, yesterday was only practise.'

'If you think you are going to be Mario, then think again.'

My head bounced up and down on his chest as he laughed.

'We aren't playing the Wii. We are going to drive real go-karts.' *Oh, Mr Clark, you are a glutton for punishment.*

* * *

We had a shower, got dressed and consumed a quick breakfast of poached eggs and toast before heading down to the garage.

'Which one?' he asked.

I looked at him, and at first I thought he was suggesting which one to fuck on. But I soon figured out that he meant 'Which vehicle shall we take?'

'Well, we can't take the Lamborghini, can we? That dent is a perfect impression of my arse.'

Bryce chuckled. 'I'm keeping it.'

'You. Are. Not!'

He shrugged his shoulders in response and gestured to his plethora of automotive porn. 'Well?'

I really wanted to suggest the McLaren, but I didn't want to draw too much attention to ourselves. I knew he liked the attention, but I was still getting used to it.

'Can we take the Charger?'

He smiled. I think he knew how the Charger made me feel. 'Of course we can.' *Yay, cue the happy-clap.*

Bryce opened the door for me like the gentleman he was and as I sat myself down the car was already doing things to my insides. *Maybe not a good idea choosing this one, Alexis. You might not actually make it to the track!* Bryce jogged around to the driver's side, sat down and roared the engine to life.

I giggled ecstatically. *Alexis, get a grip.*

* * *

I enjoyed every minute of our drive to the go-kart track, forty-five minutes south of Melbourne. There were a few envious glances in our direction, but overall it was not too bad. I could definitely handle it.

'Are you ready? You only get one chance, you know,' he taunted me.

'Oh, you don't know what you are in for. I only need one chance,' I retorted confidently.

As we entered the building and made our way to the front counter, Bryce brought the back of my hand to his mouth and pressed a kiss to it. 'You can still back out if you want. I won't hold it against you.'

'Oh, this is on, Clark. Don't you worry.'

The young man behind the counter was busy with the computer and didn't look up when he spoke. 'G'day, mate. Booking in for a session?'

'How much to hire the whole track to ourselves for twenty laps?' Bryce casually asked.

That particular piece of speech made the guy look up, but he was clearly annoyed by the request. 'We are open to the public today, mate. If you want to book a function you need to ring this number,' he added, faux smiling and handing Bryce a pamphlet.

'I will pay fifty thousand dollars now for a private function.'

The young man's eyes widened as he stared dumbfounded at Bryce. 'Are you for real?'

'Yes,' Bryce replied firmly, but I could tell he was hiding amusement.

As I stood there and watched the exchange, I could only imagine what it felt like to offer such a large sum of money and stop someone in their tracks like that. It must be very empowering. *Or obnoxious!*

'No, wait a minute!' I interrupted while turning to Bryce. 'I don't want a private session. I want to race you with others on the track. That's only if you are not afraid of obstacles?'

My sexy, competitive Mr Clark deliberated my suggestion for a short while then agreed, paying for twenty laps as general public patrons.

We were given helmets and hair nets, and I laughed uncontrollably when Bryce put his on. Even with the horrid white cap though, he still looked incredibly hot.

'Laugh all you want, honey. I will be the one laughing when we are done here.'

'Pfft, so you think!'

They say old habits die hard, and I tended to agree. When I was a teenager and raced stock cars with Dad, I had always analysed the tracks before a race. This day was no different.

I had butterflies in my stomach which wasn't necessarily a bad thing, as I'd always experienced nerves before the start of a race when I was younger. When that had happened in the past, I would jiggle in my seat. adjust my belts. check

my visor and stretch my neck. But as soon as that green flag
went down, the nerves disappeared and my focus took over.
So these butterflies infiltrating my abdomen were a welcome
reminder of what was to come.

We sat lined up on the starting grid next to each other, five
rows back with approximately thirteen other people ranging
in ages from twelve to maybe fifty. Bryce flipped up his visor
and turned his head toward me, and I could see the thrilled
but competitive glint in his eye.

He put his hand to his helmet then extended it, signifying
that he blew me a kiss. I, on the other hand, did not fraternise
with the enemy and, before closing my visor, stuck my tongue
out at him instead. I'm almost certain he would have smirked,
but I didn't hang around to find out as we were given the
green flag and off I went.

Bryce shot out quick, following his inside lane behind the
young man in front. Both of them had to go around the lady
ahead of them who apparently hadn't noticed the race had
started. I moved out of formation almost instantly, as the
young child in front of me had not yet figured out his accelerator from his brake. *Poor kid.* I wanted to stop and help
him, but my bloodthirsty racing alter ego took over, forcing
me to speed off in pursuit of the leaders.

I slotted in just behind Bryce, putting me in fourth place.
Bryce was third, the young man he followed in second and
a mystery person in first. I knew I had to stay with him to
have any chance of winning. From past experience, I knew
these karts became heavy as your arms tired. So, if the size
comparison of Bryce and my biceps was anything to go by,
I was pretty sure my arms were bound to lose strength well
before his.

With one lap down and nineteen to go, my adrenaline was pumping and I felt good. Nineteen laps was a long time, though, and if I were to have any chance of beating him, I needed to formulate a strategy. There were times, when racing, where you needed to be aggressive; assert your dominance and intimidate your opponents. But there were also times where you needed to be submissive, follow the leader and lie dormant like a sleeping volcano. The thing about sleeping volcanos, they exploded, raged uncontrollably and became quite lethal. My strategy was going to be the latter; follow the leader and quietly wait for the right opportunity.

I followed Bryce quite closely for the next fifteen laps, weaving in and out and around the majority of the rest of the field. My co-driver habit of looking past the racers ahead and into the field beyond was not lost on me as a driver. Doing this proved to be handy when there was crash or a young-ster accidentally going the wrong way. *Poor kid!* My motherly instincts kicked in yet again, and I desperately wanted to help the little guy. But I couldn't. Not now. I had to beat Bryce; there was no other alternative.

The mystery person was still out in front, and I would catch glimpses of him momentarily when we entered the straights. With three laps to go, and my arms holding their own, I decided I would pick up the pace. I didn't want to try and overtake Bryce too early on. My plan had been to do that with just under two laps remaining. However, he locked up the brakes going into the hairpin, allowing me to gain better momentum, therefore putting me in the lead whether I liked it or not.

I now had no choice but to floor it, and with my heart pounding and my adrenaline levels increasing, I sped off.

Mystery guy was now only a couple of kart lengths ahead. Either he had been held up or I had made up a lot of ground. As we entered the hairpin, I could hear the engine of Bryce's kart close behind. He gave me a little 'love' tap, bumping me forward and letting me know he was there. *That's how it's gonna be, is it?*

I kept a firm grip on the steering wheel and came as close as I could to the mystery person in front. Bryce was right up my backside now, and I had to make the executive decision as to which side he would try and pass me on. I guessed he would be his cocky self and pass on the outside, so I swung out to the right and gently nudged my front left-hand wheel into the mystery person's back right one.

This move sent mystery person drifting to the right, blocking Bryce's attempted pass route and slowing them both down.

Turning hard to the left, I then floored it across the finish line, taking my victory. *Take that, Mr I-Never-Lose Clark.*

The race steward directed me into the pits where I came to a stop, Bryce pulling up alongside of me. We both stepped out of our karts at the same time and, although I was over the moon, I was still a little nervous about beating him and felt a bit reluctant to remove my helmet.

Unable to keep it on all day, I unlatched it and took it off, watching hesitantly as Bryce did the same. He smiled from ear to ear and, as I looked at him, I mouthed the words, 'I win'. He smirked and flashed his burning approval which settled any nerves I had about how he would react.

Mystery person pulled up behind my kart and leaped out of his seat. He marched right up to me, lifting his visor and displaying an expression which was far from pleased.

'Don't look so fucking pleased with yourself, bitch. That move was a dog's act.'

'I beg your pardon?' *Who the fuck are you, dipshit?* I was shocked. How rude? And to act this way in front of children ... what a wanker. 'It's just a casual race. You might want to calm down,' I responded, stepping aside in order to get away from this nasty pile of testosterone-fuelled pig shit who thought he was God's gift to go-kart racing.

'Don't tell me to fucking calm down.'

Before I knew it, Bryce was standing in between us and was right up in the raging lunatic's face. *Go for the trachea, my love!*

'What did you say?' he hissed through gritted teeth while staring wildly at the prick.

Bryce was beyond mad. He was furious.

'The bitch spun me off the track.'

'I did not. I gave you a gentle nudge. You were holding me up.' I turned to leave. 'Come on, let's just go.'

Bryce grabbed him by the shirt. 'Apologise, now!' he snarled.

'Fuck off.' Mystery man then leaned forward and head-butted Bryce with his helmet. The knock to Bryce's head stunned him for just a second, but after that second had elapsed, Bryce was ready to take the fucker out.

He grabbed the guy's arm and swung around his back in a motion that inevitably had the guy off balance. It was obvious from Bryce's fluent motion that the guy's sudden loss of balance was not an accident as Bryce immediately had him face-planted in the ground with a knee firmly in the man's back.

'Apologise, or I'll embed your face into this helmet.'

'Get the fuck off me.'

'No, don't. Bryce stop. There are kids watching. Stop, please, he is not worth it.'

Bryce looked up, heated fury blazing from his eyes. 'He called you a bitch, Alexis.'

'I know. But look.' I pointed to four young children who looked terrified, along with their parents who were now trying to get them as far away from the fight as possible.

Three men came running down to where we were standing, ready to break the dickhead and Bryce apart.

'What's going on here?' asked a man wearing a manager's badge.

Bryce had let go of the mystery man and was now standing above him. He also had blood dripping from his forehead.

'This bitch spun me off the track. Disqualify her,' pig shit mystery-fucker explained and he rose to his feet. The guy was a complete nutcase.

Bryce moved his arm ever so slightly at the mention of the word bitch.

I grabbed hold of it and held it firmly as I whispered in his ear. 'He's not worth it, my love. Trust me.'

The manager looked to the steward and raised his eyebrows. 'The move was perfectly fine, boss.'

'Fucking pansies, the lot of you.' And with that, the nutcase wrenched off his helmet and threw it at his kart before storming off, cursing as he went.

'Are you all right, mate? Your head is bleeding,' the manager asked, pointing to Bryce's forehead.

Bryce ignored them and turned to me. 'I'm sorry, honey. Are you okay?'

He looked regretful and hurt in my defence.

I reached into my pocket and pulled out a tissue. Being a mum, I made it a habit to have at least one tissue on me at all times.

Placing it over the laceration, I reassured him. 'I'm fine. I'm more worried about you. That's pretty deep.' I blotted the tissue on the gash to his head and stared into his sorrow-filled blue eyes. 'Really, I'm fine. I'm a big girl. Anyway, I kicked that knobhead's arse, so it's all good.'

He breathed in and raised his chest, looking above me in the direction the crazy guy had disappeared. Then, turning back to the complex's manager, he finally answered him. 'Yeah, I'm fine.'

'Would you like to file a report, or call the police?'

'No, that won't be necessary,' Bryce answered, as he put his arm around me protectively.

The manager then took a step closer and slapped Bryce's back in an apologetic, manly type of gesture. 'We are so sorry for this, mate. We'll refund your money.'

Moments later, we made our way back up to the office where parents and children were standing, still looking a little worried.

Bryce walked up to a couple of the kids and bent down. 'Are you okay there? I'm sorry you got a bit frightened. Listen, how would you like to have a few more races, just yourselves on the track?'

'Cool,' said one of the little boys who was maybe Charlotte's age. He smiled.

The younger little boy — maybe aged four — held onto his dad's leg and turned away.

Bryce remorsefully glanced at their parents. 'I'm so sorry your children had to see that.' He stood back up and spoke to the manager. 'Look, I don't want my money back. Instead, I'll hire out the venue for the rest of the day, and all children and their parents are on me.' He handed over his credit card and I watched him take care of what he thought was his fault.

With all the money in the world he could choose to act arrogantly, but he didn't. He was kind, down-to-earth, and always wanting to fix things.

The mother of the two young boys stepped up to me. 'He really does not need to do that. I saw the whole thing and this was not his fault.'

I gave her a soft smile. 'I know, but he wants to do it, so take your kids back out there and go and have some fun, okay?'

She looked down at them and they smiled brightly at her. 'Okay, thank you.'

* * *

After leaving the go-kart complex, we headed toward the car.

'Show me your head,' I demanded.

'It's fine, it's just a scratch.'

'Okay, well in that case, I'll assume Nurse Summers is not needed then.'

I picked up my pace as I approached the car.

He caught up and hugged me tightly. 'On second thoughts, it's huge. Deep even, and needs a lot of attention,' he pouted, poking out his bottom lip while removing the tissue from his cut to show me.

I smiled at his adorable attempt to reverse my decision.

'Oh, yes, it does. Poor baby, but you do realise I cannot let you drive a motor vehicle in your current state.' I grabbed the keys from his hand and opened the passenger side door. He smiled and, without argument, sat in the seat.

Already, my body reacted with little tingling sensations as I grasped the steering wheel, and I could feel my face stretching into an uncontrollable smile.

'You won, honey, fair and square.'

'I did,' I stated as I turned on the engine and shuffled in my seat. 'So, what do I get for winning, Mr Clark?'

The Charger roared out of the car park, my heart roaring along with it.

'This.' He indicated the car.

'Well, if getting to drive this home is my prize for winning, then I shall challenge you again tomorrow.' *Oh, my god! This car is just gorgeous.*

'No, Alexis, it's yours.'

I shot him a what-the-fuck look, but he just smiled.

'No. Bryce, I can't accept this,' I stated with certainty. I wanted to, really wanted to, but I couldn't possibly accept.

'It's non-negotiable,' he replied quite sternly.

'But —'

'It's yours, end of story.'

I couldn't help but smile, even though deep down inside I knew I could not accept his gift. I smiled for him, smiled for my victory, and I think I smiled all the way back to the hotel.

* * *

With my hand in his, I led him up to his bedroom and directed him to sit on the end of the bed. Then, disappearing into the walk-in stadium, I returned moments later wearing the nurse costume he had bought after I sang him the 'Boo Boo Song' a few weeks prior. He had requested I dress up for him, and now was the perfect time to do just that.

The costume was made of white shiny lycra and barely covered my arse and breasts. It also came with a tie-on hat and red thigh-high PVC boots. I honestly looked like a slutty dress-up nurse — but I guess that was the point.

He was looking down at his hands when I stopped in the doorway.

'So, Mr Clark, where does it hurt?'

Bryce raised his head at the sound of my voice and, on finding my location, a huge smile crept across his face. And, might I add, he displayed absolutely no sign of injury or illness whatsoever.

'Right here,' he explained, pointing to his heart.

'I thought you had a boo boo on your head?'

'Yes, but I think my heart just stopped, Nurse Summers.'

I walked over to him very slowly, noticing him swallow quite heavily as I approached. Bending down only slightly, I put my ear to his chest, then stood back up and put my fingers over his carotid pulse. 'Your heart is just resting.'

I moved in front of him, so that I was now in between his legs, then, taking his head in my hands, I assessed the cut on his forehead. It wasn't as deep as I had originally thought, but it still needed a Band-Aid. 'First, I must see to your wound. Then we can look at ways of getting your heart beating faster.'

I raised an eyebrow, hoping it would have the very same effect on him as his always had on me. The slightest involuntary twitch of his eye told me that it did, empowering me to carry on with my little charade.

'Are you going to sing to me, Nurse Summers?'

'Yes, but only if you are a good patient, Mr Clark.'

Walking around to the bedside table, I reached inside my handbag and pulled out a tissue and Band-Aid. A sneaky self-satisfied smirk crept across my face as I realised that my pay-back for the rose petals, birds' nest-look was about to come to fruition. *Yes, good things do come to those who wait, Alexis!*

Placing myself back in between his legs, I seductively licked the tissue. A part of it got stuck on my tongue and I had to spit it out. Bryce laughed hysterically and fell back on the bed. I too had to fight back my impending laughter if I wished to remain in character.

'Mr Clark, it appears you are well again. Does that mean I am no longer needed?'

'No, Nurse Summers, my head still hurts ... BAD!' he faux whined, shooting up from the bed to a sitting position and supressing the laugh he still had within him.

I placed the tissue on his head and wiped away the remainder of the dried blood then started to sing 'Fix You' by Coldplay. My singing was distracting him from looking at the Band-Aid as I unwrapped it — which was exactly what I wanted.

I placed it over his cut and smoothed it out as I sang the last line, telling him I would 'fix' him. 'There, all fixed,' I explained with a smile, appreciating my handiwork.

It took everything I had within in me not to burst into laughter, because staring back at me was a cute little *Dora the Explorer* Band-Aid, and it was attached to his forehead. *Score! Alexis, you little payback devil.*

'No, Nurse Summers,' he smiled. 'You're wrong, I'm not fixed.' And although he was smiling at me, his eyes were speaking another language.

'Why?' I asked, cupping his cheeks in my hands.

'Because now my heart has definitely stopped beating.'

I suddenly felt awfully guilty. He was so incredibly romantic and here I was sticking cartoon character medical aids to his head.

'Oh, Bryce, I need your heart to beat.' And with that, I kissed him and we both fell back onto the bed.

13

Today was the last day Bryce and I would spend together before I reclaimed my children from their grandparents and returned home. Providing Nate and Charlotte with a sense of normality and routine would be imperative, because when I explained to them that their world was about to change, familiarity was the only thing I could provide in order to help soften the blow.

My plans were to head home first to see Rick. Facing him was almost upon me, and I was now dreading it more than ever. During the past week, I had been able to put my impending confrontation with my husband out of my head. And, because of that, the idea of seeing him for the first time was now even more unbearable.

The past week had been amazing, the most wonderful and exciting week of my life. In hindsight, though, that was probably because I had Bryce to comfort me. He took my thoughts away from the devastation I would no doubt have felt and suffered through, if had he not been with me every step of the way.

I entered my shower — or my silent confessional booth as I had so aptly named it. For some unknown reason, this little confined steamy location gave me clarity. Anxiety was one thing I felt as I stood under the stream of water, but anger was another, and it was boiling underneath my skin, bubbling away near the point of explosion. *Why would Rick have cheated back then? We were happy, we had always been happy. Or maybe we hadn't?*

The memories of our confrontation in the garage came flooding back: 'I have wondered what it would be like with someone else also. The thing is, I didn't just stop there either, Lex ... at the wondering bit, I mean.' The recollection made me shudder. Okay, so yes, I had been curious and tempted by another. I understood that part, but I had not fucked Bryce behind Rick's back while we were happily playing husband and wife. I know I had come close, but I hadn't — I wouldn't have — and if I thought it was inevitable, I would have gone to Rick and told him, or broken it off beforehand.

I tried to think of exactly what it was that went wrong with Rick and I. Was it the fact we'd been together since we were kids? Was it getting married at a young age? Was it having children at a young age? Was it the fact I was a lot chubbier five years ago and feeling sorry for myself? I couldn't honestly put my finger on it. I guess when I saw him he would have to enlighten me as to why he saw fit to fuck Claire. One thing was for certain: I could not go back to him. Not now. And to be honest, I didn't think he would want me back either after the week I'd had with Bryce. To me it was clear — we were over.

* * *

I stepped out of the shower, and found Bryce making breakfast. Or was it lunch? I honestly had no idea what the time was. We had been awake for hours after the previous night's medical assessment, Nurse Summers having administered not one, but two doses of hot, steamy sex-medicine as treatment for his wounds. Needless to say, Bryce's heart was now fully operational.

He was moving about in his kitchen and, as I watched him, it struck me that his elegant, flowing grace around this particular room was not apparent. He did not seem his normal self, and it was clear something was bugging him.

His phone rang and vibrated across the bench. He looked at it at the same time he noticed me standing there.

Scooping it up instantly, he explained that he would need to answer the call. 'I have to take this,' he apologised, passing me briskly to seek privacy out on the balcony.

I watched him as he spoke on the phone and whoever he was speaking with had him acting very nervously. His hand was placed on the balustrade railing, and I noticed it was tensing and gripping tightly. *Who is he talking to?* He turned and looked in my direction, as if he had felt my curious stare piercing deep into the back of his head.

Feeling I was intruding on his conversation, I gave him a shy smile and looked away. When he hung up, he put his finger in the air to suggest he'd be a little while longer and then headed into his office. *I hate secrets with a passion, but I guess he's entitled to them, especially if they are work related as this one probably was.*

While he was gone, my phone beeped. I lifted it out of my pocket to find a text message from Rick.

I read it out loud:

Alexis, we really need to talk. You cannot avoid me forever. It's not just about us — Rick

Don't lay the guilt trip on me. I know very well it is not just about 'us'. I typed a reply:

I'm fully aware that we need to talk, I will when I'm ready. You of all people should not try & lay a guilt trip on me, especially when it comes to our kids — Alexis

I pressed send and put the phone back in my pocket just as Bryce came through the door, both of us displaying startled and secretive expressions.

'Is everything all right?' I queried.

'Yes. I just had to do some quick banking.' *Oh, okay, I guess that could be stressful considering the copious amounts of money he has.*

'So, my love, do you notice anything different at all?'

I caught a glimpse of his very brief devilish glint which made me automatically go into survival mode. *Right, he is going to attack, but why? How? When?*

I surveyed the room, spotting a picture of the two of us at Ayers Rock which he had stuck to his fridge next to the picture of Lucy and him. *Oh, my Mr Adorable Clark, you've officially added me to your stainless steel picture board of love. How sweet.*

I pointed to it. 'Um ... you've put a picture of us on your fridge.'

'Yes, I have, but no ... something different about me?' *About him?*

I happily scrutinised him. *No ... you are as sexy as ever, right from your manly feet, to your sculpted legs, to your unbelievable package,* I leaned back from the bench to get a better view of said package, *to your glorious chest, and up to your luscious hair which falls upon your irresistibly handsome face and forehead ... which no longer has a Dora Band-Aid stuck to it ... oh shit! Look away, Alexis, look away.*

'Nope, I have no idea what is different about you,' I answered nonchalantly while glancing up at him from under my eyelashes. *Uh-oh. Shit, run!*

I took off and got as far as the lounge, stopping on the other side of the sofa. He was right behind me.

'So, you think it's funny to stick Dora the Fucking Explorer to my head?' he said, trying to hide his impressed smile.

I laughed, but kept my wits about me as the sofa did not offer much protection.

'What? What's wrong with Dora? She has a wealth of knowledge. Do you know she can speak fluent Spanish? *Hola.*'

He cracked his neck from side to side. *Fuck, I'm a goner.* I grabbed a cushion and held it up, as I needed some form of defence. He stood up on the sofa and snatched it away from me. *Uh-oh.*

I tried my best Spanish accent. 'Hey, swiper, no swiping.'

He growled and launched himself over the sofa at me. I screamed and ran for the balcony, but he had me up in his arms before I even made it to the bifolds.

'I'm sorry, it was the only Band-Aid I had. Anyway, we are even now.'

'Oh, no, we are far from even.' He carried me out onto the balcony and over to the edge of the pool.

'No, please, I just had a shower.'

'We'll have another one then.'

'You are so infuriating.' I closed my eyes and braced myself for impact.

'You are so cheeky.' He kept a tight grip, but had not yet taken the plunge.

I opened one eye. 'You are going to ruin my clothes.'

'You are making me ruin your clothes.'

Grrr, he never lets up. I opened the other eye. 'You always have to win.'

'You always drive me crazy.'

He still hasn't jumped in yet. 'No, Mr Clark, you always drive *me* crazy.'

'You mean the world to me, Alexis.'

'You make me second-guess myself, Bryce.'

'You set my heart on fire and keep it burning till it hurts.'

I touched his face. 'You, Mr goddamn breathtakingly superb Clark, are the reason I have finally discovered what true love and happiness is.'

He raised his arms and lifted me to his mouth, then whispered as he kissed me: 'You are absolutely everything I will ever want or need. Please remember that tomorrow.'

'Tomorrow?'

'Tomorrow, when you see Rick.'

I kicked my legs down and stood at the edge of the pool facing him.

'Bryce, I am not going back to him, I can't. You know I can't.'

He nodded, then hung his head.

'What? What is eating at you? I'm not stupid. I know something is wrong. Just tell me. What have you done?'

He raised his head, and the look on his face told me he could not keep his burdensome secret any longer. 'Come with me.'

He took my hand and led me to his office, then punched a code into both doors.

'What are you doing? Locking us in?'

'Yes.'

I felt the colour drain from my face. I needed to sit and sit quickly. Whatever he was about to reveal to me was serious enough for him to think it would make me want to flee.

* * *

Nervous. Repentant. Those were the words I would use to describe how he looked when he handed me a manila folder.

'Before you open it, you need to remember that I promised you I would make the impossible possible, and I never go back on my promises, ever!'

I remembered him telling me that, the night I promised I would give him a week, but at that time I couldn't see how on earth it would ever happen.

I opened the folder with trembling hands. *What the fuck is this?* The contents had my heart feeling strangled, like my outer shell was slowly caving in and engulfing everything within it. The images before me showed Claire in suggestive underwear standing in front of Rick. In one photo, her arms were around his neck and his hands were on her hips. In another, they were kissing and his hands were on her face. But it was the final photo that triggered the raging volcano inside to finally erupt.

She was looking directly into the lens of the camera wearing an expression of complete and utter satisfaction.

I dropped the folder and its contents on the floor.

'Where did you get these?' I could barely breathe let alone clearly voice the words.

'From Claire,' he said in a whisper.

'Claire? How?'

'She works in the city at a mortgage broking firm.' *What the fuck is she doing in Melbourne, and how the fuck does he know about Claire?*

I looked up, shocked and confused. 'How do you know about Claire?'

He was sitting with his arse on the edge of his desk and his arms crossed in front of him. 'Creepy research.' *Creepy fucking research, I might've guessed.*

'That is no longer an answer, Bryce. I want to know how.'

He sighed. 'I've told you before. Lucy.'

'What do you mean, Lucy? How could she have possibly known who Claire was and how to track her down?'

He clenched his fist and looked pained at the idea of answering me.

'Bryce, I want a straight answer.'

'Okay, okay. Lucy is capable of hacking computer systems. I guess you could call her a genius. She has an extremely high IQ. I told her to dig into Rick's life and find anything she possibly could.'

'You what?' I couldn't believe what I was hearing. That was not normal behaviour.

'Look, I don't want to go into detail where Lucy's talents are concerned. I will one day, I promise you, but not now, not until I have spoken to her about it. Okay?' He appeared torn;

torn between confiding in me and sharing a secret that was not necessarily his to share.

'Fine, but that's not the end of it. I want to know exactly what Lucy has dug up about me and the people in my life.'

'That's not all, Alexis.' *Oh, shit, what else?*

My head started to spin and I felt dizzy. He knelt down in front of me.

'When you were away with your friends, I ... I —'

'You what?'

'I went to see Rick.' He looked up, and I had never seen such terror in a person's face in my life. I could see now why he locked the doors, because this had to be the point at which he thought I would flee.

'You did what?' Again, I couldn't believe what he was saying.

'I went to your house and told him I loved you. I told him you had feelings for me too and that I wanted to spend a week with you, one where you could feel guilt-free and make whatever choices you wanted. He said no.'

'Of course he fucking said no. What were you thinking? You had no right to approach Rick, no right at all.' I put my head in my hands.

'I promised you. I promised I would make it happen and this was me making it happen.' He removed my hands from my face and held both of them. 'When he said no, I threatened to tell you about Claire.'

'Oh, god,' I whimpered, the tears freely flowing.

'Alexis, it doesn't change anything, it doesn't change the fact he cheated on you. Claire said herself that he initiated their whole relationship.'

Not being able to tolerate any more, I stood up. 'Enough, I don't want to hear another word.' I walked over to the apartment door and turned the handle; it didn't unlock. 'Open this fucking door. Now!'

'Where are you going? Are you leaving me?' he asked, his expression beyond miserable.

'I'm not going anywhere, Bryce. I just need air and a moment to myself.'

Nodding, he slowly walked over to the door and unlocked it.

I entered the apartment and headed straight to the balcony.

CHAPTER
14

My eyes were tear-soaked, making the view over the city of Melbourne from the balustrade quite blurry and distorted. I found myself trying to dissect how the hell my average, ordinary, everyday life had turned to fully disorganised and outrageously crazy chaos. I wasn't angry at Bryce. Okay, I was a little, because of his creepy research and his notion that he thought it his prerogative to do and say whatever he wanted. I guess I was more shocked that he would go to such lengths to ensure we could be together. In hindsight though, it really shouldn't have surprised me, especially after the week we had just shared and experiencing firsthand the amazing things he did for me, time and time again.

The salty menaces that were my tears began to escape the confines of my eyes and stream down my face. I leaned over the rail, no longer afraid of the fact I was forty-something storeys above ground. Perilous as it was, it was nothing compared to seeing photographic proof of my supposedly loving husband in the arms of another woman.

Rick and I had not just been husband and wife; we had been lovers and best friends. And five years ago, during one of the toughest times in my life, he had chosen to give in to his curiosity about experiencing someone else sexually, betraying all the things we shared and that cut very deep.

I heard slow and steady footsteps approaching me from behind.

Bryce hesitantly stepped up to where I was standing and handed me a tissue. He was also holding a cup of tea in his hands.

'I thought you might like these.' He passed over the cup of tea and touched my finger gently. 'I'm sorry. I never should have gone behind your back.'

I met his regretful and now insecure gaze. 'No, you shouldn't have.'

'Alexis, I regret hurting you, but I don't regret forcing Rick to be honest. If I hadn't, I would not have been able to experience the best week of my life, and I would not have experienced sharing every wonderful moment with you. I couldn't possibly regret any of that.'

I turned to him. 'If you and I have any chance whatsoever of a future together, you cannot keep secrets from me. I deserve better than that. I'm not angry with you, because your intentions were in our best interest, but you need to stay out of my relationship with Rick. It is none of your business, not at this stage anyway.'

A very delicate smile appeared on his face. 'At this stage? Does that mean we will experience more stages then?'

I moved my line of vision to the Yarra River and away from his. 'Yes, Bryce, I hope to have many more.'

He gently moved behind me and enclosed me with his warm, safe and secure arms. 'There is nothing else I want, just you and your happiness.'

I stood there in his arms until the tears ran dry. I realised that his revelation of the pictures and confessing his secret had made me feel ready to face Rick. Strangely enough, the shock and hurt of Bryce's disclosure had been exactly what I needed.

* * *

For most of the afternoon that followed, Bryce had tiptoed around me, and it was starting to piss me off. This was our last night together for who knew how long, and I didn't want to spend it playing silent games with him.

Dinnertime was fast approaching and he had been preparing something in the kitchen. I was also under the impression that he was hiding from me out of guilt. As I walked in, the delicious aromas of his cooking enveloped me. His graceful kitchen elegance had also returned, his movements resembling the conductor of an orchestra of simmering pots and chopping knives.

'Can I help with anything?' I asked with interest.

He shook his head. 'No, I'm nearly finished. Are you hungry?'

'Yes, a little.'

'Good.'

I could see the deep fryer bubbling away. 'What are we having?'

'It's Saturday night and I always have fish 'n' chips on Saturday night. Lucy and Nic normally join me, but I rescheduled them for next week.'

'You didn't have to do that. I feel bad now.'

'Don't, honey. Anyway, I wanted to spend tonight with you and you only,' he explained as he dished up a big plate of lightly fried tempura calamari, scallops, prawns and snapper. He then surrounded them with chunky wedges of potatoes and a homemade tartare sauce. *Looks like the best fish 'n' chips ever!*

'What would you like to drink?' I asked.

'There's a bottle of Crown Ambassador Lager in the bar fridge. Grab that and a couple of glasses.' *I love how he just assumes what I like and don't like. Assumption or not, he normally gets it right.*

I followed him into the lounge and found the lager he was referring to as he set up the plate of seafood and chips on the coffee table. I smiled at his laid-back, sit on the floor approach to fish 'n' chips.

Grabbing the fancy bottle of beer, I opened it, pouring us both a glass which I tilted as I poured. I remembered seeing this technique on TV. Apparently it reduces the froth on the surface. *Swanky beer calls for swanky pouring.* I would normally sink a stubby when consuming beer, but this particular ale was probably meant to be consumed from a glass.

We sat down on the floor on either side of the coffee table, thoroughly enjoying our fish and chip picnic. I watched as Bryce dipped his prawn in the sauce and consumed the entire thing.

I screwed up my face at him. 'You just ate the tail!'

'Yes, you are supposed to,' he laughed.

'Really?'

'Here, try it.' He picked up another prawn, gently dipped it in the sauce and moved it to my mouth. I bit down on it and consumed the first half. Bryce shook his head in response as if to say, that was pathetic.

'What? I have a small mouth,' I defensively explained, chomping the second piece from his fingers. *Yum, the tail is actually really crunchy.*

He smiled and licked his fingers. 'You have a magnificent mouth, Ms Summers.'

'As do you, Mr Clark.'

'I want your mouth now.'

'You are going to have to wait. It is currently occupied.'

'Then unoccupy it.'

My body began to react to his intense and wanting stare. 'No, I'm hungry.'

'So am I. I'm hungry for you.'

'I'm enjoying your seafood and sauce.' I selected a piece of calamari and dipped it, then licked off the sauce, and dipped it again, teasing him with my seductive display.

He crossed his arms. 'You just double-dipped.' *Oh, you are one of those are you?*

'Yes, I know, I can't help it. I like sauce.'

'Do you like my sauce?' His cheeky game-face momentarily appeared before he reined it in again.

Taking hold of the small dish containing the tartare, I poked my finger in it and swirled it around before putting it in my mouth. I then very slowly pulled it back out again, licking my lips when I was done. 'I do like your sauce.'

'I make another really good sauce, you know?' *I bet you do.* He smirked, forked a piece of snapper and downed it with a long swig of beer.

I followed his choices. 'Really? What do you dip in that sauce?' I asked with a mellow expression. I loved his ability to be able to play this game with me.

'It's not for dipping, my love.'

We both selected a couple more chips.

'How do you eat it then?' I asked, popping a chip into my mouth and raising my eyebrow, curiously.

'You savour it.' *Savour it? I'll savour you in a minute.*

'And how do you make your sauce, Mr Clark?'

My mouth was beginning to parch at the very thought of his sauce-making abilities.

'I make it with love, with passion, and I only make it for one person.'

By this point, I was biting the inside of my bottom lip, anticipating the consumption of him and his sauce. 'Will you make it for me?' I asked with a demure smile.

He lifted his finger and signalled for me to go to him. 'Only you.'

Snatching my glass from the coffee table, I drank the last of the beer in the hope it would douse the fiery burn that had formed in my mouth and throat. Then I crawled around the table to his side, climbing into his lap.

'I want you to make the best sauce you have ever made.'

'Anything for you.'

He seized my mouth, confirming that only his lips could extinguish the fire within me and, as his tongue explored me, the burning I felt for him subsided and was replaced with a purely delightful calmness.

I laced my hands through his hair, shifting a few strands away from his forehead and finding that his cut was healing over nicely. I kissed it and then trailed a few more kisses down the side of his face. As I got closer to his mouth, my kisses became more impatient and needy.

Desperately fumbling with the buttons on his shirt, I eagerly removed it and exposed his delectable smooth chest. *Holy fuck, this sight floors me every time.*

Already my pussy was responding by lusciously pulsing and moistening in preparation for his entrance. My breasts were also reacting, firming as he pulled my lemon-coloured cotton blouse over my head and exposing them within my bra. I went to assist him with my bra's removal, but he firmly moved my hands away and took control of its undoing himself, unleashing my breasts for him to devour with his mouth. *Oh, Mr Clark, you and your truly mind-blowing mouth.*

I whimpered as he tongued my nipples, one at a time, and I moaned unashamedly when he grasped my shoulders and leaned me back, allowing himself to trail his tongue from my neck to my navel.

He gripped me tightly, stood up, and began to unbutton my denim Capris as I panted from his oral exploration of my chest. I stepped out of them for him after they fell to the ground. I wrapped my arms around his neck as he scooped me up into his arms and gently laid me back on the sofa.

We paused momentarily and looked deep into each other's eyes. Here we were at the beginning of our relationship, freshly discovering each other and the burning passion that came with that process. It was not only intensely passionate, but exciting and new. However, the exchange of looks and feelings between us defied normality, because what progressed more dominantly was admiration, acceptance and comfort — the comfort that a couple who had been together for many years might display. It blew me away, the level of connection we shared. It was just inconceivable. And, as if he was thinking the same thing, he lightly kissed the tip of my nose and slowly stood back.

I sat up and watched with delight as he unbuttoned his jeans and removed them, exposing his highly desirable body. A body I both wanted and needed as close to my own as much as humanly possible.

'Bryce, you render me speechless,' I breathed out, my words barely audible.

He dropped to his knees, opened my legs, and slid me onto his ready and waiting erection, the sudden intrusion making me exhale in relief that we were again joined as one.

We stared intensely into each other's as he slowly thrust his pelvis back and forth. I could feel every inch of him as he glided in and out, satisfying the yearning sensation within me. I put my arms on his shoulders and pulled him in for a kiss. He obliged, bringing me onto him as far as I could go, forcing me to gasp aloud as his length reached further than ever before.

Bryce stopped moving and held me completely still, allowing me to engulf him entirely. The heated pause was utterly raw and pure and, while also savouring each other by mouth and eye contact, only added to this sexually precious moment.

Our motionlessness seemed to last a long time and the anticipation of when he would resume his pelvic thrusts was absolutely killing me.

I pleaded with him on an exhale of breath. 'Please!'

'No, honey. I don't want to leave you.'

'I know, but you'll be back inside me again.' I smiled seductively, but I could feel his doubt. 'You will, I promise. Now, please, give me your bloody sauce.'

He smirked and began thrusting until I was vocalising my climax, forcing him to collapse on my chest and rest his head on my shoulder.

I held him there until our breathing returned to normal. 'You'll be back, Bryce. You belong inside me.'

CHAPTER
15

Both of us were up bright and early the next day. Bryce had cooked me breakfast in bed, accompanied by roses and a gorgeous gold and diamond ring with a star on it. He had placed the ring around the handle of my fork and waited patiently until I made the discovery. It hadn't taken me long because the diamonds had caught the light, sparkling brightly and revealing the ring's hiding place.

I picked it up to inspect it.

'It's to remind you of me when we're apart,' he explained, seeming quite shy. I couldn't be quite sure whether his bashfulness was because of the ring itself or the fact he was giving it to me for a specific purpose. This gift of jewellery seemed very different from the other two.

'It's beautiful, Bryce. I love it, but I really don't need anything to remind me of you. You are permanently tattooed on my heart.'

Seeming happy with my response, the shyness he possessed moments ago began to vanish.

'Thank you,' I said as I put the ring on my finger. 'It means a lot to me.'

My smile increased when I found that it fit perfectly. 'So, Mr Astronomy Teacher Clark, what is this star called?' I asked, batting my eyelashes at him.

'Ms Summers, this is a very special star. It's known as the Brylexis.'

I giggled, then paused, taking in his uncertain demeanour. Bryce just shrugged his shoulders. *Oh, my goodness, he is just perfect. The Brylexis! He's combined our names to form a star just for the two of us. Now I'm the one in need of medical assistance for heart failure. My heart just stopped. Just stopped!*

'Oh, that's so beautiful,' I professed, tears filling my eyes. I got up on the bed, crawled across it, and placed a soft peck on his lips. 'Thank you. I love it.'

'You're welcome, honey.'

He held me tightly, and I could tell he didn't want to let go. To be honest, I didn't want him to either, but ahead of me was likely to be one of the most difficult and exhausting days I would ever endure. I had to step out of this wonderful romantic world and back into reality to face it head-on.

Pressing his lips firmly to the top of my head, he then let out a reluctant breath and released me. 'Now, I have a few things in my office to take care of, so I'll let you get ready.'

I watched him leave the room, then fell back onto the bed, holding my hand up with the ring glistening beautifully on my finger. I shook my head in disbelief and then headed for the shower.

* * *

The welcoming hot water ran over my body as I thought about what the next few hours would hold for me. Of course I was nervous, apprehensive and anger-filled, but as a result of Bryce's revelation the day before, I also possessed a degree of clarity and focus.

The pictures were definitive proof — they were what they were — and Rick could not deny them. Not that he would, because he confessed to the act in the first place. I guess what I wanted to discuss with him was why he couldn't have come to me first, before having the fucking affair. Would it really have been that difficult to set me free before freeing his dick from his pants? I also wanted to tell him to pack his shit and get the hell out of our house until we sorted out what was going to happen next. I didn't want to be arguing in front of the kids and, with the way I was currently feeling, that would be inevitable if he stayed.

I dried myself and got dressed in a pair of jeans, knee-high black boots and a tight grey tank top. There was no real need for make-up, so I only applied a gloss for my dry and overly-kissed lips.

Looking around the room, it dawned on me as to how at home I had made myself. Or more to the point, how at home Bryce had made me. I loved it here, but it was no place for my children. So I was saddened at not knowing when I'd be back to stay. *Don't worry about that, Alexis, you will sort everything out.*

I sighed disappointedly and walked out of the room, dragging my small suitcase behind me.

* * *

It was just after 8 a.m. when I walked into Bryce's office. He was sitting at his desk practically buried under a pile of paperwork.

'Wow, the price you pay for a few days away,' I stated, a little shocked at the amount of work he had to do. He looked up and cocked his head to the side, smiling at my presence.

I noticed the signs he displayed when I had a positive effect on him and they were a lovely indication that the little things that made me who I am were what he liked and appreciated the most.

'A price well worth it. Are you ready to go?'

I pouted. 'No, but I have to. On a more pleasant note, I will see you in less than twenty-four hours though.'

'It's not soon enough,' he sighed dejectedly, appearing quite miserable and flat. I presumed it was the result of me leaving and the extensive amount of business he had to attend to.

Walking over to his desk, I sat my arse on top of it, squashing his paper pile. 'Maybe you could sneak in through my bedroom window tonight?' I offered in a joking manner in order to lighten the mood.

My suggestion seemed to cheer him up and he raised his eyebrows as if to contemplate the idea.

Before he could respond, his phone buzzed, interrupting our top secret meeting about a rendezvous.

Bryce hit the speaker button. 'Yes, Abigail?'

'Mr Clark, you wanted me to notify you if Mr Summers entered the building. Well, he has and is on his way up now. Do you want him stopped?'

My eyes widened at the sound of Rick's imminent presence, and I instinctively jumped off the desk, taking a few steps toward the door. I think my initial intention was to lock it, but that would have been utterly ridiculous. *Why has he come here? I don't want to see him here. Then again, I do have Bryce as support. No, Alexis, you don't need Bryce to hold your hand. Regardless, Rick is here now so you might as well deal with it.*

Bryce shot me a look, asking the question of whether or not I wanted Rick to be allowed to continue to the penthouse.

'Let him come,' I answered resolutely.

'No, Abigail, it's fine. Thank you for letting me know.'

He ended the call and we both stared at each other. Even Bryce looked anxious.

'I'm right here. I won't leave … unless you want me to,' he asked, concern etched across his face.

'Please stay,' I said quietly. 'Although, I don't see his point in coming here. He knew I was meeting him at home today.'

'He wants to see me as well,' Bryce muttered.

I nervously wandered around the office in small steps. 'Why? This is between me and him.'

'Alexis …' he said, interrupting my pacing. He stood up from his seated position behind the desk. 'Just remember, I love you more than life itself. We belong together, and there is absolutely nothing I wouldn't do, nothing —'

Before he could finish what he was saying, the door was flung open and Rick came barging into the room. On seeing me standing there he dropped his raging bull facade and calmed down almost instantly, as though he had switched personalities. He purposely walked toward me, taking no notice of his surroundings or the fact that he had just entered Bryce's office uninvited.

Rick was not an arrogant man; he was usually quite humble. I wouldn't exactly call him placid or subdued, but he would normally be reserved and respectable. These were qualities that many men didn't have, qualities that had attracted me to him in the first place. And, it would appear in that moment, they were qualities Rick no longer possessed.

'Alexis, babe, we need to talk.'

'Don't babe me. You gave up that right.'

'Maybe. Maybe not.'

I looked at him, incredulously. *Maybe not? Are you for real?*

Rick moved toward Bryce and then turned his back to me. I think he did it to deliberately place himself between Bryce and I, kind of like a shield. It was strange.

'Your time is up, Bryce.' *What?*

Rick had been in the room for only seconds and I could not fathom his attitude, let alone what he was saying.

Pissed off by his presumptuous entry, my volcano of bubbling rage was now at the point of eruption. 'His time is up?' I exclaimed, my voice climbing an octave or two. 'I can't believe you, Rick. Is this just a game to you? It has nothing to do with time or Bryce. Do you think that after spending one week with him that I would forgive you for cheating on me? One year, let alone one week, would not be long enough for me to ever forgive you.'

The tears started to well in my eyes, but I refused to let them fall. Instead, I screamed at him with every ounce of anger in me, allowing the boiling hot lava of fury to spill out. I didn't hold back — I didn't want to. 'I can understand the fucking temptation of another, Rick, believe me I can ... but to screw Claire and then lie and cover it up for five years is just unforgiveable. You are a lying, deceitful piece of shit, and I can no longer stand being in the same room as you. You should have had the decency to come to me before fucking her if you wanted to break it off. After all you and I have been through, you should have at least done that.'

I kept my eyes fixed on his, wanting him to see what a pathetic excuse for a husband I thought he was.

'Alexis, it's not what you think, babe. Let me explain,' he said in a calm, patronising tone. I couldn't believe the stilted attitude he displayed, even after what I had just said to him.

At that point, Bryce moved from behind his desk, but stood at a respectable distance. I couldn't be quite sure if it was the due to fact he didn't like to hear Rick call me 'babe', or if it was because he wanted to get closer to me. If I had to take a guess, I would say it was probably both.

'Okay, Rick, explain to me why you chose a little whore over me? Come on, I'd like to hear it,' I demanded, putting my hand up to my ear then lowering it and crossing my arms in front of my chest.

He took a step in my direction which made me take one away.

'Don't even think about it, stay the fuck away from me,' I warned.

'I didn't cheat on you,' he said calmly. *Oh for fuck's sake. Really, Rick? Does he really think I am that naive and stupid?* If I weren't so hurt and angry with him, I would've actually felt pity for him in that moment, pity at the fact he was grasping at straws.

My anger subsided only momentarily, and I dropped my head in my hands. 'Just stop lying. I have pictures, proof that you cheated.' I walked over to Bryce's desk, picked up the folder, and shoved it at his chest. 'You might lie, but they don't.'

He opened it up, but what followed was an expression of relief which completely confounded me.

'It's not what it looks like.' *Oh please!* 'Claire is obsessive and crazy. She was fixated with me and wouldn't take no for an answer. Lexi, she set this whole thing up. Look.' He eagerly pulled some smaller pictures out of his pocket and handed them to me. 'Here are all the pictures taken that day, not just the ones she gave this dickhead.' He gestured at Bryce, not paying him the courtesy of even a glance in his direction.

I reluctantly took the photos he was offering. Not because I believed him, but because I was curious about this story he was trying to conjure up.

As I held them before me, I took note that the first picture was of Claire waiting in his office on her own. I flicked to the next one which was of Rick walking in. The one after that was the same one I had, where her arms were around his neck and his on her hips.

I looked up at him, confused. 'They are the same, Rick, how does this prove she set you up?'

He nodded to the photos and said casually, 'Just keep looking.'

The following one showed Rick with his hands on her hips, but pushing her away from him. In this particular photo, you could actually see his face, his expression not happy. The one after that was where he was holding her face while they were kissing, but what followed that one showed Rick pushing her face away in disgust. The photos after that pretty much showed her leaving with that satisfied look on her face and Rick being angry and distraught.

As the images flicked through my mind's vision, my legs gave way from beneath me and I fell onto the sofa.

Bryce came round to my side. 'What? What's wrong?'

I held out the photos for him to assess Rick's claim for himself.

'I don't get it,' I said, my voice trembling and barely audible. I was now more confused than ever.

'Claire is sick, Lexi. She came to me five years ago with the exact same photos she gave him,' he said, shooting Bryce a disdainful look. 'She threatened to show you and tell you we were sleeping together. I managed to persuade her that it was not worth it as life would then become quite difficult for her as a result. After all, her parents are your parents' close friends.

'She chose to give up and leave quietly, but before doing so, I requested copies of all the photos in return for helping her find another job. You see, babe? I didn't cheat on you, I never would. I love you, I always have and I always will.'

His explanation had me completely lost. The clarity I had felt earlier this morning had now pretty much disappeared. Instead, what now replaced it was a murky, cloudy, puddle of what-the-fuck.

Rick touched my arm, making me flinch.

'Don't touch me,' I sobbed.

Momentarily glancing up at Bryce, I noticed the colour had completely drained from his face.

I turned back toward Rick. 'I don't understand. Why would you lie? Why lie knowing I would leave you to be with Bryce, especially after I confessed to kissing him? You knew I had feelings for him. You knew that I would go straight to him. I don't fucking get it ...' I said, choking on the last words.

Tears began to stream down my face. There was absolutely no way of stopping them now. 'Why did you lie? You broke my heart. I don't understand why you would do that.'

It suddenly dawned on me that his intention was to trick me. He hadn't been with anyone else. Instead, I was the one who had now cheated on him — completely cheated — not just a kiss and some touching. *What has he done? What have I done?*

I stood up and shoved him. 'Why? Why would you do that? Why would you trick me?'

He put his hands up as if to say calm down, but I didn't want to calm down. I wanted to know why I was standing in this room and being told by my husband he had tricked me into cheating on him and sleeping with another man. It was ludicrous.

'Okay, I lied for two reasons, Lex. One: because deep down I felt that you needed to go and get this fling with Bryce — or whatever you want to call it — off your chest. And two: because he offered me five million dollars to let you spend a week with him.'

I blinked and shook my head. *Surely, I didn't just hear that right.*

Turning in Bryce's direction with a stupefied expression on my face, I was instantly met with a look of complete panic, his countenance confirming what Rick had just said. He started to walk toward me, but I put my hand up to indicate that he should stop.

I needed a moment. I couldn't speak, I couldn't breathe, my head was throbbing and my chest was aching. I'm fairly sure at that very moment my heart broke in two, and the unbearable pain I felt from it breaking surged right through me, paralysing my body.

I tried to talk, but could only gasp. The strong-willed voice that had been mine only moments ago had abandoned me.

Closing my eyes, I turned around, urging myself to find that voice once again and uncover what strength I had left in me, if any. *They set me up, both of them. The only two men I have ever loved conspired and schemed so they could both get what they wanted. I was a pawn, a plaything. I'm a whore, a fucking whore.*

I turned back to face them and directed my first question and assault at Bryce. Just looking at him was excruciatingly hard. I knew he was the type of man who got what he wanted, but to pay money to get me? Surely, this wasn't true. I needed to hear him tell me it wasn't true.

'You paid to have a week with me?' I asked, hopeful doubt escaping my throat. *Please say no.*

His expression was full of misery, but still, he kept calm. 'Yes, Alexis, I did.' *Oh god.*

'You paid to have a week with me, like I'm some whore?' I cried out in disbelief.

He shook his head and stepped up to me, placing his hands on my shoulders. My face was now soaked with tears, the hurt I felt — immense.

'No, it wasn't like that. I would never treat you like a whore.'

I knocked his arms away from me. 'But you did! You did the moment you offered my husband five million fucking dollars to sleep with me. Did you know he never cheated on me?'

'No, Alexis, definitely not, I promise you. Claire had told Lucy they were in love, but she had done the right thing by breaking it off because of Nate and Charli. We believed her.' He closed his eyes for the smallest of seconds. 'I can't fucking believe we trusted her,' he said to himself.

'You believed the stupid bitch because you wanted to, and that gave you the ultimate weapon to seal your deal and pay for my services.'

'Alexis, stop referring to yourself as a whore,' he said through gritted teeth, his anger at my self-labelling apparent. *How dare he?* 'It's not about the money, it never was,' he continued. 'I would give it all up just to be with you. If the week we just shared proved anything, it had to have proved that.'

'The week we just shared was based on a lie. A big, fat, deceitful lie.'

I suddenly felt hot and slightly dizzy. I needed to get out of here and soon. So I composed myself before I walked away from Bryce and closer to Rick.

'And you, you accepted his five million dollars?' I asked, already knowing the answer. It explained why Rick gave so much space during the past week, never once arguing about my absence.

'It wasn't about that, Lexi —'

'Then why ring me yesterday asking when it was going to be transferred?' Bryce interrupted. *Transferred? He has the five million dollars in his bank account already? I can't believe this. This is not real.*

'I accepted it because you, you arrogant fuck, deserved to be five million dollars poorer. It was going to be the icing on the cake when, after one measly week, she found out about your deal and then left you for being such an obnoxious son of a bitch.'

I'm not hearing this. I have to get out of here.

My heart was pounding in my chest due to their devious manipulation and revelations and, as a result, I couldn't stay in the room with the two of them any longer. 'I can't do this, I can't be here,' I confessed while turning to leave.

I had no bearing on which direction I needed to go so did an entire 360° turn before figuring out which way to leave.

'Lexi, come home, and we'll talk it out, just the two of us.'
Come home?

I composed myself enough to look Rick in the eyes. 'You may not have cheated, but you lied and tricked me. You tricked me into sleeping with another man so that you could cash in. You pimped me out for five million dollars. I hope it was worth it. I suggest you spend it wisely.' I walked over to the coffee table, picked up my bag and headed for the door.

Bryce tried to stop me by grabbing my arm. 'Don't leave me, you promised you'd never leave me. I told you that I would do anything in my power.'

By this stage, tears were flooding my eyes, and I couldn't help sobbing uncontrollably as I stood there in front of him.

When I woke up that morning, knowing I would get angry, confused, hurt and emotionally fucked, I never once thought it was going to be by his hand.

'You propositioned my husband with money and you bought me. I'm not for sale, I never was. If power to you is based on what you can buy, then I want no part of it, or you. You promised you'd never hurt me, and you have. More than you'll ever know. You have ruined everything.' I pushed past him and slammed the door behind me.

CHAPTER

16

Rick and Bryce

Both of them watched in disappointment as Alexis left the room and, as soon as the door slammed behind her, Rick turned to Bryce. 'I hope you're fucking happy with yourself. "Bryce Clark, the billionaire home wrecker." So ... did you enjoy your week of fucking my wife?'

Bryce wanted to pick the annoying prick up and toss him out of his office, but if he had, it would've given Rick the chance to catch up to Alexis and that was the last thing he wanted to happen. 'Yes, Rick, I did and we did a lot of it. Obviously you are not adequate in that area.'

Rick took a few steps closer to Bryce, ready to knock his head off, but instead, he stopped and mockingly laughed. 'You have no fucking idea, Bryce. She is going to hate you for what you've done. You have forced her to sleep with you and be unfaithful. Alexis will never forgive you for that.'

'I have not forced her to do anything. You were the one who gave her up. You took her for granted and decided five million dollars was a more attractive offer. I reckon you would have accepted a hell of a lot less, too.' Bryce noticed what he thought was a slight twinge of hesitation on Rick's face. 'Yeah, I thought as much. You're a shallow man, Rick, and at the end of the day, you were the one who chose the money over your wife. She is going to hate *you* for that.'

Rick dragged his hands through his hair in disbelief and took another step closer to Bryce, within reach to plant his fists into Bryce's pretty-boy face. 'I can't believe you, you're a fucking lunatic.' He shoved Bryce in the chest, but Bryce barely moved. 'You come into our lives like the cocky fuck that you are, throw yourself and your money at Alexis, treat her like a prostitute and then blame *me*.'

Bryce flexed his hand into a fist at the very mention of 'Alexis' and 'prostitute' in the same sentence. At that particular point in time, he wanted nothing more than to break Rick's filthy jaw for even suggesting such a thing. But he wouldn't. He wouldn't touch Rick. For as much as he hated him, he had no intention of causing Alexis any more pain. And breaking the jaw of the father of her children would inevitably do that.

'I have not treated her like a prostitute, and for you to even suggest that about her proves you don't deserve her. She wanted to be with me and still does. You may think that I am a lunatic, Rick, but you are the most senseless, naive dickhead that I have ever come across.'

Rick looked at the ground momentarily and then he swung his fist right into Bryce's jaw. 'You're a fucking arsehole, Bryce, and I hope you rot in hell,' Rick snarled before walking toward the door.

Bryce rubbed his jaw, then casually walked back to his desk and took a seat, tasting the blood that now coated his tongue. He kept his cool, even though he wanted nothing more than to lay into the selfish prick.

'Tell me, Rick. Do you think that Alexis would ever have come to me if what we have is just a "fling"? If you do, then you obviously don't know her very well.'

Rick was still shocked that Bryce hadn't swung back. *He looks like he could hold his own in a fight, but still, he didn't even flinch.* Rick was even more pissed at Bryce's blatant disregard of his own accountability, and gall that he would even suggest he knew Alexis better than him.

Bryce continued, in his smooth, controlled tone. 'What Alexis and I have is unbreakable. Yes, she is shocked, hurt and angry. But when she has had time to come to terms with everything, we will be together once and for all. I'm sorry that this has happened to your family as a whole, really I am, but I'm not sorry I have fallen in love with her and her in love with me. She is the best thing that has ever happened to me, and I'm not about to let her go.'

'I do know *MY* wife, you fuck. I have known her for seventeen years. We have shared half our lives together, and we share two children. You can't compete with that. And if you try to, you will lose. You've had your fun, now go back to your billions of dollars and leave us the fuck alone.' Rick reached for the door handle.

'This is not a game to me, Rick. There is no win or lose, there is no competition. Yes, you share a past and children, but you no longer share her love. I hold Alexis' heart now and you don't. You may have held it once, but you gave it up for money. I am here to stay, whether you like it or not. I'm not going anywhere, and I am certainly not letting her go anywhere either.'

Rick never turned back as he opened the door, but before slamming it shut behind him, he responded: 'We'll see.'

Bryce

I watched the self-righteous son of a bitch leave the room. 'Fuck,' I growled. *How the fuck did that happen?* I ran my hands through my hair, wanting to pull it from its roots. *What have I done?* I knew she was going to be hurt when she found out that I paid Rick. And as much as I had known it would kill me when I saw the look of pain and betrayal on her gorgeous face, I was prepared to wear it; deal with it, and do everything in my power to make up for it by taking that hurt away again.

The thing was, Rick had cheated on her. I was certain of it. And I had absolutely no idea how that vital piece of information was able to change. But it had, and he hadn't fucking cheated on her. *Again, how the fuck did that happen? Something isn't right.*

I walked over to the minibar, still plagued by Alexis' traumatised face. *I should go after her. I could easily catch up to her if I took the Aston. No, it's too dangerous.* I already felt sick at the thought of her driving in the state she was in. *Fuck!*

Opening the fridge door, I took out the ice cubes and grabbed a napkin which was neatly folded on the buffet. I wrapped the ice inside it and placed it on my jaw, feeling a slight sensation of pain as the napkin pressed against my skin. Pain or no pain, it was nothing compared to the agony I felt when Alexis had walked out the door.

Hellbent on finding out what the fuck went wrong, I made my way over to my desk, pressed speaker, and dialled Lucy's number.

'Hey, how's it all going, bro? How's Alexis?'

'She's gone,' I answered bluntly, now feeling completely forlorn. A stab of pain pierced my chest as I realised the truth in my answer. It was real, she was gone.

'What do you mean she's gone?' Lucy asked, sounding shocked.

I flexed my hand, which I often did when I was losing my shit. 'Claire fucking lied to you. Rick never had an affair with her. Those photos she gave you were only a few in a collection, a collection that showed Rick turning her down. She set him up, and she set us up as well. How the fuck did that happen?'

I could feel the onset of a major headache, so I put my fingers to the bridge of my nose.

'Bryce, settle down. Where is Alexis?'

'I think she's on her way to her parents' farm. Rick came here this morning and showed her the entire set of photos, then told her I paid him the money. She was so upset, Luce. Fuck, I screwed up.'

'Firstly, you knew she was going to be upset about the money. That was a risk you were willing to take. And, secondly, I can guarantee you Rick and Claire had an affair. He transfers $2,000 into her account on the first day of the month, every month! And he has done so for the past five years. It's hush money — it has to be. Anyway, I know a liar when I see one and she was not lying when she said they had slept together. She was a little hesitant and more than likely hiding something — I did pick up on that — but she wasn't lying. You're right though, it doesn't add up. There must be more to it.'

'Then find out what it is, Luce. I can't lose her. I can't fucking lose her. Not now, not ever. Whatever it takes, find out what Claire is hiding and do it fast. Use whatever you need, spend whatever you need to spend, just do it. Please!'

'Okay, I'll get on it right now, but Bryce ...'

'What?'

'Calm down. Alexis loves you, you know that. Pull your shit together, give her a little space, then go and fight like hell to get her back. Tell her about the money Rick is transferring. I bet she doesn't know about that.'

'No, I'm not telling her anything until we find out exactly what Claire is hiding. I'm not going to get caught out without the full story like that again. I looked like the biggest fucking prick on earth. I had absolutely no comeback and no way of easing her pain. Just find out what Claire is hiding and get back to me as soon as possible. Please, Lucy.'

I hung up the phone, feeling completely hollow. And I soon became aware that I had not felt this much despair since losing three others I loved dearly. That's why I vowed — in that moment — that I was not going to suffer to that extent this time.

The physical pain started to ease as the numbness from the ice spread into my jaw. I wished that numbness could spread to my heart, because at that point, it hurt the most — it hurt like absolute hell.

Pulling the napkin away from my face, I threw it at the wall, entered my apartment, then headed straight for my bed.

To the very spot I could breathe her in.

Rick

That felt fucking good, although my hand is now killing me and probably broken.

I quickly made my way to the elevator in the hope I could catch up to her, to tell her it was okay and that I forgave her for sleeping with him. Deep down, I never wanted her to fuck him. It was killing me knowing she was with him and that he had touched her. I guess I had thought — or hoped — that she wouldn't go that far, that the fact he was an arrogant fucker would put her off. Unfortunately, that didn't seem to be the case, especially after I saw the way she looked at him. *Fuck, I hope he's lying when he says she's fallen for him, or all this is for nothing.*

I stepped into the elevator, pulled my phone from my pocket and dialled Claire's number.

'Rick, how'd it go? Did Alexis believe you when you showed her the photos?'

'Yes, so you'll get your five hundred thousand dollars by the end of the week. Okay?'

'Yes, fine. Gee, I do you a favour and you're still pissed off at me.'

'Claire, what do you expect? You have been blackmailing me for the past five years.'

'I know, but you deserve it,' she said, with a slight tone of playfulness.

I could picture her sitting there pouting and, five years ago, that pouting lip would've been a turn-on.

'Whatever. Listen, we are done now, no more blackmailing. I'm exhausted. What we did years ago was a mistake. I fucked up and I'm sorry.'

'I'll never think it was a mistake.'

'I've made it more than clear to you that it was. Listen, I didn't mean to hurt you, you know that, but I love Alexis, I always have, and we have a family.'

'I know, Rick, but we have a ...' She hesitated.

'What? We have a what?' *We don't have a chance, we never did.*

'Nothing.'

'You got what you wanted, so hold up your end of the bargain, or you'll regret it. Do you understand?'

'Yes, I understand. You don't have to be so nasty. I didn't have to warn you about that Lucy chick, remember. I did you a favour.'

I wanted to punch the elevator wall but couldn't now that my hand was out of action. There was a small part of me that felt terrible for Claire in all this. I fucked up and made the mistake of sleeping with her, knowing that she had feelings for me, and afterward, dismissing her like a piece of shit.

She had been pissed off at me for years, blackmailing and making threats to reveal to Alexis what we had done. I couldn't really blame her. However, she has got her revenge, because I had to remortgage the house a number of times just to keep her quiet, which was a major pain in the arse. *Thank fuck Alexis has never taken any interest in our finances.*

'Claire, listen. For what it's worth, I am truly sorry.'

'No, you're not.'

'Let me finish.'

'Whatever.'

I rolled my eyes at her immaturity. This was the reason I knew I could shut her up for good when Bryce offered me the money.

'I know you didn't have to tell me about Lucy contacting you and asking about why I have been paying you, but I'm thankful that you did. In a way, we'd both be fucked if you hadn't. So both of us win, right?' *I still have no fucking idea how Lucy found that shit out.*

'I suppose.'

'Look, I'll ring you later on in the week to let you know when the money has been transferred.'

'Sure,' she answered abruptly, before ending the call and cutting me short.

My heart was beating more slowly now, and the adrenaline that had pumped through my veins moments ago subsided. *I just might get myself out of this fucking hole, once and for all.* I hoped so. Ever since the day I gave in to Claire, I had been walking a tightrope, and it had changed again the day before Bryce came knocking on my door, when Claire had rung me, asking if I knew a 'Lucy Clark'.

When I told her I did, she asked why Lucy wanted to know so much about why I was paying her each month. This unexpected news had nearly given me a heart attack. How the fuck did Bryce's sister find that out, and why?

I'd panicked. 'What did you tell her?' I had asked. She'd said: 'Nothing, but she doesn't seem like the type who is going to leave me alone.' I told her to keep her mouth shut, and say nothing or the payments would stop.

Then Bryce came knocking on my door, claiming he knew about Claire and offered me five mil. It all just fell into place. I knew I could use that money to shut Claire up, get me out of debt and reveal to Alexis what an arrogant fuck Bryce was.

I had to hand it to Claire though; she may be immature, but she certainly wasn't stupid. It was her idea to give Lucy the same photos she was going to bribe me with. It was gold and worked to perfection. The look on that rich, arrogant fucker's face when I produced the missing photos was priceless.

Sucking in a breath of fresh air as I walked out of City Towers, a small smile spread across my face. Claire would finally be out of my life for good, and I now had money to pay out my debts and buy a house ... far from here and far from Bryce.

Everything seemed great. Except now I had to convince Alexis I did it for her, that it was okay and that she shouldn't feel guilty over sleeping with Bryce. That was going to be the toughest part. Although I had not considered the fact she might now have developed feelings for Bryce. *Na, he's fucked that up.*

Opening the door to my car, my hand still hurt like a bitch. But honestly, it was the best hurt I'd felt in a long time.

CHAPTER
17

The noise of the solid mahogany door shutting behind me was like the sound of a gunshot, the loud sudden bang vibrating through my body. My breathing was ragged, and the room felt as if it were beginning to cave in around me. I needed to stop and gather my bearings, but in my current state that was not a option. One of them — if not both — would be sure to follow me shortly and I no longer wanted to be anywhere near either of them.

The only access to Bryce's private garage was via his personal elevator, which was in his apartment where I had left my suitcase. *Shit!*

I quickly made my way through the conference room and into his apartment, stopping briefly at the entryway wall where we had made love for the first time. I cried aloud and ran for the elevator, away from the very spot that had once made me nostalgic. Now, however, it showed exactly where I had cheated on my husband.

I tucked myself into the elevator and, although I should have felt better as the doors closed, I didn't. I knew from experience I was not home free until I was out of the little moving cube. The last time I had been in the process of making an escape, Bryce had manually overridden the elevator controls and forced the car to return to the apartment with me in it. I prayed that was not going to happen again, I wanted out of this building and to be as far away as possible.

When the doors opened, relief flooded my body, and the numerous cars I had grown to love and admire greeted me. I hurried out, putting my hand up to shade my eyes as I passed the Lamborghini and the Charger. The memory of what I had done on those cars, if recalled at that particular moment, would only traumatise me further.

I climbed into the safety of my Ford Territory and drove out of there as fast as I possibly could. I knew exactly where I was going and I had no plans to stop until I had reached my destination.

* * *

The amount of tears a person can cry in a short space of time astounds me. When you think your ducts are dry and emptied, they surprise you soon after by spilling over again. Mind you, it didn't help that the radio station I had chosen seemed to have their broadcast dedicated to me.

Almost instantly after turning onto the West Gate Freeway, 'Sweet Little Lies' by Fleetwood Mac started to play. That tipped off the first and heaviest outpouring. Then, about three songs after that, 'Love Bites' by Def Leppard, and Jewel's 'Foolish Games', filled my ears, setting my eyes awash again. I thought perhaps my blubbering had finally ceased when 'Big Girls Don't Cry' came on. Well ... I definitely proved that song wrong.

* * *

I had been on the road for just under an hour and, as I drove past Seymour, my drowned and traumatised state had, thankfully, started to diminish. I knew that I couldn't go to my mum and dad's house. There was no way I would allow Nate and Charlotte to see me like this. So I hit speaker on my iPhone and dialled Jennifer.

'Hey, Lex, what's up?'

'Have you left for Mum and Dad's yet?'

'No, we are about to leave though. Why?'

'Don't. I'm ten minutes away. I need to speak to you.' I started to sob.

'Lexi, what's wrong? Is everything all right?'

'No.'

'You're worrying me. What's wrong?'

'Don't worry. I'll explain when I get there.'

'Okay, drive safely, and I'll see you soon.'

* * *

Jennifer was the youngest of us Blaxlo children by a couple of years. Then it was me, then our brother Jake. Jen and I looked nothing alike: I was blonde and average height and she was a brunette and towered over me.

We were inseparable when we were little and, although I was older than her, it didn't always feel that way. She was the smart one, the organised one, the one I always went to for advice and her shoulder was the first one I would cry on if needed. I desperately needed that shoulder, and I needed it now, probably more than I ever had in my life.

I pulled into her driveway and she was already on her front porch. Switching off the engine, I watched her approach the passenger side door. Jen always did things for a reason. And because of that, I guessed that Steven was home and she had requested he stay inside to watch over the kids so that she could come outside and console her pathetic, sulky sister.

She opened the door and sat in the passenger's seat, then waited for me to pour my heart out. And, boy, did I pour as I glanced over at her, feeling nothing but utter despair. 'I'm an idiot. I'm a stupid, stupid idiot.'

'Lex,' she spoke softly, 'you are not an idiot. What happened?'

'Oh, god. Where do I start?'

She handed me a tissue. 'At the beginning, of course.'

Like me, I'm sure she had tissues stashed in every pocket and sleeve she could find.

'Thanks.' I wiped my eyes and blew my nose. 'You know I went back to work a couple of months ago, right?'

'Yeah, at that big hotel in the city.'

'Well, I was promoted to be the Personal Assistant to the hotel's owner, Bryce Clark.'

'Bryce Clark, he's the one you were with at the Tel V Awards, yeah?' *Of course, the Tel V Awards. The telecast that everybody has seen.*

'Yes. Well, how can I put this? I've fallen in love with him.' I took a deep breath and continued before she could say anything. 'I know it sounds completely far-fetched and ridiculous, especially after only a couple of months, but Jen, I have never felt anything like the way I feel when I am with him.'

I waited for her to have some input into the conversation, but she didn't, so I emptied my nasal cavity again and continued.

'I tried to ignore it, I did. I am married for fuck's sake. I kept telling myself it was the excitement of the unknown, you know, a little bit of harmless flirting and that it would just blow over. The thing is, the more and more time we spent together only confirmed what we felt for one another. It's as if we are soul mates, Jen.' Saying this aloud irritated me, because it was the truth. Regardless of the stunt the two men in my life had pulled, it didn't change the fact that, to me, Bryce was my soul mate. And now that, in itself, really just pissed me off.

Jen still hadn't interrupted in any way. She just sat there and listened, allowing me to talk until I was finished. I loved this quality in my sister; she had to be the best listener in the world.

'By this stage, we had obviously shared a few kisses and I hated myself for that. The first one was ... well ... it wasn't exactly a mistake.' I scoffed at myself. 'Well ... maybe it was? Bryce had taken me by surprise and he was terribly sorry for doing it. The thing is, Jen, that first kiss shifted the earth from under our feet and it was absolutely impossible to stop the ones that seemed to follow after that. Then I had the car accident.'

Her forehead wrinkled and her expression showed uncertainty. *Oh, yeah, I never told her.*

'Don't worry, I was fine. Anyway ... I had the car accident and Bryce came to my aid — literally — like a knight in bloody freakin' armour. He told me he was terrified of anything ever happening to me, then he said he loved me.'

I remembered lying on his sofa feeling somewhat dazed and confused and looking into his handsome face when he said the words, 'I love you.' They had been as clear as crystal, regardless of my slight concussion.

'Jen, it took everything within me not to have sex with him there and then, and that's when I realised I was in love with him too, and that it wasn't going to blow over or go away. Looking back on it now, it was obvious really. I would never have found myself doing what I did, and being in the state I was in, if I weren't in love with him.'

Saying it only reinforced exactly that: I would never have done what I had with Bryce if I had not been in love with him. It somehow made me feel less guilty. I know it shouldn't, but it did.

'I went away with the girls for the weekend to clear my head, and when I got back, Rick was acting really strange. Then, all of a sudden, out of nowhere, Rick tells me he knows I have sexual feelings toward Bryce and to go and explore them. Jen, he wasn't even angry.'

Her lips remained sealed, but the look on her face showed she did not understand Rick's thinking and suggestion.

'Trust me, I was as confused as hell, too. I told him "no", of course, but he then said that he understood the feelings of "wanting to experience another" because he'd had them years ago and, as a result, he'd an affair.'

She gasped and put her hand to her mouth, but still did not say a word.

My obviously overlarge tear-bank began to flood again as I remembered how easy it had been for him to blatantly lie to my face. 'It gets worse,' I informed her.

She instantly handed me another tissue.

'So, after Rick revealed his infidelity — which was last Sunday — I went straight to Bryce. It was as though I was on autopilot and there was a magnetic field pulling me directly to him. I couldn't help myself. So I have spent the last week staying at Bryce's apartment and, yes, I slept with him. And it was truly amazing,' I admitted, leaning forward on the steering wheel and crying more profusely, thinking of the wonderful moments Bryce and I had shared over the previous week. Not so much the sex, but those special little moments that had my heart beating frantically, then stopping completely, and then beating again.

Jen put her hand on my back and rubbed in a nurturing manner.

I didn't raise my head, just kept slouching and talking into the steering wheel. 'This past week has been the best week of my life. The way I feel when I'm with him is indescribable. I know that doesn't make sense and sounds completely crazy. In hindsight, I should have had the worst week of my life after what Rick had confessed. But I didn't. Yes, I was hurt by his revelation, but whatever pain and hurt I'd felt, Bryce seemed to heal it like magic.' I lifted my head and glanced at her, expecting a scornful look back. What I got, instead, was both a concerned and sad expression, one of understanding.

'Yesterday, Bryce confessed to approaching Rick while I was away with the girls. He told me he had informed Rick that we were in love and that he wanted to spend a week with me alone. Rick apparently told him to "fuck off", but Bryce had pictures of Rick and Claire —'

Finally, Jen interrupted. 'Claire? As in Claire Longmire?'

'Yes.'

'Jesus!' she exclaimed, shaking her head and looking out the front windscreen.

'Bryce blackmailed Rick with the pictures. Do you know what? It all makes perfect sense to me now, the little things that made me wonder why Bryce was so guilt-ridden during the week we shared, and how Rick just came out of nowhere with this bombshell.'

She still looked slightly confused, and I didn't blame her.

'Don't worry Jen, the light bulb will go off soon enough.'

By this stage, I had progressed from sadness to slight clarity, and moved on to sarcasm. These emotions were a never-ending circle, so I knew I would be back to sadness in no time.

'I hadn't spoken to Rick until this morning, when he came barging into Bryce's office. I was ready to finally have it out with him. I had the pictures of his affair and I had my mind set on being with Bryce. I had clarity — sounds weird — but I had somewhat made peace with the majority of it.'

The next stage in my circle of emotions must have been 'lack of feeling', because I had actually begun to feel quite numb. 'Where was I? I can't seem to think any more.'

'I don't blame you, Lex.' She rubbed my back again. 'Rick had just barged into the office.'

'Oh, yeah ... right ... well, he barged in and said he had never had an affair, that he had lied, which didn't make sense. He had a full set of photos showing him fighting Claire's advances. Apparently she is a nutcase and wanted to sleep with him, therefore she set him up. Like I said, it didn't make sense. Why would he lie about an affair, essentially driving me directly into Bryce's arms? Why?' *Yep, next stage in the circle is anger.*

'Do you fucking want to know why?' I shouted. 'Because Bryce offered Rick five million dollars to let me spend a week with him, that's why, and the bastard took it.'

I burst into tears again, sadness completing the emotional cycle once more.

Jen gasped and leaned over to hug me. I reciprocated and hugged her back, ignoring the awkwardness of the enclosed space and the handbrake which was now uncomfortably digging into my thigh.

'Oh, Lex, I can't believe it. Rick accepted the five million dollars?'

'Apparently it's in a bank account already. Jen, Bryce paid for me. He paid to have me like I'm some kind of whore and Rick was the fucking pimp.'

She gently broke away and sat back, still keeping a hold of my hands. 'Are you more upset that Bryce paid for you? Or that Rick chose money over you?'

I had to really think about her question at first, but after deliberating for only a second — and noticing her wise expression — I realised she was not posing a question so much as a statement.

I looked down at my fingers, and touched my wedding band then coincidentally touched my Brylexis, too. I had moved my wedding and engagement rings to the opposite hand, it being my way of signifying the separation. But what I had done — unintentionally — was put Brylexis in their place. At first, I scoffed at my mistake, but then realised the significance. Jen — I think — had only just twigged to the fact I'd switched my wedding rings to the opposite hand.

'That's pretty. Is it from Bryce?' *She's smarter than you think, Alexis.*

I let go of her hands and instinctively rotated Brylexis on my finger. 'Yes, he gave it to me this morning.' My eyes grew waterlogged again. 'As a reminder of him when we were apart.'

She pulled me in for another sisterly hug, a sisterly hug I had been blessed with many times in my life and, like now, was more blessed than ever to have.

'Right, we are going to get out of this car. I will ring Mum and tell her you are staying here tonight because you have a horrible migraine and cannot drive any further. You, Alexis, need some space and time to think about what you are going to do and, more importantly, who you want to be with, if either of them.'

'I'm supposed to be at work tomorrow.'

She looked at me, her expression incredulous. 'Seriously? Do you really want to go to work tomorrow?'

'No,' I glared at her, 'of course not. It's just there is a lot of work to do, and I feel bad.'

'Alexis Summers, you feel bad because your boss, the man who just shattered your heart, is going to have a pile of work to do without your help? Do you know how stupid that sounds?'

Yes, I did. 'Yeah, all right, I get your point. Forgive me if I'm a little fucked in the head at the moment. I think I have every right to be.'

'I'm not arguing with you there, but you need to get your head straightened out first and foremost.'

* * *

We got out of the car and Jen rang Mum. I'm not sure she bought the excuse as to why I would not be gracing them with my presence. Mum did pass on her get well wishes and said she would explain to the kids and see me the next day.

'Thanks, Jen. I just don't think I can see them all and hold my shit together, not today, anyway.'

My phone rang not long after Jen had hung up. At first I'd assumed it was Mum checking the validity of Jen's excuse. She had a habit of trying to catch us out, just like when we were kids.

I'm glad I checked the caller ID before hitting accept, though. Because it wasn't Mum at all, it was Rick.

I took a deep breath and hit decline. *Did he seriously think I would want to speak to him today?*

Jen was at the bench preparing the twin's bottles. 'Which one?' she asked without looking up.

'The five million dollar husband,' I murmured.

'Ah,' was all she said.

A small cry sounded from the nursery, my face automatically responding with a smile. Jen, too, smiled and put the bottle down.

'Come on, you can change the blue one. I'll change the pink one.'

I laughed. She amazed me, dealing with three children under the age of two. I took my hat off to her. It was hard work, no doubt, but Jen and Steven seemed to function well as a team, their crazy baby- and toddler-run life really just normal to them.

Jack and Elise were now in separate cots and had grown accustomed to each other's routines, which was just perfect for Jen. However, it wasn't like that in the beginning. She had really struggled at first. Jack and Elise had been at opposite ends of the clock; when one was awake the other would sleep, then vice versa, making it nearly impossible for Jen to get much shut-eye at all.

She had explained to me one night while we were on the phone that pillows did a good job of muffling her screams of frustration and pure exhaustion, and that dummies have a good rebound distance when thrown at the wall with force. The thing with Jen, though, was that she always managed to get her shit together and come out on top. She was 'super-mum' to those two little bundles of pure cuteness, who were now starting to open their eyes and request some tucker for their tummies.

'Good morning, little Jacko,' I said, as I beamed down at his gorgeous little chubby face.

'Ugh! I hate it when you call him that.'

'What?' *Cues baby voice.* 'How about Jackster, or Jackaroo? Does Mummy like those?' I picked him up and carried him to the change table to remove his disgustingly soiled nappy, gagging as I did so.

'Stop it. It's not like you've never smelled baby poo before.'

'It's tolerable when it's your own baby. This is just rancid. What are you putting in his bottle?'

'Aw, Jacky boy. Isn't she a nasty Aunty Lexi?'

'Pfft, I can tell you what's nasty. This nappy is freakin' nasty.'

I picked him back up after what could only be described as the nappy from hell, and removed myself from the god-awful stench that had now overtaken the nursery.

We played peekaboo in the kitchen while waiting for his sister to have her nappy changed as well. Moments later, Jen walked in holding Elise in the air, praising her for keeping her nappy clean, and giving me a suck-shit look at the same time.

'That would be right. You knew "the pink one" was clean, that's why you changed her.'

'Never!' she sweetly replied, smiling mischievously.

I remembered when the twins were about one and a half months old, and watching Jen feed them both at the same time. It was incredible and gave me a new-found respect for mothers who had had a multiple birth.

Jack was a guzzle-guts, draining his bottle dry. And, thankfully — now at age four months — he burped without following through. When he was younger, I had fed him his bottle, and the tidal wave of formula that had covered me when he attempted to eject his air bubbles could only be described as enormous.

I'd had no choice but to sit there laced with white smelly liquid from my neck to in between my toes. Jack seemed quite relieved. I, on the other the hand, was the complete opposite.

We put them on the floor for some playtime and Jen went to the kitchen to make us a coffee. While I was feeding Jack, my phone had been buzzing from within my pocket. And now that he was happily playing on the floor with his sister, I pulled my phone out to see who had been hassling me. My guess was one of three people: Bryce, Rick or Mum. Glancing at my screen, I took note that I had another missed call from Rick, but there was also a message from Bryce. *Do I open or delete it?* My finger hovered over the delete button for a second, but curiosity got the better of me and I hit open instead.

Honey, I'm sorry. It killed me to see you in pain today, pain I had caused. We are not over, we never will be. I told you that if I ever broke your heart, I would mend it and that's exactly what I am going to do. — *Bryce*

I exhaled the breath I had held from the beginning of reading his message. *He is going to mend my broken heart.* I honestly didn't know if he could. Did I want him to? Deep down, I think I did and I was glad he was going to try.

CHAPTER
18

Thank goodness for the serenity that is a rural property. There's no waking to noisy neighbours, no cars doing burnouts in the near distance and no sirens of any kind blaring their horrible emergency warnings. Instead, when I managed to finally pry my eyelids apart, I woke to the distant sound of mooing from a property down the road together with Jack or Elise's cry for a feed. *Shit, what is the time?* I felt quite drowsy, like I'd slept for days. *God, I hope I didn't sleep for days, surely not.*

Reaching out to the bedside table, I fumbled as I attempted to pick up my phone. Last night, after reading Bryce's message, I had turned it to silent with the express purpose of getting some sleep, and with the hope I would wake up with a magical makeover and no evidence of the drama-filled day I'd experienced.

Finally managing to secure the phone with my still half-asleep hands, I noticed a message from Rick.

Alexis, I am on my way to see the kids today. I know you don't want to see me, but I haven't seen them for a week and I have a feeling I won't see them for another. I would really like to talk to you, just the two of us, but no pressure. — *Rick*

The first thing I noticed after reading the message was the lack of anger that yesterday had raged within. *Wow, that must have been a good night's sleep ... holy shit, make that night, morning and midday sleep!* It was nearly 2.30 p.m. *My goodness, why didn't Jen bloody wake me?*

I pulled on my clothes from the day before and made my way out to the kitchen.

Olivia was sitting up at the table eating a bowl of fruit salad while Jen was in a Graeme Blaxlo-modified seat for twin feeding. Our dad could build or modify anything, if asked.

'Afternoon, Lex, feel better?'

'Why didn't you wake me this morning?'

'Because there was no reason to and you obviously needed the rest and recuperation.'

'Yeah, apparently I did. Thanks. As usual, my dear, you are my saviour, my confidante and my awesome fu—' I glanced at Olivia, then over to Jen whose eyebrows had risen and nearly hit the roof.

'Fuuhh ... vorite, favourite ... my favourite sister.'

Olivia giggled at my long-held 'uuhh' note, so I leaned over her bowl and pinched a strawberry.

'Your mummy is my favourite sister, Miss Olivia.'

She smiled and offered me her half eaten piece of banana and, although her donation of slimy mushed fruit was generous, it wasn't something I fancied with enthusiasm. So I screwed up my nose and politely said, 'No, thank you, sweetheart.'

'I'm your only sister,' Jen retorted.

'Well, aren't you lucky, then?'

'Hmm,' was all she could respond with.

'Well, you are my favourite. Thanks, Jen. Thanks for yesterday.' I walked over and gave her a kiss on the forehead, careful not to interrupt the two milk-devouring babies.

'I do have to get going, though. Rick is probably already at Mum and Dad's.'

'He is. Mum rang just before you woke up.' *Shit. Crap. Balls.*

I sighed and turned back to the guest room.

* * *

Jen had given me a sandwich, together with a be-strong hug as I walked out the door. The hug had lasted most of the journey to Mum and Dad's but, when I approached the farm and spied Rick, Nate and Charlotte riding around the paddock on their motorbikes, the be-strongness I had possessed in the form of a hug had now morphed into be-ridiculously-immatureness.

Rick noticed the Territory pull in and cruised over to open the gate for me.

Stupidly, I locked the doors as I watched him get off his bike. *That is going to help you how, Alexis?*

Thank goodness my sunglasses were on and offered me a slight disguise. To be honest though, I would have much preferred an astronaut's helmet or one of those biohazard suits. Unfortunately, they were all unavailable.

I drove past him as he stood by the open gate. Then, waving to both the kids, I signalled them to follow me to the house. My heart was beating off the Richter scale as I smiled at my children. I had missed them terribly and seeing them for the first time in a week had me desperate to get out and have the longest embrace ever. But, I also wanted to remain in my securely locked automobile, safely away from any form of deep and meaningful conversation with Rick. *Get out of the car, Alexis, and woman-up!*

Nate was first to my door, grabbing the handle before I had a chance to unlock it. *Shit.* I pressed the unlock button, and the door sprung open.

'Hi, Mum, are you feeling better?' he asked, excitedly. *Feeling better? Oh, yes, migraine!*

'Yes, darling, it was just a bad headache.'

Charli came to a halt, removed her helmet, and ran to the passenger side, hopping in next to me.

'Mum, I missed you so much! So where is it?'

I looked at her bemused. 'Where's what?'

'My signed napkin from Sierra Thomas.' *Shit, it's still in the clutch I took to the Tel V Awards.*

'I'm sorry, sweetheart, I left it at work.'

Charli's face transformed from sheer excitement to utterly devastated in an instant. *Quick, Alexis, what is the first rule when accidentally disappointing your children out of forgetfulness? Bribe or offer something else!*

'I do have something else for you, but you'll have to wait till later.'

The excitement of the unknown appeared to rejuvenate her spirits. *Good save!* She did her happy-clap, and it dawned on me that I often did the same thing.

It was so good to see the two adorable loves of my life, the first feeling of joy I'd had since Bryce walked in the morning before with breakfast and Brylexis. *My rings, crap!*

'Okay you two, out you get,' I said, hastily.

As they exited the car, I quickly removed all rings from my fingers, placing them in the glovebox. I exited the car and secured both Nate and Charli in my arms, giving them the biggest bear hug in history. When we separated, they both ran into the house to get a drink, oblivious to the fact that their mother might need some help with carrying her bags. *Typical kids.*

Rick pulled up moments later and approached the car. I instantly turned my back to him and reached for my suitcase.

'I'll get that,' he offered.

'I'm fine, I can handle it,' I snapped back.

He nodded and stepped away. 'Lex, I was wondering if you wanted to go to the pub tonight for a quiet drink and talk, just the two of us.'

I moved my sunglasses down my nose and glared at him. 'No.'

'We need to talk. You can't just shut me out.'

'Listen, Rick. I will play happy families with you today in front of the kids, for their sake, and that's it.'

'Alexis, I have the next couple of days off work, so I'm staying. We need to talk. If you are not ready today, then perhaps you will be tomorrow.'

I glared at him, then instantly had to turn my scowl into a smile when Nate came back outside.

'Dad, Poppa needs me to close the gate in the stockyard. Can you come with me?'

'Sure, mate. Come on then, I'll race ya.'

Nate took off, Rick deliberately giving him a head start so that he could buy some time and cement the fact he was not leaving by shooting me one of the most stubborn glances I had ever seen. *Phew, thank you, Nate. Good, now fuck off, Rick, and give me some space.*

* * *

As I walked through the door of my parents' farmhouse, Mum indicated with her head to follow her into the next room. Charli was on the sofa watching TV and Mum obviously did not want her to hear what she had to say. I had not even put my suitcase down when she wrapped her arms around me, then held me back for the mother inspection.

'Are you okay? I can tell something is terribly wrong. Your eyes have evidence of a lot of crying and now Rick has shown up unannounced and acting very strange. I'm assuming from that icy reception that you are still separated?' *I need to tell her, but if I do that now I can't be sure I will not break down again.*

I let go of the suitcase handle and touched her arms. 'Mum, I can't go into it now because if I do, I guarantee you I will lose it. Look, yes we are still separated and no, I am not all right. He wanted to see the kids, which was fair enough. They probably wanted to see him, too, and I am not about to punish them by keeping their dad away. He knows I have no intention of going home now. Not till the end of the week, anyway. Is that all right with you?'

'Of course, darling, stay as long as you need. Is Rick staying tonight, too?'

I cringed at the thought.

'Yes.' *Shit, where is he going to sleep? The kids will notice if he sleeps on the couch.*

'Okay, do you want me to put the trundle bed in with you?' She gave me her mum-can-fix-anything look.

'Yes, please. Thanks, Mum.'

* * *

Dinner was the most awkward time I think I have ever endured. More awkward than the time I accidentally joined a funeral procession on a hot summer's day with my car windows down, playing AC/DC as loud as I could and screaming out 'Thunderstruck'. I had no idea I was behind a hearse, until I looked in my rear-view mirror and noticed a good twenty cars lined up behind me with their lights on. This dinner topped that in the awkward stakes, believe it or not.

Every time Rick looked up, I looked down, then I would look up and he would look down, then Mum would look up, and we both would look down. Dad, however, just watched the news. Thank goodness for Charli and her ability to never shut up, because she managed to keep the entire dinner conversation focussed on how she was auditioning for the school play of *Robin Hood*.

The awkwardness after dinner wasn't nearly as bad though. Rick and Dad watched a movie with the kids while Mum and I played cards. It wasn't really that much different from other nights we had spent at the farm. Well, that is if you don't count the massive elephant which was invisible to the kids and standing idly in the corner of the room.

* * *

After kissing my munchkins goodnight, I headed for the bedroom in the hope I would be fast asleep before Rick came in. I'd removed my top when the door opened and he entered.

Quickly, I covered my chest with it and glared at him. 'Do you mind? Get out.'

'Lexi, I think I have seen you naked before. In fact I'm positive I have.'

'It's different now, get out.'

'Okay, okay. I'll go to the toilet.'

He left the room and my pulse automatically quickened. He was right. Obviously he had seen me naked more times than I could count, but it seemed weird and horribly wrong now.

I rummaged through my suitcase, found the nightie I had grabbed from home, and quickly put it on without removing my underwear. I jumped into bed making sure the covers were well and truly doing what they should.

Rick came back in and 'tutted' at my modest display, then showed absolutely no sign of the same bashfulness by removing his clothing entirely. He reluctantly climbed into the trundle bed and over-exaggerated his discomfort by rotating like a crocodile doing a death roll for a good minute or two. I knew he was far from impressed at the thought of sleeping on the hugely uncomfortable makeshift bed, but he had more sense than to argue this very generous arrangement on my part.

After turning off the lamp, the room was completely black and silent. You could have cut the air with a knife and I swear I even heard crickets chirp. But then again, we were on a farm, and the chance of crickets actually chirping outside the bedroom window was a high probability.

'Alexis, I'm sorry.'

'Don't,' I said firmly, not in the mood to listen to his excuses.

'Don't what? Apologise for fucking up?'

I lowered my voice, knowing from experience that the voices in this house travelled. 'Just don't even go there, Rick.'

'Where is there? We need to talk and that's what I'm doing.'

I hushed him. 'Shh. I don't want to hear your excuses.'

'You need to know why I did it.'

'It doesn't matter why. Now shut up or you can sleep in the car.' I turned over, making it obvious that the conversation was over.

* * *

In the morning when I woke, Rick was still asleep on the trundle, although his leg was half on the floor and his neck and back were uncomfortably bent and misshapen. *Suffer, I hope you ache like hell when you wake up.*

Tiptoeing out of the room, I felt a little better after having seen his obviously unpleasant sleeping position.

Mum was in the kitchen, always the first to rise, and as soon as she saw me approach, she turned on the kettle. I walked directly up to her and placed my head on her shoulder. She did what most loving mothers would and embraced her daughter, regardless of said daughter's age.

'How did last night go, darling?'

'Thankfully, sleep means you do not have to communicate with the conscious world and those who are in it,' I mumbled into her shoulder.

She kissed my head then broke away to make us both a cup of tea.

'Go and sit out on the porch. We can talk there without unwelcome ears hearing us.'

I did as instructed and waited for her to join me, which was not long at all.

'Mum, it is such a long and detailed story so I am going to break it down into point form, and I don't want you to say anything until I'm done.'

She sipped her drink then nodded.

'Okay, here goes. I've fallen in love with my boss, Bryce, and he with me. Rick told me he had an affair five years ago. I left him to be with Bryce. Yesterday, Rick came to work and told me he lied about having an affair. I asked him why? He said because he thought I needed to be with Bryce to get it off my chest. He also said that Bryce gave him five million dollars to let me stay with him ... Bryce, that is.'

Mum spat the contents of her mouthful back into her mug. *So, that's where I get it from?*

'And that's about it,' I finished, looking out over the valley and sipping my tea.

She followed my gaze, but didn't speak straightaway. 'Who do you love the most, Alexis?'

'It shouldn't be about choosing, Mum.'

'But, darling, it is if they both love and want you.' *Ah shit, she's right, but did I have to choose?*

'I don't have to choose either one of them.'

'No, you are quite right, but you will. So did Rick keep the money?'

'As far as I know, yes.'

She sipped her drink again, and the child in me thought about backwash. *Eww.*

Hearing the door creak at the hinges, I looked up to see Dad approach our seated position. He wriggled in beside me and put his arm around my shoulder. 'So, my princess, do I need to get my gun out?'

I smiled lovingly at my dad and his tough father act. 'No, but I might get it out instead.'

He pulled me in for a hug.

A daughter is never too old for her daddy's hugs. A daddy's hug being the most reassuring, precious and secure feeling imaginable. And I loved having one from my dad, even if I was thirty-five. Dad knew without a doubt that something was not right where Rick was concerned. It was like a sixth sense he had when it came to his daughters and the men in their lives. Dad chose not to meddle and not to ask for detailed information though. He was content with the fact he had raised strong and capable daughters with level heads on their shoulders, daughters who could handle their problems themselves. He was, however, always there, ready, willing and able if ever we felt we needed him.

* * *

We ate breakfast at staggered times, suiting me just fine. Another awkward meal together was not something anyone wanted.

Heading straight for the shower after breakfast, I quickly refreshed myself then got dressed in my jeans, boots and a fitted white shirt. I dilly-dallied, wasting as much time as possible in the bathroom doing my hair, and then re-doing my hair to waste some more time. *Alexis, you are being ridiculous. Just go and talk to him, get it over and done with.*

By the time I finally emerged from my shower, Rick was outside kicking the football with the kids. I ran up and intercepted a mark, praising myself as I did it. They all smiled at me, but their smiles were not ones of praise for my ball marking skills. Instead, they were smiles of ridicule at my boasting ... well, maybe not Charli's.

'Just call me "Fletcher", you know you want to,' I goaded them.

Dustin Fletcher, or 'Inspector Gadget' as he was known, was my favourite Essendon football player. The man could intercept a fly if need be.

'You wish, Mum,' Nate retorted.

I poked my tongue out and handballed to Charli who looked like she needed all the help she could get in this unfair competition.

'Your dad and I need to go for a ride,' I explained to the kids. 'We'll be back soon, okay?'

Rick walked toward me, a glimmer of hope appearing in his eyes.

'I'll take the quad. You get your bike and meet me up the top of the hill.'

I sat on top of the quad bike, switched it on and pressed the throttle, speeding off through the gate and accelerating up the hill.

The wind sailed past me with force, completely ruining my time-wasting hairstyle. *At least I'll have an excuse to do it again if need be.*

Rick wasn't far behind as I cut the engine at the summit of the hill. I swung my leg around and remained atop the quad.

He got off his bike, and I didn't bother easing us into it.

'First things first, Rick. Are you keeping the money?'

'Yes,' he answered, adamantly.

I figured as much. 'If this was not about the money, then why keep it?'

With what I thought was an aggravated sigh, he leaned up against the quad and held his helmet against his abdomen. 'Honestly?'

'Yes, fucking honestly. Do you think I need to listen to any more lies?'

'No, of course not. Look, I'm keeping the money because I need to at least get *something* out of all this,' he replied with an angry tone. *Why is he allowed to be angry?*

I shook my head and annoyance started to fester. 'You need to get something out of this? Was I nothing? Was I not good enough?'

'Of course you are good enough. But before you get fired up, Alexis, I want you tell me something honestly.'

'What?' I glared at him.

'I want you to sit there, look me in the eyes and honestly tell me that you would never have slept with Bryce if I hadn't taken his deal. I don't think you can, can you? I could see you needed to experience what it was like to be with someone else. It was obvious.'

'Fuck you. I sure as hell can tell you I would never have slept with him while we were still together.'

'While we were still together? Well, which is it? You would have, or not? In case you have forgotten, we are still technically married — still together.' *Hang on just a minute, when did this become let's blame Alexis?*

'Don't fucking blame me for all this. You deliberately pushed me into another man's arms so you could profit from it.'

'I'm not blaming you. I'm just trying to be realistic here. And for the record, I didn't do it so I could profit. I did it so this family could profit. Anyway, did you think I did not notice you flirting with Bryce?'

I lowered my anger levels just a little. I was definitely not blameless in this whole debacle. 'Yes, I flirted with him. He turned me on and made me feel things I had never felt before. Was I curious? Of course I was. I'm only human, and by the way I hope you realise this family has profited because you saw fit to "pimp" your wife. How does that make you feel?'

'I didn't see it as pimping you. I saw it as giving you an out to get this flirting shit off your chest. You admitted yourself that you had already crossed the line with him.'

I had admitted to kissing Bryce, but that was it. I never told Rick about the naked exposures and finger-fuck I experienced. I began to feel less angry and accusatory toward Rick. I was as much to blame as the both of them in all this, really. Well, maybe not as much to blame. Let's put it this way, I was not an angel, that's for sure.

'Okay, yes, it was probably inevitable that Bryce and I would have fucked at some point, but that does not give you the right, nor is it moral, to assume this scenario and strike yourself a deal where you could benefit if it did, in fact, pan out that way. It's just so wrong, on so many levels.'

He shrugged his shoulders, and for the first time seemed sad and remorseful for his decision.

'And again,' I said, with the utmost resolution, 'I would not have slept with him without breaking it off first. Let's just get that straight.'

'Okay, you say sleeping with Bryce was probably inevitable, but you also say you would have never have done it without breaking it off first. Does that mean we were headed for a break-up anyway?'

I thought about what he asked and, prior to finding out about his make-believe affair and monetary arrangement, I concluded that yes, we had been headed in that direction.

'Yes, Rick, I think we were.'

'So he isn't lying when he says you have fallen in love with him?'

I looked at my hands and the absence of jewellery that once occupied my fingers. 'No, he is not lying,' I admitted as I started to cry. 'I'm sorry, it just happened. I had no control over it and I didn't set out looking for it. I even tried to bury it, ignore it, but you can't dismiss love.'

Fortunately, I found a crumpled tissue in my jeans pocket and unclogged my now congested nose.

He looked at me with an expression of misery. 'Do you still love him? Do you still love me?'

The now calm and soft, but assertive, man I had married was standing before me. *Do I still love Bryce? Yes. Do I still love Rick? Yes, I think I do, but it is different now.*

'Yes, I love you both, but what happened has changed everything. I don't know where I stand any more. Do I stand with the man I married and have shared a life with, but who chose to give up his wife for money, therefore losing a great deal of what made us special? Or do I stand with a new man, one who has made me feel something I did not think was possible, but who has hurt me very deeply by going behind my back, paying for me as if I were a whore?'

'Alexis, if I had known for one minute you had, or would, fall in love with him, I would never have lied to you or accepted the money.'

I couldn't be quite sure whether I believed him not, but did it matter? I didn't know any more.

'But you did, Rick. You not only lied to me, you also accepted the money. None of us can undo what we have done.'

He took in a deep breath. 'So where do we go from here?'

'I don't know, but you need to leave and go home. Give me some space.'

'I don't want to leave. Being away from you this past week was bad enough.'

'Rick, you don't have a choice. I'm not saying we have a chance of reuniting or rekindling what we had, but I'm also not saying that we can't. I need time to think. So do the right thing and give me the space I need, please.'

* * *

After lunch, Rick took my advice and said his goodbyes to the kids.

'I'll call you tomorrow,' he said with a hopeful spark in his voice before driving away.

'Mum, why is Daddy leaving again?' Charlotte asked as she watched her dad's car disappear down the road.

'Because he has to work, Charli-Bear,' I concluded.

I wasn't a fan of lying, but there were times in life when a lie was needed, whether we liked it or not, and I was slowly coming to terms with that.

'Right, sweetheart. I think we have a shopping date, don't you?'

'Yes, can I get some new shoes?' *Don't look into her eyes, Alexis. It's the Charli Jedi mind-trick.*

'Yes.' *Damn it, I looked into her eyes.*

She happy-clapped then ran through the open front door to get her purse.

Nate, however, decided he would stay and help my dad with some fencing maintenance, making the trip into Shepparton a girly affair.

* * *

During the drive into town, I noticed Mum looked as though she wanted to say something to me, but she refrained.

'What, Mum?'

'Hang on a minute, give me a second.'

I glanced at her intermittently, making sure I kept my attention fixed to the road. She appeared to deliberate something in her head, and then spoke with an appreciative smile.

'Okay, so, how did the exchange of dialogue go with the male spouse?'

Furrowing my eyebrows in puzzlement, I soon figured out she was trying to use long and difficult words to disguise our conversation so that Charli could not decipher it. I smiled at her cleverness then contemplated my own choice of words in response.

'The oral exchange proved to be somewhat explicatory, although not concluded by any means, but unobjectionable for the time being.'

I could see her figuring it out in her head, as if she was counting. A smile appeared on her face, indicating she had. 'Oh, well, I guess that's a start?'

'It is,' I replied with a shrug.

* * *

We pulled into Shepparton Plaza and began browsing the shops. Charli picked out a pair of pink and purple high tops and a matching pair of shorts, while I looked at some books and a CD. Mum had nothing in particular to shop for, so we made our way to the local pub for lunch.

Just as we were about to enter the tavern, I spotted a big sign on the wall advertising a local band who were set to play the coming Thursday night.

I stopped and pointed it out to Mum. 'There's a band playing on Thursday night. I might see if Jen wants to come and reminisce about our younger years.'

'That's a good idea, I doubt she would have been out since the twins were born. It would be good to get her out of the house.'

Jen was not one to give herself some time off, so I thought I would play the sulky, needy-sister card to help her and my cause.

'I'll ring her later and grovel. It always works.'

'Yes, I know,' Mum grinned. 'Your grovelling skills come from me.'

I smiled at Mum and linked her arm with mine as we entered the bistro, while Charli stuck her little head in between the two of us.

'You guys find a table and I'll get the drinks,' I said. 'So, what would you like to drink, Charli?'

'Raspberry, please.'

'Mum?'

'I'll have a glass of chardonnay thanks, darling.'

'Okay, I'll be back in a minute.' I walked over to the bar and ordered a chardonnay, a gin and a raspberry soft drink. My phone buzzed in my pocket as I paid the bartender, so before attempting to carry the drinks back, I pulled it out to see who had messaged me.

The message was from Bryce:

Alexis, honey, I miss you so badly it hurts. I want to see you again, touch you again. — Bryce

I was so angry with him, but the thought of him touching me already had my heart rate up. I desperately wanted what he did, but I was totally confused and, after speaking to Rick, I had no idea what my next step was going to be.

I bit down on my fingernail, and then messaged him back.

Bryce, I'm hurting too, and I miss you more than you'll ever know, but you crossed the line, and now I'm torn apart. — Alexis

A response came through almost instantly.

Do you still love me? — Bryce

I didn't need to think about that.

Of course I do. — Alexis

My phone beeped again.

That's all I need to know, honey. By the way, I like your jeans. Your arse in denim does things to my cock — Bryce

I blinked a couple of times while looking at my phone. *Cheeky son of a bitch!* Then the light bulb inside my head switched on. *Oh, shit! He's here!*

CHAPTER
19

Do you know that feeling you get when you are almost certain somebody is watching you and the hairs on the back of your neck stand up? Well ... I had that feeling now, prompting me to spin around and frantically scan the busy room. *Bryce is here, I know he is, I can feel it in my bones ... or more so, between my legs.*

My heart went spastic and crazily pounded in my chest when I spotted him in the far corner, standing up against the wall. His presence parched my mouth when our eyes locked and, almost instantly, we began our silent discussion.

Walking back to the table, I placed our drinks down. It was a miracle I had not dropped or spilled them along the way, because my hands were trembling with anticipation and the fear of not being able to resist him.

'I just have to go to the toilet,' I stuttered.

'Are you okay?' Mum asked, delving deep into my eyes with her own. 'You look pale.'

'I'm fine, I just need to pee.'

'Okay, do you want me to order for you?'

'Yes, please. I'll have a warm chicken salad.'

I began my nerve-racking journey toward him, weaving in and out of tables and, with each step closer, my chest grew tighter. He walked out of the room and into a corridor which joined the bistro to the sports bar. I'd lost sight of him as I approached the exit, but as I rounded the corner, he gently grabbed my arm and pinned me up against the wall behind a rather large fake-looking palm plant.

Our bodies were against each other and our faces were only centimetres apart. I didn't think it was possible to want the feel of his lips, mouth and tongue more than I did at that particular moment. *No, Alexis, you are hurt and angry with him.*

'Hi, honey,' he breathed seductively. *Oh. shit, he still sounds so fucking sexy. Breathe, Alexis.*

'Hi,' I whispered, swallowing dryly.

'I've missed you,' he admitted as his eyes scanned my pinned body. *Oh god, I can tell.*

'I've missed you, too.' I whispered back.

He moved his face, pressing his cheek to mine. 'Do I still have permission to kiss you?' *Oh fuck, I want you to, but no, I can't let you.*

I opened my mouth ever so slightly and breathed out what little air I had taken in. The word I then spoke was barely audible as it was hugely painful to say. But I did say it. I had to. 'No.'

He rested his forehead on mine and closed his eyes. 'I didn't think so. I'm so sorry, my love, but I couldn't think of any other way. I never meant to hurt you. I never *ever* meant for you to feel like I paid for you. I know you are not for sale, I never thought you were. I just desperately wanted you to see that we were meant to be together.'

A tear fell from my eye and slowly made its way down my cheek.

He gently wiped it away with his finger. 'Please don't cry,' he pleaded. 'I hate seeing you upset.'

I fought the rest of my salty menaces back with great difficulty, not because he didn't want to see me cry, but because I simply did not want to shed any more tears. My eyes literally hurt and the muscles in my face were exhausted.

'What are you doing here, Bryce?'

There was no point in asking him how he knew where I was. I had accepted the fact that if he wanted to know something, he would use everything within his power to learn the answer. If he wanted to know where I was 24/7, then so be it. There was really nothing I could do about it.

'I can't be away from you. It's killing me.'

'You have to. I'm not ready.'

'I can't,' he said through gritted teeth. It was clearly visible in his eyes and face how tortured he really was.

'You have no choice. I need space, I need time to think.'

His expression was pained. 'To think about what?'

'To think about who I am going to spend the rest of my life with. Up until yesterday morning, before my heart was ripped in half and trampled on, I had made that decision and couldn't have been happier. I wanted nothing more than to be with you, but things have changed, Bryce.'

'Do you love me, honey?'

'Yes, I've already told you that.'

'Did you not say that my cock belonged inside you and that you promised I'd be back?' He gently pushed his body harder against mine, making me gasp very slightly.

I closed my eyes in order to gain back control of my head, my heart and my body.

Breathing in, I opened them slowly, catching a slight smirk on his face due to his attempt to sway me.

'Yes, I did, but it is no longer that simple.'

Bryce moved back again and put both his hands on the wall on either side of my face.

'It is, Alexis. It is the most purely simple thing conceivable. You and I belong together. You know it and I know it.' *Fuck it.*

I grabbed his shirt and aggressively pulled him to me, kissing him with force and biting his lip. He responded to my vigour by pushing me harder against the wall as his tongue moved with mine. *Fuck. Fuck!*

Placing my hands on his chest, I pushed him off me, then slapped him across the face.

We were breathing heavily and burning each other with our heady passionate stares.

Then, gaining a semblance of restraint, I gently replaced my hands back on his chest. *Oh, sweet Jesus, his pecs are hard and tensed and ready for my mouth and tongue to lick and ... Alexis, stop it.*

This time, I gently pushed him back so that we were no longer touching, and the urge to continue to kiss him was not so excruciating.

'Please, just give me some space to get my shit together, to get myself to a point where I don't burst into tears just thinking about you and Rick. I can't be like that, not around Nate and Charli.'

He seemed to relax a little, surrendering his aggressive need. 'I can give you time and space, but I can't promise as to how much. It is physically unbearable to be this close to you and not be able to touch you in all the places I know you like to be touched, and to taste you in all the places I know you like to be tasted. I can't promise you my restraint will last for long.'

I watched his fists clench open and closed, an indication that he was struggling. So I stepped aside and out from behind the plastic plant.

'I have to go. Mum and Charli will wonder where I have gone.' I went to turn for the bistro, but he grabbed my hand again.

'You've taken it off.'

I looked back at my bare fingers. 'I've taken them all off.'

His expression was one of heartbreak. 'I will not give up on us, Alexis. I will fix this, I promise.'

I gave him a meek smile and attempted to leave again.

'Alexis.'

'Yes.'

'I love you.'

I paused only slightly, for every single inch of me wanted to turn around and jump on him, wrap my legs around his waist, kiss him again and tell him I forgave him and that everything was fine. But it wasn't fine, I didn't trust him any more and I didn't know if I ever could. *Is love enough? Is love, without trust, enough?*

I let out a deep breath without looking back. 'I love you, too,' I replied, then I walked back into the bistro.

* * *

I sat down at the table where both Mum and Charli were more than halfway through eating their lunch.

'Are you sure you are all right? You were gone a while. Your warm chicken salad is no longer warm.'

'I'm fine, Mum, although my tummy is a little unsettled.' *That was an understatement!* I tucked myself into my seat and began to eat lunch.

Every now and then I would look up, knowing he had not left yet. But, wherever he was hiding, he was very well camouflaged. Just the knowledge of him being there, though, had me feeling things I should not feel, especially after how much he had hurt me. *I can't just forgive him this easily. It's a sign of weakness, and I am not weak.*

'Alexis, darling.'

I looked up at Mum and placed my fork down. I had been annoying a piece of chicken with it. And I'm sure if the chicken had been alive, it would have grabbed my fork and stabbed itself out of frustration.

'Yeah, Mum?'

'Do you realise how important your heart is?'

'Maybe, why?'

'Because your heart houses the love you possess, and when you open your heart and release that love, you render it fragile, and expose it to breaking. Alexis, your heart is *strong* and not as fragile as you think. Why? Because it heals, darling. It will heal if you let it. Please let it heal, okay?'

Another tear escaped my eye even though I willed it not to. Mum's words could not be more appropriate, and I loved her dearly for encouraging me to let my heart heal. I blew her a kiss, then winked at Charli while trying to wipe away the teardrop before she noticed it.

'Mum, what's wrong with your heart?' Charli asked.

'Nothing, sweetie. I'm just learning how to make it strong.'

'Why isn't it strong?'

Mum went to interrupt and divert Charli's questioning, but I stopped her.

'Charli, inside your heart is love. I have love in my heart that I give to you and Nate and Daddy, and to whoever else I want to give it to —'

'I give my love to you, too, don't I?' Charli proudly interrupted.

'Yes, you do, and it's one of my most favourite loves in the world.' This response made her smile. 'Sweetheart, sometimes when you give your love to someone and they don't give their love back to you, it hurts your heart and makes it weak. That's why we have to learn to make it strong, so that it doesn't hurt any more.'

She nodded as she tried to understand. 'So who didn't give their love back to you?' *Crap, now I've put my foot in it.*

'No one, Charli-Bear. I'm just making it stronger in case that happens.'

'Okay, well it won't be me, or Nate, or Daddy, because we always give our love to you.'

'You are adorable, my baby girl. Now hurry up and finish your lunch.'

* * *

Before we headed back to the farm, we picked up some chicken feed pellets and decided to call into Jen's house for a coffee. While Mum and Charli were playing with Olivia and the twins, I filled Jen in on the developments with Bryce and Rick.

'Bryce is here? In Shepparton?' she asked, astonished.

'Yeah, trust me, "It's what he does"!' I answered, giggling to myself as I said it.

Jen didn't get my private joke, and I didn't elaborate. She just reiterated that time and space were my best friends. Until they became annoying bitches and, in that case, piss them off and find some new ones. Preferably alcohol and dancing. Now they were friends who could show me great time. Well, not so much her analogy, more mine.

'Just pace yourself, Lex, and don't make any rushed decisions.'

'I know, I know. So, on Thursday night, we are going to the pub to check out the band, like old times. All right?' I half expected her to um and ah, but she didn't. Instead, she lowered her voice to a whisper.

'You have no idea how good that fucking sounds. I need a night out, away from crayon drawings on the wall, mushed food in the carpets and poo-splosions in nappies.'

I laughed. 'It's a date then. Pick me up at about 8 p.m. Oh, and bring some tops with you. My clothing is in short supply. I had not planned on staying up here when I packed.'

* * *

The rest of that day was pretty uneventful after our quick stopover at Jen's. When we arrived back at the farm, I gave Charli, Nate and Mum their gifts from Uluru. Luckily, I'd put them directly in my car after we returned to Melbourne and I'd collected the Territory from the repair shop.

Nate had been trying for nearly an hour to master the boomerang. Most of his attempts were a failure, but towards the end, a couple of throws were showing signs of making their way back to him.

Charli adored her necklace, and even Mum was pretty pleased with her new tea towel.

Pulling out the spoon for Tash, I realised we hadn't spoken, and knew that if I didn't call her soon, I might incur her wrath — which was not always pleasant!

I dialled her number, and she answered very quickly.

'Hey, Lex, I've been worried about you. How have you been, luv?'

'Oh, Tash, you have no idea.'

I explained very briefly what had transpired since our last chat in Yulara. She was completely shocked and at a loss for words, which did not happen to Tash. Ever!

'Shit! I'm coming there to see you.'

'No, don't be silly. I'm fine. I've got Mum and Jen and they've been a godsend.'

'Are you sure, Lex? This is a really, *really* horrible situation you're in.'

'Tell me about it. I appreciate the offer though, I do, but it is a long way to come. Listen, I'm going to head back with the kids on Friday. I have decided Rick can stay with his parents for a while, until I have at least figured out where we stand. Speak to the girls and see if they want to catch up for a drink and a dance on Saturday night. I think I need it.'

'Okay, sounds good. I'll let you know. Oh ... and Lex? I know I don't say this often, but you are an amazingly strong and level-headed person. Well ... level-headed when schnappies aren't involved.'

I laughed.

'No, seriously, Lex, you will be fine, and you will make the right decision whichever one it is.'

'Thanks, hon, I know. I just need to focus on other things and clear my head. What will be, will be.'

She began to sing. 'Que sera —'

'Don't even go there, you idiot.'

She laughed and stopped. 'Not going there, I promise.'

'I gotta go. I'll talk to you soon. Bye.' I hung up the phone and shook my head. What would I do without that crazy bitch?

* * *

The next few days went by quite quickly. I kept myself busy by helping Mum and Dad where I could. Tuesday was gardening day, and Dad showed Nate how to use the ride-on mower. Nate was a natural, so Dad got a chance to read the newspaper and drink a cup of tea while the lawns were happily mowed.

Charli, Mum and I tackled the garden beds. I enjoyed gardening — it's therapeutic. What you gained for your time and hard work in amongst the soil always proved to be a great reward. That reward could be a beautiful display of colourful blooms, or home-grown fruit, vegetables and herbs, or even just being out in the fresh air, working with Mother Nature.

Wednesday, thus far, had not been a good day. We were all indoors seeking air-conditioned relief as the temperature outside was close to 40° Celsius. The kids were restless and fighting over which movies to watch. Mum hated extreme heat and complained every five minutes and Dad was frustrated at the fact he was now forced to sit on his arse and forgo the jobs he had lined up. I, however, found myself pondering. I couldn't help it.

Keeping busy and diverting my mind from thoughts of Rick and Bryce — who I had now collectively named 'Brick' — had been a successful way to avoid any pondering. Unfortunately, with the stifling heat and lack of anything to do because of it, I had no choice but to contemplate my situation, and it was depressing me. *This is what you are here for Alexis, to ponder, to decipher and to figure out what to do.*

It was probably the most difficult decision I would ever have to make, and I couldn't just make it on a whim. I was in love with Bryce, but could I trust him not to keep things from me in the future? I wanted to be with him more than anything, but I had two children who would have to want to be in that life, too. Not to mention Bryce would have to want them in our life, and I had no idea if he did or did not. It wasn't something we had ever discussed.

Then there was Rick. I loved him also. He was stupid, naive and money hungry, but he had never cheated on me. We had shared a wonderful life together before all this happened. It was just so complicated. *Single life isn't complicated, Alexis.* Yes, if I were single I wouldn't have to deal with any of this shit. *Single again?* The thought actually terrified me. I hadn't been single since I was seventeen. Not to mention the dreadful thought of being a single mother; that would be no easy task. But maybe that was what I needed to do: wipe the slate clean, be free to make the best decision for me and the kids. *No, Alexis, it's ridiculous.* But was it?

The idea of declaring myself single actually felt good ... liberating and somewhat exciting. I guess it also felt empowering. A way of saying, 'hey, fuck the both of you, now I'm up for grabs.'

I honestly had no idea what it was like to be single. What would I do? Technically, I would not commit myself to either of them at this stage. *I like it already. I can think more clearly.*

I needed to break this down into steps, and step one was to ask Rick to stay with his parents when the kids and I returned home. *Then again, he now has five million dollars. He can fucking buy his own house!*

Step two was to get advice, and I knew just who to get it from.

I grabbed my phone and dialled Carly. Apart from Mum and Jen, her voice was one I knew well when it came to discussing problems.

'Hey, whore, how's your love triangle?'

If anyone but Carly — okay, or Tash, Jade, Lil or Steph — had said this to me at this point in time, I would have unleashed hell upon them. But, one: this was Carly and I never took any insult she said to heart. And, two: she had absolutely no idea what had happened to me since our night out at Opals.

'Hey, yourself. The love triangle has ruined my marriage.'

She didn't respond at first then opted for the I-hope-you-are-kidding approach as a lifeline to her now inappropriate directness.

'Ha, ha, you're joking, right?'

'No, hon, I'm not. I have left Rick and have distanced myself from Bryce. I am now officially single, so to speak.'

'Fuck off.' *As always, Carls, your audacity is priceless!* 'Where are you, Lex?'

'At Mum and Dad's farm.'

'Right, I'm on my way. Tell your mum I'll bunk with her and Graeme. I'd rather hear her snore than listen to you fart.'

I cracked up laughing even though it was an awful insult. 'Carls, I'm fine, you don't need to come up here.'

'Bullshit, I don't. I'm coming! Anyway, I need a break from this shit-hole I call work.'

'All right, but if you insist on coming, you are sleeping with me and you are going to have to put up with my flatulence whether you like it or not, bitch.'

'Deal. I'm only at work for a short time today, so I'll see you just before dinner. What is for dinner, by the way?'

I loved her shamelessness.

'I don't know. I'll ask.' I shouted out to Mum who was in the kitchen. 'Mum, what's for dinner?'

Moments later, she was standing by the bedroom door. 'Roast, why?'

Carly heard the selection and continued to talk. 'Ask her roast what? It had better be lamb.'

I moved the phone away from my ear. 'Carly wants roast lamb.'

Mum smiled. 'She does, does she?'

Carls' voice squawked through the phone again. 'With mint sauce.'

Eww, yuk. I couldn't eat mint anyway, so I wouldn't be touching that shit.

Mum rolled her eyes and turned for the door. 'Tell her yes, it's lamb, but she can bring her own bloody mint sauce.'

I smiled. I loved my mum. She was always welcoming and her door was never closed. Carly was like a daughter to her anyway, so Mum's refusal of Carly's self-invite was never going to happen.

'Did you hear that, Carls?'

'Yeah, hold the phone out toward your mum.'

I did what I was told then heard Carly squawk again. 'Thank you, Maryann. I love you and your roast lamb.'

When Carly was finished yelling, I put the phone back to my ear. Mum shook her head and smiled as she walked off.

'You finished?' I asked.

'Yeah. I'll see you later with the mint sauce.'

'Bye.' I ended the call and felt better almost instantly. I didn't want anyone to drive to Shepparton and help poor me get out of this hole I had put myself in, but I couldn't deny my relief at Carly's stubbornness and her dash to my aid.

* * *

Carls turned up before dinner and handed Mum a bottle of mint sauce. Mum responded by giving her a light slap on the arm together with a quick hug. Carls enjoyed her roast lamb and after a glass of wine out on the front porch, bed seemed to be calling everyone's names.

Carls and I both lay in bed, whispering for hours that night like we had when we were teenagers. It was just what I needed, filling her in on every tiny detail. She was blown away by the complexity of the entire situation and advised me to tread carefully. She was very carefree, unattached and not held down by anyone or anything, so her laid-back approach to life and situations came naturally. My dilemma, however, seemed to bring out her cautious side, which was a side of her I did not often see.

'I seem to be over my initial emotional rollercoaster, so that's a good sign. I guess I'm just at the stage of weighing up my options. Sounds terrible, doesn't it? Like putting the two of them on a scale and seeing which way it tips.'

'If weighing up your options is what you have to do, Lex, then do it,' she said with conviction.

We finally fell asleep after one of our longest deep and meaningful conversations ever.

* * *

Carls had been snoring which woke me up earlier than usual. *Maybe she should have slept in with Mum after all.* She was so cute in her pink leopard print PJs, so much so, that I wanted to give her a kiss. I leaned over and pulled a lipstick out of her make-up bag. *Ravishing Rouge. Perfect.* I put it on thickly, and with a wet wipe in hand ready to wipe the evidence off my lips before she noticed, I forcefully placed a kiss on her forehead.

'Wake up, bitch.' I turned my head instantly and wiped the red residue off my lips.

'Fuck off, I was sleeping.' She grumpily turned over, so I pulled the blankets off and flicked the elastic band on the waist of her pyjama pants.

'Get up! You are going to help me bake a cake today. Then we are painting each other's toenails, while eating popcorn and watching *Bridesmaids.*'

She opened her eyes, ever so slightly, and scowled at me. I had to refrain from laughing. Instead, I grinned at her like the Cheshire Cat.

'There's no way I'm eating popcorn while painting your toenails, that's just foul.'

'What? You know what I mean, get up.'

* * *

Charli, Nate, Carls and I trashed Mum's kitchen as a result of making the yummiest lemon-lime meringue cake to have ever existed. Poor Carly had no idea what was so funny during breakfast and the cake making process. You see, my family had all been at the end of one of her jokes at more than one point in our lives. So we all thought it appropriate not to inform her of the set of red lips on her forehead.

Dad decided he would take the kids to a clearance sale just outside of Shepparton for a couple of hours, allowing the three of us to conduct pedicures and watch *Bridesmaids*.

In hindsight this was not a very bright idea, because every time we tried to complete a perfectly steady brushstroke, we would start laughing hysterically and cover the entire toe. Mum was absolutely hopeless at both the painting and the receiving, especially during the moment in the movie when the girls were trying on their dresses and, unfortunately, having to suddenly deal with a horrible bout of vomiting and diarrhoea as a result of food poisoning.

Mum laughed so hard that she kicked me in the face with her foot, smearing the bit of polish I had put on her toe across my cheek. Carls had thought it was hilarious, of course, and mentioned that 'Karma was a malicious bitch who always had the last laugh'.

* * *

As we were readying ourselves for our night out at the pub, I smiled genuinely for the first time since my heart had been torn in two. I may have been in the love triangle from hell and in the midst of a fucked-up combination of lust, love, bribery and lies, but, strangely enough, I was also grateful. Grateful and thankful for my family and friends. I loved them dearly, and was blessed to have them in my life.

At the end of the day, there was always somebody far worse off than oneself, and what you feel to be like the end of the world was probably only trivial to them.

CHAPTER

20

The pub wasn't enormous by any means, but as pubs go this one was definitely on the larger side. I guess it probably had to be, considering it was the only pub in Shepparton that had a decent band.

As we walked through the door, we stopped at a counter where a bouncer scanned our ID, which I found hilarious. *Hello, Mr Bean on steroids. I'm thirty-five, not seventeen!* I should've been flattered really, but I found it laughable when he scrutinised my licence with the utmost detail — then my face — then my licence again. He almost gave me a complex to the point where I was about to haul arse to a mirror and check to see I hadn't morphed into another person. Once he was satisfied that we were who our licences said we were, he waved us through the door.

We walked down maybe six or so steps and along a corridor into a spacious underground room.

Instantly, I noticed not only how busy the pub was, but also the large stage, and I saw that on it was a lovely black grand piano, a drum kit and all the equipment required of a band. It faced the bar which was approximately fifteen metres to our left, spanning that entire wall. We headed straight for it, and were lucky to secure the last three seats available.

Jen had chosen to be the designated driver as she wasn't in favour of a hangover with a 5 a.m. feed scheduled. And she and Carly had found a complete outfit for me to wear. I had on a pair of dark denim skinny jeans, black pumps, a white drapey singlet top, and a long, layered gold necklace. Carls had also put long loose curls through my hair, giving me a new look. She had, however, tried to convince me to chop it short, but to trust her with a pair of scissors, especially after the 'lipstick lips' I had left on her forehead that morning, would have been a stupid decision on my behalf.

Jen hadn't seen Carly for approximately a year, so while they caught up on each other's lives, I thought I'd catch up on a much needed trip to the toilet.

'I'll be back in a minute,' I informed them as I made my way to the ladies room.

Beginning the treacherous journey to the loo, I began weaving in and out of person upon person when I happened across a small group of tradesmen. When I see groups like this, I always know when at least one of them is going to make a smartarse remark, because they snigger amongst themselves and then look at the one who either has the biggest balls or who has had the most to drink and thinks he is God's gift to women. I spotted the particular 'tool' in this bunch and prepared myself for the derogatory comment which would be fired my way.

'Hey, I like a hot cougar. If you are looking for a seat, I've got one right here,' he offered, pointing to his lap.

I kept my steady pace and, as I passed them, I stared him down. 'Cougar? Really? If I were a cougar I'd bite your fucking head off, you stupid shit.'

I smiled mockingly at him, and continued on my way to the toilet.

* * *

Pub toilets are always very interesting. Upon entering, you are automatically greeted with a queue of at least three other women, because for some reason, there are never more than two cubicles. Then, while you wait, you become passively informed by the many who are waiting along with you of their personal lives. If that is not riveting enough, when you finally get into the cubicle, you put your quadriceps through hell as you squat, hovering just above the filthy toilet seat for fear of touching it. And, while your thighs tremble and burn, you gain the life-changing information written on the cubicle walls.

So far, I'd read, 'Shaz Luvs Mick 4 Eva', 'Sally Jones was here in 07', and how to play 'Shithouse tennis'.

After looking from one side of the cubicle to the other and back again, stupidly falling for the idiot game in the first place, I soon discovered there was an absence of toilet paper. *Fear not, Alexis, you are a human tissue box at the moment.* I secretly applauded myself for having a tissue and not having to vigorously shake.

Finishing up the wonderful ritual of pub-toileting, I squirted the liquid soap, not in my hand, but on the vanity top and then made my way back to the bar. But not before being greeted with a wolf-whistle from my tradesman 'friend'.

I politely flipped him the bird and stepped up my pace, now desperate for something alcoholic.

'Fuck, I hope that clear-looking drink is either gin or vodka and that it is for me?' I stated and, before waiting for an answer, consumed it.

The look on my face must've said it all, because Carly burst into laughter and Jen looked annoyed.

'Jen. Water ... really?' I flagged down the barman.

'Yes, water. And I'll have another one, thanks.' She was clearly annoyed that she was now without a drink. So I ordered two shots of Black Sambuca for Carly and me, followed by Malibu with Coke, and replaced Jen's water supply.

All three of us tapped our glasses together, toasting to a good night ahead, but were interrupted by a god-awful squeal from a microphone, along with the annoying tap that usually followed.

'Excuse me, everybody, but I need to inform you that Rural Science will not be playing tonight due to unforeseen circumstances,' a balding middle-aged man explained.

A few of the patrons voiced their disappointment with boos and hisses.

The man put his hands up to reassure the rowdy crowd. 'Now, now, the replacement band, Live Trepidation, are very good and they will be starting in just a minute.' *Ah, crap! I was looking forward to Rural Science.*

The man, who I assumed was the manager, exited the stage as the members of Live Trepidation began to make their way onto it.

Grabbing the microphone, the lead singer repeated the aggravating tap before introducing the rest of the band. There was something about him that looked familiar, but I couldn't place it. I'd probably seen them play before, elsewhere.

Tapping his drumsticks four times, the drummer counted the other members in, and the sounds of 'Vertigo' by U2 filled the room. Already I liked the replacement band. What a great song to kick off with. It appeared that everyone else seemed to think the same as the atmosphere in the room went from doubtful to relief almost instantly.

They played another six songs or so then took a break.

'I really like them, they're great! I wonder if they are local or from Melbourne?' I said, more to myself than anyone else.

'I'd say they are from Melbourne, Lex. They don't look like a typical country town band,' Carls replied.

'Yeah, you're probably right.'

I reckoned Steph would've liked them, too, so I made a mental note to look into it when I returned home.

Spinning our chairs back round to where the barman was already standing before us, I noticed he was patiently waiting to serve the next round.

'What's it going to be this time, ladies?'

He was sort of cute, in a boy-next-door kind of way, but with an edge to him. Instantly, I thought he could be just the type of guy Carly might like to have a bit of fun with. I looked at her, but she was fixated on someone across the room, so I gave her a nudge.

'What do you want to drink, Carls?'

'You pick. I've got my eye on that hottie over there in the black shirt.'

Jen and I both looked in the direction she was pointing.

'That's Leigh. Sorry, he's engaged,' cute barman said in response.

We all spun back round to face him, and he shrugged his shoulders apologetically.

'Aw, shit. Right, I'm scanning again.' Carly rotated once more and began searching the room.

I smiled and raised my eyebrows at the barman. 'What about you, Mr Barman, are you taken?'

He gave me a cheeky grin. Carls, however, was oblivious to my matchmaking session, so I kept my scheme alive by gathering further information.

'What's your name?'

'Lucas.'

'Well, Lucas, are you single or not?'

Jen laughed, seeming to enjoy herself a little more after I had convinced her to have at least one drink. She was no longer breastfeeding so there was no harm. And one drink would not lead to a hangover, not even for her!

'Single,' he replied with a smile. *Excellent!*

'Hey, Carls, meet Lucas.'

She didn't turn round. Instead, she hit me on the arm just as the band began their next set with 'November Rain' by Guns N' Roses. I recognised the song straightaway because I loved it; it had to be one of my all-time favourite songs. And whoever was playing the piano was very good. I would've glanced over at them, but I was having too much fun with Lucas.

'Lucas, Carly is thirty-five and single. She likes dancing, beaches, and long walks on the sand ...'

Jen and I began to giggle. Even Lucas thought it was funny.

'Alexis.'

'Yes, Carly?' I said in a playful tone. I then raised my eyebrow at Lucas. 'Now it's your turn.'

'No, Alexis —'

'What?' *It's just harmless matchmaking.* I looked at her, but she was looking at the band. 'I'm just having a little fun. Anyway, he's cute, what have you got to lose?' I winked at Lucas.

'No, Alexis, isn't that Bryce? Up on stage?' *What the fuck?*

I spun round far too quickly and if had it not been for my legs slamming into the person next to me, I would have performed a complete 360. I frantically scanned the stage, but didn't see him. The only people with spotlights on them were the lead singer and the pianist. So it was the brunette sitting at the piano who I recognised first.

I gasped. 'It's Lucy, oh my god!'

She looked up, finding my position, and displayed the smirk that she and Bryce must have inherited at birth. *What the hell?* My cheeks flushed. Then, I spotted Bryce, standing on the stage in shadow, and my entire body reacted to his presence.

There was no way I could mistake that silhouette, let alone mistake the sensation that now pulsed in between my legs, a sensation only he could trigger.

My heart started pounding in my chest as I realised he was on that stage for me. But it wasn't until the lead singer began his vocals that I also realised this song was chosen to deliver me a message, the message contained in the song's lyrics.

I listened to the words Bryce was delivering through the song. He was telling me that when he looked into my eyes he could see my love for him was now restrained. Which it was, and I hated that it was. But he had gone behind my back and, when I had given him the opportunity to confess what he was hiding, he had chosen not to.

I desperately wanted to close my eyes so that he could not read me so easily, but it was impossible. I removed my stare from his shadowy figure which looked sexy as hell.

Knowing that he was looking at me, I felt the heat that radiated from his shadowy, burning gaze as he watched my reaction to the message he was delivering.

Jen raised her voice just enough to ask Carly which one he was.

Carls pointed directly at him. 'That taller one. Over there, with the guitar.'

'I can't really see him, it's too dark,' Jen complained.

'Just wait, you won't miss him, I promise.'

Carly was spot on. There was not one woman in that room who would miss him when those lights switched on. He was like a magnet that drew you to him. And right now I was magnetised by him and his message, a message that continued to convey his understanding of how I felt.

He knew it was hard for me to love him now, but I had done it before and I could do it again. And he was telling me that he would wait for me and give me the time on my own if I needed it. *Jesus, he's good, he knows just how to communicate with me.*

The lights came on and he began to play. *Oh, holy fuck! He is sensational. He is up on stage, playing the guitar in a song that gives me chills and he is playing it for me.*

Jen made a strangled, moaning noise. 'God, you're right, I know what you mean.'

From out of the corner of my eye, I could see her fanning her face, then stopping abruptly when she realised what she was doing.

Feminine wolf-whistles started sounding throughout the room, along with a few shoutouts about the 'hotness factor' of the guitarist. He, as per usual, was oblivious to the salivating women around him and only had eyes for me as he made his way off the stage, casually playing his chords and heading my way. *Oh, shit!*

I watched the amp cord connected to his guitar unravelling as he made his way toward me with a security guard in tow, making sure the extra-long cord did not get in anybody's way.

The muscles in between my legs started to tremble and wake up from their many days of solitude. And as I watched his damn sexy as hell, slow and seductive walk in my direction, my heart skipped a few beats.

'He's coming over here,' Jen whispered to Carly.

Everyone in the room seemed to follow him, as this was an unusual display from a pub band. It was also due to the fact he looked unbelievably hot, and everyone knew the guitar solo was not too far away.

Stopping his sexy walk directly in front of me, he gave me one hell of a smirk. I held my breath and offered one back then watched as he played the solo.

Again, I was in awe, watching with sheer pleasure as his fingers move with fast precision up and down the fingerboard, like they were simply put on this earth to do only that. Of course, I knew that was not the case, as his fingers were quite capable of performing many other wonderful things; things that I knew I had to experience again and, in order to do that, I had to forgive him.

He finished the first solo, stood back and eyed me ferociously. *Oh, Mr Clark, you know I will cave for you, and you know just how to make me do it.*

I remembered what that look meant the last time he finished playing for me, and I desperately wanted it to mean the same thing. Just the thought of it had me aching for his cock. It was simply uncontrollable. *I hate you right now. I hate you.*

I let out my breath, a breath I was not sure how long I had been holding. I'm assuming it was a while though, because my chest was hurting and I was panting for the need of more oxygen. *Fuck, I must look like a bitch in heat. Stop panting like a dog, Alexis!*

He finished the second solo, leaned in, kissed me on the cheek and then whispered in my ear: 'I will give you time on your own, if you really want it.'

Pulling away, he searched my eyes. I could see his sorrow and hope that I did not need the time he was offering me, so I shook my head slightly and mouthed the words 'kiss me'. He didn't hesitate and grabbed my face, planting a passionate but quick kiss on my lips.

Pulling away again, he displayed his irresistible smile then basically jogged back to the stage ready for the end of the song — the security guard frantically scooping up the amp cord behind him.

I turned to Carly who had nearly fallen off her seat, and then looked at Jen who resembled the big mouth at Luna Park.

'He is good, really good,' Jen said, simply stunned. I had tried to warn her of the enormity that was Bryce, but I guess she hadn't taken me seriously.

Lucy began to emphasise the piano lead-in to Bryce's finish as he stepped up onto a chair then on top of the piano just like Slash had in the song's film clip. I laughed and clapped my hands at his showmanship. Then, right before he began the coda to the end, he pointed at me, winked and played the absolute shit out of it.

I was in love. It was one of the best performances I think I had ever witnessed, and that wasn't because his performance was for me. It was simply because he was superb.

Everyone cheered for the spectacle he had just put on in front of them, but they also cheered at the sheer brilliance of his guitar playing. He was fantastic and everyone loved it.

Bryce held that last note till it died down then jumped off the piano and put his Les Paul guitar on top of it.

Turning around, he made his way toward me. *What do I do?* I knew exactly what I wanted to do and couldn't help myself. I pushed off my stool and ran to him, jumping up and wrapping my legs around his waist.

I swear the room went completely silent as our lips met and, as they met, the unbearable torment of waiting for their reunion — together with the desperate craving and withdrawal I had felt over the last few days — vanished. At first, it felt as if we were the only two people in the room, until I realised the room was not silent at all. In fact, the roar and applause were deafening.

I had been physically and mentally empty for the past few days. But now, as Bryce thrust his tongue into my mouth and clenched my arse with force, he filled the void, making me feel somewhat satisfied again. And he seemed to do it so easily.

Walking me out of the room and into the area the band went for intermission, we continued the reunion of our mouths, desperately and aggressively ravaging each other. I ran my hands through his hair as he pressed me to him tightly, and if it weren't for the fact that we needed to inhale oxygen, I probably would not have pulled away.

Our noses were resting on each other's as we caught our breath, and as he went to revive our kissing, I stopped him.

'Wait, Bryce,' I panted. 'We need to talk.'

'Then talk, my love.'

'Not here.'

'Where?'

'Upstairs.' I caught his fiendish smile so raised my eyebrow at him. 'It's not what you're thinking.'

'It's only a matter of time, Alexis,' he said confidently.

I had to agree. It would be only a matter of time before we were fucking each other senseless again. Our cravings and need for one another were just too strong.

Unwrapping my legs, he set me down, and we walked back into the still-cheering and crowded room. As I led him to the bar, he signalled the band with his thumbs-up. They all reciprocated, even Lucy.

We stopped in front of Carls and Jen and, as per usual, no one could find any words.

'Jen, this is Bryce. Bryce this is my younger sister, Jen.'

He took her hand and kissed the top of it, prompting her to turn a shade of crimson and look to me in horror. I smirked. *I think that fucking smirk is now contagious.*

'Carls, you've met Bryce.'

'Yes, I most certainly have.' She shot her hand out ready for it to be kissed, too. Bryce humbly obliged her forwardness.

'We need a few moments upstairs,' I explained, looking at Jen apologetically.

Jen knew exactly what I wanted to discuss with him, so smiled in return. Carls, on the other hand, had her mind well and truly in the gutter.

'Yes, it appears the two of you definitely need a room.'

I glared at her as Bryce hastily led me upstairs.

'Do you know where we are going?' I asked as he practically dragged me out of the room.

'Up.'

'Yes, I gathered that, but where?'

'Anywhere.'

* * *

Moments later, we were heading up a few flights of stairs, past the accommodation levels, and to a door which read 'Rooftop Garden'. Fortunately, there was nobody else up there. So, as I stepped out onto the rooftop and into the warm autumn night air, I watched as Bryce rolled a rather large, heavy potted plant in front of the door in order to prevent anyone from disturbing us. Then, taking a step back, he brushed his hands together, looking quite happy with himself.

Our eyes met and it was all the invitation he needed to make his way toward me, once again displaying a sexy expression of desperate need.

As he closed the gap between us, I threw my arms around his neck, our lips and tongue reuniting automatically. I went up on tiptoes for the need of additional height which was when he wrapped his arms around my waist and lifted me, spinning us both around.

Deep down, I knew I needed to stop him, to let him know that I now had boundaries and rules. I also had to let him know that I was not putty in his hands and that I could resist him if I wanted to. The problem was, I obviously did not want to resist him, and he knew it.

'Bryce?'

'Uh huh?' he murmured, clearly not wanting to separate our mouths.

'Stop kissing me.'

'No, are you crazy?'

I giggled, which seemed to do the trick and broke the kiss. So I pulled away while I had the chance and looked into his compelling eyes, eyes filled with complete joy, eyes filled with love for me.

'Sit down. I have a few things I need to say.'

He sighed then conceded. 'I know.'

We walked over to the patio setting near the brick balustrade and took a seat. I inhaled a few deep breaths and quickly ran over a few things in my head before actually opening my mouth to speak. *Right, do it.*

'Rick came up Tuesday and stayed over,' I informed him while watching his body turn rigid.

'He needed to see the kids, and they needed to see him. It also gave us a chance to talk.'

He didn't move. Instead, just sat there quietly, letting me speak.

'I'm not angry with him any more, and I'm not angry with you any more either. Don't get me wrong, I'm fucking hurt by what you both did, but I've also come to realise it's partly my fault as well.'

Bryce went to object, so I hushed him, not only with my finger and a sharp 'Shh', but also with my piercing stare.

'Yes, *I am* partly at fault,' I reiterated. 'I flirted with you and crossed too many lines when I shouldn't have. And that was wrong. Rick deserved better. That being said, he knows he fucked up, and he knows he should never have accepted the money. He also realises that you and I are in love, and pointed out that if he had recognised that fact before accepting your money, he would never have taken it.'

I watched Bryce roll his eyes and it pissed me off. 'Don't sit there and fucking mock him,' I snarled, my tone seeming to shock him. 'Rick and I have been together for a very long time, Bryce, and he loves me very much. So, yes, I believe him when he says he has made a huge mistake.'

I glared at him and he shifted in his seat, showing the first sign of worry.

'You should never have offered him money. Did you not stop to think for one second that I would find out eventually?'

'I knew you would find out.'

'Yet you did it anyway, knowing how disgusting, hurtful and wrong it was. I knew you were hiding something from me, and I gave you many opportunities to confess. Instead, you chose to lie to me by omission.'

He leaned forward and clasped both his hands together.

'Yes, I knew how wrong it was. It tore me apart every time I saw the hurt you felt, and every time you blamed yourself. It fucking killed me, Alexis. And it frightened the hell out of me to think that when you found out what I had done, you would leave me. I couldn't tell you because I had to show you just how much I loved you first, to make you see that no matter what happened we would overcome anything. Honey, don't you see? All I could do before the truth came out was to convince you that we belonged together, and that I couldn't possibly love anybody as much as I love you. You know that, don't you?' *I do, how could I not?*

'Yes, I know you love me. But things have changed. Rick did not cheat on me, and that was a big factor in deciding I was going to start a new life again.'

Bryce glared his eyes and clenched his fist.

'What?'

'Nothing, I just don't believe it.'

'Don't believe what?'

'That Claire set him up.'

'You saw the photos, it was clear he didn't want her there.'

'Things aren't always what they seem, Alexis. I will find out the truth.'

'You need to stop with the creepy research. It's wrong.'

'No. Research plays a vital part of what I do and who I am. What I need to do is make sure my research is foolproof, which obviously it wasn't in this case.'

'No, Bryce, it wasn't,' I snapped.

We sat there in silence for a minute, stubbornly assessing each other.

'I've decided I am now single ... unattached ... neutral. Switzerland if you like,' I said resolutely, breaking a silent war of stares.

He let out a laugh and sat back, smirking.

'Do you find that funny?' I asked, trying not to smirk myself.

'Yes, very.'

'Why?'

'Because you are not single, Ms Summers, you are mine.'

He eyed me possessively which made me lean forward with a confident, lust-fuelled stare.

'Correction, Mr Clark, I was yours. I am not any more. I am no one's; not yet anyway.'

CHAPTER
21

Bryce grabbed my face and sealed my mouth with a hungry kiss. I gave into him for a second, then bit his lip and pulled back. He clenched his fist and twitched his eye but still looked amused, obviously not taking me seriously.

'Bryce, I'm serious. I am now single. Rick will stay at his parents' house until he has bought himself a nice new home with the money you gave him. Therefore, I am now single and officially on the market.'

He ran his hand through his hair, contemplating what I had just said, then raised his eyebrow and shook his head in conceit. 'In that case, can I ask you out on a date?'

I felt my face morph into a smile, even though I willed it not to. 'Yes, you can, anybody can.'

'No, they can't.'

'Yes, they can,' I said scornfully. 'It's up to me whether I say yes or no.'

'Can Rick ask you on a date?' *Ah, now you are getting it.*

'Yes, Bryce, he can and he will. He has told me he is not going to give up on us. He wants a new start, and like I said before, I am now unattached and available.'

He leaned forward, grabbed hold of my chair and dragged it closer to him, until we were practically nose to nose. 'You are not available, my love. If he wants to fight for you, I will show him exactly what a fight is.' *Oh, shit, he is so lusciously protective and sexy and possessively hot.*

'Tell me something, honey. When he touches you here ...' he said in a low, alluring voice while placing his hand on my thigh. 'When he touches you here, do you feel what you are feeling now?'

I whimpered at his touch. *No, not really, not for a long time anyway.* I didn't say anything because he already knew the answer. He opened my legs and ran both hands up them, then grabbed hold of my arse and lifted me onto his lap.

'Do you honestly think he can fight for you over me?' *Don't answer that, Alexis.*

I ran my hands through his hair and he gave a low groan, making me clench my pelvic floor muscle.

'I have to give him a chance,' I said softly. 'Our whirlwind romantic week is over, and it's now back to reality for me. I have a home to keep, kids to clothe, feed, wash, love and play with. I cannot just abandon all that.'

He gave me a curious look. 'Why would I think you'd abandon that?'

'I don't know. We've never really discussed me as a package.'

He gripped me tighter and looked me up and down. 'And you are quite the package, my love.'

I smiled at his compliment. 'Seriously, Bryce, I know you want me, you have made that very clear. But do you want me *and* my children? That's the question.'

I hopped off his lap and walked to the brick balustrade. The view from this rooftop was somewhat ordinary compared to the penthouse, as it did not have the dramatic effect, nor the perspective that being forty-three floors up can give you. Instead, when I looked down from my current position, I found one man taking a piss which was no assistance whatsoever when trying to untangle my head. *Nice!*

Bryce walked over and put his back to the wall. 'I want you, only you ...'

My heart sank, what did I expect? That he would want to wake up one day and automatically have two children?

'I want you, honey, and your children are a part of you. So, yes, I want your children, too.'

I turned to look at him.

'I love kids, and although I've only met Nate and Charlotte once, I can see so much of you in them both. There is no way I would not want them and love them.'

The relief I felt at his words was enormous.

'They would have to want you too, you know? You might have impressed me with your incredible good looks, hot body, mind-blowing bedroom antics, guitar playing and cooking skills, but that will not work on them.'

He crossed his arms. 'Two words my love: helicopter and 4Life.' He raised his eyebrows at me, which made me laugh.

'Funny that, because that's probably all it's going to take.'

Pulling me to him, he secured me in his arms. 'I will do anything to have you in my life. Whatever it takes, I will do it.'

I kissed him again, not wanting to wait a second longer. I missed the taste of his mouth, the smell of his skin, the feel of his hair through my fingers as I grabbed it. I missed his sometimes short, rough stubble that prickled my cheeks and tickled my neck as he made his journey south. I missed the way my body responded to his touch, from the tingling in my lips to the moan that resonated from within my throat. I missed how the muscles in my pelvis would clench and pulse, the way my nipples would firm and how my leg would sometimes automatically lift for him to take hold of. All these things came to life from just one simple touch.

'I want my cock inside you,' he groaned.

'I want your cock inside me, too,' I panted, 'but I don't sleep with men before I date them.'

He broke away from me. 'Well, let's go on a date, now!'

I laughed at his plea. 'Sorry, I'm busy.'

Bryce's smile indicated that he found my playfulness amusing. 'When are you available, Ms Summers?'

'Well, let's see ... tomorrow is out. And Saturday I'm going dancing with my girlfriends. Sunday is a school night —'

'You don't go to school,' he interrupted.

I retorted with squinted eyes. 'Monday, I go back to work.'

He smiled.

'Um, I'll call you, okay?'

'Monday. I am not waiting any longer than Monday.'

'Well, that depends if my boss keeps me late on Monday.'

'He might just do that.'

'Good. Now come on, I need to go back downstairs. Plus there is a really good band on tonight and the lead guitarist makes me wet when he plays.'

I went to leave, but he held my hand out at full stretch.

'I will not lose you again, *ever!* If you want me to fight for you I will, but it will only prolong the inevitable.'

I stepped back toward him. 'Bryce, it's not about you fighting for me or proving your love. It's not about a competition between you and Rick. It's about me and my children finding our feet without their father, about reassessing what we want and need as a family.'

'You need and want me.'

I turned and pulled him to follow. 'Fuck, you are infuriating.'

He laughed and trailed behind, grabbing my hips and whispering in to my ear, while rubbing himself against me. 'Fuck, your arse in denim does things to my cock.'

I loved his sexy compliments. 'Shut up and move this potted plant.'

* * *

We walked back into the bar and a couple of slightly intoxicated men gave Bryce their manly approval by commenting on our absence.

'Nice work, mate. That didn't take you long.'

'You showed her how it's done!'

He tensed ever so slightly, so I squeezed his hand to reassure him that they did not bother me at all. If anything, their behaviour was laughable.

We stepped up to the bar and if my eyes were not deceiving me I swear I'd just caught Carls writing something on the back of a coaster before slipping it to Lucas. *Nice work, Carls!*

We found Jen in deep discussion with Lucy, the two of them seeming very comfortable with each other. Well ... until we stopped right next to them, and they both stopped talking.

'Lucy, I've missed you,' I confessed, giving her a hug. 'You were fantastic up on stage.'

'Well, the performance obviously worked!' she said while shooting her brother a knowing smile.

'Yes, but we have a lot of things to work through and sort out. So let's just say it is a work in progress,' I answered.

Jen smiled and nodded in approval.

'So, Alexis, seeing as we are now dating, can I buy you a drink?' Bryce asked, in a somewhat sarcastic tone.

I rolled my eyes at him but secretly loved his naughty little stab at me. 'Yes, I'll have A Good Fuck thanks.'

Jen dropped her jaw in surprise and then realised that I had actually asked for a drink. *Well, technically a drink ... yes. But truthfully ... I want the non-liquid form.*

Bryce squeezed my hand again, this time, a lot firmer. And, guessing that was not the only thing that got a lot firmer, I strategically moved ever so slightly, placing myself in front of him and subtly pressing my arse into his groin. His dick twitched against me, confirming what I had thought.

'What's in A Good Fuck?' he asked, still playing along. *Only two ingredients: you and me, Mr Clark.*

'Vodka, sambuca, orange juice and crushed ice,' I answered, turning to him and smiling satisfactorily.

He recognised that I knew this was not the 'Good Fuck' he was referring to. 'Very well, anyone else?'

'I haven't had A Good Fuck since the baby, so yeah, count me in,' Lucy replied.

Bryce turned to his sister — his face priceless — but also giving the impression that he did not know whether to laugh or cup his ears with his hands.

'Yeah, me too. It's been a long time in between Good Fucks for me, so I'm in.'

Jen's acceptance of Bryce's offer also had his face slightly twisted.

'I'm always up for A Good Fuck,' Carls interjected.

With all of us on board, we were now set for a round.

* * *

Bryce and Lucy joined the band for their last set on stage, and I watched with thorough enjoyment their interaction as they performed — they really did share a special bond.

The other members of the band were also good, and I was really looking forward to getting to know them. If I was going to be completely honest, I was looking forward to meeting everyone who was a part of Bryce's life. I wanted to know everything about him.

After the performance, we stayed and had a couple more drinks. Jen and Bryce had a long chat while Lucy and I made another harrowing trip to the toilet. And Carly seemed to have taken a liking to Lucas, flirting with him right up until we dragged her out of the bar.

* * *

Standing outside by the car, Bryce had his arms wrapped around me.

'Where are you staying?' I asked.

'I had hoped you and I would fly back to the city tonight,' he responded as he dragged his nose up my neck.

'Had you just? Are you allowed to drink and fly?'

'Um, actually no, so I think I will need to sleep here with you.'

'Do you think that after a date at a regional pub where you bought me A Good Fuck, I'd actually then give you a good fuck? Sorry, Mr Clark, I'm not that easy.'

A low growl sounded from deep within his throat, the sexy as hell growl he always made right before he ravished me until I climaxed and screamed his name. 'Alexis, honey, you are fucking killing me.'

I stood up on my tiptoes and kissed him softly with the intention of calming his raging need for me. 'I know, I'm sorry. I have to go home tonight then wake up with my kids and take them home tomorrow, but,' I placed my finger on his lips, 'I might be able to convince the girls to go dancing at say ... Opals, tomorrow night? So, if you are lucky, you might just see me there. And if you do, you can buy me another drink, maybe this time A Screaming Orgasm.' I unwrapped his hands from around my waist and blew him a kiss, then climbed into Jen's 4WD.

* * *

'Alexis Elizabeth Summers!' was all Jen could manage to say as we drove away from the pub.

'Yes, Jennifer Ann Blaxlo-Scott?' I replied, wearing a smirk. *Yes, they are freakin' contagious!*

'I can see why you have fallen head over heels for Bryce Clark. He is such a —'

'A fucking clit-clenching, sexy beast?' Carly butted in.

I cracked up laughing.

'Well ... yes, but that's not what I was going to say. What I was going to say was, he is very charming and obviously adores you something chronic,' Jen explained.

I let out a long sigh and smiled simultaneously. 'Yes, he does.'

'So what did you talk about while you were gone upstairs? You did talk, didn't you?' Jen asked while raising a questioning eyebrow.

'Yes, Jen, we did talk. I didn't fuck him on the roof if that is what you are insinuating.'

'Why not? I would have, especially after that performance. Fuck,' Carly chimed in.

'Not helping, Carls. Yes, we talked. I told him I have forgiven him and Rick, and that I am now single and sorting my life out. I told him that if he wanted me, he would have to date me like any other normal couple would do.'

Carls started laughing. 'I love it, you little whore.'

'Carls.'

'Sorry, I love it, you little two-timing minx.'

I giggled at her correction. 'I'm not two-timing. Okay well maybe I am. But it's more to do with starting fresh and seeing who I want to be with. There's nothing wrong with that, is there?'

'I think it's obvious who you want to be with,' Jen added.

She was right, it was obvious. I couldn't resist Bryce. I couldn't resist the attraction we had, the chemistry, nor the insatiable urge to taste one another. Then there was Rick. I still loved him, I know I did. But was it a mutual respect kind of love, or was it the passionate kind? *Shit, maybe this whole dating thing is not such a good idea. It will probably confuse me even more.*

'Maybe it is, maybe it isn't. I don't have to decide right away though, that's the beauty of it, Jen. I have all the time in the world.'

She shot me an uncertain glance then drove us back home.

* * *

On Friday morning, the kids and I rose early. We packed the car and said our goodbyes but, before leaving to return home, Mum and Dad hugged me tightly, just like they had when I was a youngster. It was the kind of hug you got when you needed reminding that you were still their little girl and could turn to them for anything. I thanked them for looking after the kids and for being wonderfully supportive, and for just being them, really.

Jen had driven home the previous night after she had dropped me and Carly off. I had kissed and hugged her through the driver's side window, thanking her for being 'Sister Of The Year' and my rock during times when I completely screwed things up.

She had kissed my cheek in return and told me to take my time when deciding who I loved the most, but to also be careful with Rick and Bryce's hearts. 'They obviously both love you,' she had explained. 'And you would not cope knowing you had destroyed one of them.'

Those words of advice had played on my mind as I drove the two-hour drive home. *No, I would not cope knowing I had destroyed one of them. It would, in turn, destroy me. But how do I avoid doing that? I can't be with them both, and I don't want to, I'm not like that.*

* * *

Rick greeted us after I parked the car in the garage.

'Dad!' Charlotte squealed as she unbuckled her seatbelt with lightning speed, launching herself out of the car and into her father's arms.

'Hello, my princess. Did you miss me?'

'Of course.'

Nate casually walked up to Rick and gave him a quick hug. 'Hi, Dad.'

'How's it going, mate?'

'Yeah, all right.' He dropped his head and went inside.

Rick shot me a confused expression. 'What's wrong with him?'

'He crashed his bike again. He's not hurt, but the bike is. Dad is going to have a look at it during the week.'

Rick shook his head and turned to go inside, still carrying Charlotte on his hip.

'Don't shake your head,' I called out. 'He's your son and, just like you, he has no fear on that bike.'

'You should talk. I think you have crashed more vehicles than me.'

'I was supposed to back then. It was called Crash 'n' Bash racing, remember?'

He opened the door and went inside. 'I rest my case, Alexis.'

Frustrated, I called out after the three of them, 'So I guess I'll bring in the bags then?'

Rick came back out, minus Charlotte, and leaned up against the car as I started to unload it. 'Did you get some time to think?'

Yes, but not enough time. 'Yes, I did.'

'And?'

'And what? Are you asking if I played "eeny, meeny, miny, moe" with the two of you?'

'No, babe. Have you made any decisions since Tuesday?'

'Yes, I have. The first one being, you cannot stay here. I want to be on my own.' I lifted the suitcase up and went to drag it, but he intercepted and placed it gently on the ground.

'For how long?' he asked, taking over the unloading of the car and not looking at me as he did it.

'For as long as I need to decide who I want to be with. You might not like to hear this, but I am torn between you both, and I am not ready to commit to either one of you. That's why I'm becoming single again.'

This statement caught his attention, because he stopped grabbing the bags and turned to look at me, his face displaying a little anger.

'You can't be serious?'

'Yes, I'm very serious. My wedding rings are off and staying off. I'm now officially single. So, if you want to ask me out on a date, go for it. If not, then I guess that is it. I'm not promising you anything, and I'm not promising Bryce anything, either. I will continue to work and support myself and if you don't like it, Rick, well, you now have five million dollars. I'm sure you will figure something out.'

'So, you want us to both fight it out for you?'

'No.'

'That's what it sounds like.'

'It can sound however you think it sounds. All I'm saying is I'm no longer tied to you. You untied me when you sold me, remember? If I want to go out with Bryce, I will. If you want to ask me out and I accept, then I accept. I'm starting fresh, with a clean slate. I don't know how else to do this. It's either that, or we end this now.'

He leaned back on the car. 'Lexi, I don't want to end it now, but I don't want to share you with Bryce, either.'

'And he doesn't want to share me with you. So it works both ways. I'm not trying to play both of you, really I'm not.

I'm just trying to assess who and what I want, and I can't do that unless I'm free to do it.'

'What have you told the kids?'

'Nothing yet, but you can stay here tonight in the spare room. Then stay wherever you like tomorrow night and the night after that and so on and so on. You can stay at your parents' house or a nice ritzy hotel room — apart from City Towers of course. Tomorrow night, though, I think perhaps you should take the kids to see your parents. They haven't seen them in months. I'm sure they would appreciate it.'

'And what are you going to do?'

'I'm going to go out with the girls.'

'So, it's going to be like that, is it?'

'Yes, I told you. I'm serious, you need to move out.'

He shook his head again. 'Fine, I'll take the kids to Mum and Dad's house tomorrow night. You do realise you are going to have to tell the kids something soon though. Nate is not stupid.'

'No, *I'm* not going to tell them anything. *We* are going to talk to them together, and we can do it on Sunday when you bring them home.'

I grabbed a few of the bags and went inside.

CHAPTER

22

After unpacking the kid's suitcases and tackling the laundry, also known as Mount Washmore, I was completely drained. I had to determine what we would have for dinner, let alone cook it, and I still had to ring Tash to find out if we were set for a night of dancing. I was actually looking forward to a day to myself, and thought maybe I could just soak in the bath for most of it with my favourite book. *Yes, you can ... but that is tomorrow, now is the time for dinner. Argh.* I missed my smirky chef. *What would he cook? Probably some delicious gourmet dish with something encrusted or infused with something else. Maybe I could conjure up something gourmet?*

I went to the fridge. *Nothing in here ...*

Nearly expired milk, a half-eaten packet of Tim Tams, the usual jars of condiments and a banana that looked like something that needed flushing down the toilet. *Well, there goes that idea. Guess what I'm doing tomorrow? Food shopping, how wonderful.* I kept searching through the kitchen in the hope there would be at least one thing edible. Thankfully, I found a tray of lasagne in the freezer. I had made it weeks ago, so we ate that and all watched a movie together.

The movie had been my idea, as a way to sit as a family without actually having to communicate with Rick. It was stupid, really, because if I was going to give him a fighting chance, I needed to do just that — communicate with him.

To be honest though, I was struggling, as the dynamics in our relationship had shifted. It was obvious that something between us had died and I was not sure if we could resuscitate it.

Watching the movie had been slightly awkward for two reasons. One: because *50 First Dates* was the only movie on TV. And two: Charli and Nate had both fallen asleep halfway through it, leaving Rick and I to watch it on our own.

Rick carried Charli into bed, and we both tucked her in after moving the pile of stuffed animals out of the way. Nate was next and I could see Rick strain as he lifted him.

'He's too old for this,' he complained.

'You try and wake him up. It's next to impossible sometimes. I guess he takes after you,' I said with affection for my not-so-little boy before turning out the light.

Rick closed the door behind us and then followed me to our room.

'You are sleeping in the spare room, remember?'

'Yes, I know. I'm just getting my pillow. Is that okay?'

I felt like such a bitch. 'Sorry, of course it is.'

Pulling out my hair tie, I noticed in the reflection of the vanity mirror that he had not yet left the room. I smiled at him. 'What? Did you forget something else?'

'You're worth fighting for, Lexi. If Henry could make Lucy fall in love with him every day in that movie we just watched, then surely I can make you fall in love with me again, too.' He stepped up to me and kissed me, slowly.

At first, I wanted to push him away. But there was something different in the kiss, and it left me feeling strangely uneasy, like I was now cheating on Bryce. *Fuck!*

'Good night, babe,' he said as he left our room.

* * *

The next morning Rick seemed different. He wasn't moping or shitty. Instead, he seemed relieved and happy, which I found to be really strange. He explained to the kids that they were going for a sleepover at their other grandparents' house.

Nate was not impressed that I would be missing the sleepover and asked why.

'I'm going out with friends, sweetheart.'

'You always go out!' he complained and stormed off to sit in the car, his arms crossed over his chest.

I blew him a kiss as Rick pulled away, but he turned his head, which broke my heart. He was right, I had been going out a lot lately, and I felt terribly guilty. But I had been cooped up at home for the past nine years, rarely going out at all. *He'll get over it, he always does.* I hoped he would. I had a lot to deal with at the moment, and the last thing I needed was having to sort out Nate's slight attachment issues. Don't get me wrong, I loved that he was a 'Mummy's boy', but at times, it got a little overbearing.

Right, to-do list: grocery shopping, vacuuming, bath and defuzzing with a razor. I grabbed my bag and shopping list and headed to the shops.

* * *

I hadn't planned on doing a full grocery shop as I was only going to get the bare essentials, but before I knew it I had piled in enough food to completely fill the trolley. Most of it was ingredients to attempt my own gourmet cooking, and I had also had to stock up on back to school lunchbox snacks.

Having a hell of a time trying to manoeuvre the over-stacked trolley that had a bung wheel, I groaned in frustration as I weaved up and down the aisles of the store. At first, I thought people were looking at me strangely because of my exasperated cart handling, but I soon realised the double takes and hushed whispering as I passed had absolutely nothing to do with the awkward trolley movements at all.

With a big heave, I swung the aggravating metal cart around the corner and nearly slammed into Lil.

She stepped back against the shelves, as if to insinuate I needed the entire aisle to get past. 'Coming through, coming through! Crazy lady with trolley!'

'Shit! Sorry.'

We gave each other a quick hug.

'How are you doing, Lex?'

'Yeah, not bad. Mind you, I feel like I have a note stuck to the back of my head or something. People keep giving me the weirdest looks and are whispering as I go by.' I pointed out two whispering women who were standing not too far from us.

'It's not a note, hon. You are somewhat of a celebrity around here now. The thing is, rumours and judgments go hand in hand with stardom.'

I gave her an odd look. 'What the fuck are you talking about, Lil? In English, please?'

'The whole town thinks you are having an affair with your rich boss.'

'What!' I shouted, then lowered my voice. 'What do you mean the whole town? Why? How?'

'You were on TV looking very cosy with Mr Hottie Clark. Plus, you know how the mummy mafia at school works.'

'It's the school holidays, Lil!'

'Since when does that matter? They spread gossip in their sleep. The fact it is school holidays is redundant. Look, don't worry about them, luv. It's all lies, anyway.'

I gave her a sheepish glance.

'Oh, maybe it's not then?' she enquired.

'So much has happened in the past fortnight, you have no idea.'

'I reckon I could have some idea?'

'I doubt that. Anyway, I promise I'll fill you in tonight at dinner.'

'You'd better.'

I gave her another quick hug then took off to face the rest of the judgmental idiots who knew nothing of my life.

* * *

After putting the shopping away, quickly tidying up the house, performing a complete top-to-toe wax session, soaking in the bath, reading half a book and drinking a nice cup of chai, it was time to get ready for my night out.

Flicking through my dresses, I came across the navy sequin batwing dress that I had wished I'd worn last time we went to Opals. *Perfect, that was easy.* I stewed over which pair of shoes to match with it, but eventually settled on my navy high heel Gucci's that I had bought myself for my 30th birthday.

Looking at my lifeless hair, I suddenly wished Carls were here with me, curling it like she had when we went to Shepparton. Instead, I went with my natural wavy locks and pinned some of it back.

Tash pulled up at 6 p.m. and let the entire neighbourhood know she was there with a rendition of 'Pop Goes the Weasel' from her car horn.

I opened the front passenger door and took a seat. 'Do you freaking mind? You're a lunatic.'

'What? Would you prefer the Minions 'Banana Song'?'

I laughed. 'Actually, I would.'

'You got it.' She started honking again while singing.

'Stop it,' I chided.

She stopped pressing the horn and, instead, we both sat there and finished singing the song ourselves.

'Okay, glad we now have that out of our system. So, how are you?'

I leaned over and gave her a hug. 'Good, hon, much better now. Minions make everything better!'

Tash and I absolutely adored the Minions from the movie *Despicable Me.* All four of our children had been watching it while we were away on holiday, and as soon as Tash and I had heard the little high-pitched voices coming from the TV, we were hooked. They were hilarious, and I believe that we had now watched the movie more times than the kids.

'Yes. That they do, Lex, but seriously, how are things going?'

'Tash, really, I'm fine. I've spoken to Brick and —'

'Brick?'

She gave me a quizzical look, and I couldn't help but laugh at my own stupid collective name for them.

'It's my collective name for Rick and Bryce.'

She laughed, too. 'I like it, but you're an idiot.'

'Thanks, I think? Anyway, I've spoken to Brick and have told them that I'm Switzerland.'

'You're Switz-a-what?'

'Switzerland. You know … neutral. I've kicked Rick out, and I am now single and available to date.'

She glanced over at me, unsure of the concept. 'What does Brick think about that?'

'It doesn't matter, hon, it's not their choice. Let's just say they have both asked me out on a date.'

She choked a little. 'Shit, if it wasn't so fucked up, it would be funny.'

'I hear ya. Oh, hey, I got you a present while I was away.' I reached into my bag and pulled out the spoon I had bought for her. She took it from me and unwrapped the tissue paper. The look on her face at first glance was one of 'gee, thanks, a spoon'. But when she figured out why I had bought it for her, she smiled brightly and started laughing.

'They look like boobs. That's great! Thanks, I'll add it to my rude-bits cutlery collection.'

I smiled. 'You're welcome, hon.'

She happily placed it in her glovebox and reversed out of my driveway.

* * *

We called past and collected Steph, Lil and Jade then made our way into the City Towers precinct for dinner. There were over twenty different restaurants in the complex, so the options were endless.

After much discussion, we all voted for Thai and made our way into The Green Pearl.

'A table for five, please,' I asked politely while glancing around the restaurant. It looked very busy.

'I'm terribly sorry, ma'am, but we are fully booked tonight.'

I turned around and pulled a sad face at the girls. 'Do you fancy Italian?'

They screwed up their faces, not keen on the idea.

'You could always drop Bryce's name,' Tash hinted.

'You're so funny, Tash,' I said, sarcastically.

'No, I'm serious.' She ignored me and started to speak slowly, like talking to a baby. 'Excuse me, sir. This is Mr Bryce Clark's girlfriend. You know, Mr Clark, the owner of the hotel?'

I was mortified but Steph, Jade and Lil were giggling.

'Tash, stop it,' I hissed, pinching her arm.

'What? Call him.'

'No, I'm not going to call him and stomp my feet like a spoiled brat because I can't get a seat.'

'You're dating him, aren't you?' she blurted out.

The girls all gasped.

'I knew it! I knew you'd shag him, Lex,' Jade declared, seeming pretty pleased with her prediction.

'Thanks a lot, Tash.' I glared at her.

'When were you going to tell us you'd split with Rick?' Steph huffed in an offended manner.

'Over dinner. It's very complicated.' I noticed that Tash had suddenly disappeared. 'Where's Tash gone?'

Lil pointed in Tash's direction. 'Over there, she's on her phone.'

I squinted at Tash, who was on the phone, except her phone did not have a silver case and my phone did. 'Hang on a minute, that's my phone. What is she doing on my phone? How the hell did she get it?' I quickly rummaged through my bag and confirmed that she had, in fact, stolen it. *What the fuck? She's the friggin' Artful Dodger.* Then it occurred to me why she had stolen it. 'You sneaky little bitch. Natasha Jones, you'd better not have done what I think you have!'

Her head shot up like a meerkat and she laughed while trying to get away. *Oh, my god, how old are we, again?*

'Come back here, I can't run in these shoes!'

She stopped and held the phone out to me with a satisfied look on her face, so I snatched it from her.

'You are going to pay for this, bitch.'

She smiled and kissed my cheek then skipped back to the girls. Hesitantly, I put the phone to my ear.

'Hello.'

'Hello, my love,' Bryce replied, his rich, sexy voice filling my ears. *Fuck, I knew it.*

'I'm so sorry. Tash is going to die for this.'

'You look so fucking hot in that short navy dress.' *What?* I looked around, my face already expressing my excitement with a rather large grin.

'You won't find me.'

'Where are you?'

'Not telling. I'll reveal myself when the time is right.'

'And when will that be?'

'You'll have to wait and see. You might just feel my hand on your arse when you least expect it.'

'What if it's someone else's hand that I feel?'

'Then whoever's hand it is, I'll break it. Your arse belongs to me, honey.'

'It does, does it?' *He is so possessively hot.*

'Yes, it does.'

'So what you are saying is that you are going to stalk me all night?'

'Yes. Now go and have dinner. Your friends are waiting for you.'

I spun back around to find that they were no longer standing at the door. Tash shot her hand up from a table within the restaurant and waved. I glared at her again and turned around once more.

'I didn't want to bother you with this, it's stupid.'

'Oh, honey, you eat anywhere you want to eat. You go anywhere you want to go, you got it?'

'No.'

'I'm going to make sure every employee in this complex knows you by sight so that this does not happen again.'

'Bryce, you wouldn't.'

'Yes, I would. You are dating the owner, after all.'

'Am I? We haven't officially gone on a date yet.'

'Alexis, stop arguing with me and go and have your dinner, or so help me god I will walk over to you now, pick you up and haul you over my shoulder.'

The idea excited me very much, but I knew not to call his bluff.

'Okay, you win. Oh, and by the way, thank you for this.'

'No thanks necessary.'

'Okay, I guess I will see you tonight sometime?'

'You can count on it.' He ended the call and I revelled in his exciting game, quickly scanning my surroundings one more time to try to spot his hiding place. Unfortunately, there were too many people, and I knew he would not show himself until he was ready.

Suddenly my phone rang, startling me. It was Bryce again. 'Yes, Mr Clark.'

'Stop looking for me.'

'How did you know I was here?'

'Tash rang me.'

'I know that, but how did you get here so quickly?'

'Who says I'm there?'

I looked around again and noticed the black domed security camera. 'Are you watching me on your security CCTV cameras?'

'Maybe. Maybe not.'

'You are so infuriating, now leave me alone. I'm hungry.'

He growled into the phone as I hung up, making me both giggle and involuntarily shiver, so I opted to tease him further by performing a catwalk and wiggling my arse as I walked over to the table where the girls were seated. Before I was able to make the complete journey to my seat, I received a text:

Fuck, I love your arse. — Bryce

I stopped and quickly typed a response:

If you're lucky, I might let you spank it. — Alexis

I'm the luckiest man alive. — Bryce

We'll see. — Alexis

I love you. — Bryce

I love you, too. Now seriously, leave me alone xo. — Alexis

Never. — Bryce

I decided I wouldn't respond, or we would be there texting each other all night. Putting my phone back into my bag, I sat down at the table with the girls.

I shot Tash a daring look. 'You, missy, are going to pay for that.'

'What? If you have the connections, use them! Anyway, I'm sure Bryce would've been pissed if he found out you were refused a table.'

She was right, of course, but that was not the point. I glared at her again just as a waitress came to the table with a round of cocktails.

'Four Beautiful Ladies for four beautiful ladies,' she said as she placed the drinks in front of the girls.

'And for you, Ms Summers, A Screaming Orgasm, courtesy of Mr Clark.'

The girls laughed as she placed it down in front of me. Granted, I did put in the request for this particular drink when we were saying our goodbyes in Shepparton, so I couldn't help but drop my head to the table in embarrassment, but of course, secretly loving his cheeky side. *He never ceases to amaze me.*

'If you don't want his Screaming Orgasm, Lex, I will take it!' Steph offered, already downing her Beautiful Lady and now eyeing my drink.

'Oh, no, hon. I'll have all his Screaming Orgasms, thanks,' I said, denying her request and sculling my drink.

'So are you going to fill us in or not?' Lil asked, waiting patiently for my response.

Steph put her drink down, and Jade dropped the menu. I looked at Tash and she shrugged her shoulders. Then, taking a breath, I let it all out in one fell swoop.

'Okay. Got back from our weekend. Rick said he'd had an affair. Went and fucked Bryce for a week. Rick came to hotel and said he had lied about the affair. I asked him why? He said Bryce paid him five million dollars to spend a week with me. So, long story short — I'm now single and sort of dating them both.'

Lil was dead silent.

Jade swore I was having them on.

And Steph thought it was hilarious, whether it was a lie or not.

'No, I'm serious, obviously there's more to it, but that's it in a nutshell.'

Jade looked confused, and seemed to be trying to get her head around the story. 'Hang on, so did Bryce pay Rick to tell you he'd had an affair? That arsehole! I'm not drinking his Beautiful Lady then.' She pushed it aside.

'No, again it's a long story. But essentially, Rick lied about the affair himself so that he could get the money. Bryce just offered to pay it as an incentive to have Rick let me spend a week with him.'

Steph was eyeing Jade's cocktail.

'Well, in that case, I will drink it.' Jade dragged it back in front of her.

The waitress came back and we ordered our meals. I explained a little more about what had happened, but I also kept a few details to myself.

'So, single Alexis, eh? Does that mean you can date anyone? I mean, other than Brick?' Tash asked with a mouthful.

'Brick, ha! I love it!' Jade laughed, obviously fond of Rick and Bryce's collective name.

'Well, yes, I suppose I could, but I don't want to.'

'Why would she want to date anyone other than Bryce, Tash?' Steph asked, looking dumbfounded.

'I don't know. She's single again. She could date anyone.'

'Hello, I'm still here,' I proclaimed. 'And no, I couldn't date just anyone. I'm not in my twenties, nor would I want to date just anyone. Can we change the subject, please? I'd really like to hear about your lives for once.'

'I'll start. I found the best pair of ruffle butt's today. They are so awesome. I am going to have my name embroidered on them.'

We all rolled our eyes at Tash.

'Anyone else, please?' I begged.

'Yeah, the concrete slab for our house will hopefully be poured on Monday.'

'That's great, Jade,' I replied excitedly, knowing she has been waiting so long for this turn of events. I forked a prawn from within my bowl of Pad Thai and put it in my mouth. 'How exciting, the house will be built in no time after that.'

'I'm getting a tattoo,' Lil chimed in, also forking one of my prawns.

I playfully flicked her fork away. 'Get out!'

'I'm getting some freedom and putting Holly in day care,' Steph added.

We continued our catch-up discussion over dinner, chatting about different tattoo designs, various house facades and the pros and cons of day care. Thankfully, they did not revert back to the topic of my love-life. Don't get me wrong, I was happy to fill them in, but to elaborate and discuss it exclusively was just a bit too much.

When we were ready to leave, I signalled the waitress for the bill. She smiled and bent down to speak to me discreetly. 'It has been taken care of, Ms Summers.' *Taken care of? Of course it has.* I stood up and patted my dress down.

'You're very lucky, Lex, lucky to have an obscenely rich man in love with you.'

'You know what, Steph? You're wrong. I'm lucky to have an obscenely romantic man in love with me. At the end of the day, I couldn't give a shit about the money.'

CHAPTER
23

Opals was packed to the rafters. There were people absolutely everywhere. It was a little too crowded for my tastes but we decided to go in anyway. I had not even made it a few metres through the door when a security guard approached me. *Shit, what have I done?*

He shouted over the sound of music. 'If you'd like to follow me, Ms Summers, we have a booth reserved for you and your friends.' *Mr Fuck-Me-Senseless-Clark, you think of everything.*

'Oh, thank you.' I turned to the girls. 'Follow us.'

We made our way through the crowd to a booth situated against the far wall. 'Security guy' motioned a barman to the table before leaving.

'Hi, I'm Kyle. I'll take care of your drinks tonight. So, what would you ladies like first?'

I wasn't really paying much attention. Instead, I was scanning the room, looking from wall to wall.

'Alexis?'

'What? Sorry.'

'What do you want to drink?' Lil asked.

'What you're having.'

I didn't normally drink what Lil did, so that answer was more than likely a mistake. Not that I really cared, though, because standing against the far wall near the bar was Bryce, looking terribly sexy in a black shirt. Or was it navy? *Who cares, he would look just as hot if it were fluorescent orange.* His sleeves were rolled up and the top two buttons undone, revealing just enough of his chest to make my mouth dry.

'I'll be back in a minute,' I explained, standing up quickly and taking off before any of them could ask where I was going or if they could come.

I zigzagged through a plethora of people on my way to the wall, catching a glimpse of him, only to have my view obstructed by someone else blocking my way. When I finally reached the spot I saw him standing in, I found it now vacated. He was gone. *I'm sure I saw him. No, I'm fucking positive.*

My phone vibrated in my hand and I second-guessed myself:

Honey, you fucking drive me wild. — Bryce

Mr Please-Fuck-Me-Now Clark, you are driving me wild. I tried to ring him but he didn't answer.

My phone buzzed again:

Uh-uh, Ms Summers. I think I will play with you just a little bit longer — Bryce

I typed a response:

Mr Clark, I want you to really come and play with me — Alexis

I kept scanning the crowd, aware that he couldn't be far. It was unbearable knowing he was close but not close enough.

Suddenly, I felt a tap on my shoulder. I spun round, ready to launch myself on him. Instead, I found Jade who would have gotten more than she bargained for.

'What are you doing?' she shouted over the music, cringing at the same time.

'I thought I saw Bryce, so I was just texting him,' I shouted back.

'You're a goner, aren't you?'

I knew what she meant. I was gone, gone way over the edge when it came to him.

'Yes, I think I was a goner from the first moment I met him.'

'I can't hear you, come to the toilet with me.'

She grabbed me by the hand and led me to the ladies room.

* * *

When I walked into the toilets at Opals, I was first struck by some minor comparisons to the ones at the pub. The queues were the same, regardless of the fact there were more cubicles ... and the simple reason for that was because there were a lot more people. The conversations overheard while waiting in line were also the same topics. It seemed that it didn't matter where in the world you were, there was always one backstabbing friend coming onto another girl's boyfriend.

The walls of the Opals toilet cubicles were spared the graffiti of Shaz loves Daz and, thankfully, there were no requests for a match of 'Shithouse Tennis'. However, the absence of toilet paper was unavoidable and, unfortunately, I had no pockets or stashed tissues this time around.

'Fuck!' I said, just a little too loudly.

'No toilet paper either?' grumbled Jade.

'Yeah.'

A high-pitched voice sounded from the cubicle next to me. 'Oh, I've got some.' Then, almost instantly, a tiny manicured hand appeared beneath the wall with a big bunch of toilet paper.

'Thank you, you're a life-saver,' I said gratefully, passing some under the wall to Jade.

'Thank fuck for that,' she exclaimed. 'I hate having to pretend I'm spinning a Hula Hoop.'

'You spin a Hula Hoop? That's great! I do a Tina Turner.'

She laughed. 'What, the fucking Nutbush?'

'No.' I laughed, nearly having to pee again. 'The little open-legged run on the spot.'

'Oh ... I'll try that one out next time.'

We both exited our stalls at the same time, unable to refrain from laughing when we looked each other in the eye. I didn't know about Jade, but I now couldn't help but picture her standing over the toilet bowl, moving her hips round and round. *Get that image out of your head, Alexis!*

'So, as I was saying out there in that noise, you are completely smitten with him, aren't you?'

I washed my hands — managing to catch the soap — and then looked up at her reflection. 'Yes, I have been all along.'

'What are you going to do about Rick?'

'I don't know. He was different last night, though. I can't put my finger on it. It was actually bugging me today.'

'Maybe he still has a chance, then?'

'I honestly don't know, Jade.'

My heart was telling me 'no'. Even my head was telling me 'no'. But there was something that was telling me 'maybe'.

And for the life of me, I couldn't put my finger on what that something was.

'Don't take this the wrong way, Lex, you know I love you dearly. But don't lead them on. Decide who it is going to be and do it quickly. Or stop seeing them both and take your time. You can't date them, fuck them, love them, whatever them, at the same time. It's not fair, and it's just not you.'

I moved on to the hand dryer. 'I know, Jade. The biggest part of me wants to continue what I've started with Bryce. We are so in sync with each other, it's not funny. We can communicate with just our eyes and mouths, and he just simply satisfies me in every way possible.'

I kept drying my already dry hands.

'But?' *Is it that obvious there is a but?*

'But, I don't know how to say goodbye to Rick, especially after this fuck-arse feeling I got last night.'

'Lex, sweetie. Your hands are already dry.'

Jade was waiting and leaning against the wall. *Oh.* 'You feel this way about Rick because you have spent half your life with him. Saying goodbye to someone you have been with that long is not easy.'

'Exactly, not to mention that I'm still confused.'

'Why?' she asked with her arms crossed.

'Really? You need to ask why?'

'Well, no, but I want you to say why you think you are confused out loud. Sometimes saying it out loud can help clarify it.'

I sighed. 'Okay, Rick never actually cheated on me, right? Therefore I shouldn't feel the reluctance toward him that I do. The thing is I can't seem to help it. Last night, when he kissed me, it was different. Not in a way where I thought, "Oh my god, I want more," but in a way where I thought, "Who are you? I don't know you any more." When I forgave them both, I still harboured anger toward Rick, but not so much at Bryce, which in hindsight, doesn't seem fair. I guess I'm confused because I think that Rick and I have both changed and, because of this, I'm not sure I can give him an equal chance.'

'Well, maybe that's your answer.'

'But I owe him a chance, don't I?'

'Do you? It seems to me he had a chance and he blew it. I mean, who allows their wife to sleep with a hot billionaire just so they can get money?' She put her arm around my shoulder. 'Come on, stop torturing your conscience about it, and let's get out of here. I want to burn some calories on that dance floor.' *Yes, I think I definitely need to do that.*

As I followed Jade out of the bathroom, my phone buzzed again:

Where do you think you are going, sexy? — Bryce

I quickly typed as I continued to walk:

Keep watching, my love, and you'll find out. — Alexis

We sat down at the table and I gagged as I swallowed the Bourbon and Coke Lil had ordered for me. My little talk with Jade had given me a new perspective on my Brick situation, and I was now ready to clear my head and have a good night.

'So, who wants to dance?' I asked, eagerly.

They all put their hands up.

'Excellent! Let's go!'

We made our way onto the crowded dance floor, crowded being a euphemism — it was freakin' crazy! Regardless, I loved going dancing with my girlfriends. The thing was, when you were in a busy nightclub such as Opals, there was nothing worse than a drunk sleazeball sliding on over to where you were dancing and completely getting up into your face. Granted, tonight's particular sleazeball was stacked with dance moves.

Lil and I faked a smile at him as he tried to shake his chest in our direction, then, picking up on our reluctance to reciprocate, he turned to Steph.

I couldn't help laughing, because it was love at first sight. Well ... maybe for him — definitely not for Steph.

He grabbed her hand and kissed the top of it which made me burst into hysterics and bury my face into Lil's shoulder. Sleazeball tried to impress Steph by picking up his pace and popping his hips and, as a result, I swear the poor girl was struggling not to vomit into her own mouth.

The good thing about sleazeballs, though, is that they are normally alone. You do you get the rare group of sleazeballs who are quite difficult to escape. But one sleazeball? Well ... we could handle him. In fact, I think we could actually have some fun with him.

Tash could sense Steph's need to regurgitate, so stepped up in his face and performed some disco moves of her own. First, she rolled her hands in front of her body really fast then she shot them out, John Travolta style. I chimed in with a 'woot-woot', but sleazeball turned to me. So I buried my head back into Lil's shoulder for protection.

Sleazeball didn't know what to make of Tash's brazen moves, a stupefied expression appearing on his face as he lost his groove factor. But, to be honest, I think he didn't like the fact she was drunk-dancing better than him. So, as all good sleazeballs do, he slowly wiggled his way out of our circle and found a new group to try and impress.

'Oh. my god! I thought he would never leave. Tash, I love you,' Steph sighed.

'Come here, Steph.' Tash put her arms out and pulled Steph in for a hug. Jade, Lil and I were still laughing, and we were now mimicking his chicken-head dance move.

'She Wolf' by David Guetta and Sia sounded through the speakers, thrilling me immensely.

'I love this song,' I squealed, grabbing Lil and twirling her around.

It seemed everyone else loved the song, too. Because the dance floor became so busy that we were involuntarily separated as people fought for whatever dance space they could find.

Trying to push back to where my friends were dancing, I felt a hand grab mine from behind. Instantly, I knew whose hand it was, now accustomed to his body as if it were permanently imprinted on my skin. Bryce gently pulled me toward him until I could feel his hard chest against my back. Then, placing his hands on my hips, he moved them with his, sending my pelvis into pelvic-arrest.

I felt his warm breath on my neck as he whispered into my ear. 'Don't look back.'

Slowly moving his mouth across the back of my head, I heard him take in a sharp breath, inhaling my hair, before breathing into my other ear. 'You fucking drive me wild, honey. Do you know that?'

I nodded.

'Good,' he whispered while moving my hips and making me do what Sia was only singing, 'fall to pieces'.

I dropped my head back against him and closed my eyes as I let go.

He kissed my neck and moved his hands further down so that his fingers were now splayed across my pelvis. 'My cock is going to be inside you soon and you are going to scream my name,' he murmured into my shoulder.

I wanted to scream his name right there on the dance floor, I wanted desperately to spin round and stick my tongue down his throat, but I didn't. I did what I was told and didn't look back.

Reaching above my head, I put my hands on either side of his face then flexed my nails into his hair. He growled and pulled my arse into him as hard as he could, making me gasp. We stood there grinding against each other to the music while his lips made love to my neck. It was one of the most erotic moments of my life.

Hearing the music start to slow down, I felt his hips relax and his grip loosen. Then, all of a sudden, I was left standing there alone ... and panting.

Almost instantly, my phone buzzed:

You look a little breathless, my love. — Bryce

I struggled to type as my fingers were slightly shaking:

Breathless ... and incredibly wet. — Alexis

Good, you better be. — Bryce

Rhianna's 'We Found Love' came on, prompting Tash to bounce up and down. So I shuffled back to where they were.

'Where'd you go?' Jade asked.

I opted to lie. 'I got squished out, then sleazeballed.'

'Ha ha, suffer!'

'I'm going back to get a drink, you guys coming?'

They all agreed and followed me back to the table.

'Okay, where is Kyle?' Steph stood up and wolf-whistled, getting Kyle's attention.

He quickly made his way over. 'Yes, what would you like, ladies?'

'Tash, what time is it?' I asked, raising my eyebrows at her.

She caught my drift and bellowed. 'It's schnappies time,' holding the 'eeeeee' sound for her longest go yet. Poor Kyle had no idea what we were shrieking about.

'Ten Cocksucking Cowboys, please,' I requested in lingo he actually could interpret. He nodded in response and then turned for the bar.

'Ten?' Lil exclaimed, looking slightly shocked.

I started dancing in my seat. 'They're not all for me.'

'I figured that. Tash, you'd better slow down after these. I want to actually get home tonight,' Lil warned.

I smiled at her and poked my tongue out, then, feeling as if I had been sent a subliminal message, I looked up to the second level.

Leaning over the railing and watching me was Bryce. There was no mistaking his expression; it spoke nothing but pure love, want, and need for me. He was my magnet, my other half. And right now, I needed nothing more than to be with him.

'I don't,' I muttered, keeping my eyes fixed on his.

'You don't what?' Lil asked.

'I don't want to go home tonight, because I'm going home with him,' I declared, pointing toward Bryce.

They all looked up. He smiled and waved to them, but our eyes never left each other's.

'He is hotter than I remember.'

'That's because you were drunk the last time, Steph,' Jade explained.

'I'm drunk now,' said Steph, causing Tash to giggle.

'Go, Lex. Go and see him.' This time Tash was cheering me on.

'No, not yet. I'll make him wait.'

'You are such a tease.'

'He deserves it. Little do you all know, he has been watching and texting me the entire night.'

'Fuck, that's hot.' *I know, Jade, tell me about it, I'm pretty sure my underwear is damp from excitement.*

I started to type him a text:

I've had a bit too much to drink, Mr Clark. I hope no one takes advantage of me tonight — Alexis

I watched the look on his face as he read the message, then waited eagerly for the response as he typed:

I plan on taking full advantage of you, honey — Bryce

That's my cue to go. 'I'm afraid I'm going to have to love you and leave you, girls.'

'What, already?' Lil asked.

'Yes, I am going to have a night full of hot and heavy sex. I love you dearly, but even you guys don't trump that.'

'Fair enough. You go, Lex,' Jade cheered. 'You go and screw that sexy son of a bitch until you hurt.'

I laughed, but strangely enough that's exactly what I planned on doing.

Downing my two schnappies in succession and making sure he was still watching as I did it, I licked my lips and typed a message back:

If that's your plan, my love, you'll have to catch me first. — Alexis

I grabbed my bag and kissed the girls on their cheeks, then walked into the middle of the crowd and pressed send.

While he was looking down at his phone, I moved very quickly, sneaking in behind a large pillar. He read the message and jerked his head up to look for me. The look on his face suggested he had lost my whereabouts. But damn ... did he move quickly.

CHAPTER
24

I could not be one hundred percent sure that he hadn't spotted me sneakily hide behind the pillar. So I kept moving through the crowd, stopping under the stairs as they offered a little bit more shelter. I then quickly typed him another message, looking up every second to make sure I had not yet been found.

If you want me, come and get me. — Alexis

Standing on tiptoes, I scanned the dance floor for his sexy, dark-blond head then tilted my head up to look through the stairs in case he'd decided to come down them. As I stood there waiting and looking at my phone, my excitement started to climb, bordering on reaching its summit.

Suddenly, I felt his hands and fingers slide across my stomach where they interlaced and held me tight. He pressed his lips to my ear and breathed his luscious warm breath as he spoke.

'I want you more than you'll ever know, and now that I have you, I am never letting you go.' He dropped his head slightly and mouthed my neck. *Oh, fuckity fuck.*

I closed my eyes as my head fell back on his shoulder, taking in every single sensation around me. The touch of his soft lips and tongue as he caressed my neck; the smell of his hair and aftershave which blended with the aroma of him; the feel of his hands as they secured me tightly; and the sound of the music which was now unobtrusive in comparison to the sound of my beating heart.

Wrapping my arms across his, I hugged him to me, tightly, pressing my nails into his skin and making him growl.

'Walk,' he said, with an urgent tone. I moved forward with him still hugging me, and made my way toward the door. 'Not that way,' he whispered then steered us in the direction of the bar.

'Where are we going? I want to go upstairs, now!'

'Oh, we are going upstairs. This is just a short-cut.'

He directed me through a door next to the bar which led into a corridor and past a few other doors.

'If you let me go, Bryce, we can walk faster.'

'Honey, I promised you I would never let you go.'

'You might want to rethink that. How will you make love to me if you never let me go?'

We stopped in front of his private elevator. He removed one hand, still gripping me tightly with the other. Then, pulling his keycard from his pocket, he swiped it. The doors slid open.

'Get in. I intend to show you how,' he growled, nudging me gently with his groin and provoking me to enter the lift.

From the moment he placed his hand across my abdomen in the club, it had not moved; not even an inch. And, as we walked into his elevator, it still remained securely in place. He impatiently fisted a button with his free hand, closing the doors behind us, all the while wrapping his hand around me with possession.

'Best you show me then, Mr Clark, because I don't believe you can pull it off.'

I could see our reflection in the mirrored panelling, the look in his eyes far more intense than I had ever borne witness to. And without speaking or taking his eyes from mine, he gently drove me closer to the wall with his groin, one hand still fastened to me as promised. He used the other to place both of my hands on the rail.

'As you wish,' he vowed.

Gently, he moved my hair away from my neck then dragged his tongue along my skin. 'You take my breath away, Alexis,' he murmured as he reached down with his free hand and lifted my dress.

The groan that then left his throat at the sight of my navy, lace underwear, shook me to my core. 'I like these, but they are coming off.'

I released a long hard breath, waiting for him to destroy them, but he didn't. Instead, he ran his finger along the seam, back and forth, until I watched it slowly slide across my skin then disappear underneath.

My mouth fell open and I licked my lips, trying to replenish the moisture that had all but disappeared from my mouth. This man was programmed to my every need, mentally, physically, and even more, sexually.

His finger found my clit and I couldn't help it — I let out a moan.

'That's right, honey, let me know you like it.' *I fucking more than like it. Holy shit!*

He continued swirling in a repetitive motion, intensifying the sensation that was gradually climbing to its peak. Then, sensing my quick rise, he stopped his finger's vigorous tease. Instead he plunged it inside of me and then slowly slid it in and out.

'Mm, you have missed me, haven't you?' he whispered into my ear before biting down on my lobe and securing me tighter with his other hand.

'Yes. I have, more than you'll ever know,' I admitted, watching intently as my answer pleased him, forcing his adorable smirk to appear on his face.

He withdrew his finger and pulled my underwear down, stopping just above my knee. If he were to bend down any further, he would have to let me go and I knew from experience that he never broke his promises.

'It appears you have a problem,' I asserted, my sneaky smile creeping across my face. 'You might have to let me go, after all.'

'That's not going to happen.'

He lifted his knee and pressed it in between my legs, stopping briefly to apply pressure to my pussy. His amused expression was sly and it intrigued me to see what he had in mind.

Placing his foot on my underwear, he then dragged it down my legs until it hit the floor. *Clever boy.*

He smiled, knowing that I was impressed.

I stepped to the side and opened my stance in invitation as his reward. 'You, Mr Clark, have earned your entry.' I tilted forward ever so slightly and wiggled my arse, bidding him to prove he could make love to me without letting me go just like he said that he could.

'Fuck,' he groaned before slapping my arse with his free hand.

The mirror reflected his sheer determination and carnal desire as he wrenched at his belt, ripping his trousers open and unleashing himself onto my backside. I felt his smooth hot crown drag along the crease of my arse until he held it excruciatingly still at the very tip of my entrance.

Gripping the railing, I anticipated the sensation I was about to experience. Not just the sense of physical satisfaction that I desperately longed for, but the emotional fulfilment I had been without since the last time he was inside me.

I looked deep into our reflection, knowing he was drawing out the very thing we both wanted the most. And, to be honest, I understood why. I could see in his expression that he was relishing this moment, grateful that it was occurring. So I allowed his pause of gratification for just a few seconds before pushing back and enticing him to enter. Seemingly satisfied with his feelings, he gave in and inserted himself entirely.

I cried out at the sudden change in pressure between my legs, and the pace at which he moved within me.

I cried out at the sheer delight of being able to feel him once again, as the absence of him had been truly dreadful.

And I cried out because he asked me to, to let him know that I liked it.

Bryce growled harshly and placed his free hand on my shoulder, firmly massaging it and holding me in place while his other hand remained unmoved, still secured around my waist.

'Fuck,' he said, through gritted teeth as he slammed into me with intensity, quickening his pace and strengthening his hips.

I was right on the cusp of my climax, a blissful release set ready to explode. And as that delightful tickle of pleasure commenced, he dropped his hand from my shoulder and fingered my clit, blossoming my frenzied spasm until we were both moaning in exquisite rapture. *Holy fuck of all fucks, that was intense.*

Pulling out from within me, he lifted me up and turned me around. Then, like mirrored images, we pulled each other in for an embrace.

I wrapped my arms around his waist as he pressed my head to his chest.

'Don't ever leave me again,' he murmured.

'I don't want to leave you,' I replied, honestly.

'Then don't.'

I squeezed him tighter, unable to conjure any words, and when he realised they weren't forthcoming, he pressed the button to his apartment and hugged me in response.

* * *

As the elevator doors opened, he stepped out of his trousers, bent down and lifted me into his arms. My first instinct was to roll my eyes at him, but I caught a glimpse of what seemed like elation and relief on his handsome face so held back on my response.

'Bryce?'

'Yes.'

'Believe it or not, I have missed being here with you like this,' I confessed, resting my head against his neck. He smiled appreciatively and carried me to his room.

Expecting our destination to be the bed, I was surprised when he walked straight past it and continued into the bathroom. As we entered, I was met with golden candlelit hues, flickering across the tiled walls. The bath was full of hot steamy water and, floating on top, were several rose petals. I could see the steam rising from the surface, and it occurred to me this had only been set up within the last half an hour, if that.

He set me down gently and unzipped my dress.

'The water is still hot! How did you pull this off?' I asked, slightly confused.

He chuckled. 'Housekeeping. I rang them after our dance.'

'How did you know I would come back here?'

'You didn't have a choice.'

'Is that right?' I questioned, turning around and crossing my arms in front of my chest. 'Technically, I shouldn't be here. We haven't even gone on a date yet! You made me break my rule. I think I should leave.'

I smirked at him. *Yes, my smirk will rival yours very soon, you wait and see.*

With a resolute smile, he placed his hands on my shoulders and threaded his fingers underneath my bra straps. 'Honey, you are not going anywhere right now other than into that bath. Then I am going to kiss and lick every single bit of your body, make love to you again, fall asleep with you in my arms, wake up and stare at you for a while, go and make you breakfast, make love to you again ... and then we can go on a date.'

Without waiting for my response — which was more than likely redundant where he was concerned — he moved his hands behind my back and unhooked my bra.

I stepped out of my shoes. 'It's supposed to be the other way around. We are supposed to go on a date first.'

'That's just stupid.'

I smiled at him while holding his hand as I stepped into the bath. 'Why?'

'Because if my date sucks, then I have already slept with you.'

He shot me a satisfied look, so I playfully punched him in the arm then lowered myself into the water, which was gloriously perfect in temperature. Bryce climbed in after me and moved toward the opposite end.

We sat there staring and grinning at each other for minutes, and with an amused expression on his face, he watched as I tried catching the rose petals with my toes.

'Tell me something, Bryce. If I decide that I want to spend the rest of my life with you, what happens next?'

'You've already decided that,' he said with a cocky look on his face.

Smartarse. 'I haven't decided anything.'

'Yes, you have. It's written all over your face.'

'You are so unbearably cocky, Bryce.'

'And you are so unbearably beautiful, Alexis.'

'Stop trying to distract me with your compliments.'

'I'm not,' he laughed.

'Okay, say I have already decided it's you and only you. What happens next?'

'We live happily ever after.'

'Where do we live happily ever after?'

My eyes softened from playful probing to seriously seeking an informative answer.

'Where do you want to live?'

'I don't know, but I'm not sure this apartment is child-friendly.'

I waited to hear his response, not sure he had even considered what changes he would have to make in order to have me and my children in his life.

Grabbing hold of my foot and stilling it from swirling the water in front of him, he lifted my toe and rested it on his lips. I glared at him with a warning that if he even tried to stick it in his mouth, I would unleash some form of fury on him.

'It's simple. We can live anywhere you want. Whether it be in a house by the sea, on a mountain, in the city or on the moon. If you want to live here we can, and I'll do everything possible to make this place just as much a home to you and the kids as it is for me. You just have to say the word, that's all.'

'So you have thought about this?'

'It's all I think about. I will live, breathe, eat and sleep anywhere you want me to. So long as it is with you. That's all I care about.'

'Why?'

'Why what?'

'Why give up your life for me? That's a lot to ask.'

'I'm not giving up my life at all. I'm simply starting a new one.'

He gripped my foot tighter and put my toe between his teeth.

'Bryce Edward Clark, I'm warning you.'

Closing his mouth, he ignored my caution, the tip of his tongue now caressing my skin. *He is still so fucking sexy, even with a foot hanging out of his mouth.*

I dipped my head down under the surface and opened my mouth to fill it with water. He watched me curiously as I positioned my head on an angle — an angle I hoped was perfect for what I had in mind.

With a hard push of breath, I expelled the water from my mouth, launching it like a fountain in his direction. It hit him in the face, my accuracy surprising even me.

Holding my breath and impending laughter, I waited for his reaction, a reaction which could have been anything from amusement, to disgust, to anger or arousal. Or he could, quite simply, be impressed by my marksmanship.

Waiting in anticipation, he gave nothing anyway, not even his devilish glint as he wrenched my legs toward him. The sudden movement had me under the water again before he pulled me back up to sit upon his lap.

During my time submerged, I had managed to scoop a little more water in my mouth, once again fountaining it toward him. He pulled me aggressively to his lips and wrapped his arms around me. Then, after what felt like minutes without oxygen, we separated our mouths.

'I don't care where I am, Alexis, as long as it is with you.'

'I know, I just want you to realise that it's not always going to be like this, like how we are now in this bath. Young children don't want to see their naked mother in a bath full of water, straddling her new boyfriend's lap.'

'Oh, what a shame.'

I laughed and kissed the tip of his nose. 'Even though Nate and Charlotte are well-mannered and well-behaved, I really don't know how they are going to react to seeing me with you. It might get pretty ugly at times. Nate can be quite jealous and punishing.'

The thought of how my kids would take this sudden, monstrous change in their lives terrified me. But I was their mother and could handle their wrath and lashing out if need be. Bryce, on the other hand, did not have to put up with it.

'Stop worrying about things that have not yet happened. We will deal with it when and if it has to be dealt with.'

'Why are you always so optimistic and relaxed?'

'I'm not, well ... not always. I guess it's because of something Mum said to me once, not too long before she passed away, actually. It was just after my year twelve school exams, when I had been overcome with stress.'

He rested his head back on the rim of the spa, and I watched him delve deep into his mind, recalling a very personal memory. I wanted nothing more than to comfort him as he did it, so I trailed my fingers down the sides of his face as he continued.

'I had been stressing and panicking about my results, making everybody's lives a living hell — mine too, obviously. Mum had dragged me into the garden; her favourite place in the whole world. She told me to lie down on the grass and look to the sky, and I remember rolling my eyes at her, thinking it was ridiculous. She then held out a beer, a cigarette and a paper bag. 'Choose one,' she'd said.

'I thought she'd gone nuts, because I didn't smoke, nor was I eighteen yet, and a paper bag? Why would I need a fucking paper bag? Opting for what any seventeen year old would, I choose the beer. She opened the bottle and handed it to me then lit up the cigarette. I had no idea Mum smoked, so again, I thought she'd gone nuts. Mum then lay down beside me and touched her head to mine. "Bryce," she said, "life is too short to worry about things that are out of your hands. Take these results, for instance. You've completed your exams and now have to wait. So wait. Don't stress about them, don't think about them, just put them out of your mind for the time being." I remember telling her that was stupid and naive as I watched her blow a smoke ring just above us. I laughed as I thought to myself, *Who is this woman and what has she done with my mum?*

'"It's not stupid, Bryce," she'd continued, "it's the smartest thing you can do. It allows you to keep your calm, your sanity and your wits ... something you will need. Because if the result or the situation does not pan out the way you want it to, you are then fully prepared to dive in and do whatever it takes to change it. Remember that, Bryce. Do not dwell on the negative or the unknown, it's foolish."' He lifted his head and looked into my eyes, as though he had been somewhere else while he was talking — I guess he had.

'Your mum was a very smart woman by the sound of it.'

'Yeah, she was, and slightly nuts.' He smiled and lifted me up. 'Now, get out of this bath! I want to taste you for the rest of the night.'

* * *

Bryce did exactly what he said he would. He kissed, licked and tasted every part of my body, and then we made love once again. I fell asleep on his chest and woke to him centimetres from my face, taking in every part of me with his stare. He cooked me bacon and eggs for breakfast which, as per usual, stimulated my taste buds to the brink of explosion. Then, hungrily, he devoured me on the kitchen bench.

'You are lucky, Mr Clark.'

'I know, Ms Summers.'

I rolled my eyes at his cheeky answer and smile. 'No, you are lucky because you got screwed without having to take me on a date.'

Frowning, he walked over to me and cupped my face. 'I told you I would take you on one today.'

'I know, but you can't. I have to go home and spend time with my family.' I placed my hands on his, removed them from my face and replaced them on my arse. 'But I'll take a raincheck, and let me tell you, it better be the best date in the history of all dates or you'll find yourself off my kissing permission list, for ... hmm, let's say a full twenty-four hours.'

'That sure as hell is not going to happen.'

'We'll see.'

* * *

I stepped out of the walk-in stadium wearing a pair of jeans and a light pink fitted shirt. Bryce was sitting on the end of the bed and appeared to be sulking, so I walked over to him, pushed myself in between his legs and ran my hands through his hair.

'Stop sulking. I will see you tomorrow.'

He wrapped his arms around my backside and pulled me to him so that we both fell onto the bed.

'Bryce, let me go, I have to go.'

My phone rang from within my handbag which was on the bed just above our heads. I stretched over him to retrieve it, exposing my breast which was virtually pressing into his face. He gripped the edge of my bra with his teeth and yanked on it, then kissed and licked my flesh. 'Stop it,' I giggled while trying to reach my phone. I grabbed hold of it to find that Rick was calling. 'I have to answer it. It's Rick.'

He reluctantly let me go with an angry look on his face.

'Hey, what's up?' I answered.

'Lexi, where are you?'

'I went out with the girls last night. I'm on my way back now.'

'Oh, okay. Listen, I'm ringing to ask you out on a date.'

An awkward smile crept across my face. Not because I was excited about his proposal, but more so that I found it strange he was doing it over the phone.

'Why didn't you just wait and ask me when I got home?'

'Because I didn't want to wait.'

'Oh, okay. Um ... what about the kids?'

'They are helping me with it.'

'With what?'

'The date, babe. How much did you drink last night?' *It's not the minor traces of alcohol in my body that are confusing me, Rick. It's your weirdness right now.*

'Not much. Sorry, I'm just confused.'

He laughed. 'Don't worry, just tell me you'll accept my date and I'll see you when you get home.'

'About that, Rick. Have you arranged for somewhere else to stay?' I turned slightly in Bryce's direction. It was obvious that he was listening carefully and dissecting my every word in the conversation.

'Yes, I'm staying in a hotel in town for now, but I don't plan on doing that for long. So, do you accept my date proposal or not?'

'Yes, okay.' I lowered my voice. 'I'll go on a date with you.' Out of the corner of my eye, I noticed Bryce flinch. 'Look, I've got to go.'

'Okay, see you soon. I love you.'

'Okay, bye.' I hung up, unable to bring myself to reciprocate and tell him that I loved him too, which said something in itself.

Turning back around, I reinserted myself in between Bryce's legs, noticing that his fists were clenched and his knuckles now white.

'I have to go,' I said, sadly.

'You're going on a date with him?'

'Yes. Well, sort of, he was actually quite weird about it. Anyway, the kids will be with us, so technically I don't think it is a date.'

'Do you want to go on a date with him?'

Bryce looked devastated, and I hated that I was torturing him in the way that I was. I couldn't help but remember what Jade said to me the night before. 'Lex, decide who it is going to be and quickly. Or stop seeing them both and take your time. It's just not fair, and it's just not you.'

'Honestly, Bryce, I don't want to leave here at all. I want to grab my kids, bundle them into the car, bring them here and start our new life together. But I can't. I have to give him a chance, a chance to see if there is anything left between us. He didn't cheat on me, so I owe him at least a chance.'

Bryce dropped his head. 'He doesn't deserve a chance, honey. He gave you up.'

'He fucked up just as much as you did, Bryce. He deserves just as much a chance as you do.'

He stood up, looking angry. So I wrapped my arms around his waist. 'I'm sorry.'

It was killing me. I knew deep down that my intent wasn't to try and play them off against each other, but it felt that way. And it felt horribly wrong.

He unwrapped my arms. 'You don't need to be sorry. Go home and give him that chance if it makes you feel better. I know you are now mine, and deep down I know you will stop this when you realise that.'

A tear started to roll down my cheek.

He lifted his finger and gently wiped it away. 'Don't cry. I love you and I'll see you tomorrow.' He started to walk me to the elevator, and I felt he was now in a hurry to kick me out.

Pulling a set of keys out of his pocket, I instantly recognised that they belonged to the Charger.

'Here, take your car.'

I smiled at the word 'your'. 'It's not my car, Bryce.'

'Like hell, it isn't.' He placed the keys in my hand then closed my fingers around them. 'I'll see you in the morning.' Then he kissed me on the forehead and helped me into the elevator.

'Why do I have a feeling you are anxious for me to leave?'

I didn't like it. I couldn't help but feel that I had upset him, hurt him and he now just wanted me gone.

Bryce put his hand on the door to stop it from closing then walked into the elevator car and cupped my face, kissing me deeply.

'Understand this, my love. I am *never* anxious for you to leave, *ever*. And if you feel that way, I'm sorry. It's just ... I desperately need to speak to Lucy, which is exactly what I am going to do as soon as these doors close.' He stepped backward out of the elevator, hit the button, and at the same time, blew me a kiss.

'I love you, Ms Summers.'

'I love you too, Mr Clark,' I responded quickly before the door closed.

And it was in that moment that I realised, by being able to say it so easily, that Rick really did not stand a chance.

CHAPTER

25

Pulling into our driveway quietly or inconspicuously was nearly impossible behind the wheel of my Charger. *My Charger, Oh my god, it's really mine.*

As I stepped out and looked at the stunning purple beast, I couldn't help but smile at the personalised number plates that Bryce had arranged and put on the car for me.

Nate, Charli and Rick came through the front door, and my smile faded just slightly when I saw the look on Rick's face as he spotted the Charger and the number plate that said 'Alexis'. I was sure he knew where I had been and it seemed to have drained the colour from his face.

'Mum, this car has your name on it! Is it yours?' Nate asked as he opened the door and took a look inside.

'Yep.'

'Cool, where did you get it from?'

'Bry— um ... Mr Clark. It was my prize for beating him in a race,' I answered honestly and smiling to myself as I remembered my sweet victory.

Rick turned around and headed back inside the house. 'Come on, kids, let's go inside.'

'I love the colour, Mum. Purple is my favourite.' *And so is pink, yellow, gold and silver, Charli-Bear.*

* * *

The absence of Rick from the kitchen, lounge and dining room indicated he was in our bedroom, waiting for me to explain.

As I entered our room, he was standing by the window, looking out at the car with a furious and disgusted look on his face. 'You were with him last night,' he snarled.

I didn't lie to him. 'Yes. The girls and I went out for drinks and dancing at Opals. So, yes ... I ended up staying with Bryce.'

He turned to me and glared.

'What, Rick? I told you that you and I had separated. I told you that I was now single. And I told you that if I wanted to date either of you, I would.'

'So the first chance you get, you go there and fuck him again.'

'I beg your pardon? Don't speak to me like that. You know what? On second thoughts, maybe you should just go, Rick.' I went to leave the room, but he grabbed my hand and wrenched it back.

'I'm sorry. I didn't mean to yell at you like that. It just sickens me that you are being intimate with another man.'

'Yeah? Well, it sickened me that you sold me to another man for money, so I guess we are even.' I took back my hand, walked around to the other side of the bed and kicked off my shoes.

'I'm sorry, babe. Please give me a chance to fix this. The kids and I have a special surprise for you.' He followed me round to my side of the bed and wrapped his arms around me. I literally went rigid. I couldn't help it. Maybe it was because he had just chastised me, or maybe it was because I no longer felt anything for him, I wasn't sure. My reaction confounded me, yet enlightened me at the same time, if that were at all possible.

He pulled back and gave my body a shake, as if to shake me loose. 'Come on, Lex, loosen up. You're going to enjoy our date.'

I smiled briefly.

'Now, put something nice on and meet me out in the dining room,' he explained in a soft and excited tone.

'Put something nice on? Where are we going?'

He shook his head with a secretive expression. 'Nowhere.'

'Then why do I have to put something nice on?' I asked, a little annoyed.

'Because we are on a date. Work with me, babe. This was your idea, remember?'

'Okay, I'll put on a dress.'

'Good.'

Rick scooted off down the hall and disappeared into the spare room. *Fuck, what have I gotten myself into? I don't think I want to date Rick any more. God! I don't know what I'm doing? My life is such a mess.*

One minute, Rick was kissing me like he's never kissed me before, and the next he was hurling hate at me. I looked down the hall toward the spare room, at the door he was behind, then I glanced down at my arms where he had just grabbed me. When he touched me, there was just nothing there. Zilch. He paled in comparison to Bryce.

Rick had only just seconds ago embraced me, but I didn't feel the lingering effects of his touch. Instead, my skin still buzzed with thoughts of Bryce, of him consuming every piece of it, and that was hours earlier.

I rifled through my wardrobe with no enthusiasm to dress up for the date. *Alexis, make an effort. You asked for this and he is doing it. The least you can do is make an effort and try and enjoy what could be your last romantic meal together.* I sighed but agreed with my annoying mini-me conscience who always invisibly sat on my shoulder.

Begrudgingly, I pulled out my plain black slip dress which sat just above my knee and sported a split to about halfway up my thigh. I couldn't be bothered doing my hair, so ran the brush through it quickly, before putting on a little lip gloss and mascara.

Taking a deep breath, I practised my smile in front of the mirror for a second and then left the room.

* * *

When I walked into the dining area, Charli was dressed in her best party dress.

She smiled sheepishly and then cleared her throat in order to begin her act. 'Mrs Summers, your table is just over here,' she explained as she held up her arm, suggesting I link mine around it.

I wrinkled my nose at Charli's cuteness, but she opened her eyes wide and tilted her head as if to say that I needed to take her seriously. So I swallowed my humour and linked my arm around hers.

'Thank you, ma'am,' I replied.

Charli escorted me to a table that was set with my best dinner wear, two candles, two gerberas and wine glasses.

She pulled my chair out and pointed to it. 'Please, take a seat.'

'Thank you.' I sat and she tried desperately to push me in. Leaning backward, I whispered to her. 'It's okay, I'll do it.'

She whispered back. 'Cool, thanks.'

Moments later, Nate rounded the corner in black slacks and a plain white shirt. He had even put some hair gel through his hair and combed it back. My heart started to thump heavily in my chest at the sight of these two incredibly adorable children who were revelling in this charade for their mother. It was just so sweet.

Nate walked into the kitchen, opened one of the drawers and pulled out a tea towel. He meticulously draped it over his left arm and then carried a bottle of wine to the table, displaying it to me like they would do in a restaurant.

'Would you care for a glass of wine, Mum ... I mean, Mrs Summers?' He closed his eyes and shook his head, embarrassed at breaking character.

I giggled and reassuringly squeezed his leg. 'Yes, please, sir.'

A look of shock and horror passed over Nate's face and, as a result, I nearly panicked myself. *Shit, what did I do?* His eyebrows lifted, as if to display that he'd had an epiphany and, before I knew it, he'd run out of the room.

'I'll be right back,' he called out behind him. I heard the noise of a cork popping and watched Nate enter the room again, looking relieved and holding a now open bottle. *Oh, you two gorgeous, gorgeous little loves of my life. I just want to break character and hug you both.*

Nate poured wine steadily into the two glasses on the table while Charli approached with a smugness about her. 'Mr Summers will be joining you shortly.' She nodded, curtsied then walked backward, awkwardly, into the kitchen.

I laughed and placed my head in my hands, hiding my amusement in fear of offending them.

Suddenly, there was a hand on my own, pulling it away from my face.

'May I have this dance, Mrs Summers.' Rick was standing before me in a tuxedo, grinning, but trying to keep an air of seriousness about him.

'Sure,' I replied, looking around and listening for any sign of music.

He led me to the lounge where he had cleared the space and created a makeshift dance floor. Then, picking up the remote control for the stereo, he pressed play.

Bryan Adams filled the room and a memory of our first dance as husband and wife popped into my head. He firmly pulled me into his arms and we began to dance to '(Everything I do) I do it for you'.

Rick and I had taken dance lessons before our wedding so that our first dance together would be special. Rick was exceptionally good at dancing, so we continued to go to the lessons and classes for a couple of years after we got married.

When I became pregnant with Nate, the lessons stopped. I'm not really quite sure why we never went back to them, we just didn't.

I put my head on his shoulder, not saying a word as we danced. It was kind of strange. Nice — but strange. For me it felt a little like closure, being that it was our first dance as husband and wife, and it would more than likely be our last.

I lifted my head from his shoulder as we twirled around the room. There were pictures on the walls of us on our wedding day looking happy, which we had been. When he had placed my wedding band on my finger and promised to 'love and cherish' me 'for as long as we both shall live', I had believed he would. And when I had put his wedding band onto his finger and promised to 'love and be faithful for as long as we both shall live', I believed I would, too.

Standing there in his arms and dancing like we'd done twelve years ago after pledging those vows to each other, I came to realise those vows had now been broken. We had broken them and we had taken them for granted.

A tear rolled down my cheek just as Nate and Charli peeped around the corner. Nate's smile faded to confusion, but it was Charli, as always, who opened her mouth.

'Mum, why are you crying?'

Rick pulled back from me to see for himself. He looked concerned, unsure if it was a happy or sad tear. I didn't want to ruin the date that the kids and he had planned for me, so I lied. 'It's a happy tear, ratbag.'

Rick sighed with relief and Charli smiled, but it was Nate who showed a small sign of hesitation.

The atmosphere in the room needed a desperate shift. So when the stereo changed, delivering Elvis Presley's voice throughout the room, Rick stood back and threw his hands in the air at the same time as pointing his toes to the ground. Then, as if he were born to do it, he flicked his knees into each other simultaneously as he swung his hips from side to side.

Charli made herself comfortable on the couch and started clapping, whereas I pulled Nate over to me, bear hugged him, and whispered into his ear, 'I'm okay, little man.'

He squeezed my arm, then we watched his dad do what his dad did best: dance!

Rick paraded his 'Jailhouse Rock' moves for a few seconds more, then grabbed my hand. Nate quickly jumped out of the way so that Rick and I could jive around the lounge. He really was a fantastic dancer; I'd almost forgotten. We hadn't danced together for years, the last time being at his brother's wedding just after Charli was born.

He spun me around and pulled me back to him, repeating the motion until the song finished.

Now in need of catching my breath, I sat myself on the arm of the couch and laughed. 'You've still got the moves, Rick.'

'You're not too bad yourself, Lex.'

'Ha, that's the most exercise I've had in a long time. I'm stuffed.' *The non-sexual kind, anyway.*

'Well, I hope you've worked up an appetite then. Come on.' He took my hand and led me to the table, where, unlike Charli-Bear, he successfully pushed in my chair.

Momentarily, he disappeared into the kitchen with the kids, leaving me alone to sit in a state of confusion and emotional ruin. I'd gone from anger when I first came home, to reluctance and unwillingness, to closure and sadness, then to recognition, reminiscing and fun. Now, I was sitting there clouded, muddled and in complete disarray as to how I was going to break his heart and end our marriage for good.

As I contemplated my complete head-fuck, the kids walked out of the kitchen and toward the family room, each holding a bowl of pasta. Rick followed behind and closed the family room door behind them, giving us complete privacy. He then made his way to the dining room table carrying two plates of Veal Scallopini and vegetables. 'Your favourite,' he said proudly as he placed the dish in front of me.

I looked at the plate. It *was* my favourite. I loved Rick's Veal Scallopini. 'Thanks, that's sweet.' I forked a medallion of veal and some mushrooms then popped them into my mouth. As always, it was delicious. But I couldn't help myself, and wondered what Bryce's Veal Scallopini would taste like in comparison to this. *Alexis, you're a bitch.* 'Yum, it's beautiful,' I said gratefully.

'No, you're beautiful.'

I forced a smile then looked back at my plate, tears threatening to fall again.

He reached over and grabbed my hand. 'I fucked up big time. I noticed early on you were forming an interest in Bryce. And instead of persuading you otherwise and showing you how much I loved you, I ignored it. I let you down. You are smart, talented, beautiful and funny. You are a wonderful mother and wife. You're sweet, shy and bashful, but you also have a raw don't-mess-with-me side. You're perfect, Lex. And I don't blame Bryce for falling in love with you. Instead, I blame myself for encouraging it when I could've stopped it.'

I let go of his hand and spoke as calmly as I could. 'Rick, in all honesty, I don't think you could've stopped it even if you had tried. Bryce and I share a connection that I cannot explain. I felt it the first day I bumped into him, before I even knew who he was. Listen, you can't blame yourself for "letting" this happen, because you didn't — it just happened of its own accord. Our connection is unstoppable. Could you have stopped us from taking it any further when we did? Well, yes, perhaps. But you chose to risk it in order to profit and that is not something you can take back.'

I looked down at my plate, then drew a deep breath and looked back up again.

'Honestly, though, and this may hurt you to hear, and if it does, I'm truly sorry, but Bryce and I were inevitable ... and ... we still are.' I let out a breath, knowing I had just ended our marriage for good.

He didn't say anything, just sat there, letting it sink in. Then, finally, after a few minutes of silence he broke down and started to sob. Seeing him fall apart like that really hit me hard. I had never seen Rick shed a tear, let alone sob. It just wasn't him; he didn't get emotionally distraught over anything.

I was about to get up and offer what relief I could when he spoke through his grief.

'I don't deserve you, anyway, I never have.'

'Rick, I —'

'No, let me finish, because if I don't say it now, I probably never will ... and you deserve better than that. Our family deserves better than that. You need to know, though, that I love you. I always have and I always will, and I love those two kids in there more than anything.' He pointed to the family room. 'I don't want to lose them as well. I've already lost you. Please don't take them away from me. Promise you'll never take them away from me.'

'I would never keep Nate and Charli from you, ever!' I affirmed, my heart clenching in my chest.

'You might when you hear what I'm about to say.' His face went pale and he wiped the tears from his eyes. I watched him suck in a deep breath then blow it out harshly, composing himself to deliver something I knew I did not want to hear, but strangely enough, knew I could handle.

'I did sleep with Claire all those years ago, I couldn't help myself. She was young ... beautiful, and she threw herself at me. You were dealing with your own self-esteem issues after having Charli and you shut me out. I'm not saying it was your fault, not at all, because it wasn't. It was mine. Instead of helping you with your demons, I abandoned you and succumbed to temptation and have regretted it ever since.'

I went to say something.

'Please, just let me finish.'

I nodded.

'Claire has been blackmailing me ever since, and I have been paying her monthly to keep her quiet. I know that's fucking stupid but on the flip side, Lex, you and our marriage were worth more to me than money. That's why when Bryce came to me and offered me the five million, I saw it as a means to an end with Claire once and for all. That's the only reason I accepted it.'

We sat there staring at each other for what felt like minutes, not saying anything at all. I felt relieved that he had, in fact, cheated on me. *How seriously fucked up is that?* I was so relieved that, in a sick way, I cackled in my head like a witch on crack.

My new-found craziness continued when I broke eye contact with him, picked up my fork and persisted with my dinner. Why? Because I was hungry.

* * *

After our silent meal, Rick and I cleaned up together, still not uttering a word. The atmosphere wasn't tense, it wasn't even awkward. It just wasn't anything at all apart from the weirdest kind of calm I had ever experienced.

The kids went to bed, so I grabbed my bottle of gin and went out to sit under our pergola.

Rick opened the sliding door and finally spoke. 'I guess I'll get going. The kids won't know any different. They'll just think I woke up early and went to work. But tomorrow, afterward, we might have to tell them something.'

'Rick, can I ask you something?'

He stepped out and took a seat opposite me. 'Yeah.'

'Do you feel relieved?'

I watched him search for the answer within his head and, not to my surprise, he found it quite quickly. 'Yes, really relieved. I've held this horrible secret for so long and it has been killing every part of me.'

'I reckon it would have. I'm actually relieved myself. When you confessed before, I thought the relief I felt was because your infidelity justified my own, but it wasn't that at all. I'm relieved for you. I'm relieved that you no longer have to carry this around with you, and that you can finally go back to being the person you were before this happened.' I took a sip of my drink. Rick looked at my glass, so I slid the bottle over to him. 'Knock yourself out.'

'Nah, I've got to drive to the hotel I'm staying in.'

'Sleep in the spare room. Really, what's the difference? It's not like we will ever repair this. We are done.' Those three words tumbled out of my mouth so easily, but they did leave a twinge of pain in my chest. 'You might as well crash in there until you find yourself a new place, and that way the kids can see you like they normally do.'

He nodded and put the bottle to his lips. 'I never thought you'd react like this.' *Pfft, neither did I.*

I took a swig of my gin. 'I've been angry. I've been upset. I've been confused. I've been hurt. I've been depressed, and I've been fucked in the head. I've pretty much felt everything one could feel since you first told me you had an affair. And then you didn't have it. And now you have had it again. The only thing left for me to be is just how I am right now. I can't explain it. I am just ... blah.' I laughed and drank some more. *Alexis, the crazy witch on crack.*

Rick gave a rueful smile. 'That actually makes perfect sense.'

'Hmm ... I know.'

* * *

I woke the next morning still feeling 'blah', but when my head cleared enough to realise that I was on my way to see Bryce completely free to be with him, unattached or hindered in way shape or form, I smiled. I smiled then cried. I cried tears of joy, tears of pain, tear of loss, tears of exhaustion. And I cried tears of fulfilment.

Parking my Charger in its normal parking spot, I then assessed the panda-eyes that looked back at me from the rear-view mirror. *Shiiiiit!* I wiped my eyes with a tissue and patted my cheeks. When I did this, I noticed Brylexis sparkle at me. I had put it back on my finger this morning, but not on my ring finger because that was not where it belonged. Brylexis now belonged on the opposite hand and it looked perfect.

Sitting there and staring at it for a few minutes, I smiled as much as a person could smile. Then, looking back at my reflection in the mirror, I spied that the panda was now a cub.

Somewhat happy with my appearance, I stepped out of the car and made my way to Bryce's apartment.

* * *

When the doors opened, I could smell the superb aroma of a cooked breakfast that I was slightly jealous I had missed. I could hear Bryce's voice outside, but he wasn't alone. I skipped toward the balcony and found him and Lucy at the balustrade in deep discussion. She was in the middle of saying something when I approached the bifold doors. They didn't see me at first.

'... you are just going to have to be careful and delicate with how she finds out.'

'I know, Luce, but she has been hurt enough. I can't bear to see her beautiful face struggle to deal with what I have to tell her. Fuck! She's been through enough already.'

'I know that, Bryce, but Alexis deserves to know.'

My smile faded and I stepped forward. 'Know what?'

CHAPTER
26

There's a sensation that formulates in the pit of your stomach when you go from feeling sheer happiness to utter dread in the space of a second. It's an awful feeling, one I don't like to experience, but after hearing what Lucy had said, I was experiencing it now.

'Know what, Bryce?' I asked again.

He walked over to me and cupped my face. 'How long have you been standing there?'

'Long enough to hear that you have to tell me something that you know will upset me.' I laughed. *Fuck, I really am a crazy cackling witch on crack.*

'Are you okay? You look like you have been crying.'

'Yeah, I have, but trust me, there are no more tears alive in this body. I have completely and utterly evicted all salty menaces. So, whatever you have to tell me, say it. Fire away.' I ran my hands up my face and interlaced them on top of my head, waiting for his bad news.

Bryce grabbed them and pulled them down into his own hands, then smiled. 'You're wearing Brylexis!'

'Yep.' I smiled back.

'What's Brylexis?' Lucy asked as she made her way over and looked at my hand. 'Oh, that is Brylexis. Weird, but cute.' She put her hands on both our shoulders and looked at her brother. 'What do you want me to do? Organise it now, or for later?'

He looked at me with sorrow, then back to Lucy. 'Now. Organise it now. I want to get it over and done with.'

'Okay, I'll be back shortly.' She squeezed his shoulder and gave me a reassuring smile then hurried out the door.

I released my hands from his and wrapped them around his waist, bringing myself into his peaceful arms. 'So, are you going to tell me what's wrong? Trust me, after the night I have just had with Rick, I can pretty much take anything you throw at me.'

He pulled away, concern and fear on his face. 'The night you had with Rick? What happened?'

'You first.'

'No, you first.' He was stern and conflicted with his new secret, but I was still harbouring crazy witch crack and burst into laughter. 'Alexis, are you okay? You seem a bit ... I don't know. A part of me wants to hug you because you seem sad, but a part of me wants to haul you over my shoulder, take you upstairs and have my way with you because you also look deliriously happy.'

'Well, why don't you do both then? Right after you tell me what you have to, of course.'

'Once I tell you, you may only want the hug, which is fine, I'm more than happy to have just a hug, I —'

'Bryce, just fucking tell me! You're starting to piss me off.' I narrowed my eyes at him and stood back.

He ran his hands through his hair, clenched his fists and twitched his eye. *Shit, all three in succession, I'd better sit down.*

'Fuck,' he growled. 'Okay, come with me. I need to get you away from this balustrade.' He led me into the lounge and sat me on the sofa, then paced back and forth a few times before stopping and kneeling at my feet.

Just as he was about to say something, Lucy walked through the door.

'Thank fuck, your timing couldn't be better. Did you get what you needed?'

'Yes, what I needed is in the foyer.'

'Good.' He turned back to me. 'Okay, honey. I'm sorry you have to hear this from me, but you have a right to know the truth. Shit, here goes. I know you hate how we conduct creepy research, but we do it for a reason. We do it to protect ourselves and the ones we love, and we love you. Damn, do we love you. I love you more than it is fucking imaginable.'

I smiled at him and touched his face.

'Stop smiling at me. This is hard enough to say to you as it is, let alone if you are smiling at me. When Rick said he didn't have the affair, I didn't believe him. So I asked Lucy to dig deeper. I was sure he was lying. Things just didn't add up.'

I went to interrupt him, to tell him he was a good judge of character, but he put his finger to my lips.

'Please, don't stop me, honey ... So, Lucy looked into his bank accounts and found he was transferring money into

Claire's account every month and has been doing it for five years.'

I tried to speak again, because I was now interested in finding out just how much Rick had been paying her. I'd never found out that piece of information.

He kissed my lips to prevent me from speaking. *Where's baby Alexander?* I wondered, suddenly noticing his absence. I scanned the room quickly looking for the little adorable bundle of cuteness. I didn't know where he was and it began to bug me.

Bryce carried on talking while I searched for Alexander. 'I know, my love. I'm sorry, this must be terrible to hear, but I'm not done yet. So —'

This time I did interrupt. 'Lucy, where's Alexander?'

Both Bryce and Lucy looked at each other with profoundly shocked expressions. They then returned their gaze back to me.

'He's upstairs asleep in his cot. Why?' She shook her head briefly.

'Oh, no reason. I was just wondering where he was, that's all.'

'Alexis, are you listening to me?' Bryce pleaded, while putting his hands on either side of my head and turning me to face him.

'Yes, I'm listening. You didn't believe Rick was telling the truth. So you got Lucy to conduct more creepy research. She did, and found Rick was paying Claire money to keep her mouth shut about their affair five years ago. Yes, I'm listening.'

He leaned back on his knees and stared wide-eyed at me.

'Oh, by the way, how much was he paying her? I forgot to ask him that last night.'

Bryce turned to Lucy who shot him a blank expression. 'Two thousand dollars a month for five years,' she said slowly.

I started doing the math in my head. *So, $2,000 times 12 equals $24,000, times 5 is around $125,000. Fuck, I really should've paid more attention to our banking.*

'You already know?' Bryce asked, slightly shocked.

'Yes, I told Rick last night that from the moment I spilt my drink on you, I was yours. I told him that you and I just have something that cannot be explained, that we were inevitable, that we still are inevitable ... and always will be.'

Bryce's jaw basically hit the floor.

'Once Rick let that sink in, the unbearable guilt he had held for five years just spilled out. He told me what they did, why they did it, how she blackmailed him, how he paid her, how when you came along with your offer he saw a solution — and he told me how sorry he was, for everything.'

Lucy took a seat and both she and Bryce sat there in silence.

'It's fine. I'm fine. Rick is fine ... well, at least I think he is. I didn't see him this morning when he left for work.'

'He stayed at the house?'

'Yes, Bryce he did, and will continue to do so.'

Bryce's demeanour changed, uncertainty now covering his features.

'He is sleeping in the spare room and the kids have no idea. We are going to tell them tonight. But for now, he can stay in the spare room until he finds a new place. It's just easier that way.'

I watched Bryce dissect everything I had told him.

He looked up at Lucy with pleading and desperate eyes. 'Fuck, what do I do now, Luce?' He dropped his head in my lap.

'Do about what?' I asked, lifting his head. He had so much regret in his eyes; there was more to the story, I could see it right there.

'Fuck, I have to tell you, honey. No more secrets, I promised. The problem is, Rick doesn't even know about this one.' He looked over to Lucy and nodded. She stood up, leaned forward and gave me a quick hug before heading out the door.

Confused by her caring, but strange, actions, I asked the obvious question. 'Where's she going?'

'To get Claire.'

I stood up abruptly. 'Claire is fucking here?'

'Yes, and there's someone —'

Lucy reopened the door, and moved aside for Claire to walk in. The first thing I noticed was that she looked different, somewhat grown-up and more mature, tired even, and she didn't carry the self-righteousness like I remembered from all those years ago.

My anger was bubbling near boiling point, and I was just about to lose control and hurl abuse at her when she put her hand down and encouraged a small child to come out from behind her legs. His little innocent and slightly nervous eyes met mine. *Oh, my fucking god! He looks just like Rick!*

* * *

I'm not exactly sure what happened next. Well, at least for a few seconds, anyway. My mind seemed to go into survival mode, and I couldn't help but imagine a teeny tiny drill sergeant standing in the centre of my brain, barking orders, telling some emotions to go this way and the others to go that way. *Right, Anger, you go stand over there and keep at bay until told otherwise, understand me? You, Fear, yes you, you are no longer needed here, be on your way. Sadness, you pussy, pull your-self together and stand tall. Composure, you are going to lead by example. Do you all hear me?* My inner drill sergeant blew its teeny tiny whistle, snapping me back into reality.

With hesitation, Claire stood there and searched my face while holding her son in front of her. Bryce had stood up and was now next to me, waiting for my reaction, which appar-ently hadn't really come yet. I sat back down on the couch and put my head in my hands.

'Alexis.' Bryce knelt back down in front of me. 'Alexis, I'm sorry, honey, I —'

I lifted my head and looked into his eyes, then put my head back down and held up one finger to indicate I needed a moment. *You can do this, Alexis.*

Mustering whatever strength I had left in me, I placed my hand on Bryce's shoulder for support while rising, and to reas-sure him that I was good. I walked over to my handbag and pulled out my iPod, then flicked through the screen until I came across the app I was looking for. As I walked toward Claire I noticed her grip tighten on her son's shoulders.

I bent down so that I was eye level with him. *Shit. Crap. Balls. He has Rick's eyes.*

'Hi, what's your name?' I asked, trying to sound as pleasant as I possibly could, given the situation. He looked up to his mother as if to ask permission to answer. Claire nodded and smiled gingerly.

'R ... RJ,' he said nervously with a stutter. *RJ? Rick Jr. Fuck!*

I looked up and glared at Claire. The hatred that was fester-ing within me was bordering on the brink of explosion. *Anger, stay in that corner, man. Do you hear me? I said, do you hear me?* I closed my eyes for the smallest of seconds then looked into

RJ's, feeling just a tiny bit of familiarity ... as if I had looked into those eyes before.

'RJ, do you like Angry Birds?' I asked.

He nodded.

'Good, how about you come sit over here on this sofa, and you can play it on my iPod.'

He glanced up at Claire and she nodded again in response.

I handed him the iPod. 'If you can get past level seven, I'll be your biggest fan.'

He smiled and seemed to relax a little as Claire led him to the lounge.

I, however, was far from relaxed. Standing back up, I walked straight out to the balcony, desperate for the view of the city that had once before helped calm my nerves and find clarity. I sure as hell hoped it would do the same today, but I couldn't be sure as to how I was going to react when Claire and I were alone.

Moments later, and from out of the corner of my eye, I noticed Claire standing at the balustrade only a metre away from me.

'I'm sorry, Alexis, but it is what it is.' Her voice was shaky as she said the words.

I stared at her and gripped the railing. I wanted to pick her up and flip her over the fucking side and dangle her there. 'It is what it is because you made it that way,' I hissed from between my teeth.

'I know and I'm sorry. But I'm not sorry for RJ. I love that little boy and I don't regret what I did for a second, because if I did, I wouldn't have him,' she explained as tears began to well in her eyes.

'I know the love a mother has for her child, Claire. I'm more than fucking aware of it.' I was still hissing, but understood what she was saying. No matter how your children come to be, there is no possible way you could regret them.

I turned to look at her. 'Why have you kept RJ a secret for five years?'

She didn't answer straightaway. Instead, a lone tear streaked down her cheek and dropped, falling forty-three storeys below. I wondered if it ever made it to the ground.

'Because I didn't want to ruin your perfect family.'

'You did ruin our perfect family. You ruined it the moment you decided to sleep with my husband.' I relaxed my grip on the railing. 'But none of that really matters any more, does it? What matters now is Rick has a son he knows nothing about.'

'He doesn't have to find out,' she said, clearly fidgeting with uncertainty. 'He'll hate me and RJ, and RJ doesn't deserve that.' She looked down at her fingers and picked at her nail.

'You don't know that. Rick is many things, but an arse of a father is not one of them. You never even gave him a chance. You've robbed him of five years of RJ's life, five years he can never get back.'

She turned and looked at me for the first time since meeting me out on the balcony. 'I panicked, Alexis. I was young. I had slept with a married man, a man whose wife I had known since I was a kid. A man whose wife I respected, and a man whose wife I envied and wanted to be more than anything in this world.' She turned back to look across the city and then sighed. 'I was so disgusted with myself ... but I loved him. I couldn't help it. I knew it was wrong, but I wanted him more than anything. And because of that, I didn't care what I was doing.'

My stomach wrenched as I realised I could relate to what she was saying. I also knew how wrong it was to have feelings for someone you shouldn't. I also knew how wrong it was to cross the line and not care as you did it, because when you love somebody like that, you can't help yourself.

'Claire, I can understand that ... but why blackmail him?'

'Because I needed the money and I couldn't exactly ask him for child support, could I?' She pulled away from the railing and tilted her head to see if RJ was still captivated in Angry Bird land.

He was smiling as he ran his finger along the screen, and a happy little 'Yes' escaped his mouth, suggesting he was successful in his actions. 'He is my everything. I fucked up and brought him into this world. A world where his father didn't know he existed. And a world where his mother was an immature slut who had no money to her name. That little boy deserved more than what he was given. I'm already a worthless excuse for a human being, so why not accept that and resort to blackmailing. That's why I did it.' She started to cry and something inside of me broke.

I took in a deep breath and did the thing I thought was never possible for me to do. I grabbed her and hugged her as an act of comfort. 'You are not a worthless excuse for a human being. You made a terrible, terrible mistake. One that you could not take back ... but your mistake resulted in that adorable little boy in there, and there is nothing worthless about that, you said so yourself.'

She pulled back from me, her mouth wide open in disbelief. She wiped her eyes and laughed mockingly. 'I deliberately slept with your husband, had his child, kept it a secret and bribed him. And here you are hugging me and telling me I'm not worthless? I think you are slightly crazy.' She laughed again.

'Yeah, you could be right.' I mimicked her laugh. 'Look, like you said when you first came out here and back when I wanted to push you over the edge ...'

She stepped away slightly, and I smiled to myself.

'Like you said, Claire, "It is what it is." You fucked up, but now you need to make it right. And I can't believe I am going to say this, but I am.' I sighed. 'I will help you.'

'Why, Alexis? Why would you help me?'

'It's really quite simple, Claire, because you need it, because Rick needs it, because RJ needs it, and because Nate and Charli should know their half-brother.' I walked back into the lounge with her following behind me. 'I will ring you in a few days.'

I knelt down by RJ. 'How did you do, RJ?'

He turned the iPod around. 'I'm up to level ten.'

'Wow! Good job, I'm now your biggest fan.' I put my hand up for a high five. He slapped it hard and smiled.

'It was really nice to meet you. I'll see you next time, okay? And maybe then, you can get up to level fifteen?'

'Yep, I will.'

'I reckon you just might.' I gently placed my hand on his head, then smiled and walked upstairs.

* * *

As soon as I closed the door to the spare room behind me, I let go. I knew I could no longer hold in the anger and hurt I had kept at bay while downstairs. It took everything in me not to let loose the inner ball of fury I was harbouring in front of RJ. I, too, was a mother and there was no way I would allow that poor little innocent boy to see me berate his mum.

Picking up the pillow, I pressed it to my face and screamed into it with as much rage as I possibly could. Then I threw it across the room. I pulled my blouse over my head, scrunched it into a ball and slammed it on the ground. I wrenched off my shoes and launched them at the door with as much fury as I could. I needed my shower, and I needed it now. I needed the clarity it had brought me once before. I needed to see the anger wash down the drain so that I could be content with the fact I had let it go.

Wrestling with the zip on my skirt, I yanked and screamed at it to come down. Suddenly, Bryce had his arms around me tightly. I fought them, trying to push him away, but he was too strong.

'Shh, honey. It's okay,' he whispered as he pressed his lips to the back of my head.

I surrendered the fight and went limp. 'I can't do it. I can't get my skirt off. I can't do it any more. I just want to get in that shower, Bryce.'

'Okay. Let me help you.'

He gently released his grip and eased down my zip, allowing my skirt to fall to the floor. I felt his hands undo the clasp of my bra, then it was on the floor as well. He pulled down my underwear, lifted me into his arms and carried me into the bathroom.

Gently, he set me down on the bathmat, then removed his own clothes as I stepped into the shower. I put my hands against the wall with my arms locked, just staring down at the drain. I was exhausted, emotionally depleted, and completely fucking shattered.

Bryce put his hands on my shoulders and gently massaged them. He didn't say a word to me, knowing I would talk when

I was ready. He knew that by just being there with me was all I needed.

When I was sure I had finished watching all the anger from my body wash away, I turned around and hugged him tightly. 'Thank you.'

'It's what I do, Ms Summers.'

I laughed, but thankfully not the 'witch on crack' cackling laugh. That laugh had started to worry me. 'It is, Mr Clark.'

'You are beyond incredible, honey. Have I told you that?'

'Yeah, I think you might have mentioned that a couple of times.'

'Oh, well, in that case, you are fucking incredible.'

I laughed again. 'So are you.'

* * *

We spent a little while longer holding each other in the shower. I came to the conclusion that not only was that shower my miracle mood clarifier and enhancer, but when Bryce was in there with me it helped with the healing even more so.

Bryce had offered to take me out for the day to take my mind off things, but I knew his work was piling up. Apparently, Lucy had been doing most of my work since the Tel V Awards. I told him 'no' and that working was probably the best thing for us both at that moment. But, unfortunately, my ability to focus was quite minimal, therefore I wasn't as productive as I might have been. When 5 p.m. rolled around, Bryce emerged from his office.

'That's it. Enough. I can't fucking wait any longer.' He walked over to my chair. 'Get up.' *What? What have I done?* I hesitantly stood up. He wrapped his arms around my waist and hauled me over his shoulder.

'Bryce, what are you doing?' I laughed, slightly surprised.

'What I should've done hours ago.' He carried me into the apartment and upstairs to his room then laid me down on his bed.

I started to remove my shoes when he stopped me.

'No, you just lay back and relax. I've got this.'

Slowly, he removed my shoes and clothes then he did the same with his own. He kissed up one of my legs and across my clit, back down the other, then back up again. He was so gentle and soothing in his actions, it was perfect.

'You know,' I hummed, 'if I continue to work for you, we will never get anything done.'

'I know,' he agreed, smiling.

'Well, that's not good.'

'No it's not,' he quickly answered, still smiling.

I giggled.

He continued trailing kisses up my stomach until he reached my breasts. I shivered when the tip of his tongue touched my nipple. Almost instantly, he engulfed it with his mouth while massaging my other nipple between his thumb and finger. I pulled his head up to mine and kissed him tenderly, looking into his eyes and letting him know I appreciated everything about him.

He entered me gently, rocking his body into mine in slow deep thrusts. I gripped his back as hard as I could, pulling him into me as far as he would go.

'Bryce,' I whispered, breathing heavily as he continued to move deep inside me. 'Promise me you'll never hurt me.'

He slowed his momentum only slightly and raised his head from where he had been kissing my neck. His sincere stare penetrated my core. 'Alexis, I will never hurt you.'

'No, I mean it. Promise me you'll never go behind my back and do things like Rick has done, no matter how bad it is. Promise me you'll always tell me first. I ... I don't think I could handle it. I ... just don't.'

'Honey ...' He paused long enough to tell me what he needed to. 'I promise I will never hurt you, never keep anything from you. I promise I will do everything in my power to make you the happiest woman alive, because you make me the happiest man alive.'

I nodded. 'Okay, I'm yours then, Mr Clark. Forever.'

He smiled. 'I know.'

Pulling him back down to meet my mouth, I kissed him reverently as he increased his rocking until we were both giving each other over to one another, entirely.

CHAPTER
27

Leaving Bryce at the apartment after our wonderful lovemaking session was terribly difficult. I felt at home falling asleep and waking up with him. And knowing that it was not going to happen this night had dulled our moods.

I made it home before dinnertime with the intention of cooking us one of the gourmet meals I had planned when I did the food shopping. However, when I opened the front door, barbeque fumes wafted in from the backyard and quashed that idea very quickly.

Dropping my bag on the buffet table, I headed out to the pergola where Rick was standing over the hot plate turning sausages and hamburgers. Charli was on the trampoline and Nate was shooting hoops. I decided I wouldn't mention anything to Rick about Claire and RJ. Not now, anyway. My first priority was to tell the kids that their father and I were separating. I was dreading the fact I had to speak such words to my children. My heart felt as if it were clawing at my chest. But I had to do it. At the end of the day, it was for the best and it could not be avoided.

As I stood there watching them, I felt strangely separated from the scene. This wasn't my life any more. The man at the barbeque was no longer my husband. He was no longer my lover, or a man I could share my life with. Instead, he was a man who gave me two beautiful children and, for half of our life together, had been a wonderful companion. I didn't hate him — I could never hate him — but at that moment when I looked at him, all I could see was a man who had lost faith; faith in me and faith in our marriage. And for that, I felt sorry for him.

It was very clear to me that he had not lost faith in himself as a father though. He might not have known how to be a faithful husband, but he clearly knew how to be a loving dad. And I knew that when we told the kids we were no longer going to be husband and wife, I could confidently say that we would still be Mum and Dad. Our separation was not going to change that.

He looked up and noticed me standing by the door. 'Hi. I figured I would barbecue. Save you worrying about dinner when you got home.'

'Thanks. Good idea, it smells wonderful.' I walked over to the trampoline to give Charli a hug, then called for the ball from Nate and sunk a three-pointer from the mark near our swing.

'Mummy Jordan, swish!'

'You're so embarrassing, Mum.'

I winked at Nate. He was impressed despite his statement, I could tell. *Sure, keep telling yourself that, Alexis.*

As I headed back inside, I called to Charli. 'Charli-Bear, come and help me set the table.'

* * *

We ate our dinner outside under the pergola as it was the perfect night for it. The kids did their homework then had a minor argument over which channel to watch on TV before going to bed. After they had both settled, Rick and I went back outside to talk about how we were going to handle breaking the news to the kids.

'Lex, you do realise Nate will want to know why?'

'All he needs to know right now is that we no longer love each other like a husband and wife should.'

'Well, that's not really true, is it?'

I gave him a slightly disappointed retort. 'Rick, please don't make this any harder than it has to be.'

'Well, it's not true. I still love you like a wife, I always will.'

I tried to brush off his comment; it was a bit late to tell me he loved me like a wife. I didn't dispute it now, but he didn't love me like a wife five years ago, and that could never be taken back.

'We'll tell them that you are still going to live here until you find a new home to buy, but after that they can stay over with you whenever they like.'

He nodded, but I could sense he was deliberating telling me something.

'I'm going to tell them about Bryce in a couple of days, but on my own.'

'Are you planning to move into his apartment?'

'I don't know. I haven't decided yet. Maybe.'

'Well, what's the point of me buying a new house if you are going to move out?'

'I don't know. You've got five million dollars. Wouldn't you like to buy something a little nicer? Something bigger, perhaps?'

'No, wouldn't it be best if I lived here and you moved in with Bryce? That way the kids still have the stability of this house, the only house they have ever known.'

'I'm not going to live away from my kids, Rick. Forget it!'

'No, I'm not saying that. I'm saying that if you plan on moving in with Bryce, the kids can stay with you and with me, whenever they like. They could go between us, I guess. I don't know, I don't fucking know what to do any more.' He started to get up to leave.

'No, sit. I understand what you are saying, and I think that it might be a good idea to try at first. That way, it is not so much of a change or transition for them. Look, I think we should just take each day as it comes, okay?'

It actually was a good idea. They were going to have to deal with the shock of hearing we were splitting up — that was going to be hard enough. So sparing them the shock of having to leave their home as well, I agreed was sensible. At least if I were to come and go, then ease both of them into coming and going, the notion of moving might not hit them as hard.

'I'm not about to pack my bags and move in with Bryce straightaway. I will stay over there every now and again, and then wean the kids into it until it just becomes what it is. If you want to keep the house, then fine. I would not have been able to stay here anyway. There are just too many memories.'

'I know, Lexi, that's why I want to keep it.'

'You might as well start accepting this. Torturing yourself is not going to help you move on. You need to move on for the kid's sake, at least.'

He raised his eyebrows at me.

'Now, I'll be staying with Bryce tomorrow and telling the kids I have a late meeting, which I do. Then we will sit down with them and talk to them about it on Tuesday. All right?'

'Sure.' He stood up and headed inside.

'We have to work together on this, for the kids.'

'I know, but that doesn't mean I have to be happy about it.'

* * *

The next day — in the eyes of Nate and Charli — was no different from any other. Rick had slept in the spare room and left for work before they had woken up.

'I won't be home tonight, munchkins. I have a late meeting at work. Mummy is helping with the marketing of the family-friendly rooms in one of the hotels.'

'What's marketing, Mum?' Charli asked as we all climbed into the car.

'Well, it's about making something both sound and look good. I have to help make the new family-friendly rooms at the hotel sound and look good so that people will want to stay in them.'

'What is so good about them?' *Charli, you are a question-asking little monster.*

'Well, some of the rooms might have carpet patterned like a Twister game, and a built-in dial selector so you play Twister whenever you like.'

'Cool, what else?' *Grrr.*

'I don't know, missy. Why don't you tell me what you would like in a hotel room?' I looked in the rear-view mirror at Charli who was now thinking of suggestions in her head. *That will buy you maybe thirty seconds of silence, Alexis.*

'I know,' Nate said from the passenger seat beside me, 'arcade games, the ones you can sit in and drive, or the ones where you have to hit the hedgehogs on the head.'

'I know, I know!' Charli squealed. 'I want baby animals I can take care of.' *That was barely five seconds of peace and quiet.*

'So, arcade games and a petting zoo. I'll mention it, thanks. Anything else?'

'A treasure hunt around the hotel,' Nate said with an expression similar to a greedy pirate.

'A girly pampering salon,' Charli beamed as she held her hand in the air to inspect her nails. *Hmm, not bad, kidlets. Maybe I could suggest some activity programs for kids, programs conducted by the hotel.*

'Good work, my little brainstorm-troopers. Get it Nate? ... Brain ... Stormtroopers. You know ... *Star Wars*?'

Nate sighed and rolled his eyes. 'I get it, Mum. But that was so not funny.'

'Oh.' I said, with a sad-child face.

I received a handful of other suggestions in the time it took me to drive the kids to school. A trivia challenge on things around the complex, and the guest with the most correct answers got a prize of some kind. We actually formulated this idea together. Nate had the idea of the challenge — or a test as he called it. I had the idea of it being a competition amongst guests, and Charli came up with the prize. Charli also suggested goodie bags for kids upon arrival, which I thought was a great idea. And Nate suggested themed rooms, which could be worked on, too.

* * *

All in all, my drive to school that morning had resulted in some great suggestions for my meeting. A meeting I was terribly nervous about. The last time it had only been me, Bryce, and Patrick, the head designer. This evening, though, it was going to be the three of us, plus Chris from marketing, and the entire board including Gareth.

I hadn't seen Gareth since the Tel V Awards, not including that time I overheard Bryce arguing with him in the office. I was slightly nervous about having to be in the same room with him, knowing he had Dissociative Identity Disorder and that I was the probable trigger for his psycho alter, Scott. I just hoped I wouldn't let the nerves I might feel at his presence render me useless, like a babbling sweat-beaded mess, resembling a drug addict in withdrawal.

I parked my Charger then exuberantly made my way up to see Bryce.

When the doors to the elevator opened, he was standing there with a rose for me. I paused for a second to take in the sight of the incredibly romantic and drop-dead gorgeous man standing before me. I licked my lips because, as per usual, the sheer sight of him depleted my mouth of moisture — that very moisture being transplanted to the spot in between my legs.

I didn't give him a chance to prowl toward me wearing his extremely smouldering gaze, a gaze that had the ability to send my pussy into a seizure. Instead, I made the slow cat-like walk toward him, wrapping my arms around his neck and planting a kiss on his lips that would hopefully send his cock into full-blown cock-assault.

We kissed hungrily just outside the elevator for a minute or so.

'I missed you,' I mumbled as our tongues tasted one another's.

'Not as much as I missed you,' he replied in a similar mumbled tone.

I reached down and caressed the bulge that was pressing into my hip. *Full-blown cock-assault achieved! Good work, Alexis.* 'I think you might be right.'

He slid his hand up my leg and wasted no time inserting his finger inside me. 'No, I'm definitely wrong.' He pulled his finger out then stuck it in his mouth. *Shit, that's hot!* I had been there less than five minutes, and already my body was crying out for his.

'You are so bad,' I giggled.

'And you are so sweet, literally.' He wrapped his arms around my waist and pushed me up against the entryway wall, which had returned to being one of my favourite spots in the apartment.

I fumbled desperately with his trousers, wrenching them undone and being rewarded with his long hard cock. He groaned and lifted my dress, wasting no time in yanking my underwear down.

Ferociously, he mouthed his way up my leg with frantic need to get to the top. My legs almost buckled as his tongue slid up and down my clit. He was anxious today, bordering on frenzied and desperate in his actions. It worried me slightly, but the overwhelming pleasure I was experiencing as a result shelved the worry. I decided that after he had released whatever emotions this frantic performance signified — because let's face it, it was fucking hot and felt great — I would return to the shelf in my mind, take back the worry I had tentatively put there and find out what it was all about.

'Bryce Clark, you are sensational,' I confessed as I threw my head back, delighting in the feeling his mouth had bestowed upon me.

His desperation did not ease as he made his way up to meet my lips, caressing them aggressively with his own. My leg automatically lifted for him and instantly, he was inside me, pinning me to the wall. *Sex Up Against the Wall. Yes, I'll order another of these. It's been a while.*

He pulled away from my mouth and penetrated me with his eyes as he thrust deep within. I closed mine as the intensity of his reach was almost too much to bear.

'Open your eyes. I want all of you with me when I bring you undone.'

'You already have brought me undone.'

'Not yet I haven't.' He increased his pace and pressure, and it was just about impossible to grant him the request of staying open-eyed. The pure bliss he was conjuring inside me was boiling to the point of explosion. I couldn't help it, my lids closed, covering my eyes and disobeying his instructions.

'Alexis!'

I flung them open at his demand.

'That's it, honey. Look at me,' he said with a salacious smirk as he thrust into me harder.

I opened my mouth. 'I can't. Oh fuck, I can't.'

'Yes, you can.' He smiled and grabbed my breast, massaging it within his hand.

'Please,' I pleaded, piercing him with my stare, now hell-bent on keeping it.

'That's it, beautiful.' He kissed me quickly then relinquished his control so that we both exploded at our thresholds simultaneously.

As our bodies relaxed, I finally closed my eyes, shuddering against him.

'Holy fuck,' I exhaled.

He chuckled and picked me up, then sat on the couch and laid my head on his lap.

'I'm supposed to be at work in five minutes, but none of my limbs are now functional,' I explained, completely sated.

'This is work. I've put it in your job description. The memo is on your desk.'

'It is, is it?'

'Yep.'

'So does that mean I have to start my day like this every day?'

'Sure does. And you have to finish it like this, too.' He traced his finger down my cheek then lightly dabbed my nose.

'In that case, I need to go back to the gym.'

'Good, we'll start now.'

'What?' *Are you for freakin' real? My muscles have just completely cracked the shits and gone on strike.* 'What part of "limbs no longer functioning" did you not understand, Mr Clark? Anyway, don't you have a self-defence class this morning?'

'Yes, I do and you're coming with me.' *Shit. Crap. Balls.*

'I'm not going to be your guinea pig again.'

'We'll see.'

I nearly fell asleep while he sat there and trailed his finger up and down the side of my face, but after half an hour or so of resting on Bryce's lap, my muscles finally decided to cooperate again.

We went upstairs, and I reluctantly changed into my gym clothes which, just coincidentally, happened to be in my half of the walk-in stadium.

* * *

Self-defence class was pretty much the same as the last time, except after spotting Chelsea in the group of drooling women I was more than happy to be his assistant. I think he got frustrated at one point when he had me in a bear hug hold from behind, and I reluctantly refused to fight him off. He had whispered into my ear, 'What are you waiting for? Stomp on my foot,' and I'd replied with, 'No, I like your arms around me,' to which he then responded with, 'Do it or you're off my kissing list.'

No longer reluctant, I'd reacted abruptly by slamming my foot hard on the top of his, which resulted in him having a limp for the rest of the day.

We didn't even shower together. By the time he had made it upstairs after talking to the lingering flies disguised as women, I was already showered and seated at my desk. He had walked past without saying a word, stopping only briefly to plant a kiss on my head.

We were then both quiet with each other as the day progressed. He had back-to-back meetings, so I had my lunch with Liam and Samantha. I hadn't seen Liam for quite some time, and found it a delight to be in his bright and slightly sarcastic presence, which I just loved. But Sam, on the other hand, was quiet and a little off. I'd asked her if everything was all right, and she'd said that it was. But, clearly, she thought I'd come down in the last shower.

* * *

After Bryce's last meeting had finished, I knocked on his door and entered. From his position behind the desk, he looked absolutely drained, so I didn't say anything to him as he watched me enter the room.

Walking over to the minibar, I poured him a Scotch and walked around to his side of the desk and, still not uttering a word, I spun his chair to face me and put the Scotch into his hand. I slowly knelt down before him and gently removed the shoe from the foot I had crushed. When I took off his sock, it revealed a huge bruise on the top of his foot. I put my hands to my mouth and gasped, then tears began sting my eyes. *Oh, shit, what have I done?*

'I am so sorry. I ... I didn't mean to do it that hard. Shit,' I offered regretfully as I picked up his foot and kissed it, hoping to take away what I had done. I kept kissing it like a crazed sicko, when he chuckled, so I looked back up to find a rather large smile plastered across his face.

'I thought you didn't do feet, Ms Summers?'

I tried to suppress the smile that was forcefully breaking its way through my worried expression. 'I don't, Mr Clark.' I kissed it one last time, then knelt up and crawled into his lap. 'But I will do your feet. I will do anything you want me to do. In fact, I know something I can do for you right now.'

Placing one last kiss on his lips, I climbed back off his lap and scooted down to my knees. I gave him a seductive glance and unfastened his belt from his pants, releasing his already swollen cock into my hands.

Wriggling myself into the opening underneath his desk, I began to stroke his shaft with my tongue. He moaned deeply and caressed my head with his hands.

'Please, do not let me distract you from your work,' I offered in a sweet voice.

'That's fucking impossible. You distract me even when you are in the next room.'

I giggled and licked his crown.

'Fuck, maybe you should stomp on my foot more often.'

I retracted my tongue. 'Don't, that's not funny. I hurt you.'

'It's fine, honey. Please don't worry. It looks worse than it feels. Anyway, I shouldn't have threatened you with no kissing. I know what that feels like.'

My tongue slid across his warm, soft skin once again. 'Regardless, I'm sorry.'

'Alexis, stop apologising and keep sucking.'

I giggled and mouthed as much of his length as I could. The more of him I pulled into my mouth, the more he stiffened and tensed.

'You like that, my love?' I asked around his dick, teasing him with his own amatory question.

'Mm,' was all he could manage.

There was a knock at the door, and as casually as one would, he announced 'come in'. *What the fuck, Bryce!*

I let go of his soldier who was obediently standing to attention and I put my hand over my mouth.

'Sorry to bother you, Bryce.'

'No, it's not a bother at all. How can I help you, Arthur?' *Shit. Fucking crap. Balls. It's Santa.* I heard the seat opposite

Bryce's desk crunch as Santa placed his arse on it. Holding my breath, my heart rate took off like a rocket through the roof.

'I just wanted to get these proposals signed off before the meeting this evening,' Arthur explained.

'Sure, not a problem.' The noise the pen made as Bryce autographed the paperwork was louder than normal. I think the sheer fear of discovery had heightened my senses. 'So, Arthur, how is Geraldine?' *Bryce Edward Clark, small talk, really? I am not only going to stomp on your other foot now, I am going to bite down on your tasty hot dog like I would if it were slapped in between two pieces of bread and covered in mustard and sauce.*

'She's been a little miserable lately, not being one for the heat.' *Best you be on your way and go see to her, Santa. Quickly, run along.*

'That's not good to hear. Maybe you should take her on a holiday, somewhere where it is cooler, perhaps?' Bryce politely suggested. *Bryce! Argh!*

Being scrunched up on my knees in a space no bigger than a cardboard box, and fighting my body not to make any sound, was killing me. *Why is it, that when you are desperate to be quiet, your body ignores you and instead wants to vocalise in any way it can? Right now I could probably laugh, cough, sneeze, pee and fart all at the same time.*

'Yes, we were thinking of taking a short trip to Tasmania.'

'Yeah? That would be nice. Have you been there before?' Bryce asked, leaning back on his seat.

I noticed through the small gap between him and his desk that he had comfortably put his hands behind his head. *Oh, for frigs sake. Why not ask him about the weather, or if he is the real Santa?* I shifted a tad, making scarcely a sound, then reached my hand to Bryce's groin and plucked one of his hairs.

'Shit!' Bryce blurted rather loudly.

'What?' exclaimed Arthur.

'Nothing, it just felt like something bit me on the leg, that's all.' *Oh, you'll get bitten, just not on your fucking leg.* He reached his hand down and pretended to rub his leg. 'So, Arthur, have you been there before?'

Obviously my little hair removal threat did nothing to persuade him to forego his annoying small talk. *Right, Mr Hot Dog-Dick Clark, you are in trouble now.* I wriggled quietly and got as comfortable as I could, then reached over and took hold of his still semi-firm erection. He tensed slightly and dropped his hand to try and fight me off. *Oh, no, you don't, you wanted this.*

I held his hand at bay and drove him into my mouth, forcing a low murmur to come out of his, as he hardened in response. I would've loved to have seen his face at that moment — it would have been priceless.

'Yes,' Arthur answered. 'We went there twenty years ago. Such a lovely part of the world.'

'Twenty years —' Bryce choked out as I enveloped as much of him as I could, compelling him to hesitate and stutter in his sentence. 'Twenty years, that's a long time.'

I continued to devour him under his desk until I could feel and taste his salty escalation. Then, without warning, I clenched my teeth around him. Not too hard, not hard enough to hurt him. I'd already done that this day and I felt terrible. No, I clenched hard enough to warn him to get rid of Santa.

'Sorry to be rude, Arthur, but I've got a pile of paperwork to get through before the meeting. So, if there is nothing else?'

Standing up from the desk, Arthur got the hint. 'Oh, certainly. I'll leave you to get back to your work.'

'Thanks, Arthur, and pass on my well wishes to Geraldine.'

'Of course, I'll see you in a couple of hours.'

Santa must have shaken Bryce's hand, then shortly after, I heard the door close.

'Alexis,' Bryce growled, his tone menacingly stern.

My teeth were still pressing into his smooth skin, so my response was slightly muffled. 'Yes?'

'Release my cock, please.'

'No. You are in trouble,' I mumbled.

'Release my cock, *now*! I want to plunge it so deep inside your pussy, it may never come back out.'

My jaw automatically opened, releasing him from my grasp. He pushed back from the desk and got down on his hands and knees so that we were now facing each other like two dogs about to introduce themselves and sniff each other's butts. I tried not to laugh, but the position we were both in at that point in time was hilarious.

I dropped my head and let the laugh roll out of me. 'I hate you.'

'No, you don't.' *No, I don't.*

We christened his desk like oversexed teenagers. Paperwork was scattered across the floor, and some even found a way to stick to my arse. I hoped to god that those particular pieces were not needed for our upcoming meeting; I could see it now, speaking in front of the board and holding up a piece of paper with an outline of my sweat-stained arse on it. *Hmm, explain that one.*

* * *

Just before the meeting was due to be underway, I ordered refreshments and some light snacks from the hotel's kitchen, and then set up the conference room for the meeting. While I was going over some notes with Chris, the board members started making their way in, including Gareth, who was last through the door.

We sat at a large rectangular table, Bryce at the head of it. Santa was to his left and Gareth to his right. The other members, I'm guessing in order of importance or share stake, were then seated both sides of the table right down to Chris, Patrick and me. Once everyone had finished getting acquainted, Bryce welcomed us and got the meeting underway.

'So, gentlemen and lady,' he smiled and winked at me, 'as you are aware, today's meeting has been arranged to discuss some prospective ideas for the renovations of levels three through to eight in the City Promenade building. These renovations are designed to make them more family-friendly. For those of you who don't know Alexis, she is a mother of two and has been kind enough to brainstorm ideas in order to help make the rooms more attractive to parents with children of all ages.'

I sheepishly smiled at the board members who were kind enough to reciprocate the gesture, with the exception of one person whose smile was as natural as a silicon implant. *Ignore him, Alexis. He's sick and can't help it.*

'So, without further ado, I'll hand it over to Patrick and Chris.'

Patrick and Chris stood up in front of a presentation screen powered by the iPad in Patrick's hand. I had no intention of removing my arse from this seat. I was simply there to offer advice and information from a mother's point of view, and answer any questions about the ideas I had already put forward. Standing in front of the room was about as appealing to me as shit on toast, so it was not going to happen.

Patrick began describing some of the major structural renovations, including converting a number of rooms into multiple-bedroom apartments. The board members seemed to be in agreement on the importance of having a large number of different room configurations.

'We want to divide the rooms into different categories, the reason being that there is not a typical family model. So trying to cater for all families in one room could be rather difficult. Therefore, we want to produce rooms designed to fit into categories for families with babies and young children; families with older children; and families with teenagers.

'Now, again this will not cater to everyone, so we also want to produce a number of rooms that can be easily reconfigured as needed. For instance, bedding configurations that can accommodate younger children as well as older children would be highly desirable. This could possibly be addressed by using bunk beds and portable cots. When discussing these options with Alexis, she was of the mind that flexibility in terms of bedding configuration was a key factor for parents looking at booking a holiday.'

Gareth interrupted. 'Why is that?' he asked, looking directly at me and displaying an inquisitive expression. *I knew he would try and put me on the spot.*

I cleared my throat. 'It's really quite simple, Gareth. When you have children, you realise that when they sleep everyone is happy. No one wants to go on holiday only for it to be ruined by grumpy children because their sleeping arrangements have been less than perfect.' I smiled politely at him.

A few of the men nodded their heads. Bryce smirked at me, and his eyes held something much more than approval that only I could read.

Patrick then went on to discuss interior design in the form of paint colour schemes and carpeting. 'Alexis came up with a brilliant suggestion of having carpet that resembled a Twister game laid down in either the living area or children's room. I have looked into a few businesses that can produce such a design.' Patrick touched the screen and showed a projection of what the Twister carpet might look like in a renovated room. A few of the board members raised their eyebrows and one even said he'd like to get something like it for his own home. I laughed. I wouldn't mind some too, actually.

Chris then interjected his expertise of what a great selling point this particular idea could prove to be. 'I've done some research, and although I have found some mats on the Internet that grasp the same concept, nothing like this has been implemented into permanent flooring. Nor has it been done anywhere in the world in a hotel — that I am aware of.' The board unanimously agreed to go ahead with the idea, including Gareth. However, he was not as enthusiastic as the others.

Patrick flicked through some more pictures of possible room designs then put forward the idea that Nate had come up with that morning. 'I haven't had a chance to look into this, but Alexis also mentioned maybe having a couple of special rooms that have themed bedrooms for the kids. Like a princess room decked out in pinks and with a princess bed etc. And a room designed for boys, with maybe a car style bed and race track.'

Gareth interrupted again, 'That is not going to work.'

It was Bryce who spoke up this time. 'Why is that, Gareth?'

'Because a girl is not going to want to sleep in a car room, and vice versa. We do not have enough rooms to cater for a large number of "specially themed rooms", it would be costly, and you would find some rooms will not be used simply because the family does not have the right gender of child to fit the availability of the room.'

A small number of the men tended to agree, which was fair enough. I could see his point. But he was not thinking about ways of getting around this, or simply compromising.

Bryce looked to me; I think he could tell I had something on my mind. 'Alexis, did you want to add anything?'

'Well yes, if I could.'

Gareth leaned back and crossed his arms.

'I completely understand what Gareth is saying, but there are ways you can get around that. Look, I think the idea from a marketing point of view to have extravagantly themed rooms could definitely be a big selling point. It's different and special, and parents want their holidays to be special. They want their children to remember the experience.

'Obviously, you don't want rooms being unused simply because of a painted theme not suiting. But you don't necessarily have to just have boy-themed rooms or girl-themed rooms. Why not have universal unisex rooms to suit multiple personalities.' *Shit, did I just say that? Shit, keep going.* 'Um ... for instance, a room designed like a magical forest, or a safari, or a beach, a circus, etc.' *Shit, I don't want to speak any more.*

It was obvious Gareth had noticed my choice of words, as his look toward Bryce then back to me was bordering on furious. A part of me thought Gareth was no longer in the room, Scott instead having appeared in his place. *Who is he right now? Maybe he needs a collective name too. Maybe in circumstances like this he can be Garott!* A chill went up my spine, and I looked away.

'Exactly,' said Patrick. 'There are definitely ways to avoid being gender specific or as Alexis put it, to suit multiple personalities.' *Oh, Patrick, shut the fuck up.*

Bryce sensed my unease and pushed to move along. 'Okay, Patrick, maybe you could work on some designs of rooms showing these unisex themes and we can decide on them at the next meeting?'

'Sure. Okay, moving along then to safety. As you can see on the tablets in front of you, there is a list of some minor changes and implementations which will need to be addressed in order to comply with Australian safety standards.'

The board members all perused the list and Patrick proceeded to go through some figures in terms of cost projections. This basically continued until the end of the meeting. Overall — apart from my stupid, stupid Freudian slip — it went quite well.

Afterwards, Patrick and Chris smiled and congratulated me on the board backing my ideas. A few of the board's members introduced themselves properly and asked about my role as a mother.

Bryce was going over some of the cost projections with one of the men, so I decided to pack up the drinks tray and take it to the kitchenette while he was busy. I didn't really need to as housekeeping would've cleared it up. I think my instinctive response as a mother to tidy up after people must have kicked in.

Placing the tray down next to the sink, I turned and went to leave the room when Gareth blocked the door. *Oh, fuck. Play it cool, Alexis. Don't bait him.*

'Hi, Gareth,' I said in greeting, as placidly as I could. *Now that's not playing it cool. He knows you don't like him, Alexis.*

'Did you enjoy yourself in there?' he sneered.

'Um ... no ... I wouldn't say I enjoyed myself. I'm just happy to be able to help.' I walked closer to him as if to say I was finished and wanted to leave the room, but he didn't move from the doorway.

'I think you are more than happy to stick your nose into things that don't concern you.'

'Look, Gareth, I think you and I got off on the wrong foot. Maybe we could just put it behind us and start over?'

'I don't want to start over, Alexis.' When Gareth said my name, he emphasised the 'S', hissing like a snake. 'I want you gone. I want you to stay away from Bryce. He doesn't belong to you.'

Shit, it's Scott. 'Gareth, I'm not a threat. I don't know why you think I am. I love Bryce and I would never hurt him.' I took another step closer, not sure if it was in the right direction. Every part of me was saying I should be stepping backward, as far away from him as possible. The problem was, I was boxed in, and I thought that maybe if I could show him that I was not afraid of him and not a threat, he might relent.

'Do you think he loves you?'

'I ... I ... I'm not sure,' I answered, not knowing whether to answer honestly and say yes, or lie and no.

'Well, he doesn't. So if you know what's good for you, you'll fuck off and get out of his life!' He glared at me with a look I could barely describe. It was terrifying, the most hate-filled expression I had ever seen in my life.

Gareth turned and left the room, leaving a chilly, frosty sting that bit at me, all over. I leaned over the sink and put my head down, trying to bury my fear and gain back control of my nerves.

'Alexis, what are you doing? Shit, are you okay?' Bryce asked, rushing to my side and lifting my head from the sink.

I was still trembling from Gareth's presence.

'What's wrong? You're shaking.' *Don't tell him, he'll go insane. He'll probably do something that neither of us wants him to do. No, Alexis, you can handle this.*

'I'm fine. I was just nervous and had a moment.'

'You were terrific. The board was very impressed.'

'I fucked up about Gareth, though. Where is he?'

He hugged me tightly. 'I don't know. He disappeared and so did you. I panicked for a second.'

'I'm fine. Honestly, I'm fine. I'm just exhausted. I think I need something to eat and a long hot bath.'

His face lit up. 'You're staying tonight?'

'Well, yeah, if it's all right with you. I can always go home, though,' I playfully pouted.

'If I had my way, honey, you would be calling here your home.'

'Hey, about that,' I said softly, unsure whether to continue with what I wanted to tell him. 'I spoke to Rick yesterday, and he suggested he keep the house and I move in with you —'

'Hang on. Rick suggested you move in with me?'

'Well, yeah, sort of. I told him I was going to move in with you at some stage, but where? I wasn't sure. He said there was no point in the both of us moving out and selling the house when he wanted to keep it. So, I was thinking that I would start staying over a few nights a week and then easing the kids into staying over as well. They could switch between us and Rick. What do you think?' *Oh, fuck, is it too much, too quick? I know he said he wanted me to live with him, but now that it can happen, he might no longer want it.*

He grabbed my face, placing an eager kiss on my lips, then lifted me into his arms and carried me out of the door. Most of the men were still in the foyer, together with Gareth. I giggled and blushed as he whisked me past them.

'Good evening, gentlemen,' Bryce said with pride.

'Good evening,' I said softly, still embarrassed by his bold display.

I tried not to look at Gareth, knowing that what I would see in return would churn my insides.

The men smiled and headed for the elevator as Bryce walked toward his apartment. As he punched in his security number, I looked over his shoulder. Gareth was standing there watching us, so I kissed Bryce, lacing my tongue with his. Gareth didn't move and continued to stare at us until the door closed. The intent behind my action was a message, figuring that he needed to see it. Maybe he'd back off.

* * *

'Welcome home, my love,' he declared, holding me in his arms while standing at the entryway to his apartment.

I looked around and smiled. 'Say that again.'

'Welcome *home*, my love.' *Home, could this really be my new home? Yes, I think it could. Maybe when the evidence of me and my children become a permanent part of the decor, then it could be home.*

'We will change whatever you want to change ...' He stepped down into the lounge and swung me in his arms as he turned to look at the apartment. He was speaking quickly and excitedly as he went over its features. 'If you want to change the colour and the furniture, you can. We can go shopping together and you can pick whatever you like. I have already organised contractors to fence off the pool for the kids and to reinforce the balustrades to make them higher. Do you want Twister carpet? We can get that too —'

'Bryce, Bryce, stop.' I laughed at him. 'I don't want to change much at all. I love it as it is. Maybe some photos up on the walls? And yes, Twister carpet,' I laughed again. 'But other than that, it's perfect, you're perfect, and we're perfect.' I leaned closer to kiss him again.

'Yes, we are,' he smiled. 'Perfect together. Thank you.'

'For what?'

'For giving me a chance.'

'You didn't need it. The moment you smirked at me while wearing hot, white chocolate was the moment that cemented our future together. I didn't know it at the time, but now I know it could not have been more clear.

'You had me at "Shit! Shit! Jesus, that is hot!" I couldn't have agreed with you more, honey. You were the hottest thing I had ever laid eyes on.'

I looked at him with a strange expression and then remembered that that was the first thing I had ever said to him.

'You still are the hottest thing I have ever laid eyes on, and you always will be.' He pressed his lips to mine, neither of us separating them for longer than a second, until we were naked and lying in his bed — our bed — together.

* * *

The next day was just as busy as the previous one. I'm not sure if Bryce's heavy workload was due to our time away, or whether it was inevitable from the storm that followed the calm ... or was it the calm that followed the storm. I hardly knew any more.

I had been busy organising meetings for Bryce for the rest of the week, so I had not thought much about the task of breaking the news to the kids this evening. I guess there was no real point in trying to plan it, because the kids reactions would likely be completely different from each other. I did feel that I wanted to tell Nate first, and alone. For some reason, I felt he already knew, that he would understand it better and that he would appreciate being treated more like the eldest child. I also felt that maybe he could then help Charli understand it, too.

After 6 p.m., I sucked in all my courage and made my way home, which really wasn't my home any more. Bryce had walked me to the car and kissed me through the window, hesitating to let go even while I was reversing. I watched him stand there through the rear-view mirror, his hands in his pockets, looking glum, which only dampened my mood further.

* * *

Rick and I had already decided to organise pizza for tea, our way of lightening the mood around the house and showing the kids we were still friends.

When I walked in the door, I pulled Rick aside to tell him my thoughts about breaking the news to Nate first. He agreed with me, so we put our plan into motion.

'Charli, have you got homework tonight?'

'A little bit.'

'Well, why don't you do it now? Then, after dinner, we can paint our nails and put on a face mask together.'

'Okay, cool!' She skipped off to her room. *Good, that has Charli-Bear organised.*

'Nate —'

'I don't have any homework. I did it yesterday.'

'No, sweetheart. Can you come into our room for a minute? We want to talk to you about something.'

'Sure.' He slowly and with uncertainty made his way into our room. I sat down on the bed next to him and put my arm on his shoulder. Rick stood opposite him, leaning up against the wall. Before Rick began to speak, he smiled at me. *That's right, Rick. Smile, like we said.*

'Mate, your mum and I have something we need to tell both you and your sister. We thought that seeing as you are the eldest and more mature, we would tell you first. But also because your little sister might need you to help her understand.' Rick ran his hand along his chin.

'You're breaking up, aren't you?' Nate's words came out so matter-of-factly, yet his head was down and his shoulders had slumped.

I squeezed him tighter. 'Yes, little man, we are. We just don't love each other like a husband and wife should any more ... but we still love each other as friends, and we still love you and Charli just as much as we ever have.'

'Is that because you now love Mr Clark?' *Oh, holy fuck, he is so tuned-in sometimes.*

'No, that's not the reason ... but yes, I do love Mr Clark.' I kissed the top of his head, and Rick shot me a dirty look. 'Rick, he deserves to know the truth, he is obviously mature enough to hear it.'

Rick's eyes widened and I realised that he thought I was going to tell Nate about Claire. I shook my head as if to say, 'Good on you, as if I would do that.'

'Nate, your dad and I stopped loving each other years ago. It's just taken us a long time to realise it and move on.'

'So what does that mean?'

'It means that you will now have two homes, and you can choose when you want to stay at either of them.'

'Are you going to live in that big apartment with Mr Clark?'

'Sweetheart, you can call him Bryce and, yes, eventually I will ... but not straightaway. We can go and have sleepovers a few times a week until you decide you want to stay there more often.'

He didn't say anything, just shrugged his shoulders. Charli called out to Rick, so he left the room to see what she wanted.

As soon as the door closed, Nate looked up at me. 'Mum, why don't you love Dad like a husband any more?' He searched my face for a truth he knew was there but was not being given to him. I knew that if I didn't give him just a part of it, he would feel hurt. And I didn't want him to feel any more hurt than what he was feeling at that moment.

'Nate, sometimes husbands and wives do things that hurt each other, and when they do hurt each other, it's hard to forgive them and love them as much as they used to.'

'Did Dad do something to hurt you?'

He was going to find out soon enough, so I guess preparing him just a little would not hurt. 'Yes, he did, darling. A long time ago, but he was sorry because he hadn't meant to do it. Then I did something to hurt him back. You see, it's not good doing things to hurt each other and that's why we need to move on.'

He nodded and pressed his lips together as if to give me the impression he understood.

'Not much is really going to change, Nate. You will still go to the same school every day. You will still go to the footy with Dad. Hey, I might still go with you, too. Someone has to cheer for the Mighty Bombers louder than Charli, don't they?'

'I don't think you are louder than Charli.'

'I can be.'

He smiled.

'Do you have anything else you want to ask me?'

'Are you going to marry Mr Cl— I mean Bryce, one day?'

'Maybe, but that's a long way off. You don't have to worry about that.'

'I'm not worried about that, Mum. I was just wondering.'

I gave him a huge hug, and he wrapped his arms around me, squeezing me back, tightly.

'I love you, my little man.'

'I'm not little.'

'No, you're not. And you know what? You've just proven that. Maybe I should call you my "big man" or my "incredibly brave mature man"?'

He rolled his eyes in response.

'Can you do me a favour?' I asked.

'Yeah?'

'Help Charli understand if she needs it. I have a feeling it might be hard for her.'

'Yeah, I know, Mum.'

* * *

We sat Charli down after dinner and explained it to her. Of course she didn't understand how Rick and I didn't love each other like we should. She cried when I said that we would eventually not live here, because she thought she would have to leave all of her things behind. Nate had cuddled her and said that she would now have two lots of everything, which brightened her eyes. He also told her she could have a pony, which made me nearly pass out.

I had to explain that no, she could not have a pony. Unless it had the words 'my little' in front of it, was approximately ten centimetres high, purple and smelled like grapes.

When I tucked Charli into bed that night, she begged me to 'love Daddy again'. It destroyed me internally because it was just something I could not do — not in the way she wanted me to. I told her that everything was going to be okay. Although, I knew it wouldn't be for her, not for a long time, especially after little RJ was introduced.

I decided I would call Claire while Rick was in the shower and tell her that the time to tell Rick about RJ probably wasn't right just yet.

I dialled the number Lucy gave me.

'Hello.'

'Claire, it's Alexis.'

'Oh, hi.'

'Listen, I think we should wait to tell Rick.'

'You've decided you don't want to help me, haven't you?'

'No. It's not that at all. I just don't think it's the right time to tell him. A lot is happening at the moment, and we need to sort it out first.'

'Yeah, I get it. It's been five years, what's a few more months?'

'Claire, you were the one who wanted to keep it from him, remember? Look, just let us sort out what we have to first, then I'll ring you. Probably in a few weeks.'

'I have a feeling you might not ring me.'

'Claire, I promise you, when I've settled my children into this new chapter of their life, I will help you tell Rick about RJ. I said I'd help, even though it killed me to say that, but I will. I'm true to my word. Just sit tight for now, please. The least you can do for me is wait a little longer.'

'Okay, Alexis. I'll wait until I hear from you.'

I hung up the phone then sunk onto the bed. *Fuck, my head just cannot take any more.*

'Alexis?' Rick asked from the doorway. 'Who's RJ?' *Oh, shit!*

CHAPTER

29

If there was ever a time I wanted the earth to just open up and swallow me whole, it would have been this moment. The crazy emotional weeks leading to this point could have been a top rated episode on *Jerry Springer*.

Jerry! Jerry! Jerry! Thank you, thank you, and today on the show we are talking to Alexis. She has been told by her husband that he'd had an affair. Ooooooo. So she went off and fell in love with a billionaire, only to find out that her husband lied. Ooooooo, I know, but Alexis found out it wasn't a lie, and today she has brought him here to the show, to tell him that the woman he had an affair with has a five-year-old son to him. Jerry, Jerry, Jerry.

'Alexis?'

'Yes.'

'Who is RJ, and why were you talking to Claire?' He took a few steps closer, looking like he was almost ready to lose his shit at me.

'Sit down, Rick,' I ordered in a calm tone. He ignored me. So I said it again, harshly. 'Sit down.'

This time he did.

'Now, before I even start with who RJ is, you need to understand that I only found out myself on Monday. I wanted to wait a few days to tell you. Only because so much has happened in the last few days, let alone in the past few weeks. I thought it was best to let things settle a bit before this particular shit hit the fan.'

'Alexis, who the fuck is RJ?'

'RJ is Rick Junior. He's Claire's and your five-year-old son.'

I watched the colour completely drain from his face until he was practically transparent. His mouth was agape, and any fight or fury he had in him had completely vanished. What was left was a man whose entire inner core had been torn from him, leaving an empty shell behind.

I touched his hand, which was lying limp on his lap. My touch triggered him to slowly meet my gaze with his own and his eyes filled with tears.

'Claire found out she was pregnant shortly after you told her you had made a mistake and wanted to end it. She didn't want to cause any more trouble than she already had, so she decided to raise RJ on her own.'

'How?'

'How what?'

'How did you find out?'

'Lucy.'

'Oh.' He didn't question how Lucy found out. He just accepted it and dropped his head back down.

'I've met him.'

His eyes darted back up to mine. He looked so confused, it was heartbreaking.

'He looks just like you. He has your eyes.'

'My eyes?'

I could see the colour return to his face with a red flush of anger as the realisation of what he had missed started to sink in.

'I have a five-year-old son who has my eyes?' he shouted angrily, while standing up and punching the wall, leaving a big hole in the plaster and bloody cuts on his knuckles. 'Fuck!' He stormed out of the room and grabbed his car keys.

I ran after him and snatched them back. 'No, Rick,' I pleaded, pushing and ushering him outside to the pergola area. 'Shh, you'll wake the kids. Look, I know this is a terrible shock. Trust me, I know. But there is no use in driving to Claire's house and hurling anger at her in front of your son. You need to calm down. Sit, I'll get you a drink and some ice for that hand.'

I walked back inside, my heart pumping in my chest. I fixed him a Bourbon and Coke and grabbed some ice and a tea towel for his hand. As I went to sit down, my phone buzzed in my pocket. I pulled it out and there was a text from Bryce.

How did it go with kids? I miss u like fucking crazy xo — Bryce

'Excuse me, Rick. I won't be a second.' I walked back inside and typed a response:

Hey, I miss you, too. But now is not a good time. Rick found out about RJ. I'm trying to explain it to him xo — Alexis

Do you need me to come over there, I'll take the chopper. — Bryce

Fuck no. Definitely not!

No, thank you. I've got this. It's fine. I'll ring you later. I love u xo — Alexis

Okay, but if you do, just let me know. I love u more xo — Bryce

I walked back outside. Rick didn't need to ask who the text was from, because he knew. I could see it written on his face.

He had wrapped his fist in the ice and tea towel, so I walked over to take a look.

'Give me your hand.'

He offered it to me, so I unfolded the towel to look at his knuckles. They were cut, but nothing that a bit of ice, pain-killer medication and rest wouldn't fix.

'Lucky for you, the wall came off second best,' I said as I sat back down. 'I understand you are angry, but from what Claire explained to me the other day, she was young, scared and ashamed of what she'd done. And she did not want to ruin our family. That's why she chose not to tell you. Listen, I am not making excuses for her, that's the last thing I would do. But you have to put that little boy first. He is innocent in this and does not deserve his father — a father he has never known — going over there and yelling at his mother. You need to keep calm around him, Rick.'

'I know, I'm not stupid.'

I raised my eyebrows at him. *Yeah, well I beg to differ. If you hadn't been stupid we would not be sitting here having this conversation.*

'If I were you — which I sure as hell wouldn't want to be — I would drink that drink slowly, then give Claire a call and speak with her calmly. I'm going to have a bath. Are you good?'

'Yeah, I'm good.'

'Good.'

The camera pans up close to Jerry Springer's face. 'Take care of yourselves, aaaannd each other.'

* * *

Rick had called Claire on the Wednesday morning and they'd arranged to meet for coffee which apparently had gone well, because Rick was now due to meet RJ the very next day. I decided that seeing as Rick was about to meet his son for the first time, I would give him space and have the kids stay with me at the apartment that evening.

I wasn't sure who was more nervous about the whole sleepover thing, because when I rang Bryce on the Wednesday shortly after speaking to Rick, he'd asked all sorts of questions. Questions like, 'What's their favourite food?', 'What Wii games does Nate like?', 'Does Charli need any specific "girly" type decorations?'

I had laughed at him and asked if his 'creepy research' abilities had diminished, then hoped he hadn't taken that literally, because he said he would be calling Lucy after he hung up. *He'd better not have!*

Nate seemed quite calm about the idea, although I could tell he was a little nervous as he had been fidgeting in the front seat of the car. Charli had been asking questions the whole drive, wanting to know everything about the apartment, like where was the toilet? Where would she be sleeping? And where would I be sleeping? I seemed to be the only one who was relaxed and looking forward to it, knowing deep down that the kids would love it there. My theory was about to be proven.

'Nate, I have a little surprise for you.'

'What?' he asked dubiously.

'Well, when I turn this corner and pull into Bryce's private garage, you are going to have a fit. Are you ready?'

He looked at me anxiously with an expression that suggested he was half expecting something to fall from the sky and land on his head, but that the particular falling object in question was to be something amazing.

I turned the corner and, as I expected, Nate went into awed nine-year-old boy mode, pressing up against the window of the car as we drove past Bryce's extensive car collection.

'Sick! This sick! Totally the sickest!' he babbled.

'Wow, they are so pretty. Lots of different colours like a rainbow,' Charli cooed, also pressed up against the window.

I parked the Charger and Nate was out of the car like a rocket.

'Don't touch!' I yelled out after him.

'Of course he can touch,' Bryce said while walking toward the car. He had been waiting for us in the garage and — if my eyes didn't deceive me — I would say he was definitely nervous as hell. 'Hi, Charli, how are you?'

'I'm good and bad.' She looked at me and I gave her a reassuring smile. 'I like your cars. They remind me of a rainbow.'

'Do you like rainbows?' Bryce asked, quickly. *Oh god, what's he going to do, try and buy her a freakin' rainbow?*

'Yes, they are my favourite. Mum, can I go and have a look at the gold one?'

'Yes, just be careful.'

She ran off.

'So, Mr Clark, how are you coping?'

'Coping? I'm coping just fine, Ms Summers.' He lowered his voice. 'Although, I desperately want to taste those lips of yours right now.'

We had discussed that there would be no public displays of affection in front of the kids during their first visit. I didn't want to upset them, and I believed baby steps were the key.

'You're just going to have to control yourself.'

He groaned and grabbed Nate and Charlotte's little suitcases from the car.

'Aw, sick! I love this one!' Nate exclaimed. He had stopped at the McLaren alongside Charli.

'We can go for a ride in it, if you like?' Bryce offered quickly.

'Yeah?'

'Let's go up to the apartment first. Then we'll talk about joyrides, okay?' I stated firmly, before the three of them went driving around town.

We all stepped into the elevator and headed directly to the apartment, Bryce stopping us on the second floor of the private residence. I stepped out after him, curious as to why he would opt for the second level first.

'Now, I didn't know where you would want to sleep. So I organised a few different options for you,' he explained to the kids as he opened a bedroom door.

Inside was a room with a single bed and desk, decked out in greys, reds and blacks. There were signed pictures of the Essendon football team on the wall, together with a large mounted TV. My eyes nearly bulged out of my head.

'Sick! I bags this room.' *Bags? Is this his new word of the month?*

'What the hell is "bags"?' I asked my son.

He rolled his eyes at my apparent lack of modern-day lingo. 'It means I'm having it, you know ...' *No, I don't bloody know, obviously.*

Nate walked in and flopped on the bed, then shot back up and scrutinised one of the pictures. 'Hey, Mum ... this Bombers picture is signed and it has my name on it.'

I walked into the room to take a closer inspection of the picture and, sure enough, it was personally signed for Nate. Turning back around, I dropped my mouth wide open. Bryce just shrugged his shoulders.

'You didn't tell me your football team was the Bombers,' I said with a smile on my face.

'It's not,' he replied with a smirk while crossing his arms.

'Oh. Well, what team do you support?' I asked inquisitively. 'Please don't say Collingwood. I think I will have to leave if you say Collingwood.'

He laughed. 'The Cats. I support the Cats.'

I looked at Nate, then to Charli. 'What do we think of that?'

'It's better than Collingwood or Carlton, Mum,' Nate said in Bryce's defence.

Charli turned to Bryce and gave him the thumbs-down.

He laughed and led us out of the room and down the hallway.

'When did you organise this?' I queried in a quiet tone.

'Right after I spoke to you on Wednesday.'

I quickly pinched him on the arse before he opened the next door. 'You are amazing.'

Turning around, be knelt down so that he was eye level with Charlotte. 'Charli ... if you'd like, you can sleep in here, or with your mum. It's up to you.'

Standing back up, he opened the door for her, and we were all hit with what could only be described a princess's paradise, a princess who was obsessed with 4Life. *That reminds me: the video Bryce recorded for her, and the napkin!*

She screamed. 'Mum, there is 4Life stuff everywhere and it has my name on it.'

'No way!' chimed Nate.

'That's not all, Charli. I've got a surprise for you.' Bryce switched on the TV which — like in Nate's room — was mounted to the wall.

Instantly the scene from backstage at the Tel V Awards came up on the screen. *Oh, shit! Quick! Record it, Alexis.*

'Hang on, hang on.' I yanked my phone from my pocket and pointed it at Charli and pressed record. 'Go.' I indicated to Bryce to press play, which he did.

Harry's voice filled the room.

'Charlotte, we are sorry you couldn't be here tonight, so we've put together something especially for you.'

If I thought she'd screamed before then I was wrong, because the shrill noise that radiated from that tiny little mouth had my eardrums begging for mercy. She bounced up and down on the bed as 4Life sang her favourite song, 'Anything'.

Holding my phone up and capturing every single second of her reaction, I watched the sheer excitement and joy plaster her little face. A tear sat teetering on the edge of my lid, undecided on whether or not it would fall. Her reaction was just so emotional. I giggled when the footage on the TV filmed the roof for a second, remembering that was the moment I leaned back and kissed Bryce while he recorded it.

I glanced over at him, to see if he remembered that moment too, only to find him standing there filming me with his phone. I gave him a what-are-you-doing look then put my hand up to shield my face.

When the recording finished, Charli ran up to Bryce and wrapped her arms around his waist to say thank you. It took us all by surprise, especially Bryce who didn't know what to do at first. He sort of stood there with his hands in the air, as if a police officer had just sprung into the room and shouted 'stick 'em up'.

By the time he realised he could relax and hug her back, she had let go and had run straight for me, practically barrelling me over.

'Thank you, thank you, thank you! That was the best thing EVER! Can I watch it again?'

Bryce handed her the remote control. 'Sure.'

'Don't you want to come and see my room, Charli, in case you want to sleep in with me?' I asked, worried she might find sleeping on her own in a not so familiar place a bit daunting.

'No, I'm good. This room is awesome!' She pressed play and bounced up and down again as she replayed her person-alised footage.

I laughed at her. 'Okay, quickly, one more time.'

She watched it again, then reluctantly put the remote down and left the room. I wanted to secure Bryce in my arms and show him just how much I loved him and appreciated him. It was almost unbearable that I couldn't. We had made a pact that there would be absolutely no displays of affection in front of the kids, and whoever broke that pact would owe the other 'anything'.

I opened the next door. 'This is my room, kids.'

'Where's Bryce's room?' Charli asked, squinting her eyes as she searched the hallway.

He pointed down the hall to the last door. 'Down there, Charli.'

'Okay.' She nodded, then followed her brother downstairs.

I walked up behind Bryce as we followed them, and gently whispered in his ear. 'So, what were the other sleeping options you had arranged for them, if these ones had not worked out?'

'Your bed, or the couch,' he said matter-of-factly. I laughed.

We finished showing the kids the entire apartment, and they were quite excited about the prospect of spending a lot of time there. I didn't want to overwhelm them with the thought of it permanently being their new home, because as Bryce had said to me the other day, 'It doesn't have to be here, we could live anywhere.' Just the notion of being able to live anywhere still hadn't quite sunk in. I knew Bryce was incredibly wealthy, but it was not the dollar signs I saw dripping from him. It was his determination and passion, not to mention the sweat and soapy lather — I couldn't forget those either. *Alexis, you've gone off subject.*

Right ... I knew we could live anywhere, but I really did like it at the apartment. This was the special place that had changed my life for the better.

* * *

Bryce and Nate spent most of the morning in the man cave, playing the rather new and large collection of Wii games Bryce had organised. Charli spent a good hour in her room, replaying her footage and staring starry-eyed at her signed pictures and memorabilia. I was so glad the school had scheduled a pupil-free day as it was nice to see the kids settle into their new environment so well.

Deciding to put on my bathing suit, I opted to soak up the sun's rays as the cooler weather was only just around the corner.

The weather in Melbourne often resembled a woman's temperament during that lovely time of the month when it was evident fertilisation of her egg had not happened. One day it was sunshine, butterflies and rainbows, and the next it was grey, miserable and ready to attack and unleash hell on all of those in the vicinity. So I had every intention of enjoying this particular sunshine and butterflies day by lying on the sunlounge by the pool and reading my extremely funny book. During the past nine years at home, after my domestic duties had been sorted, attacked and accomplished, I would increase my caffeine and sugar levels and get lost in the world of literature.

'Mum?'

I looked up from my book still giggling at its content. 'Yes, sweetheart, have you finished watching 4Life?'

'Yes,' she blushed. 'Addison is going to be so jealous when I show her. Mum, can I bring my friends here?'

'Um, I guess —'

'Of course you can, Charlotte,' Bryce said as he and Nate walked out onto the balcony looking like new best friends.

'I kicked his butt, Mum. Seven games to three!'

'He did, fair and square. Unlike his mother.' Bryce gave me a cheeky look.

I dipped my sunglasses to my nose. 'I do not cheat, Mr Clark.'

'Mum, it's Bryce, remember?' Charli shook her head at me then changed the subject rather quickly, as six year-olds tend to do. 'Can we go for a swim?'

'Yeah, did you pack your bathing suits?'

Charli's face dropped. 'No.'

'That's okay, I can get Michelle —' Bryce was already reaching for his phone when I interrupted him.

'No, no. We can go downstairs to the shopping precinct and pick some out ourselves, then we can get some lunch.'

Charli jumped up from the end of my sunlounge. 'Can we have McDonald's?'

'Sure.' I looked at Bryce who displayed a look of distaste, but then quickly smiled.

* * *

We made our way down to Rip Curl and chose both Nate and Charli a new bathing suit. The friendly shop assistant smiled and said hello to Bryce.

'Can you please charge it to my account?' he replied.

'No,' I stated, handing over my credit card.

Bryce turned to me and cupped my face. 'Honey, you have to let me look after you and the kids if, in fact, you want me to look after you and the kids.' He leaned down and placed a soft, quick peck on my lips.

My eyes widened, and so did his at the realisation he had just broken our promise, unintentionally. He dropped his hands and we both quickly looked at the kids. Nate was smiling and trying to cover Charlotte's eyes. She was also smiling and peeping through the crack of Nate's not-so-big fingers.

My smile rose to match my children's. 'Come on, let's get lunch.'

I gently pushed them toward the door.

'I'm so sorry, my love. I just completely forgot and couldn't help it,' he whispered into my ear.

I slipped my hand into his. 'It's fine, didn't you see their faces? Anyway, now you owe me "anything".'

His eyebrows rose. 'I've already pledged "anything" for you.'

'Good, I hope you've got your Channing Tatum on.'

'Channing what?'

I laughed. 'Have you seen *Magic Mike*?'

'No.'

'Best you Google it then.' I lifted his hand to my mouth, kissed it and pulled him along to catch up with the kids.

* * *

We stopped in front of McDonald's and Charli sat on a park bench which had a fibreglass, life-size statue of Ronald McDonald sitting on it. Charli draped her arm around him and posed, prompting me to pull out my phone to take a photo.

'Go on, Nate, sit with her,' I suggested.

He reluctantly sat beside his sister and pulled a stupid face. I took the picture.

'Come on, Bryce, you can sit here too,' Charli smiled, pushing Nate across the seat and patting the spot in between them. I looked up at Bryce, thinking what fantastic progress we were making in the space of only a few hours. I had never in my wildest dreams thought that the kids would be so great about this massive alteration to their lives.

Spying Bryce's hesitant face, his expression shocked me.

'Go on,' I encouraged, putting my hand on his back and directing him to the seat. He sat down with a horrified look on his face and my heart fell to the floor. *What's his problem?*

I glared at him. 'Smile, Bryce.'

He forcefully smiled, making me furious. But it wasn't until I caught his subtle sideways look at the Ronald McDonald statue, that I realised what his problem was. I couldn't help it ... I burst into laughter. He, on the other hand, shot me a deadly look, and I wouldn't have been surprised if he had sat there and crossed his arms.

'Come here,' I offered, giggling at him.

He shot up and I handed him my phone.

'I'll trade with you,' I said as I continued to laugh.

'It's not funny,' he whispered.

I sat down in between Nate and Charli and put my arms around them, hugging them in tight.

'What's wrong with Bryce?' Nate asked, a little sad and offended.

I laughed again. 'Oh, it's nothing, Nate.'

'Alexis, stop it,' Bryce scolded. He tried to look seriously at me, but even he was starting to break.

'Mum, tell me,' Nate pleaded.

'Bryce is afraid of clowns, and Ronald McDonald here was freaking him out.' I choked again, mouthing the word 'sorry' to Bryce before burying my head in my hands.

Nate looked up and replaced his concerned and offended face with a broad smile then he, too, laughed.

Charli on the other hand, stood up and wrapped her arms around Bryce's waist. 'Don't worry, Bryce, I understand. I'm afraid of bees.' She squeezed him tightly.

He placed his hand on her head and gave it a light rub, the gesture stopping my laughter in its tracks and replacing it with a smile filled of love and relief.

Nate rested his head on my shoulder and spoke quietly. 'She likes him, Mum, and so do I.' *Oh, thank Christ for that.*

CHAPTER
30

Life hands out challenges that we sometimes unwillingly accept. We have no choice in the acceptance really, because that is essentially what life is: a series of unavoidable challenges thrown our way. And how we assess them, deal with them and progress through them, shapes our life to be what it will be. Some of us assess challenges in different ways, either seeing them as a hurdle that one can easily jump over, or as a brick wall that seems impossible to climb.

For less than a year, I seemed to have faced a lot of life's brick walls. Brick walls that I was eventually able to climb over, but not without reluctance, struggle and a strenuous effort. Now, after being dished a platter of challenges in such a short space of time, I hurdle over them with ease, ready for the next row and the endless rows after that.

* * *

The latest hurdle I had to overcome was settling my children into a new life with me and Bryce. This hurdle at first seemed a bit higher than usual, but I didn't have to jump it alone. As a family, we all took it together, and now that hurdle was behind me, along with the others. The one I approached this particular day, though, was not really mine. It was Rick's, but because it involved my children, I had made it my hurdle as well and I intended on jumping over with Nate and Charli as quickly and as easily as we could.

'Stop scratching your head, Rick, you'll get dandruff.'

He glanced over at me, looking slightly annoyed. 'I'm about to tell our children they have a brother they have never met, and you're worried about dandruff?'

He scratched his head again.

'They are stronger than you think. They dealt with our break-up and me moving on with Bryce so much better than either of us could ever have anticipated. So try and relax and think about how you are going to break it to them. You need to choose your words carefully.'

The school bell sounded and children came barrelling out of their classrooms, filtering in different directions as they escaped the confines of another day of education. I poked my head out of the window and waved, getting Charli's attention. She picked up her pace and skipped toward the car.

'Mum! And Dad!' She smiled but seemed confused at the idea of us both being there.

Charli opened the back door and jumped in then wrapped her arms around Rick and the driver's seat he was sitting in.

'Hi, princess, how was school?'

'Good, we made grass cups.'

'You made what?'

'Grass cups, silly. You put some seeds in the cup and then you water it. Oh ... and you put it in the sun. That's when the grass will grow. It's not ready yet, because we only put the seeds in today.'

'How exciting, watching grass grow,' Rick muttered under his breath as he looked at me.

I shot him a nasty look. *Geez, he's a nightmare when he's losing his shit.*

'Sounds like fun, Charli-Bear,' I replied, encouraging her gardening aspirations.

I spotted Tash and Steph parked a few cars away. 'I'll be back in a minute,' I informed them before climbing out of the car and jogging toward my friends.

'Hey, Lex, did you have the day off work?' Tash asked.

'No, I finished early so I could pick up the kids with Rick.'

'So, are things going well with Rick?' Steph asked, slightly disappointed.

'No, we have definitely split up. He really did have an affair five years ago.'

Tash stumbled and nearly fell into the car parked beside her. 'What? Since when?'

'Since he told me nearly two weeks ago.'

'And you're here picking the kids up like nothing ever happened? Can anyone else see a problem here?'

'Again, it's a long story that I will fill you in on soon. We have split up and I have moved in with Bryce ... well, not completely moved in. I spend two or three nights at home still, to help with the transition for the kids. But, essentially, they will predominantly live with me and stay with Rick whenever they like. It's actually been going really well.'

Tash was still shaking her head and blinking at me in astonishment.

I noticed Rick signalling me to come back, so I touched her arm. 'Hey, hon, it's fine. It really is. I'm a hurdler now.' I kissed her cheek, gave Steph a quick hug and jogged back to the car, pretending to jump a couple of hurdles.

'You're insane!' she called out.

'I'll ring you tomorrow,' I replied, blowing them a kiss.

* * *

We drove the kids to St Kilda and ate fish and chips on the beach. Rick was silently stewing on how and when he was going to break the news about RJ. I didn't want to probe him, but if he didn't man up and let it out soon, the seagulls would not be the only things annoying us. Mosquitos would venture out as they always did when the sun dipped over the horizon. I hated mosquitos with a passion. They were devils with wings and soon to be conducting their ritual of blood theft and saliva distribution, resulting in a red welt which was as itchy as hell.

Charli had been tossing our leftover chips to the seagulls and watching them turn into vicious, crazy, potato, salt and oil devouring machines. Nate was more particular with his chip tossing, trying to bounce them off as many of the birds' heads as possible.

'Nate,' I warned him, but smiled to myself at the desperation of the seagulls running for the damned chip even after it bounced off their heads.

'What? I'm not throwing it hard.' *Fair enough.*

I slapped my leg. 'Bitch!' *Fucking mosquito.* 'Sorry for the language, guys,' I apologised, putting my finger to my mouth.

'Why's it a bitch?' Rick asked, his voice dripping in gloom. 'What?'

'Why is the mozzie a bitch? Why is it not a prick?'

'Rick, seriously?' I screwed my face up, annoyed with his attitude. 'If you must know, only the females bite.' I leaned over and whispered: 'And if you don't hurry up and say what you have to say, this female will bite, too, and it won't be pretty.'

He took in a deep breath. 'Nate and Charli, come here, please.' The kids wriggled in and sat between us. 'Listen, I have something really important to tell you both.'

'I knew it. I knew something was up when you both picked us up from school.'

'Nate, let your father speak,' I said sternly, furrowing my brow and pulling my 'smart son' closer to me.

'This might come as a shock at first.' *Really, Rick? Don't tell them it's shocking before you even bloody say what it is. Men, hopeless!* 'But, it is also really cool.' *Ugh, it's so not 'cool'; it might be 'new', possibly even 'good' (possibly not), but it was definitely not 'cool'.*

I could tell that he was struggling bigtime, but I had no intention in doing it for him. He had to get it out then, as 'Mum', I would smooth it out.

'A few years ago, your mum and I had some problems.' *Pfft, that was news to me.* 'I met a nice lady ...' *Fucking nice, my arse! Alexis, shut up and let him do this.* 'and ... well, we had a baby together. His name is RJ and he is now five. He's your half-brother.'

Nate stiffened against my side. Charli went red and scratched her head. *I now know she gets that from her father.*

'So, do you want to meet him?' *Oh, Rick.*

Nate got to his feet and stared at his father. 'I hate you.' Then he took off toward the car.

I screamed out after him, 'Nate!'

'I'm waiting by the car.' He turned back around and walked off.

'Come on,' I said to Rick and Charli, 'we're leaving.'

We all followed Nate to the car.

'Nate, I'm sorry. I made a mistake five years ago when I met that lady. But I can't change that. You have a half-brother now, and he is really a sweet young boy. You would like him.'

'I hate him and I hate you,' he yelled at Rick. 'Mum, I want to go home.'

I looked at Rick and shook my head slightly as if to say, 'let it go'. 'Okay, sweetheart, we'll go back to the house.'

'No, not that home, my new home.' Tears filled his nine-year-old eyes, and it tore my heart to shreds. I gave him a strong hug, then opened the car door. Charli, I assumed, had no idea what this all meant, but seemed concerned by Nate's reaction.

'Hop in, sweetheart.' I helped her into the seat and closed the door.

Rick was leaning against the tailgate. His cheeks were damp and his knuckles white.

I lowered my voice and turned my back on the car. 'Rick, calm down and get yourself together. Nate is in shock and he is hurt. Give him some time to process this. I will take the kids to the apartment tonight and talk to them. Nate will come around eventually, Rick, I promise.'

* * *

We drove back to the house in silence. It was horrible. Nate went straight to his room and packed a bag. It was the weekend

the following day so at least he would not have to go to school
in the state that he was in.

'Charli, sweetie, can you go and pack some clothes in your
bag?'

'Mum, can I stay here tonight?' She almost looked scared
to ask.

I glanced at Rick, then back at Charli. 'Yes, but don't you
want to come with Nate and me?'

'I do, but I think I'll stay here with Dad. He looks sad.'

Rick bent down in front of Charli. 'Princess, I'm fine, you
can go.'

'No, I'll stay here. We can go shopping tomorrow.' She
smiled and walked to her room.

'If you're happy for her to stay, she can,' I said. 'I'll take
Nate and have some one-on-one with him, then I'll be back
Sunday night.'

'Yeah, that's fine.'

I kissed Charli goodbye and told her to look after her dad.
She seemed pleased with her new task and was checking to see
if he needed anything as I closed the door.

* * *

On the way to the apartment, I asked if Nate wanted to talk.
He had said 'no', but I could tell that he did. I thought I
would give him the option to ask me when he wanted to, but
when we pulled into the garage, he started to cry.

'Nate, sweetheart. I know it's a shock. Trust me, I know.'
I gave him a reassuring smile. 'But it's going to be all right,
you'll see.'

'Why did Dad want another son? Am I not a good son?'

'Oh, darling.' I got out of the car, walked around to his door, opened it, and knelt down beside him. 'No, not at all. You are the perfect son, the best son in the whole wide world, and you absolutely did nothing wrong. Dad just made a mistake. We all make mistakes, sweetheart. It's just some mistakes are bigger than others, and this one was a pretty big one, wasn't it?'

'Yes.'

'Listen, the thing about mistakes, is that most of them can be fixed. What Dad did was a mistake. But do you want to know how to fix it?'

He nodded.

'You can fix it by giving yourself some time to get used to the new changes. But what you need to understand is that RJ, himself, is not a mistake. He's a lovely little boy who had no idea his Dad had other kids. He even had no idea who his Dad was until a few days ago. And, sweetheart, Dad didn't even know RJ existed until a few days ago, too.'

'Why?'

'Because the lady who is RJ's mum thought it was best if she didn't tell anyone.'

'I don't get it.'

'I know, and that's okay. All you need to know is that your dad and I love you so, so much, and that you have a half-brother now who is really nice. And you know what? He is probably a lot more scared to meet you than you are of meeting him.'

'I don't want to meet him,' he said stubbornly, crossing his arms. This was a typical sign that he didn't mean what he had just said, but too proud to admit it.

'Well, you don't have to right away. But you will eventually, mate. Now, come on it's getting late.' I helped him out of the car and found Bryce leaning up against the concrete pillar.

He walked over and kissed the top of my head. 'Sorry, I didn't want to interrupt.'

I placed my hand around his back and hugged him to me.

'Hi, Nate. Do you want a game of Mario Kart before bed?'

Nate shrugged his shoulders but I could tell he did.

'You can have one game,' I said to my son with an encouraging smile. 'Then it's bedtime, okay?'

* * *

Despite my strict instructions of one game only, Nate and Bryce played Mario Kart for an hour. I called Rick to tell him not to worry about Nate; that he seemed to be calming down.

He told me Charli had fussed over him and asked if 'RJ looked like Nate', and 'Why did he give a baby to another lady and not to Mummy'. I asked him what his response was to that question and he said he had asked Charli, 'Do you want a hot chocolate?' *Typical.*

Nate had reached a state of unconsciousness as soon as his head had hit his pillow.

I walked down the stairs in search of Bryce when he suddenly grabbed my arm and pinned me up against the entryway wall.

'I can't wait another fucking minute, honey. I need to be inside you now!'

I looked at my watch. 'It's only been five hours and fourteen minutes.'

'Yeah, I know. That's too long.' He pressed his mouth to mine and lusciously explored my tongue with his own.

'Hmm, I have to agree, but we can't here,' I slurred with what sounded like lustful intoxication.

'Where? I honestly don't care where, just pick a place and quickly.'

He moved his mouth to my neck, and at the same time, slid his hands underneath my top to fill them with my now firm breasts. 'Fuck, I love your tits.' *Fuck, I love that you love to love my tits.*

'I need a shower,' I breathed heavily. 'Do you want to join me?'

'Jump up,' he said. So I jumped up and wrapped my legs around his waist. He took to me to the elevator where we continued to hungrily consume each other. We almost didn't make it to the shower, but I'm glad we did. It had to be one of my favourite spots to make love to him. I adored the feel of his wet mouth as it pressed into mine while water cascaded all over our bodies.

He lifted me up, securing me to him with one hand pressed firmly on my arse and the other pressed against the tiles just to the side of my head. He slid in and out of me with ease as he groaned harshly into my ear, sending shivers of raw pleasure right through me. I was fairly sure he had no idea what his groans actually did to me.

'Bryce, are you happy?' I asked, searching his eyes.

'Yes, but I could be happier,' he admitted, kissing my chin as he said it.

My heart skipped a beat, wondering why?

'I would be happier if you married me.' *Phew.*

He pumped into me harder, making me bounce against the wall, my voice jerking as I responded.

'I will marry you, but not yet. Anyway, we still haven't gone on a date. I'm not marrying you or even properly saying yes to a proposal without a ring and a date.'

He laughed. 'We really did do the whole date thing backwards, didn't we?'

'Yep,' I moaned, my voice climbing. My breathing also escalated as he rolled into me many more times. His pace and rhythm were fucking sensational, so much so that I sunk my teeth into his shoulder blade and buried my outburst of pleasure into his skin.

We slowed our breathing and relaxed. Then, letting me go, he leaned up against the wall and watched me as I proceeded to wash my hair.

'How was Nate when you were playing the Wii with him?' I asked.

'He was alright. He did ask me if I was going to be his "new dad" though.'

I turned my neck so quickly in his direction that I pulled a muscle. 'Ow, fuck!'

Bryce chuckled. 'You all right?' He pushed off the wall and placed his hand on the sore spot, then rubbed.

'What did you say to him?' I asked, now feeling a slight twinge of discomfort.

'I said "no", that he "already has a dad who loves him". But I did say that, "One day I would be his second dad if he ever wanted me to be."'

A smile crept across my face. 'And what did he say to that?'

'He said, and I quote, "Sick!"'

CHAPTER

31

Bryce and I fell asleep together in his bed, but in the early hours of the morning, he carried me back to my room and told me he would see me in a couple of hours. When I woke for the day and sat up, I felt horrible and only just made it to the toilet before hurling the contents of my stomach. *I'm never eating fish and chips ever again, unless Bryce makes it with his special sauce.*

Groaning, I made my way back to the bed and flopped facedown.

'Mum, Bryce wants to know how you want your eggs: poached, boiled, fried or scrambled?' *Eggs, white and yellow, soft, slimy ... oh, no, not again.*

I ran back to the toilet and projected another fountain of stomach interior decoration. When that was down, out and flushed, I washed my hands and face then brushed my teeth.

Bryce burst into the bathroom with Nate following closely behind. 'What's wrong? Are you okay?'

'I think it was dodgy fish and chips. How do you feel, Nate?'

'Fine.'

'Well, I had the calamari and you didn't ... so maybe it was that? I need to ring Rick and see if he and Charlotte are okay.'

'I'll get your phone, Mum.' Nate handed me the phone and I dialled Rick.

'Hey, how did you and Charli go last night?'

'Yeah fine, she is still asleep. How's Nate?'

'Yeah, he's fine, don't worry. Listen, have you or Charli been sick at all?'

'No, we are fine. Why?'

'I must've had a dodgy calamari ring. I feel awful.'

'Shit, that's no good. Make sure you rest.'

'Yeah, I will. Thanks. Oh, by the way, when Charli takes you shopping today, she does not need another pair of pink, purple or silver sparkly shoes, nor does she need another hairbrush. Don't be fooled by her blue, twinkly eyes.'

'Got it. No shoes or hairbrushes.'

'And avoid the eye contact, trust me. Okay, got to go, bye.' I threw the phone on the bed and ran back into the bathroom.

Bryce was there rubbing my back as another, smaller version of my fountain spilled into the toilet bowl.

'I'll call Janette and see if she can come and take a look at you.'

'I'm fine, it's probably food poisoning. I just need some water.'

'Okay, I'll get you some water.'

I cleaned up again and got back into bed.

'Mum, it smells like spew in here. Can I go?' *The amount of times I've had to smell your spew, young man, let alone other bodily excretions you have blessed upon me throughout your nine years, and yet you can't handle this? Lucky you.*

'Yeah, go, mate. I'm fine.' I watched him deliberate whether or not to give me a kiss, so I made his decision easy by blowing him one. 'Go, sweetheart.'

He walked out the door as Bryce walked in with a glass of water and some dry toast.

'Here. Janette is on her way up.'

'Bryce, I'm fine. You're just wasting her time.'

'Time I pay her for, so shh.' He handed me the water, which I guzzled, then I took small nibbles of the toast. He was smirking at me as I made tiny baby bites.

'What?'

'You're even beautiful when you vomit, you know that?'

I rolled my eyes at him. 'You're funny, Mr Clark.'

'No, I'm not. You are all kinds of green right now, yet you are still the most beautiful creature I have ever seen.'

'I'd kiss you right now if I didn't have vomit-breath.'

'I'd let you kiss me right now if you didn't have vomit-breath. You might be breathtakingly beautiful, but I don't do vomit-breath.' He kissed his fingers and pressed them to my head.

Moments later, the buzzer to his office door rang.

'That will be Janette. I'll be back in a minute.' He rushed out of the room and, within minutes, he was back with the City Towers precinct nurse.

'Alexis, dear, I'm not going to ask how you are because obviously you are not too well.'

'Hi, Janette, I've definitely seen better days.'

She sat down on the edge of the bed. 'Okay, so what's been happening?'

I looked at Bryce who was leaning up against the wall. 'Well, I had fish and chips last night, and I think the calamari rings might have been a bit suspect.'

'Right, have you had diarrhoea at all?'

'No.'

'Stomach pain?'

'No, not really.'

'Okay, I'll just take your temperature and blood pressure,' she said reassuringly as she pulled a thermometer from within her bag. She placed it in my ear until it beeped.

'37.8 ... that's slightly higher than normal, but not high enough to indicate a fever.' She took out the blood pressure cuff and wrapped it around my arm then placed the stethoscope across the crook of my arm and pumped away.

'125/90. Your blood pressure is also slightly high. Do you normally experience high blood pressure?

'No, not that I am aware of.'

'Have you been stressed lately, or over-exerting yourself?' *Ha, stressed? Well you could say that.*

'Just a little a bit,' I admitted as I smiled studiously at Bryce.

She removed the cuff and placed it on the bed. 'Are you on birth control, Alexis?'

'Yes.' I blushed and quickly looked at Bryce, because he had never asked me this question. 'Yes, I'm on the pill.'

As I said it, a wave of heat resonated at my toes and slowly rolled through my body until it hit my face. *My period, shit! I haven't surfed the crimson wave in ... in a while. Fuck fuckity fuck, when was I due?*

'Bryce, can you show me how to do that trick on Mario Kart?' Nate asked, poking his head in the door.

'Sure. That's my cue to leave.' Bryce followed Nate out. *Thank you, my little angel boy.*

'Alexis, when did you last get your period?'

'I don't know. My pill is in my bag, but I missed some just over a month ago when I went away for a couple of days. Shit!'

'How many did you miss?'

'Um ...' I remembered back to the day before I first came here. I had taken my pill away on the girl's weekend, but when I came home that night I put it on my dresser. After Rick fake-confessed to having his affair, I had grabbed my bag and forgot all about it until I went to the house on my way back from the airport. *So that would be one, two, three, four days.* 'Four days.'

'Okay, I think we should do a urine test.' *Shit. Crap. Balls.*

She handed me a cup, so I went into the bathroom and very awkwardly placed it between my legs, closing my eyes and hoping I wouldn't pee on my fingers.

Looking around the en suite, I tried to push away the thought that I was about to catch the amber liquid that would determine the use of my uterus for the next nine months.

Opting to instead focus on the task at hand, I clenched my pelvic floor and removed the cup, holding it before me to stare at it. *There is no baby in there, Alexis. What are you doing? Get off the toilet.* Washing my hands, I then handed over my cup of possible gestation.

'This will only take a minute, Alexis,' Janette explained as she dipped the test strip into my pee. *Longest freaking minute of my life ... I'm sure it's been, like, ten or fifty even. Hurry, hurry, hurry, hurry uuuuuup.*

She pulled the strip out, took the cup to the bathroom and tipped the sentencing fluid away. 'Alexis, you are pregnant,' she said in slow motion. Well, at least I thought she had said it in slow motion. Maybe it was my brain that heard the protracted tone of each and every syllable that left her mouth. *A l e x i s   y o u   a r e   p r e g n a n t. Oh, holy shit! Fucking crap. Crappity balls.* 'When did you say you were due for your last period?' she asked.

'What? Oh, I think maybe two weeks ago, thereabouts.' *Shit, how did I not realise this? Well, you have been slightly preoccupied, remember?*

'I'd say you are approximately four to six weeks along then. You'll need to book in to see your doctor as soon as possible.' She packed up her stuff. 'Make sure you start taking folic acid as of today and good luck.'

I followed her out of the room and escorted her to the door.

'Thank you, Janette.'

'All the best.'

Closing the door behind her, I fell against it and shut my eyes. *No, no, no. My womb is in retirement. She cashed in her superannuation and has been holidaying on Alexis Island.*

'Honey, what are you doing?' *Shit.* Bryce walked over to me. His face was awash with concern. 'What did Janette say?' *Oh, nothing really. Just that I'm brewing a human in my uterus and you are going to father it.*

'Probably food poisoning.'

'Probably?'

'Yeah, my tests were all good. She said to drink plenty of water to help wash it out of my system, and I have to get some folic acid.'

'Folic acid? What's that for?' *Oh, shit. Alexis, you're an idiot.*

'It's just a vitamin to help boost my immune levels,' I lied. *Please fall for it, please fall for it.*

'Okay, go back up to bed and I'll bring you some more water.'

'Actually, I'm going to have a shower.' I went to kiss him, but we both stopped and leaned back simultaneously. I pulled a sad face and turned. 'I hate being sick.' *And pregnant, right now.* As I walked off he came up behind me and moved the hair away from my neck, then trailed kisses over it, stopping to whisper in my ear.

'I might not do vomit-breath, honey, but I definitely do every other part of your body.'

I let my head fall back on his shoulder. *No, goddamnit, this is why you have baby Clark in your belly, Alexis. Baby Clark! Hmm.*

'I'm going to have a shower,' I murmured with a delicate smile, then made my way upstairs.

* * *

I turned on the shower, put my hands against the wall, and watched the water go down the drain. *Baby Clark is not going to wash down the drain, Alexis.* Automatically, I placed my hand on my stomach. *Oh, my god! I'm pregnant. I'm having another baby. I'm having Bryce's baby. It is Bryce's baby?* I quickly racked my brain again. *Did I sleep with Rick after my girls' weekend away? No, definitely not. So yes, it's positively Baby Clark.*

I had no idea how I was going to tell him. Would he be happy? I hoped so. He'd told me before he loved kids, and he was fantastic with Nate and Charli and absolutely adored

Alexander. I couldn't tell him yet though; we would need to be alone. I was going to have to wait till Nate went back to stay with Rick which would be tomorrow night. *Fuck, how do I keep it from him? I'm not very good at this shit. I should ask Rick for pointers! No, definitely not.*

'How's it going, beautiful?' Bryce asked, his voice breaking me from my excessive analysing. I turned and found him standing in the bathroom holding another glass of water. I reached my hand around the shower glass and took it from him, then guzzled some more.

'You make food poisoning look sexy as hell.'

'Stop it, I do not.'

'Yes, you do. Are you feeling any better?'

'Yeah, I think the vomit express has moved along.'

He screwed up his nose. 'Good. That means I can kiss you in a day or so.'

'What? A day or so?' *I can't wait that long. I need his tongue in my mouth, like minutes ago.* 'Pass me my toothbrush,' I scowled.

He put toothpaste on it for me then handed it over, together with a smirk. I scrubbed and scrubbed as much as I could then spat the minty foam down the drain. Growling, I basically threw the toothbrush back at him while poking out my tongue.

'I'm kidding, my love.'

'I hate you.'

'No, you don't.' *No, I don't.*

* * *

I took it easy for the rest of the day and, thankfully, no longer felt sick. My Jerry Springer lifestyle and row of hurdles had completely drained me, and obviously had not subsided for the time being.

Bryce had spent a good part of the day showing Nate how to play pool, and when Nate was confident enough, he asked me to join him and challenge Bryce to a game. I'm not sure whether Bryce deliberately played under his capabilities or not, but the end result was a hell of a lot closer than what I had predicted it to be.

Nate watched a movie in bed and when I went up to check him, he was fast asleep and drooling on his pillow. I tucked him in and wiped his mouth with a tissue while giggling.

Bryce was standing at the door, watching me. 'You are a wonderful mother, Alexis.'

'No, being a mother is wonderful,' I corrected him.

'It suits you.'

'It better.' *Ah, the irony.*

He cupped my face and kissed me passionately.

'I thought you said you wouldn't kiss me for a day or so.'

'There's no way I could wait a day to have your lips on mine.' He swept me off my feet and carried me down the hall to his bedroom, then gently placed me on top of his bed and scooted down next to me, laying his head on my chest.

'How are you feeling?'

'I'm fine. You can stop asking me that now.'

I ran my hands through his gorgeous blond hair. *I hope Baby Clark gets his hair chromosomes.*

He propped himself up onto his elbow, facing me, then slowly began to drag my dress up until it was bunched underneath my bra, exposing my legs, underwear, and stomach. He moved closer and kissed my abdomen.

I smiled. *Little do you know you just kissed your offspring, Mr Clark.*

Continuing to trail his finger around my stomach in large circles, he looked up to me with his alluring, blue seductive eyes. *Oh, I hope baby Clark gets your eye chromosomes, too.*

'I love you,' he said with renewed sincerity.

'I love you, too.'

He looked back at my stomach and kissed it again. 'So, honey, when are you due?' Slowly, he tilted his head and smirked at me. *What? How? Oh, I hope Baby Clark does not get your smirking chromosomes.*

'Um ... um, at the end of November. How did you know?' I choked.

'Well, you turned a shade of beetroot at the mention of your pill. Then you asked for some folic acid. I took care of Lucy's supplements for her during her pregnancy, so I know what folic acid is for.' *Alexis, you dumbarse.* 'Why didn't you want to tell me?'

'I did, I just wasn't sure when, or if you would even want this baby. I really didn't mean for this to happen, Bryce. I was taking my pill, but when I walked out on Rick and came here I left it at home. I didn't take it the whole time we were away, I just completely forgot. I'm so sorry,' I sobbed as the tears started to fall.

'No, don't cry. What are you crying for? I couldn't be happier. Well, I could. I'll be the happiest man alive when you say "I do" to me. But to know that our baby is inside here ...' He kissed my stomach again. 'Growing bigger as each day goes by. That just has me at a loss for words.'

'So you're happy?' I asked, wiping the tears from my eyes.

'More than happy ... I'm in love. I'm in love with you, our baby, our life and our future together.'

Relief flooded through me, so I grabbed his face and dragged him up to mine. 'We're having a baby, Mr Clark.'

'Yes, Ms Summers, we're having a baby.'

EPILOGUE

Gareth
Three months earlier

I don't think I can wait till 10 a.m. I need to speak to Bryce now. Maybe if I ring back he will be there. Yes, I'm sure he will, I will ring back.

'Bryce Clark's office, Alexis speaking. How may I help you?'

Alexis, who is Alexis? What is she doing answering Lucy's phone?

'Alexis, is it?' I asked.

'Yes, can I help you?'

'I just spoke to Lucinda, is she available?' *Where is Lucy? Where is Bryce? I need to speak to Bryce.*

'She's just stepped away from her desk. Can I take a message for you and get her to call you back?'

'Yes, my name is Gareth Clark. Is Bryce in the office yet?' *He has to be. I need to speak to him.*

'No, he's not back yet, sir.' *No, where is he? I have to go and see him.*

'Let him know I'll be there shortly.'

'Yes, I will pass that on for you. Thank you, goodbye.'

I hung up the phone and stared out my eighth story window. I hadn't seen Bryce for nearly a week, which wasn't normal — I usually saw him every day. *Why is he avoiding me? Have I done something wrong?* It was worrying me. The last time he avoided me, I'd had an episode because I decided to stop the medication Jessica had given me. I didn't want to take the pills any more, I didn't know whether they were brainwashing me or making me worse. *Sometimes I just don't know. I hate it, I hate feeling like that.*

Something felt different with Bryce, and I needed to know what it was, so I stepped back from the window and headed to the penthouse floor.

* * *

The elevator doors opened, and I stepped into the foyer. *I don't know what I have done wrong. I have been taking my meds, I know I have.*

Lucy was standing in the middle of the foyer with her hands on a blonde's shoulders. *Maybe this is her new girlfriend? Good, I hate Nic. She's a bitch.*

'Good morning,' I greeted them. *I hope this new girlfriend doesn't watch me like a hawk, it makes me nervous. Nic is always watching me, I hate it.*

'Gareth, this is Alexis. She'll be taking over for me when I have the baby.' Lucy winked at Alexis. *Shit, that sucks. I hate Nic.*

'Ah, Alexis, it's always nice to put a face to a name.' *She's beautiful. Why didn't Bryce tell me he had filled Lucy's position? As far I knew he didn't want a replacement.*

'Likewise, Mr Clark,' she smiled nervously. *Why is she looking at me funny? No, not you, too.*

'Please, call me Gareth.' I held the door for her, but sensed she wanted to get as far away from me as possible. *She knows something? What does she know?*

She nodded sheepishly as the doors closed. *Something is wrong. Something is wrong.*

'Good morning, Lucy. Is Bryce back yet?'

'Yes, he's just having a shower.'

'So, Alexis is his new PA. Where'd you find her?'

'She was our Concierge Attendant. Bryce offered her the job today. You can wait in his office, Gareth. He won't be long.'

I walked into Bryce's office and made my way to the window. The view from up here was so much better than the eighth floor. From here you could see across Port Phillip Bay, but when you looked out my window, you could only see directly across to the Metropol.

I glanced at his desk and noticed a manila folder with the name Alexis Summers written on it. Curiously, I opened it up. There was a picture of her attached to her résumé, a police check, credit check, a medical report, then lots of sheets of paper printouts from Facebook. *What's all this Facebook shit?*

I was about to have a better look when the door to Bryce's apartment beeped. I quickly shut the folder and turned back to the window.

He walked in, freshly showered and smiling from ear to ear.

'Someone looks happy this morning, was it a good class?' I asked. Something was telling me it had nothing to do with his class though.

'Yeah, something like that. So, Gareth, what's up?' He walked over to his desk, picked up Alexis' file and put it in his drawer.

'Not much, just haven't seen you around lately. Anything new going on, Bryce?'

'No, not really.' He still had a smile on his face.

'I see you've replaced Lucy.'

'Oh, you've met Alexis?' He raised his eyes then tried to play it down.

I've known Bryce nearly all my life, and I know when something is different. Something about this Alexis woman was different.

'Yeah, just a minute ago,' I replied. 'She seems nice and all, but is she going to be right for the job? Wasn't she your trainee CA?'

'She'll be perfect,' he snapped. 'So was there anything else, Gareth? I've got a shitload of work to do.' He sat down and turned his laptop on without looking at me.

'No. I just wanted to see how you were. I'll let you get back to it.' I went to turn, when he looked up.

'I'm all good, mate. Listen we'll catch up after work and have a beer, all right? I'm just swamped right now.'

'Yeah, all right. I'll see you later.' I walked out of his office and said goodbye to Lucy.

'Are you okay, Gareth?' she called out.

'Yeah.' I rushed to the elevator. My ears were beginning to throb and my head was all of a sudden killing me. The last time this happened I ... *Oh, shit, not again.*

Scott

I knew this elevator, I knew these walls and the mirrors on them, and I knew the reflection looking back at me. *What the fuck have you done to your hair? And this suit makes you look like a pussy.* Obviously something else had happened in Gareth's miserable life; the wanker couldn't handle his own dick let alone anything else. So, he'd called upon me, again, knowing I'd help him out. He also knew I was not afraid to get us what we wanted, and he knew that I always knew best. I was glad to be back, actually, because I could finally see Bryce again. *Why is the elevator going down? I need to go back up?*

I hit the stop button, then the penthouse button.

Lucy was at her desk when the doors opened, and she gave me a strange look when I walked into the foyer.

'Did you forget something?' she asked as if she suspected me to be a criminal. *Shit, think.*

'Yeah, my phone.' I walked past her and noticed her stomach was as round as a fucking beach ball. *Fuck, she's pregnant. How did that happen? Ain't she a lesbian? Then again, it wouldn't surprise me if that Nic bitch had a dick and was packing some swimmers.*

I didn't bother knocking on Bryce's door before I opened it to let myself in. Hopefully I would find him relieving his built-up sexual tension, and I could help him with it.

Unfortunately, he wasn't. Instead, he was concentrating on some paperwork in a manila folder. *Fuck, he looks good. He gives me a hard-on so easily, I love it.*

'Did you forget something, Gareth?' he asked, slightly annoyed.

'Did I leave my phone behind?'

'No, not that I can see. Why don't you ring it? Here, I'll do it.' He pressed a button on his phone. *Fuck, it's in my pocket.* I quickly put my hand in there and flicked it to silent.

Instantly, it started to vibrate and assist my already hard dick. I smiled.

'I can't hear it, Gareth. It obviously isn't here.'

'Yeah, sorry.' I stood there admiring him, while enjoying the silent vibrations of my phone.

Bryce looked agitated. 'Okay. Well, I'll see you tonight.'

'Yeah, where?' *I had no fucking idea where.*

'Here,' he snapped, now looking pissed off.

I decided that I'd better go.

'See you later.' I walked back out of the office and past the beach ball. 'Later, Lucy.'

* * *

Why am I looking into a fucking fish tank? Gareth had obviously managed to return during the night, but once again he needed me to save his wimpy arse. I noticed a blonde walking up the stairs and away from me. She glanced back over her shoulder and looked at me as if I'd just told her I slept with animals. *Fuck, that bloody Gareth has swallowed his balls again. Maybe it had something to do with her.*

I waited till she'd turned the corner, then followed. She opened the door to the staff kitchen. *She obviously works here.*

'Hello, Mr Clark,' a short, dark-haired woman said as she smiled at me politely before entering the kitchen after blondie.

'Hello,' I replied. *What's her name again? I've seen her before.*

Stopping just outside the door, I listened to their conversation.

'Alexis, how are you, dear? How's Lucy doing? Did she have the baby?'

'Yes, Abigail, she did. She did a wonderful job, I'm hoping to go and see her tomorrow.' *The blonde's name is Alexis and she obviously knows Lucy. And Abigail ... the old bird is Abigail.*

'Oh, that's wonderful news. So how is your new position going?' Abigail asked Alexis.

'Great, Mr Clark is a lovely person, and very easy to work for.' *She works for Bryce! Maybe that's why Gareth has summoned me because she is trying to bed him. It's not the first time he's wanted help for something like this.*

I hid around the corner and watched Alexis leave the kitchen. *Over my dead body you'll bed him. He belongs to me.*

Furious that this Alexis chick could have the audacity to lure Bryce into her clutches, I make my way to Gareth's office to check out her file.

Soon, I have found out that she's married with kids and had started at the hotel as a Concierge Attendant alongside a Samantha Taylor. *Might just have to meet this Samantha Taylor, I think.*

* * *

It had been a few days since deciding to make sure Alexis didn't get her claws into Bryce. And since that point, I'd made a lot of progress. Samantha was easy. All I had to do was flash my smile and credit card, and she was ready to open her legs. Not that I wanted anything to do with what was in between her legs. They weren't Bryce's legs.

I sat in Gareth's office, bored shitless. I didn't know what he fucking did and I didn't really care. I flicked on his TV, hoping there would be a rerun of Seinfeld. Instead, there was a news update. Some dickhead had had an accident on the freeway that morning, and it made me glad I had decided to sleep in the hotel. I watched the chopper zoom in on a crazy guy running up the off ramp then scooping a blonde into his arms. The chopper zoomed in some more, then 'Bryce Clark, a knight in shining armour' flashed across the screen. *Fuck, what's he doing? That slut has fucking brainwashed him.*

I got up and stormed out the door with an idea of how to get rid of her for good.

* * *

When the elevator doors opened, I saw the slut sitting at her desk, looking disappointed.

'Good afternoon, Gareth. Bryce is not in. He's out with Dale going over some security checks.'

I go to speak. *Remember, talk like Gareth.* 'Oh, bugger ...' *Yep, that sounds like the wimpy son of a bitch.* 'I needed to have a quick word to him about a new proposal. Never mind.' I walked over to her desk, making sure I got right into her personal space. I wanted to make her feel as uncomfortable as hell, and I wanted her to never want to come back here again. 'So, how are you feeling, Alexis? That was some bump you took this morning by the looks of your car and the fact Bryce had to carry you off the road.'

'I'm fine, thanks. It looked worse than it actually was. Bryce was good enough to come down and see if I was okay. It was very kind of him.' *She's lying, does she think I'm fucking stupid?*

'Oh, come on, Mrs Summers. You and I both know he didn't just come down to see how you were. What he did went far beyond the expectations of an employer.' I waited for her reaction to my not-so-subtle dig at her.

She stood up. 'What are you getting at, Gareth?'

'Feisty! I can see why he likes you. Tell me, are you feisty between the sheets, too?'

I felt a hard, sharp sting to my cheek as she slapped me across the face. *You fucking little slut.*

'How dare you,' she shouted as she tried to leave.

I managed to grab her on the back of her head. 'Listen here, you little whore. You just keep spreading your legs for Bryce, because you are doing me a favour. You want to know why? The board won't be too impressed that he is fucking a married woman. It doesn't look good for the company.' I figured I'd try and guilt her into believing she'd be the cause of Bryce's demise. If she really liked him, she'd leave him alone, but if she didn't and just wanted what she could get from him, then I'd need to scare her a little more.

I licked my lips and went for the kill, grabbing her tit. 'You are a sexy whore, I'll give him that much.'

The next thing I knew, I had a fucking sore eye and my balls were killing me. 'You bitch! You'll fucking pay for that.' I went to get up and teach the slut a lesson, but I was grabbed from behind and flung into a wall. Bryce then picked me up by my collar and punched me in the ribs, then again in my jaw. *Fuck, that hurt. But man, he just gave me a massive boner.* He kicked me again in the stomach, when Alexis screamed for him to stop, which he did.

'Get the fuck out of my building now, you piece of shit.' *He is sexy when he's angry.*

I laughed. *That was fun.*

For dramatic effect, I spat blood at his feet and looked into his gorgeous eyes. I could see it, I could see he knew, and I loved it. I could see he knew I was back. *Yes, Bryce, Scott has come back for you.*

* * *

Alexis had been staying with Bryce on and off since the Tel V Awards. I saw them walk to his elevator that night after a few drinks, practically fucking each other before the doors had even closed. It was in that moment that I realised she was a major fucking problem I needed to take care of. He was mine, and no one else's, and I was not going to allow that bitch to take him away from me.

I had to be smart, though, and not let my anger get in the way of my plan. Scaring her away or making minor threats obviously was not going to work any more. I needed to take action, action that would see her out of Bryce's life for good. *Alexis Elizabeth Summers needs to have an accident. Yes, an accident, one that will fortunately render her no more, and I know just how to do it.*

Loved *Satisfaction*?

Turn over for a sneak peek of Book 3 in the series —

Fulfilment

K.M. GOLLAND

Alexis and Bryce are finally happy, in love, and expecting their first child together. But one person does not share in their happiness and could destroy everything...

Out September

harlequinbooks.com.au

PROLOGUE

Bryce

I've always had goals to strive toward in life. Goals that, with hard work and initiative, were achievable regardless of how remarkably high they were set. But damn, it was amazing how quickly your lifelong goals, aspirations and priorities could change when faced with new information — information that had the capacity to blow existing plans right out of the water. In my case, all it took was the news I was about to become someone's father.

The night before, when Alexis had confirmed she was carrying our baby, everything I had previously been working for my entire life seemed meaningless in comparison to what my life held next. Leading up to that moment, I had been hell-bent on expanding and building my family's legacy, as a kind of tribute to my father.

Now, I didn't only see it as a tribute to him, but also something I could pass on to my family, and this new revelation excited the fuck out of me.

* * *

As always, when I stare at Alexis' naked back lying before me, she fucking takes my breath away and even more so now that she is carrying our baby.

I gently trace my finger down her back, careful not to wake her, as she needs her sleep. She had got up three times during the night to piss. Three times! I can't figure out how a person can possibly piss so much. Although, I did have to chuckle to myself last night when the bed dipped for the second time, waking me, and I heard her curse to herself and, I quote, 'pathetic bladder, you need to harden the fuck up.'

She makes me laugh. My heart literally hurts at how much I love and adore her, to the point where I think she somehow has some form of supernatural hold on it, controlling whether it beats or not.

* * *

The moment Alexis confirmed that she had feelings for me, I knew that I would do absolutely anything for her, and ever since, I have made it so that my world revolves around the very spot on which she stands — and I wouldn't have it any other way.

She is just everything I have ever wanted: beautiful, kind, smart, funny, nurturing and feisty, my favourite part of the day being when she challenges me. Of course, I know that I will always win, because that is just something I cannot and will not change. She doesn't know that though.

God, just thinking about her — let alone being in her presence — makes me so bloody happy that my cheeks ache. I'm even sitting here right now, staring at her and grinning like the fucking Cheshire cat. I should be ashamed of myself.

Sometimes I think I need a good reminder, tell myself to man-up and stop acting like a fucking lovesick teenager. After all, I am thirty-six years of age and have a fucking decent set of balls between my legs.

* * *

When Alexis confirmed that she was pregnant, I couldn't say that I was shocked. In fact, to be brutally honest, I had hoped she wasn't on birth control in the first place. It wasn't something I had ever discussed with her for a reason. Why? Because I hadn't really given a shit. She was the woman of my dreams and I had fallen in love with her from the word go, so the idea of her possibly falling pregnant with my child was … well … fucking great!

Now I know that sounds completely fucked up and bordering on evil, because on paper she was still married and she already had two wonderful children of her own. But I make no excuse for getting the things I want in life, and I certainly make no excuse for how I go about getting them.

I made myself a promise the day my parents and brother died, the very day my life was ripped out from beneath me. I decided I would take care of the ones I loved, and instead of wallowing in self-pity asking 'Why me?', I would make it my lifelong ambition to get what *I* wanted. After all, I fucking deserved it.

I've never been one to say that life will hand you what you want on a silver platter or that fate will bring you what you deserve. No, I've always said life is what you make of it. That you rule how your existence in this world plays out; that no one else controls the decisions you choose to make. When you think about it, it's quite simple really. The direction in which you head is determined by your own conscious decision to go there and no one can take that away from you.

I wanted Alexis. I'd never wanted anyone or anything more in my life. So I knew I would do whatever it took to have her, regardless of what or who I had to overcome. Yes, it was selfish and callous, but I didn't care. I knew only too well that life was too fucking short to spend it wasting time accepting the second-rate dividends that are handed out.

Essentially, life is what you make it, and I have one more thing I need to accomplish in order to make mine the best it could possibly be. I want to marry Alexis, make her my wife, and make her the happiest woman on earth. I want to wake up next to her every day because, fuck, she makes me the happiest man alive. So, as soon as I get the green light to do so, Alexis *will* become my wife.

ACKNOWLEDGEMENTS

As always, I have to first and foremost thank my amazing husband — you not only picked up the duties I dropped to write this book, but you also allowed me to bounce ideas off you in the middle of the night when I woke up slightly crazy. Not only did you share the lack of sleep with me during the writing process of books one and two, you also brought me a cup of tea every single night before you went to bed as I sat in front of my laptop and typed into the early hours of the morning. I honestly couldn't have finished *Temptation* or *Satisfaction* without you and my nightly caffeine shot. Thank you for your support and for always being my rock you wonderful, wonderful man.

The two little loves of my life — you were told many times during the writing of this book, 'Shh, Mummy is trying to type' and 'Mummy is busy right now'. I am so sorry for saying that over and over, and I promise to go back to nail painting and Lego building now.

My parents — you have encouraged me and been my biggest fans since I decided to follow my dreams and become a writer. Your support is unwavering and profound and I am thankful for it every day.

Mum — you read and reread, and then reread some more, in order to help edit my first draft. You even picked up on a typo that would have mortified me had it been published (yes you know which one I am talking about, the one that had you snorting like a little piggy). Thank you for always being only a phone call away.

My close friends and sister-in-law; also known as Fran (Tash), Gab (Lil), Lea (Jade), Jules (Steph), Kate (Carls) and Renee (Jen) — you support and encourage me on a daily basis and provide me with material every time we get together. Thank you xo.

Cherra, Sarah and Heather — thank you for beta-reading during the early stages of this book and for helping me tidy up the mistakes I made through lack of sleep and caffeine consumption.

To Annabel, Sue and the team at Harlequin — you have helped make *Temptation* and *Satisfaction* be the best they can possibly be and, for that, I will be forever grateful.

And lastly, but certainly not the least — my fans and followers on social media. I love reading all your comments and feedback, and knowing I have given you something to laugh about, gasp over and blush from, is essentially why I do what I do.

talk about it

Let's talk about *Satisfaction*.

Join the conversation:

 on facebook.com/harlequinaustralia

 on Twitter @harlequinaus & @KellyGolly

#TemptationSeries

Golland's website: www.kmgolland.com

If there's something you really want to tell

K.M. Golland, or have a question you want answered,

then let's talk about it.